DARK DISCOVERIES

Summer 2016, Issue Number 35, www.DarkDiscoveries.com

Publisher
JournalStone Publishing, LLC

Editor-in-Chief and Art Director
Aaron J. French

Contributing Editor
K. H. Vaughan

Assistant Editors
Russ Thompson (Senior Submissions Editor)
Stuart Conover (Assistant Reviews Editor)

Layout and Design
Paul Fry

Contributors

Aaron J. French	Lisa L. Hannett
K. H. Vaughan	William Simmons
Joe Hill	Colleen Wanglund
Douglas Wynne	Mike Davis
Laird Barron	Donald Tyson
Gary Raisor	Robert Morrish
Ann Christy	Joe Donnelly
Nick Mamatas	John Shirley
Kane Gilmour	Nick Antosca
Jeremy Robinson	Geoff Brown
A. Scott Glancy	Chris Kelso
Angela Slatter	Bryan Thao Worra
Richard Dansky	

Founding Publisher and Editor
James R. Beach

Special Thanks

Joe Donnelly	Jen Salt
Joe Hill	William Simmons
Douglas Wynne	Lisa L. Hannett

Contributing Artists/Photographers
Jen Salt (front cover and interior photographer)
Jen Salt (cover art)
Greg Chapman (pg 33 & 63)
Steve Santiago (pg 17 & 47)
Luke Spooner (pg 85 & 95)

DARK DISCOVERIES
(ISSN 1548-6842) is published (Qtrly) by
JournalStone Publications
3205 Sassafras Trail, Carbondale, IL 62901

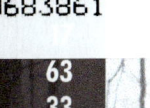

I0683861

EDITORIAL

The world is coming to an end, both literally and figuratively. Things we've taken for granted, ideas we have come to associate with modern society, even concepts like binary opposites—all of it is being called into question. New technology grows more and more amazing every day and increasingly invisible and subtly interpenetrated with the natural environment. Meanwhile, hard-toed boots march toward conflict everywhere across the globe. Truly, this must be the sign of the times, proclaiming that the Apocalypse is nigh.

Or is it? Perhaps we are simply vaulting through an abyss toward some further stage in our shared human evolution. Welcome to issue #35 of *Dark Discoveries*, where it's wartime and conflict and End Times *all* the time. Lace up your desert-colored tactical boots and get your butt in here so we can start the fight!

But in all seriousness, we're thrilled to be exploring War and Apocalypse this time around with our theme. While you will find plenty of military action and guns-a-blazin', I have endeavored to gather content for this issue that also explores the theme through other perspectives. If you're like me, the sci-fi action of slaughtering zombies, aliens, and evil cultists can be great fun, but the "action" takes on a whole new dimension when it's human beings killing other humans *en masse*. Sure, it feels great to have one's team prevail in a game of war, but what happens after the killing? What changes did that war produce in the cognitive structures of the surviving soldiers? How about their psychological condition after the tour of duty is over? Or the civilians or innocent bystanders, how are their lives affected? And what about the daily life and interactions in the groups of soldiers, even those members of revolutionary cells, how might those be worked into a horror story? These are some of the questions surrounding warfare that I wanted the issue's authors to explore.

Still, fear ye not, because within these pages you'll find plenty of weird aliens and creatures who need to be mowed down for the sake of mankind's survival. One of our authors, A. Scott Glancy, asked me about "competency porn," and after laughing at the apropos phrase, I said we would be including some of that for sure, since competency and triumphal good are key ingredients for military horror. I think those kinds of stories connect with some primal human instinct: watching a group of ass-kickers shoot their way out of an impossible situation reestablishes a sense of hope for the dark world in which we all reside. But that is only one part of human history.

Of course, the world will be ending, too. The world is *always* ending, and so we are thrilled here at DD to bring you an exclusive Joe Hill feature while we're all still cohabiting this planet, a conversation about his bestselling apocalyptic book *The Fireman*, as well as an excerpt. You don't

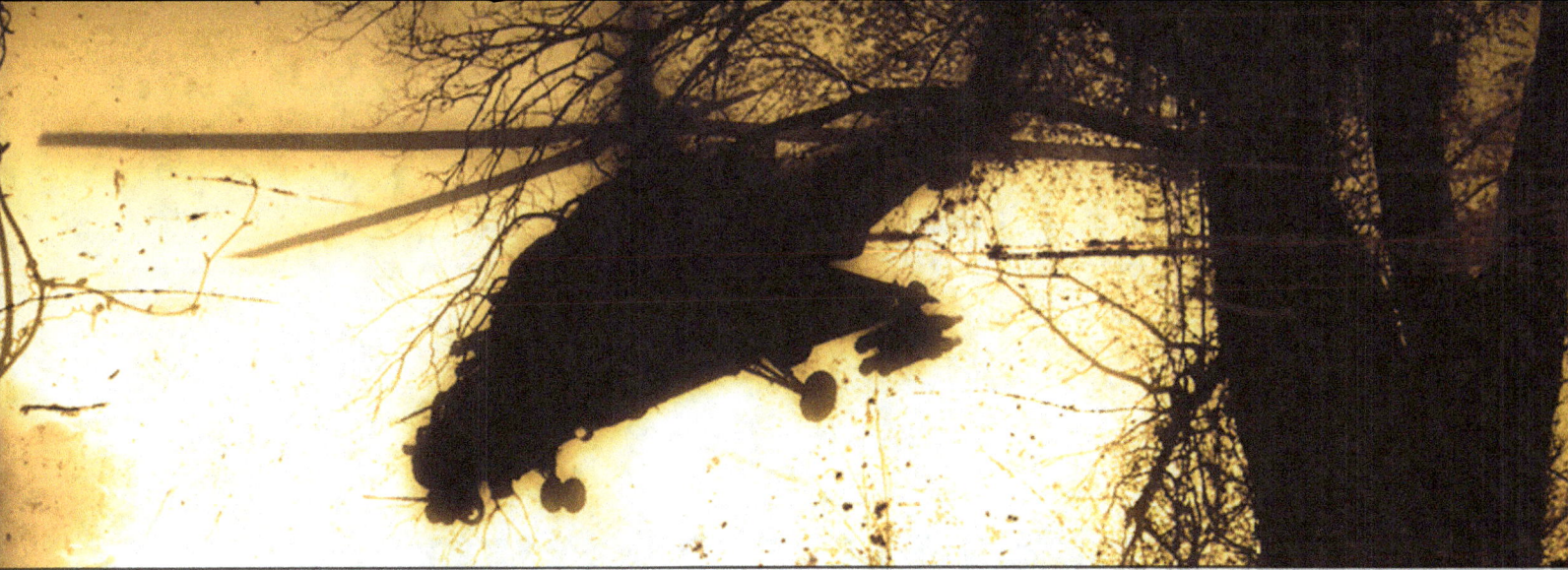

want to miss this, a brand new interview with Mr. Hill conducted by JournalStone's own Douglas Wynne. All of us in DD's Editorial Department are *huge* fans of Mr. Hill, and we're excited to bring our readers exclusive photos of him and an awesomely unique cover shot.

In addition, the fiction in this issue explores the end of the world, its aftermath, and the effects of warfare in various creative ways. The always excellent Angela Slatter looks at the consequences of a war-without-end in a future eerily familiar; Nick Mamatas pairs together Communism and the supernatural for a haunting conclusion; A. Scott Glancy gives us an awesome new Delta Green story with Lovecraftian baddies galore; Kane Gilmour offers an interesting take on those creatures who need mowing down that I mentioned earlier; Ann Christy's Captain Wygone is a badass female Navy senior officer fighting a future technology as the world collapses around her; and finally, Gary Raisor concludes his vampire story from issue #34 with part 2 of his exclusive *Less Than Human* novella.

For our nonfiction, besides the new interview with Joe Hill, we have a fascinating interview with Lisa L. Hannett, in which she discusses writing and her new book. Jeremy Robinson and Kane Gilmour elucidate their popular Jack Sigler thrillers. A. Scott Glancy talks about the amazing Delta Green series, and Chris Kelso chats with John Shirley, Nick Antosca, and Geoff Brown (Cohesion Press)

about their horror and military fiction. Donald Tyson in his column Murmurs in the Dark explores how swords have been mythologized as magical weapons throughout time. Mike Davis in his Weird Reflections column gives us a list of some recommended Lovecraftian post-apocalyptic reading, and the always insightful Laird Barron in his recurring column The Black Barony discusses post-apocalyptic themes in horror fiction and film. We're happy to present more dark poetry this issue from Bryan Thao Worra, and Richard Dansky and Robert Morrish deliver great new columns, including an interview with Joe Donnelly. Plus there are two military horror film features by Colleen Wanglund. And don't forget the extensive reviews section!

Well, let's get to it then. Cock back your piece (sexual innuendo intended), suit up, and let's face the end of the world through the imagination of these talented authors…

— AARON J. FRENCH
EDITOR-IN-CHIEF

Tales of horror, suspense, adventure and mystery take readers to the troubled little town of Pine Deep, to the feudal Japan of the Samurai, to the angry red planet of John Carter of Mars, and elsewhere.

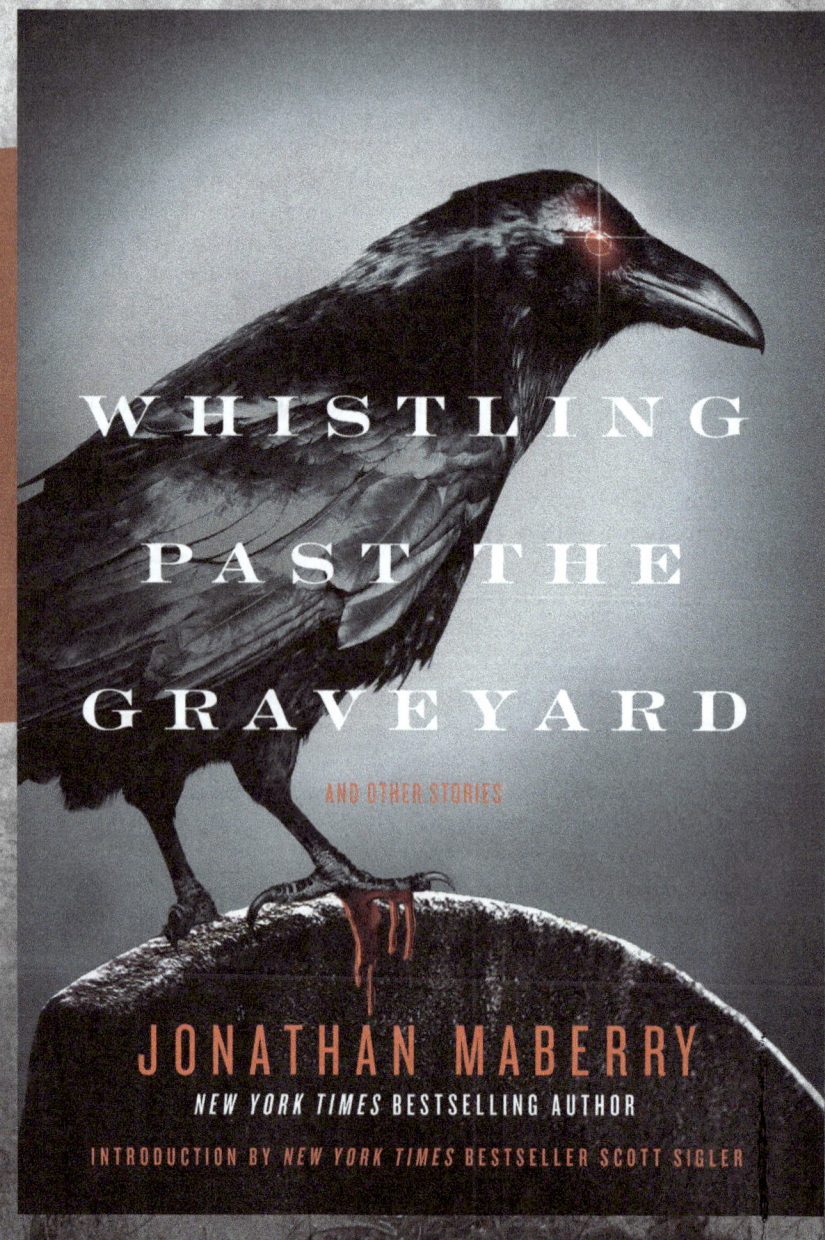

WHISTLING PAST THE GRAVEYARD

AND OTHER STORIES

JONATHAN MABERRY

NEW YORK TIMES BESTSELLING AUTHOR

INTRODUCTION BY *NEW YORK TIMES* BESTSELLER SCOTT SIGLER

Publication Date: July 22, 2016

JOE HILL

FIREMAN

Photo courtesy of Jen Salt

SPONTANEOUS COMBUSTION:
A CONVERSATION WITH JOE HILL

BY
DOUGLAS WYNNE

Joe Hill is the author of the novels *Heart Shaped Box, Horns,* and *NOS4A2,* as well as the short story collection *20th Century Ghosts* and the comic series *Locke & Key.* His fourth novel, *The Fireman,* was released in May and debuted at #1 on the NYT Bestsellers list. It's a high-tension apocalyptic thriller that you won't want to miss. Just before the book hit the shelves I had a chance to sit down with the author on the back of a fire truck and then over lunch at a riverside restaurant to discuss his creative process, the art of suspense, and mob psychology.

Douglas Wynne: Was there a particular moment or juxtaposition of ideas you can point to as the genesis of *The Fireman,* when you first glimpsed the potential of the story and knew it would be your next book?

JOE HILL: I can't identify a single place where the idea for the story came to me. I know that I heard about spontaneous combustion when I was 12 years old and immediately became terrified of dying that way. It just seemed like such an unfair thing that you could be wandering around and your chemistry would turn against you and suddenly you become like a human stick of nitroglycerin and just explode into flames. And I was convinced from the age of 12 to about the age of 15 that I was going to die of spontaneous combustion and… I didn't. I made it through, fortunately. So spontaneous combustion was a thing that was in my head for decades. And at some point about 8 or 9 years ago, I saw the first scene of the book. I saw in the opening scene, you have a young school nurse named Harper looking out the windows into the playground, and she sees a man stagger into the playground with smoke pouring from the sleeves of his coat. And I saw that whole scene play out very clearly. And I wasn't sure what the story was, I just knew that I had an opening that I liked and wanted to write. But I can't say at what point I knew that scene was going to be about a runaway plague that caused spontaneous combustion. At some point the pieces fell together and I thought: I could run with this. And probably I imagined it would be a novella, 'cause almost everything I write I think will be a short story or a novella until suddenly I've got 350 pages

and I think, "Oh, I guess maybe it's not."

DW: You wrote the first draft longhand in journals.

JH: Yeah, it's a *huge* stack of journals.

DW: It's a 700 plus page book. Why did you choose that approach? What were the advantages and challenges of working longhand?

JH: It's the first book I've written that way, which has its advantages and disadvantages because it forces you to work a little bit slower, and I remember I spent all of one month writing this one scene where a character needs to get a message to someone out on an island, and she decides she's going to do it by taping the message to an arrow and shooting the arrow out to the island because she can't get to the island herself. And she sneaks past all of these sentries and gets up into a church bell tower, and she's shooting arrow after arrow. It's a tremendously suspenseful scene, and it took me 3 to 4 weeks to write. Fifty pages, this major action set piece, you know. And after I finished writing the scene, almost the day after I finished writing it, I thought: or she could just have one of her friends carry a note over in secret… And so I never even ended up typing that scene up. It just became completely unnecessary and I dumped it.

So that was a little weird. There are moments like that when you're working longhand when it almost seems like, is it really worth the trouble? But I think it *is* worth the trouble. I'm best friends with Gabriel Rodriguez, who is the artist on *Locke & Key*, and from watching him create pages I was fascinated by the way a page of *Locke & Key* would start as a very loose rough sketch with just shapes placed on the page and the panels loosely framed out. And I had this moment, this sort of flash of insight, when I realized *that's* what the first draft of a novel should be like, too. It's just a personal sketch for yourself where you're framing out where the big moment should come, and you are sort of getting a sense for how your characters look and act, and

the whole overall movement of the story. And by writing it in long hand I'm really reinforcing that idea that the first draft is just for me, it's not for anyone else, it's just a sketch of the book to come. I don't outline, but I do sketch, I do that sort of first draft sketch work where things are a little bit more skeletal and very open to change, and I'm just sort of getting a sense for how it should flow.

DW: Does that involve some stuff where you might literally be writing what might sound like stage direction or summary for yourself? Is it that sparse?

I do that in the margins. One of the things that I do, and it's another reason why I love working in a notebook, is I'll be writing the scene and I'll put down one pen and get out a red pen and begin writing notes to myself in the margin. Like: this scene should actually come earlier in the book and it would be better if Harper was actually talking to *this* character instead of that character. And in first draft maybe Harper will be talking to Allie Story, say, and suddenly mid-scene she's talking to Renée Gilmonton instead because I'll suddenly realize it would be so much better if those were Renée's lines and that Allie doesn't belong in this scene. And you could do that working on the computer too, there's no reason you couldn't, but for some reason something about the nature of working longhand tricks my brain into claiming a freedom for itself that it doesn't seem to have when it's on a computer when I'm typing up a document.

Furthermore, there is no Internet on a notebook. There's no Twitter, there's no Instagram, there's no Huffington Post. So your opportunities to be distracted are substantially reduced. And I do some other stuff, like I don't keep the phone in the room with me. I don't listen to my music on my phone. I have a record player, and if I want to listen to music, I listen to vinyl. Because the record player just does one thing, it just plays music. It doesn't also give me text messages, and so I can't get distracted by text messages when I should be creating a scene. It's very selfish, but it's very satisfying.

DW: Music plays an important role in *The Fireman*, and there's a character in the book who lives in what's referred to as "the House of the Black Star" because of a folk art ornament mounted on the front of it. At that house, we also encounter a minor character who resembles David Bowie. And yet I'm pretty sure the book was finished before his death and before the release of *Black Star*. Synchronicity or tribute?

Um, you know, I've never even thought about that until just now. So synchronicity. It's true Harper is at one point brought to the house of the Black Star where she meets a David Bowie like character. That is very peculiar. That makes me seem smart, you know I like that, that's cool.

DW: A few years ago, in a blog post called Pour Me Another Draft, you offered a glimpse into your revision process, including the discipline of manually retyping the entire book because it forces you to be a more discerning editor than if you were just scanning through the text. When I read that you did that, I thought you were crazy. So, of course I immediately took up the practice. But I've found that after a few books, I'm writing more economical first drafts from that training. Do you still retype an entire draft in revision?

Absolutely. Twice if possible. One thing is, when you have to copy a manuscript over from longhand, you literally have to retype every single sentence. In the process, you get rid of stuff you don't need. You look at a paragraph that's a huge paragraph and you'll type in the first two sentences and then you'll be looking at the next 10 sentences and you'll be like, "Eh, I don't really need any of that. I don't really feel like typing any of that."

DW: Laziness is your ally.

🏢 Yeah, being lazy is your ally. I got it all in the first two sentences, I don't need the rest of that crap. Hit return, onto the next paragraph. And until you test each sentence by writing it again, you don't really know which sentence is worthy of staying there, and I think when you're just cutting and pasting stuff those sentences remain very unexamined. You know, it's always been there and you just clip it into a new document and it hasn't been forced to prove it deserves to stay.

David Mamet who said that when you write a screenplay for a film you always want to have at least one building explode. And the reason why, he said, is because the film crew really loves when the building explodes. It's a big night when you're shooting and everyone shows up, they got the explosives all set up, the building explodes… it's awesome. Everyone has a great night. And I thought, you know, I write novels not films, but that feels right. Sooner or later you blow some shit up and everyone loves it.

DW: Your action scenes are fantastic, and I've noticed that part of what makes them so kinetic are what I think of as great *auditory verbs*. The sound of the word often contributes to the action. Do you make a point of collecting great verbs? (I hear you're a fearsome Scrabble player.) Or is that

Photo courtesy of Jen Salt

DW: You seem to enjoy burning shit in your books. Did you go through a pyro phase growing up?

🏢 *Yeah*… I mean there is a lot of fire in the books, a lot of fire. I've thought about this very carefully, and I do sort of wonder: if I wasn't writing would I be in jail for arson? Would I be a firebug?

DW: You found a socially acceptable outlet.

🏢 I'd be locked up in jail and every time someone lights a cigarette near me I'd wet myself with pleasure. I'd be like, "*Ahhh*, the sweet cleansing flame." I think it was

something you bring from your work in comics?

🏢 Actually, I was working on a comic the other day and I wrote an unforgettable line of dialogue. It was, "HURKKKKK!" And after writing it I just thought, "Damn, you just never get to write a line like that in a novel." I think the right verb tweaks a reader's thrill centers, it pokes that excitement center in a way I don't understand, but if you nail it with just the right verb, the reader kind of feels an interior shudder in response. Or at least *I* do.

DW: And it saves so many other words.

🔥 And it saves so many other words. That's right. One of the things I noticed when I was in high school and I read Louis L'Amour westerns—I was interested to learn how rarely Louis L'Amour described how things looked. Instead he described how things *sounded*. The sound of horses breathing. The sound of dry firewood snapping in the flames. And I thought it was interesting how immediate that made scenes feel. The visuals tended to be static, but the sounds tended to electrify the reader's attention. So I'm always wondering how can I get away from the visual and get under the reader's skin.

DW: Give them the right sound and they can see it.

🔥 Exactly. The other thing to remember is you don't want to be too controlling. You want to let the readers do at least half the work. Let them cast the movie. Don't cast the movie for them. Let *them* decide what the characters look like. So I do try not to step all over what the reader might have the potential to imagine. With John Rookwood in *The Fireman*—one of the lead characters of the novel—I think there are three sentences where I remind people he wears glasses sometimes, and I described him as small and sort of sinewy, and that's about it. Otherwise, I hope the reader will build their visual off of the way other people talk about him and his own dialogue, and let them sort of shape the image in their mind. Elmore Leonard said once, "I want to know how a character looks from what he says." I always thought that was such an interesting idea. Why should the way a person talks suddenly give you a visual of what they look like? But it never fails. The right dialogue always makes you picture a character.

DW: This is your second book with a female lead, and you also included some Easter eggs that pay homage to female horror and sci-fi legends. My favorite was a little girl's "cup of stars" right out of Shirley Jackson's *The Haunting of Hill House.*

🔥 Yeah, I love that cup of stars. That thing in *The Haunting of Hill House* about the cup of stars is like one of the most beautiful passages ever written in an American novel. Don't let them take away your cup of stars. I love that.

DW: It seems to me that we're in the midst of a golden age of female horror authors who are bringing new perspectives and voices to the genre, particularly in short fiction.

Who are some of your favorites?

🔥 Karen Russell and Kelly Link have both done astonishing work. I really learned how to write short stories from studying Kelly Link's fiction, in particular "The Specialist's Hat," which I think is a classic of horror—speaking of Shirley Jackson—on par with "The Lottery." Just a total masterpiece of formal construction and imagination. And I love Karen Russell. *St. Lucy's Home for Girls Raised by Wolves* is terrific. Recently I've discovered Seanan McGuire. She is a terrific writer, and more of a fantasy writer than a horror writer, but she does really incandescent work. Beautiful sentences, beautiful ideas. She has a really brave imagination that takes her into unexpected directions. So those are a few writers who come to mind, and they've all done some of their most exciting work in very compact form, in short stories or novellas or short novels.

And I would just say about that, as a guy who's written two very long novels back-to-back, that I often think that mastery is revealed in miniature. When you're seeing someone really at the height of their powers, it tends to be in short novels or short stories. And then I guess my defense at having written two long novels is that especially *The Fireman* is a series of short novels stitched together. Novels about the same character stitched together into one overarching narrative.

Photo courtesy of Jen Salt

DW: In the dedication you thank J.K. Rowling "whose stories showed me how to write this one." Is there a particular thing you learned from her approach to storytelling that you could share?

🔥 Anyone who loves the Harry Potter novels—and I love the Harry Potter novels, I've read all of them twice and I guess I've read a couple of them three times and seen the movies multiple times and I just adore J.K. Rowling both as a writer and as a public figure, I love the stories—anyone who's familiar with the Harry Potter novels who reads

The Fireman might be able to see how the structure of *The Fireman* mimics the structure of most of the Harry Potter novels.

In Harry Potter you have a hero who's coming from a very unhappy domestic situation and who is different. Different and strange. And then he goes away to a community where everyone is different and strange like him, and there he wrestles to learn to control unexpected powers, and is confronted with a series of mysteries. And also makes friends and makes enemies. And then each of the mysteries in the book are resolved in a series of escalating confrontations that will force Harry, the hero, to make use of his newfound education and powers, to take control of his own specialness, his difference, and use that to confront his enemies and to resolve these puzzles.

And that's basically *The Fireman*. You have this hero, Harper, who is coming from an unhappy domestic situation. There's something very different about her from other people, which is that she's contaminated by this illness that could cause her to burst into flame at any moment. She goes to a comunity where people are different; like her, everyone is sick with the same illness. It's not Hogwarts, it's Camp Wyndham, but it is a place where the strange is commonplace. There she makes friends, she makes enemies, and is confronted with a series of mysteries and puzzles. And she's forced to grapple with her own difference, her strangeness, and to take possession of her own powers. Those mysteries are all resolved in a series of escalating confrontations that force her to use the things she has learned from the people who care about her. So it is in many ways a mirror, it is a weird mirror to the structure of the Harry Potter novels.

DW: You mentioned mysteries. One of the heroes in the book says, "Any writer who works by outline should be burned at the stake. Possibly with their own outline and note cards used as kindling." As a fellow seat-of-the pants writer, I find the spontaneous approach is great for suspense but tricky for mystery. Do you forecast plot events at all? And I'm thinking of two revelations in particular from your books: the mystery regarding a thief in the middle of

The Fireman and Merrin's secret in *Horns*. Did you know in advance how those mysteries would be resolved, or is it a discovery for you almost as much as for the reader?

JHb One of the things people have mentioned is how surprised they were that I gave away who the killer was in the first hundred pages of *Horns*. Because it looks like it's going to be a mystery and then actually at page 80 I say no, this is the dude that did it. And in that case I revealed who the murderer was because I didn't think I'd fool anyone. I figured everyone would just say, "Oh, it's this guy." And so the job is to create suspense. You want to keep people turning the pages, to keep them excited. And Hitchcock once said the difference between surprise and suspense

Photo courtesy of Jen Salt

is simple. Surprise is when people are sitting at a dinner table and suddenly the room blows up. That's surprise. Suspense is when you see the bomb ticking under the table and they don't. So I thought, instead of keeping it a surprise who the killer is, I'm going to say it right up front and then I'm going to create suspense because we know he's out there hunting our hero and that his powers might be overmatched by this guy's resources.

DW: But then we find out something about Merrin.

JHb Right, we find out something about Merrin that we didn't know right off.

DW: And it changes everything. I wondered if you knew that about her before you got there.

🔥 Actually I didn't. I discovered it as I went along. And I didn't know who the camp thief was in *The Fireman* originally. But I began to suspect. Before that revelation came out, I began to suspect who it might be and why. But then, the beauty of doing five or six drafts is if something is painfully obvious in the first draft you can retrofit it to make it harder to spot. And, especially about the identity of the thief working in Camp Wyndham, in the last three drafts I was literally down to playing: can I keep this one sentence in without giving it away? Can I have this one thing, this one detail on this one page, or will it give it all away? And I would take it out and I would put it back in and I would take it out. I think I left it in. Were you surprised, or did you see it coming?

DW: I considered it as one of several possibilities, but I wasn't sure until I got there.

🔥 Okay. I talked to one reader who said, "Oh, I knew who the thief was on page 250." But then this reader said, "But I grew up reading Agatha Christie novels, and I'm impossible to fool." And a couple of other people were surprised, and my dad said he didn't see it coming, so I thought, "Well, I got my dad. I got someone."

DW: One technique that makes *The Fireman* so suspenseful is how you buy yourself the space to develop characters and relationships by dangling high stakes consequences before stepping away, so that the whole time people are sharing their backstories or falling in love, I'm biting my nails about what's going on off-screen. And that tension is often enhanced by how Harper's rationality and concern for others gives her a blind spot to certain dangers. She continues, in many ways, to operate from a pre-apocalyptic mindset while everyone around her is going crazy. Did those strategies for keeping suspense in the red come intuitively in early drafts, or did you have to play with the story structure to strike the right balance?

🔥 That's really why the book took three years to write. I'm not a fast writer and often times I'll encounter a problem somewhere in the course of writing a book that's like this. Here's the problem that had to be solved: Harper arrives in Camp Wyndham where suddenly the book opens up with a huge cast of characters and an interesting setting with a lot of mysteries and puzzles and big ideas to wrestle with. Somehow you have to provide all that and anchor the reader and introduce all these characters, introduce the setting, introduce the problems, but you still have to keep the gas pedal down. Because if it becomes expositional, if it becomes information, the reader begins to flip ahead and say, "My God, is anything good going to happen in this book again?" So you can't slow down. And the process of the work in the book was tuning and tuning and tuning so that when Harper gets to Camp Wyndham we learn about who these people are and we get to love them, we get to care about them, but still there is suspense,

the pressure is still on, there is still danger, people are still dropping dead left and right. You know, Harper is always still scrabbling for resources to survive, scrabbling to escape the next dire situation. Maybe I wouldn't feel the need for that if I wasn't so insecure. But I am very insecure about the reader quitting the book, losing interest and then saying on Goodreads or Amazon, "I gave up after page 250 because not enough was happening." So you have to accelerate, you have to keep the danger coming or people lose interest.

DW: You expanded on *NOS4A2* in the *Wraith* comics. Do you have any plans or see any potential to revisit the world and characters of *The Fireman* in other media?

🔥 I don't know about other media… *The Fireman* is the first book I've ever written where I thought there was a chance that there might be another book about those characters. Although, I think if I were to return, I probably wouldn't return for maybe a decade. But I could see 10 years from now writing another story about some of those characters because I can imagine a little bit more, and I've given some thought about what might happen next. Also, the rights to *The Fireman* were bought by Temple Hill and 20th Century Fox, and they're developing it as a feature to be directed by Louis Leterrier. They're talking to a screenwriter right now, so fingers crossed that something happens there.

DW: Cool. What book would you rescue the last copy of from a burning building?

🔥 That assumes there are no more copies anywhere in the world. I think this is like, if you were going down into the bunker and knew we were going to have to start civilization over, which books would you bring with you? I think that you'd have to bring *The Riverside Shakespeare* because it's got all of the plays in it. It's a little bit of a cheat because it's got all of the plays, it's got the complete poems, and some academic analysis. I just don't think you could rebuild a humanistic society without Shakespeare. Probably Shakespeare over the Bible, really. And I don't say that to bash religious people, but given the world's track record with religion, I assume if you're going down into the bunker to escape the apocalypse it's because of some kind of religious war, so maybe you leave the Bible behind and just take Shakespeare because that would make for a better fresh start.

DW: On Facebook, Christopher Golden—a champion of your work since long before he knew you were writing under a pseudonym—called *The Fireman* "the novel in which Joe seems to have both fully embraced his legacy and fully processed it, successfully moving beyond it in a way a lesser writer never could."

🔥 Chris has a good heart.

DW: *The Fireman* seems to especially have some DNA from *The Stand* blended into it. Of course, most apocalyptic novels do, but I think I detected intentional references in the naming of certain characters.

JHb Oh yeah.

DW: For me as a fan, it's fun to see, and it feels sort of like recognizing little ornaments in the craft of someone like a woodworker, who learned the family trade and then in many ways surpassed that foundation by making the work uniquely his own. Is your father's influence something that you feel you can acknowledge more comfortably at this point in your career without it being a distraction?

JHb: I retrofitted a lot of *The Stand* stuff in the second and third drafts because, to be honest, when I was writing the first draft I didn't really think about *The Stand* that much, but at some point very close to the end of the book I thought, you know, this has a lot in common with *The Stand*. And my joke about it, when I've talked to people about it, is to say that this is basically my version of *The Stand* soaked in gasoline and set on fire. I mean I did make this decision, when I started out writing, to write as Joe Hill. Not as Joseph King. And to keep it a secret for as long as I could. And I did that because of insecurity and because I wanted to have a chance to learn the craft, and when I finally did publish, I wanted to get published because people were genuinely excited about my fiction and not because I had a famous last name. I was worried that if I started writing as Joseph King, and if I was writing stuff that wasn't very polished or very good and I was getting published because of who my dad was, people would say he only got published because of who his dad was and he's riding on his coattails. And so I did write as Joe Hill and I was able to learn some things and publish some stories, get some stories accepted by people who didn't know, and that was a big confidence booster for me and it was a very useful period of my development. That said, I love my dad's books and I'm a huge Stephen King fan, and my mom and dad are always the people who look at my first drafts. Actually, they don't usually look at the first draft, they look at the third drafts—I don't want anyone to see the first two drafts. But they are my first readers and still the best writing teachers a guy could want.

DW: But *The Stand* related material actually came in as finishing touches?

JHb There is a character, a child named Nick, who's deaf. And of course, one of the heroes of *The Stand* is a deaf man named Nick Andros. Actually, the kid was named Travis in an earlier draft and it was only when I was two thirds of the way through the book that I remembered there was a deaf character in *The Stand*.

DW: Your Harold also reminded me…

JHb Yeah, he was named something else as well, and I thought, you know, this character is so much like Harold Lauder. So one of the things I started to do was, I thought: so this book does have echoes of *The Stand* in it. What do you do? Do you try to distance yourself from *The Stand* or do you embrace it? I thought, you know, as an artist I always think it's better to be loud and proud and embrace what you are about than to run from it. This is why when someone directs a horror movie and it gets time to release the preview to theaters, you show the chainsaw. You don't pretend you made an art film. Embrace what you did, okay? And so then, instead of running from *The Stand* I kind of went back to the book and said, "Where can I strengthen the notes? Where can I strengthen the echoes in interesting ways?"

DW: Bring it up in the mix.

JHb I kind of look at it as its own song that at some point in the song has some musical references to a pretty good song that we remember from a few years back.

DW: It kind of harmonizes with *The Stand*.

Photo courtesy of Jen Salt

🔥 Yeah, it does.

DW: In the book, you refer to the hormone oxytocin as the "social media drug." This real neurotransmitter plays a key role in how the fictional Dragonscale spore is either transmitted or kept in a state of equilibrium. And one quote that I love is: "A chorus or a firing squad: either would serve to satisfy the 'scale." You do a very deft job of showing us both sides of that coin, how the social bonds that give us civilization can also fuel mob violence. It's a theme that feels very prescient in foreshadowing the energies of our current election cycle. But the book was written before things got so crazy. Did your own social media observations inspire you to explore those themes? And when you look at the crowd psychology on display in this election year, are you optimistic that our better natures will prevail?

🔥 I spent years on Twitter as a guy who spent an hour a day every day on Twitter. I've backed off from the social network quite a bit over the last year, but I was really into that community, and I had some really great times there. I had all these great conversations and had a chance to talk with artists I admire and fellow bookworms and people into the same kind of weird historical stuff that I'm into, and I had moments when I thought: this is a very inspiring place for bringing people together and sharing joy and really all geeking out together about the stuff we love. And so that was very inspiring and moving.

But then you also see all of the stuff around Gamer Gate. And the hideous way women were persecuted by mobs of trolls in a really horrible way, essentially for daring to have an opinion about video games. And those two things exist together. The Gamer Gaters who were savaging women are in their way embracing their own community. It's a vile community, but you know… And think about when you see the Bernie Sanders rallies, and you see this outpouring of joy and humor and people are essentially geeks for Bernie and they're wearing funny Bernie Sanders T-shirts, and then you contrast that with the Donald Trump rally

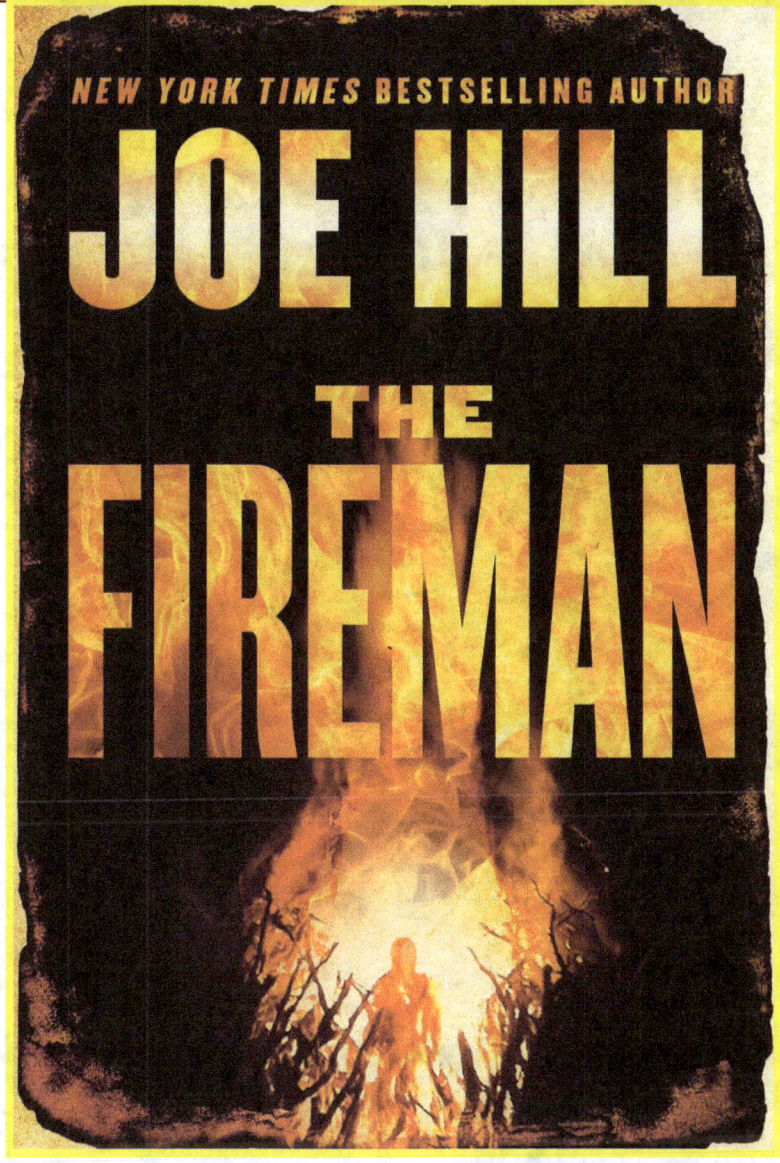

where there seems to be this seething rage, this desire to break something, to spread some hurt around. And on the one hand, the two communities are clearly very different. On the other hand, both are demonstrations of group dynamics. You have the beautiful and the hideous very closely paired together.

DW: Chemically, people may be getting a similar experience.

🔥 Almost exactly the same experience, right. And so one of the things I did want to explore in the book is I wanted to show the way communities can heal and support and love… but the problem with having a tribe is it gets tribal. And people who are not of the tribe, you have an excuse to hate, demonize them, be cruel and savage, and sort of have the safety of the crowd, too. And you know, if I could change just one thing in the book, if I could go back and add one thing, I'd give The Marlboro Man a 'Make America Great Again' hat.

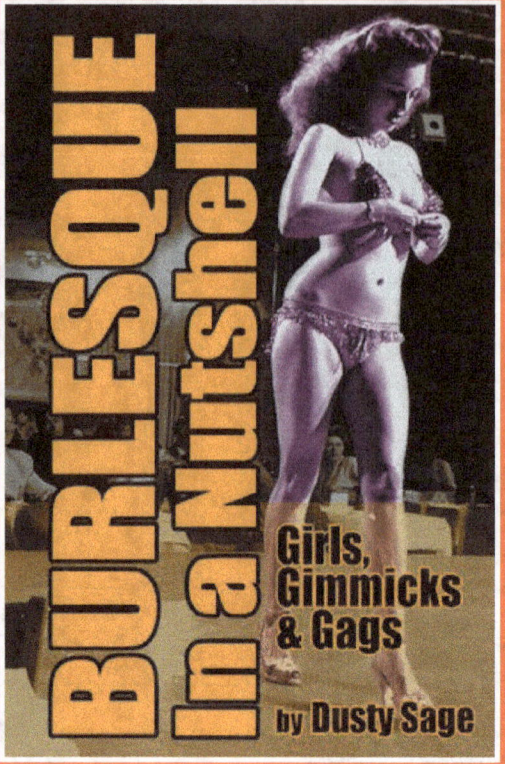

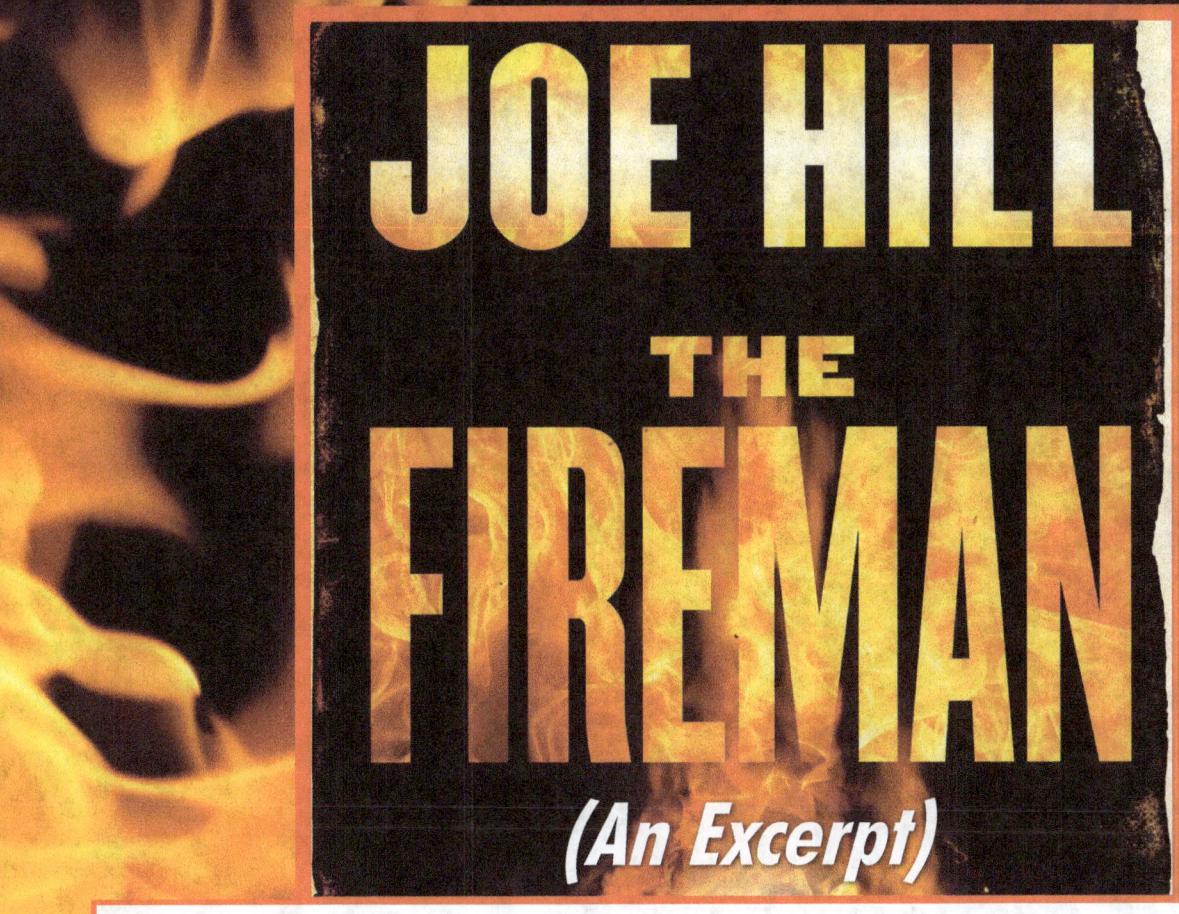

JOE HILL
THE FIREMAN
(An Excerpt)

I t was first period and no kids were out now, the only time of the day there wasn't a flock of screaming, rioting, laughing, colliding children rushing about in sight of the health office. There was just the
man, a guy in a baggy green army jacket and loose brown work pants, face in the shadow of a grimy
baseball cap. He crossed the asphalt at a slant, coming around the back of the building. His head was
down and he staggered, couldn't seem to hold to a straight line. Harper's initial thought was that he was
drunk. Then she saw the smoke coming out of his sleeves. A fine, white smoke poured out of the jacket,
around his hands, and up from under his collar into his long brown hair.

He lurched off the edge of the pavement and onto the mulch. He took three more steps and put his
right hand on the wooden rung of a ladder leading up into the jungle gym. Even from this distance,
Harper could see something on the back of his hand, a dark stripe, like a tattoo, but flecked with gold. The
specks flashed, like motes of dust in a blinding ray of sunlight.

She had seen reports about it on the news, but still, in those first moments, she could hardly make
sense of what she was looking at. Little candies began to fall out of the Mary Poppins lunch box, rattling
on the floor. She didn't hear them, wasn't aware she was now holding the box at a crooked angle, dump-
ing out miniature candy bars and Hershey's Kisses. Raymond watched the potato drop with a fleshy thud
and roll out of sight under a counter.

The man who walked like a drunk began to sag. Then he arched his spine convulsively, throwing his
head back, and flames licked up the front of his shirt. She had one brief glance at his gaunt, agonized face
and then his head was a torch. He beat his left hand at his chest, but his right hand still held the wooden
ladder. His right hand was burning, charring the pine. His head tipped farther and farther back and he
opened his mouth to scream and black smoke gushed out instead.

Raymond saw the expression on Harper's face and started to turn his head to look over his shoulder
and out the window. Harper let go of the candy box and reached for him. She clamped one hand to
the cold compress and put her other hand behind Raymond's head, forcibly turning his face from the
window.

"Don't, dear," she said, surprised at the calm she heard in her own voice.

"What was that?" he asked.

She let go of the back of his head and found the cord for the blinds. Outside, the burning man sank
to his knees. He bowed his head, like one praying to Mecca. He was engulfed in flames, a mound of rags
pouring oily smoke into the bright, cold April afternoon.

The shade fell with a metallic crash, shutting out the whole scene—all except a feverish flicker of
golden light, glimmering madly around the edges of the blinds. ◊

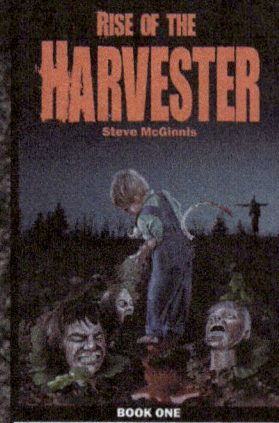

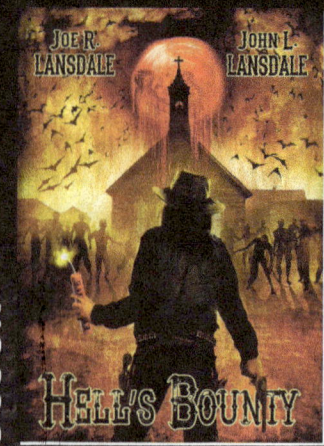
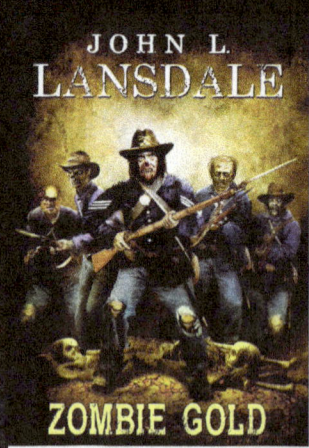

The Great Armored Train

Nick Mamatas

So, this is what Communism means? Gribov thought. The train was magnificent. It seemed too heavy to move, but it fairly glided along the tracks. It was the smoothest ride Gribov had ever been on, and it bustled with activity—warehouse, restaurant, barracks, even a Politburo office and telegraph station, a two-car garage and a small biplane among its twelve wagons. Never mind the armored engines with gun turrets. *All this, and doesn't even have a name!* It was just the train of the *Predrevoyensoviet*, Leon Trotsky. Didn't the War Commissar have a wife or a girlfriend to name his personal armored war-train after?

But really, it was the workers' train, and there was much work to be done. Gribov was a soldier, but no longer just a standard peasant with a rifle and a children's book on the Russian alphabet to help him learn to read. He was one of the Red Sotnia, the hundred soldiers who made up Trotsky's bodyguard and rushed out to join pitched battles. Not long before, he'd been in the cavalry train that followed behind Trotsky's, shoveling horseshit. But the train, and the Bolshevik efforts, had taken some hits lately and now Gribov was decked out in black leather, presumably ready to give his life for the world proletariat, and for comrade Trotsky. Gribov dutifully collected the train's newspaper, *V puti*, but mostly used it to insulate his boots. It was cold tonight on the Polish border, and he was glad that Trotsky wrote so much. *Almost toasty*, he thought, as he leapt from the roof of one car to another, watching the forest for Mensheviks, for Cossacks, for Poles.

One of the sharpshooters stationed on the roof whispered harshly to him. "Comrade! Step lightly! You'll bring them down upon us."

"Comrade," Gribov said, "we are on a giant train. Steam is billowing from the engines. Even idle, even under the new moon, we're obvious."

"And an opposing army flooding from the wood should be more obvious still," another sharpshooter said.

"When I was a soldier under the czar, we would never have dared to banter so," said the first shooter.

"Thus I am thankful now more than ever for the Revolution, and the 2nd Latvian Riflemen's Soviet Regiment," said the second. The others, five in all, giggled. "But be quiet anyway," the second shooter said to Gribov. "I'm working on my poem." More chortling emerged from the dark.

"Poem? What?" Gribov frowned.

"Don't you read the paper?" the first shooter asked. "How do you know where we are *on our way* to?" More laughter, this time for the pun on *V puti*—*en route* or "on our way."

"Comrade Fancy Dude has called on the poets of Poland to write poems denouncing the landlords and the bourgeoisie," a new voice explained.

"Perhaps I will write a poem then," Gribov said. He laughed, once.

"What rhymes with *pshek*?" the second shooter asked, and he got a round of chuckles from the shooters arranged on either side of the train car's roof. The new Communist mentality had not quite taken hold in the men of the Red Sotnia. After all, the Polish workers spoke as funnily as the Polish bourgeoisie. But Gribov couldn't blame them for

their elitism. They were an elite! It was a very nice train after all, complete with cloth napkins for Trotsky's personal staff, so perhaps being part of the "One Hundred," living aboard a futuristic conveyance, had confused them. Gribov could write a poem too, and a poem that would be understood by the Polish proletariat! Working man to working man, something these careerists from good families would never understand. The poem could be about the train, and its many magnificent attributes—the Rolls Royce liberated from the czar's garage and outfitted with a pair of machine guns! It was always a thrill to hear it roaring forth from its special train car, metal flashing under the sun, lighting and thunder at once…

"Carry on," he announced to the sharpshooters, and moved on to the next train car, jumping lightly and expertly over the gap. It was a risk, but Gribov knew there would be no insults shouted at his back, for fear of alerting the enemy. There was no way the train was secret, but a sudden yelp could give away a comrade's position to a Polish sniper.

A poem, a poem… What would inspire the Polish working class to rise up, to greet the Red Army as liberators? No poem had been needed to persuade Gribov. His family were dirt-poor peasants and when he crawled into Petrograd to look for work on the piers, he was treated worse than his father had treated the animals on the farm. Nobody else offered anything but misery, and the phony promise of a heavenly reward. The heavens were dark tonight. No moon, no stars; the clouds were low and the color of slate.

A rush of wind almost sent Gribov's spine tearing out of his back. Bursting from the trees had come a great gray owl, flying low and nearly silent just under the dome of the sky, wings stretched a meter and a half from tip to tip.

Incredible! This would go into the poem, Gribov decided, but then the owl banked and turned, its claws wide and gleaming. Gribov couldn't decide between drawing his pistol and just raising his arms. The owl took his face. Screaming, Gribov flailed and fell from the train. An alarm was raised, but from the woods Polish irregulars rained small arms fire down on the train.

***

Who would wake Trotsky? "The man would sleep through the Proletarian Revolution were he not in charge of scheduling it" was the common joke, but it wasn't quite fair. Trotsky was awake twenty hours a day, so the four he slept were extremely necessary. He was difficult to awaken, and ornery when he finally arose. Even under Communism, whoever knocked on the door had better have his boots polished. Nechayev drew the short straw and was poised to knock when the door opened. Trotsky was already dressed, complete in leather coat and hat.

"We're not under way, I presume," Trotsky said, "because the tracks ahead have been destroyed. And we are concerned that if we head back along the line, we'll encounter a Menshevik train. The cavalry train is also pinned down."

A near-perfect set of wrong conclusions. Under any

other circumstances, Trotsky would have been correct, but…

"We have an infiltrator. She has sabotaged the engines. We were able to repulse the Poles, but we expect reinforcements by morning," Nechayev said.

"She—" Trotsky began.

"So…we've heard," Nechayev said.

"*She*'s not been captured yet? A woman? An individual woman?"

"It's hard to explain," Nechayev began. A few words later and Trotsky pushed past him, his own sidearm drawn, orders spilling forth.

The woman looked like a Pole; fair, with a round face, though there was something else about her coloration too, the bone structure around her cheeks. She wore the black leather uniform of a Red Sotnia fighter, though it was far too big for her. She'd made it as far as one of the supply cars. The men she had already dispatched slumped amidst piles of shoes, loose piles of tobacco and potatoes spilling forth from the sacks they'd been stored in. Four guards had rifles trained on her. For a moment, Trotsky thought she was weeping silently, but then realized that the squint was just her eyes—she was a Tatar, or had some Tatar ancestry anyway.

"Anyone have any Polish?" Trotsky asked. Then he tried, in Russian, then German, and even bad French, and English.

"Comrade Commissar," one of the guards asked. "What shall we do? Shoot her? If we approach, she just…" he trailed off.

"…turns into an owl," Trotsky finished. "Keep her pinned. Rotate comrades in and out of here. Let her stand there, looking foolish. Kick a bucket over to her so she can urinate without making a mess. If she does anything else… *interesting*, seal her in the car and detach it from the train on both ends. We'll rendezvous the hard way."

After hasty scrambles around tracks and over coaches to the restaurant car, everyone was full of questions, but only Trotsky was able to complete his sentences without interruption.

"You'd sacrifice the train, but—"

"Seal her in and set it on fire! That way—"

"How many more…"

"Why are you even taking this seriously?" Pozansky finally demanded of Trotsky. He was the senior of the commissar's secretaries, and broad-chested, so his voice both metaphorical and literal carried like no other. "It defies all we know of science!"

"That is why," Trotsky said. The room quieted. "Why am I on the verge of sacrificing our train? Because if a woman can metamorphose into an owl, our cause is lost. The proletarian dictatorship depends on proletarian revolution. The proletarian revolution depends on a dialectical understanding of history. The dialectical understanding of history—" the soldiers began shifting in their seats, as Comrade Fancy Pants was gearing up for one of his extensive speeches it sounded like—"and the dialectical understanding of history is built upon a bedrock of materialism."

Trotsky tugged on his van dyke. "We're at war, so I'll say it quickly. If she is some sort of mystical or supernatural being, our cause is lost. If magic is real, then Marxism is not. We may as well go home and light candles by the family icon."

"What are the chances that this woman can turn into an owl in a way not possible to explain by some science, even if only the science of the future?" Pozansky asked. "And what are the chances that vodka and philosophical backsliding led to a certain level of embarrassment among our troop over the fact that a single, female, saboteur eluded detection, damaged both engines, and killed several men with what was obviously a garden fork of some sort?"

"Low," Trotsky said.

"Lower than the possibility that magic and superstition is real? That a fairy out of children's tales attacked our train for the glory of Polish imperialists?"

"That depends on the nature of reality," Trotsky said. "Which we will now investigate. Men, take the motorcars out. Find me a Pole who speaks Russian. Find me a Tatar familiar with the superstitions of his race. Find a book, a journal, anything, even if for children, on the subject of local folklore or avifauna. And try to make sure the Pole who can speak Russian is literate. Shoes and food and cigarettes and liquor are to trade, and if the marketplace doesn't meet our demands, well then men, remember that you are Communists."

When the troop dispersed, Trotsky raised an eyebrow at Pozansky. The senior secretary smirked back, and young Nechayev just look confused.

"We cleared the train of anyone who might have been bamboozled by this stage magic," Pozansky explained.

"Obviously, she is wearing one of our uniforms. If she turned into an owl and then back, she would be nude," Trotsky said. "What I am interested in, primarily, is finding out how our captive performs these tricks. It might make for a useful wedge between Polish workers and reactionary, credulous, peasants."

Nechayev said, "I thought we were never to lie to the working class."

Trotsky shrugged. "We wouldn't be. We'd be lying to the backward elements of the peasantry. The Poles are lying to our people, of course, which is why this social-reactionary split has occurred." Nechayev had the strong feeling that the only split that had occurred was that Trotsky was getting ready to have him demoted, arrested, or thrown off the train for passing on the owl story with such credulity.

"And we need to find out from whom she got one of our uniforms. We've not been through this part of the front before; we've had no recent casualties outside of the train from which the leathers could have been salvaged. If the Poles had decided to infiltrate, surely they would have sent a male, and a Russian speaker. I suspect some sort of love affair concocted by local peasant militias," Trotsky said. "You two, move my desk over to the train in which our owl has been penned."

***

A handful of comrades discovered Gribov on their way back from their mission. He was cold, bloodied, probably blinded and one eye was missing entirely, but he lived. Much of his uniform was missing as well. They created a makeshift gurney from rifles and coats and brought him aboard, to the infirmary car.

Gribov was not a weak man, and he had fallen into a snowbank, so soon enough he was able to testify, haltingly. Pozansky took notes, argued closely over the advice of the medics.

"The owl? Not a small kite, or even an aeroplane of some sort?"

"It was warm, alive, smelled like the woods and dead prey…"

"Feathers would do that!"

"She took off my clothes. Just one little girl…"

"One? How do you know there was only one if you are missing one eye?"

"Just a pair of little hands…"

"Did they say anything?"

Gribov laughed. "Pshek pshek…you know how Poles sound. All consonants. Haha."

"Comrade, there are many revolutionary Poles in our movement who might tell you that to a Pole a Russian sounds like a child," Pozansky lectured. "Shaa shaa vaa vaaa."

"Comrade secretary, please," one of the medics said. "He needs rest, not political education."

"We need to get to the bottom of the case of this infiltrator, comrade doctor!"

"Why not just shoot her and throw her into a ditch?" the medic demanded.

"Please don't…" Gribov said. "She's…"

"Yes?"

"…my poem."

"He's delirious," said the medic.

"Thank you for that insight, comrade doctor," Pozansky said. "As we thought."

***

Nechayev told Trotsky about finding Gribov, but that made the commissar only more interested in this interrogative theater. Soldiers had slowly moved in to the train car, but kept their rifles, and further the length of two strides, between themselves and the girl. She looked like a wax doll. If not for the puffs of steam coming from her mouth with every exhalation, she could have passed for a bit of whimsical propaganda art amongst the supplies.

The soldiers had found several books on folklore, and a local bilingual speaker, an older woman who had experienced the border shifting between empires under her feet several times in her long life. She was not pleased to have been awakened at gunpoint and brought here for the interrogation, but she drank her tea and ate a potato and a bit of meat from the tin plate held on her lap with some pleasure. She could even read, but her glasses had been smashed during the trip back to the train, so her literacy was of no help.

"Do you two women know one another?" was the first question.

"I don't associate with Tatars," the old woman said.

"Or Communists."

"And yet here we all are," said Trotsky. Nechayev put his hand to his forehead and sighed. Under the czar he probably would have been whipped for the gesture, but Trotsky didn't even notice.

"Ask her why she is against the proletarian revolution," he said to the older woman. With a practiced sneer, she turned toward the girl and repeated the question in Polish. The answer was short.

"She says you know why."

The interrogation went on for some time. Was she a Tatar? That depends on what you mean. Did she attack the soldier Gribov, sabotage the engine, then storm through the cars of this magnificent train, killing and injuring Soviet soldiers? Certainly she did, and she would be pleased to continue. How did she manage such a feat? The soldier had his head in the clouds; her husband, murdered by Reds, had been a machinist so she knew something of engines; Russian men are weak and easy to kill, even for a simple girl like her. Can she turn into an owl? Yes, of course. That was the fault of the Bolsheviks as well.

"How is that?" Trotsky said, clearly amused.

"Girls who are married when they die turn into owls," it was explained by the translator before the young girl even spoke. The older woman added, "It is an old story." Trotsky took a moment to flip through one of the children's books his soldiers had liberated, and grunted once when he alighted upon a certain illustrated page.

"Are there mice in your home?" The old woman turned again to ask the girl, but Trotsky raised his hand. "In *your* home, ma'am."

"There were mice in my home," she snapped, "when there was food in my home. Another achievement for the Bolsheviks!"

"Then how likely is it that Polish girls transform into owls upon their death?" Trotsky asked, ignoring the last bit of editorializing. "The moon would be eclipsed every night by masses of owl wings, and there wouldn't be a mouse left in Poland."

The girl said something testy-sounding, and the old woman translated at length, even pantomiming a mouse nibbling at some food. Trotsky turned to Nechayev. "Summon more witnesses," he said. "If they are not wounded or tending the wounded, if they are not on watch, if they are not repairing the engine, have them gather on either side of the car and peer inside." Nechayev ran to comply.

Finally the girl said something and the old woman translated it. "Her explanation is that she is only a Pole on her mother's side of the family. Her father's side are Tatars." There was a bit more discussion, then the old woman turned to Trotsky with a smile on her face. "She says her grandfather's grandfather was a…primitive."

"A shaman," Trotsky said. Behind him, a crowd was forming, four or five rows deep. With military discipline the shortest gathered immediately behind Trotsky's desk and took to their knees to not block the vision of their comrades behind them. "I presume it was the hybridity of superstitions that allows you your special ability to transform into an owl." The old woman didn't bother to translate that.

Lanterns shifted and danced on either side of the train car as comrades who couldn't fit inside jockeyed for position by the exits. Trotsky was clearly pontificating at length in order to allow everyone to get into position.

"So, why attack us? Why not be free as the proverbial bird, always, without the burdens of consciousness or the need to labor? Why not join us, allow us to better understand your ability, so that we might integrate it into the corpus of materialist science? What diseases could be cured via this form of cellular transformation? And yet, you keep it to yourself." The old woman's translations were obviously abbreviated and simplified, Nechayev could tell, but the young girl seemed to be getting the gist of Trotsky's comments anyway.

"Or, perhaps, you cannot turn into an owl," Trotsky finally concluded. "Just acknowledge this, and we'll keep you a prisoner here until our engine is repaired. We'll leave you at the next station on our side of the front for typical justice. If you continue to insist on your nonsense story, we shall gun you down—summary revolutionary justice on the part of the international working class, against a deranged member of the criminal element.

"Or you may turn into an owl and flee," Trotsky said. He glanced at Nechayev, then nodded toward the closest window. It occurred to Nechayev that the window, even were he to smash it out of its frame with the butt of a borrowed rifle, would not be sufficient for the wingspan of an owl the size of the one Gribov supposedly encountered, but he obeyed anyway as the older woman translated. Then, harshly, the older woman added something else—a message directly aimed at the girl.

The girl shifted in her outfit. A shoulder, nude, almost pink despite the cold, was visible now, and her thin little collarbone, itself like a bird's wings. Then two things happened.

The girl made a move. It wasn't a run, or a leap, but as though she had thrown her body forward, every muscle working together.

One of the soldiers fired. The train car filled with sound and smoke. Men screamed. "No!" "Don't!"

For a moment Nechayev thought something would happen. She wouldn't fall. Feathers would erupt out her back, trailing the bullet.

There was still shouting. The comrades were worried, hysterical, for themselves. Why fire into a crowded train car? Madness!

The girl fell hard. A gardening tool slipped from one sleeve of her oversized leather coat and clattered to the floor.

The other soldiers who had had their rifles trained on the woman held their fire. The old lady wasn't crying as Nechayev thought she might be. She was terrified that she would be next, her face chiseled by horror into an unnerving rictus.

Trotsky looked contemplative. Maybe it was a flash of disappointment that crossed over his eyes as he spoke. "Retrieve the coat and have it stitched up if possible," he said to nobody in particular, and there were no volunteers to strip the girl. He turned to the shooter. "Comrade Fedin,

you are relieved of duty due to reckless fire. Put your rifle down now if you do not wish it removed from you by force."

He sighed deeply. "Have the body brought to the infirmary car. We're not equipped for an autopsy here, but it might be interesting to see if there are visible lesions on her brain. So much for magical owls, eh?" Trotsky readied himself against his desk and rose. With a gesture, he told Nechayev to clear it all away. "And if I see one comrade making the sign of the cross, or hear tell of it, he will be disciplined most severely. And someone pay this woman and return her to her home," he said, indicating the old lady, who still hadn't moved, hadn't blinked.

***

Clearly, the corpse should have been stored in the refrigerated car, but Pozansky wouldn't have it, and he threatened the medics who said they'd go to Trotsky about it with hard discipline and a negative write-up in the train's newspaper.

"It's cold enough on this train," Pozansky said. "Her lesions will keep for the night, I am sure." There were a few choice items in cold storage that Pozansky liked to keep for himself, and whenever an unauthorized comrade entered the refrigerated car they would, in a burst of revolutionary fervor, take a sample of the caviar or beefsteak or decent vodka to share with the masses—that is, their friends.

And so she ended up in sickbay, next to Gribov. He suffered, awake, from his wounds, so was conscious to hear her cough out the bullet that had entered her chest. Mostly blind, he couldn't see that the bullet was coated in plant matter, feathers, and tiny bones. She slid off the examination table she had been left on, wrapped the blanket she had been given out of a sense of retrograde modesty around herself, and nudged Gribov.

"I have your eye," she said to him. "Would you like it back?" She was not speaking in the pshek-pshek of Polish. It was a strange tongue, all elongated *y* sounds.

"I…that would be hard to explain to the comrade officers…" Gribov said.

"You may come with me," the girl said. "Indeed, I insist upon it. I need a new husband, after all. I saw the world through your eye when I ingested it—you're not like these other men. You'll do. Come away with me."

"I'd be a burden," Gribov said. "I cannot fly as you can."

She smiled. "No, but you can drive."

He smiled too. Not quite like a mother giving a child a kiss, she leaned down, swept her hair away from her face, and with a significant gulp, regurgitated Gribov's eye onto his face, then roughly pushed it back into the socket with her free hand. Ten bloody minutes later, they had made it to the czar's Rolls Royce in the garage and were *on their way*, roaring, serpentine into the night, machine guns blazing as Gribov twisted the wheel to dodge fire from traintop sharpshooters.

Fire that soon tilted up into the slate-dark sky as a thousand great gray owls descended in swarms onto the train.

THE BLACK BARONY

THE DOOMSDAY REELS

BY LAIRD BARRON

Not long ago I wrote the foreword to a deluxe edition of *The Collector*, the seminal British horror novel about a psychopath who kidnaps a young woman and imprisons her in a basement dungeon. Written in the latter 1960s, the tale still packs a hell of wallop despite our societal desensitization thanks to a ceaseless barrage of violent imagery. The frame of that essay was an observation about parenting in 1970s and 80s rural Alaska: despite a laundry list of everyday hazards, such as domestic violence, alcoholism, and plain old poverty against a backdrop of short summers and long, savage winters, parents obsessed over potential child abduction by rapists and Satanists; they also lived in unholy dread of imminent nuclear annihilation.

The dread became a background hum in everyday life; not only in Alaska, where we understood full well that Fort Richardson and Elmendorf Airforce Base were prime targets, but across the entire country. You can chart the fear and paranoia in history books. You can also chart it in pop culture. While we may not have ever learned to love the bomb, we surely immersed ourselves in a bloody sea of apocalypse-oriented literature and film.

I was born in 1970. I belong to a generation that understood on a vague, albeit fundamental level, the idea of the Doomsday Clock set at roughly five minutes to midnight. One false move and the USA and the Soviets were going to blow the world to hell. Public education (at least in my state) had evolved beyond the notion that hiding under your desk might save you, but the 1950s poster checklists concerning how to survive a nuclear blast still lurked in the margins. By the 1980s, parodies of those posters arose, checklists culminating with, "Put your head between your legs and kiss your ass goodbye."

I am sure it was in such spirit that famed country and western songwriter Steve Goodman wrote and performed the 1980s Cold War classic "Watchin' Joey Glow," a short, wryly humorous song about an American family twiddling their thumbs in a fallout shelter while the eponymous Joey amuses them with absurdist side effects of radiation poisoning.

"You have to wear dark glasses if you look at him a while, Or he'll fry your little eyes out with his incandescent smile."[1]

---

1   "Watchin' Joey Glow" by Steve Goodman

Goodman satirizes not only the notion of a survivable nuclear holocaust (a myth that Soviet and American authorities were all too happy to endorse), but the fervent nationalism that presumably led to the catastrophe. This is how a broad swath of western civilization dealt with it once upon a time; we swallowed the dark humor of Steve Goodman or warmed ourselves by the more elevated satire of *Dr. Strangelove*. That's not all—it's scarcely a beginning.

An *Encyclopedia Britannica* set could be devoted to the exploration of doomsday scenarios in print and on the silver screen. I'll confine myself to a few of the best films (or at least personally nostalgic) in a stroll down damnation alley of my youth.

Planet of the Apes: Charlton Heston and Roddy McDowall starring; directed by Franklin J. Schaffner. I'm sure I watched plenty of science fiction movies during adolescence—this is among the first I recall. It's a B-movie to the hilt; Hollywood did it right back then.

The plot: Astronauts crashland on an alien planet dominated by super intelligent apes. What stands out forty years after my first viewing? Heston's physicality and relentless emoting; the genteel and benevolent Cornelius as played by McDowall; Linda Harrison as the obligatory love interest in barely-there animal skins; armored gorillas on horseback, shooting guns, scoffing in amazement at Cornelius's theories regarding Homo sapiens' intellectual capacity; and of course the Statue of Liberty reveal and Heston's supremely melodramatic reaction. Highly evolved apes turning the tables on humanity; leash in one hand, cattle prod in the other? Yes, please.

Logan's Run: Michael York and Jenny Agutter starring; directed by Michael Anderson. I had the pleasure of screening this at the Airport I Theater in Wasilla, Alaska. This science fiction classic endures as the preeminent post-apocalyptic story, albeit it qualifies more as a

"After total war can come total living"

WELCOME TO THE 23RD CENTURY.

The only thing you can't have in this perfect world of total pleasure is your 30th birthday.

LOGAN'S RUN

Logan is 29.

METRO-GOLDWYN-MAYER presents A SAUL DAVID PRODUCTION "LOGAN'S RUN" starring MICHAEL YORK · JENNY AGUTTER · RICHARD JORDAN · ROSCOE LEE BROWNE FARRAH FAWCETT-MAJORS & PETER USTINOV · Screenplay by DAVID ZELAG GOODMAN Based on the novel "LOGAN'S RUN" by WILLIAM F. NOLAN and GEORGE CLAYTON JOHNSON Music—JERRY GOLDSMITH · Produced by SAUL DAVID · Directed by MICHAEL ANDERSON Filmed in TODD-AO and METROCOLOR [NOW A BANTAM BOOK!] ORIGINAL MOTION PICTURE SOUNDTRACK ALBUM AVAILABLE ON MGM RECORDS AND TAPES

Distributed by Cinema International Corporation   MGM

dystopia given the amount of screen time devoted to life under the crystalline dome.

The plot: Long after the Earth has been destroyed and people retreat to underground cities, Logan 5, a brutal government assassin (a sandman), makes a run for the surface. What stands out? The clash of a utopian society and a ruthless dictatorial computer charged with maintaining the status quo; domed cityscapes and interiors like something out of a Jetsons porn parody; the life clock crystals and the "carrousel" where anyone aged thirty must report for execution; the cold-blooded nature of the "sandmen" who murder citizens (runners) who attempt to flee for the surface; Jessica 6, Logan's swoon-worthy fellow escapee; and that damned robot who freezes humans as a source of protein. Love, betrayal, political awakening, institutional paranoia... It's a bad ass film that manages to inject counterculture theory and elements of the sexual revolution into a run-and-gun thriller.

Mad Max 2 (The Road Warrior): Mel Gibson starring; directed by George Miller. Doesn't get much more quintessential than George Miller's take on the Outback circa a few years after the end of the world.

The plot: A widowed ex-cop drifts around a post-nuclear holocaust desert and gets into fights with assorted bandits intent upon raping, pillaging, and securing the all-important petrol. Max saves the petrol. What stands out? Gibson carries the show entirely upon his shoulders; Max is a great antihero in the tradition of Leone westerns and Clint Eastwood's Man with No Name; George Miller knows how to direct an action film like none other; Miller also depicts the savagery of man against a hostile backdrop with the same aplomb as the aforementioned Leone; and a largely nameless, fantastically-costumed cast of marauding villains. An utterly different film than its slow burning predecessor, *Mad Max 2* is one of the better and most iconic sequels ever made.

Phase IV: Starring ants, lots and lots of ants; directed

by Saul Bass. Another flick I had the pleasure of seeing in the theater somewhere between first and second grade. My parents exhibited no fear regarding the damage such a psychedelic drip feed through the eye might reckon for a child's long-term emotional wellbeing. Done is done and I occasionally pause to give thanks to Saul Bass and his giallo meets Philip K. Dick meets H.G. Wells meets Lovecraft meets a Richard Attenborough nature documentary gone pear-shaped into some kind of gods forsaken insect exploitation joint.

The plot: A mysterious celestial event near Earth causes radical changes in the terrestrial ant population. After a suitably ominous buildup, shit hits the fan. What stands out? Take your pick. Sinister intertitles of each phase of the hostile ant takeover; Uncle Creepy scientists who make the ant protagonists (yes, Virginia, ant protagonists) seem relatively sympathetic in comparison; weird and possibly insane art and music direction; a disjointed plot with a baroque, futuristic texture; super ants versus killer spiders and guardian mantises; and a cosmic horror thread that runs through the entire hot, magnificent mess. The bastard of an ending embraces nihilism (from the human pov,

anyhow) without a shred of reservation. If you can track down the original extended ending, do it.

The War of the Worlds: Starring alien tanks and plenty of screaming crowds; directed by Byron Haskin. For maximum effect, you'd need to have been on the scene, October 30th, 1938 for the radio teleplay broadcast delivered by Orson Welles as a series of news bulletins. As it stands, I watched *The War of the Worlds* for the first time on a Saturday afternoon, Cartoon Day, as we kids once referred to the sacred hours between 6AM and 4PM between the ages of five and twelve.

The plot: Martians have come to Earth to do unto indigenous people what sufficiently "advanced" civilizations have always done to those less powerful. What stands out? The alien vessels and their sinuous necks, flaming cyclops eyes and tripod legs; the horrifying sounds of the Martian tripods; nuclear blasts unable to scratch the invader ships; men and machines disintegrated by the cyclops eye beams; the utter destruction of the works of man; our hapless protagonists playing a desperate game of cat and Martian in a deserted house; the (literal) Deus ex Machina solution to the one-sided war. Dated, perhaps, and morally didactic, it holds up surprising well and hasn't been surpassed in the alien invasion genre. The only thing Tom Cruise's 2005 remake got right was the sound, the hideous, blood-chilling trumpeting of the murderous conquerors.

The Terminator: Arnold Schwarzenegger, Michael Biehn, and Linda Hamilton starring; directed by James Cameron. Here then is Schwarzenegger's second big time role to follow-up his turn as *Conan the Barbarian* in 1982. Similar to *Logan's Run,* this film doesn't slot neatly into the post-apocalyptic or disaster genres, but any tale that begins with tank treads grinding over hills of picked clean human skulls against a backdrop of the despoiled ruins of human civilization fits the theme of this essay by my lights, the remainder of the narrative's sojourn in 1980s' L.A. be damned.

The plot: An android (the Terminator) who happily resides in the hellscape of 2029 where sentient machines have overthrown humanity travels back in time to murder a woman (Sarah Connor) who will become the mother of a great resistance fighter; the only thing standing in its way is a soldier (Kyle Reese) who has also arrived from 2029 on a mission to protect the woman. Hijinks ensue. What stands out? The Terminator wearing an Austrian-American bodybuilder's skin like a suit; the aforementioned skin-suit's gradual degradation revealing the lethal and inhuman robot beneath; the Terminator murderizing an entire police station as poor Sarah Connor hides, anxiety-ridden as poor Laurie Strode when Michael hunted for her throughout the Haddonfield Memorial Hospital; "I'll be back." I'm only joking a little in regard to the Halloween II reference—the fact of the matter is, Michael Myers and the Terminator have a few things in common. It kills people who've recently enjoyed premarital sex; it's implacable and bullet-resistant; despite its ability to annihilate platoons of cops, gangbangers, and assorted riffraff, the monster proves shit out of luck when it corners the final girl.

A Boy and His Dog: Don Johnson (Vic) and Tiger (Blood) starring; directed by L.Q. Jones. Adapted from the novella by one of the great American authors, Harlan Ellison, this one is plagued by sloppy editing, uneven sound, and the murky lighting we've come to know and love in 1960s and 70s films. And for all that, the raw power of Ellison's imagination is enough to overcome a host of technical criticisms.

The plot: Vic is just a boy searching for love (sex by any means) among the irradiated ruins of the Earth. He is assisted in his endeavors by a sardonic, telepathic dog named Blood. What stands out? Ellison's eye for social commentary—in this case a pair of antiheroes whose amoral philosophy winds up indicting the audience conditioned to root for pov characters; Vic's single-minded need to get his rocks off, thus validating the cliché that men are led to doom by their peckers; Blood's cynical observations and rapier sharp digs at his human partner; the absolute horror of the underground utopia Vic and Blood discover; Vic's naiveté regarding the method of extraction of his manly essence by the science team interested in revitalizing the utopian colony's breeding stock (hint: manual insemination of the colony's eligible young maidens is not on the program). Of course there's that ending which polarized audiences and possibly annoyed Ellison himself. Whatever

the case, *A Boy and His Dog* is as gritty and uncompromising as a walkabout the wasteland should be.

I'm not bold enough to stake the claim that these seven cinematic depictions of Doomsday and after are unimpeachable—however, they played a role in shaping (for better or worse) my youthful imagination, as well as that of my friends. Horror is a strong and pervasive component of these particular films. Horror, at its best, humanizes evil and filters it so that we might interact more safely and rationally with the hazardous and the irrational. To some degree, apocalypse narratives operate similarly and offer a certain measure of consolation. In some cases, the mechanism is the absurdity of super apes reversing the power dynamic with humans, or aliens in giant tin cans wreaking implausible havoc only to be thwarted by the common cold virus. In other cases, these stories seek to render the inconceivable conceivable and the inhuman human.

The doom that comes to Earth and what happens after has become an integral feature of human civilization; it mirrors creation mythology and snaps shut the jaws of the Ouroboros on its own tail. It's a rehearsal (perhaps unknowing, perhaps not) for the potential reality that we're going to be wiped out by a meteor, a plague, or our own damned foolishness. Should the unthinkable come to pass and a few people scuttle into the dark to begin anew, it won't be long before someone chars a stick and paints the shape of the next doomsday scenario on a cavern wall. Our end has always obsessed us as much as our origin. And it will until the curtain drops for good.

FEATURED REVIEWS

BY COLLEEN WANGLUND

Men Behind the Sun

(Hong Kong/China, 1988)
Director: Tun Fei Mou (as T.F. Mous)
Runtime: 1 hour 45 minutes

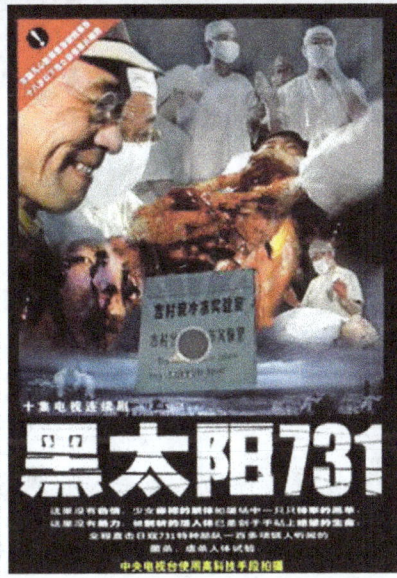

Japan and China have had a contentious relationship dating back centuries with probably the most volatile period coming during the Second Sino-Japanese War and World War II (1937-1945). Both countries have their own versions of history but nothing I've ever seen reaches the horrifying level of propaganda and war crimes accusations as the 1988 film *Men Behind the Sun*. It combines the historical atrocities committed by Japan against Chinese and Russian prisoners of war with the grotesque horror of films such as the *Faces of Death* series (1978-1996).

Based on the historical record surrounding the infamous Rape of Nanking by the Japanese military, *Men Behind the Sun* takes the viewer to Unit 731, a secret facility which experimented with the creation and use of biological and chemical weapons. Chinese and Russian prisoners of war, as well as Chinese civilians, were used in deadly medical experiments to aid the Imperial Japanese Army in finding better ways to kill the enemy. The Japanese military have also brought a small unit of the Youth Corps—very young boys—to train them in the art of fighting and killing. It is nearing the end of the war and the military is desperately trying to find a way to use bubonic plague as a mass biological weapon. During one of the experiments involving Chinese and Russian prisoners tied to crosses in a field, the experiment must be aborted because the plane with the test bomb carrying the disease is forced to retreat

due to the advancing Allied forces. The prisoners then attempt a revolt which ends in a bloody massacre.

As it becomes clear that the Japanese are losing the war, the head of Unit 731, Lt. General Shiro Ishii (Gang Wang), orders the complete destruction of the camp, including all documentation of the various experiments carried out there, and orders all of his top personnel and their families to commit suicide. Soldiers begin a killing spree of the remaining prisoners. Not all of Ishii's top scientists wish to see their work destroyed and some records remain. Ishii is persuaded to allow them to be evacuated and only commit suicide if they might be captured. The Youth Corps are sworn to secrecy about what they witnessed at Unit 731 as trains take the remaining personnel from the camp.

Men Behind the Sun would be horrifying just as a historical film due to the vicious atrocities committed by the scientists and military who operated Unit 731. But the film goes further, showing many of the atrocities in graphic detail. In one scene a woman is tied up outside in a stockade in the snow, her arms repeatedly doused in freezing water. Later when she is brought inside, icicles hanging from her frozen forearms, her arms are put into a bath where the skin and muscle completely disintegrate. Another scene shows a man in a sealed chamber while some kind of gas is pumped in. The man cannot breath and his body becomes completely distorted, limbs and torso expanding until his body explodes from the pressure. The bodies are taken to ovens where they are burned to ash. A handful of men is responsible for disposing of the bodies, but there are too many and the dead and dismembered pile up everywhere. These grotesque scenes of torture and death are reminiscent of films such as the original *Guinea Pigs* series

(1985-1988), or *Faces of Death*, but because of the documentation discovered when members of the camp were captured we know they really happened. It may have been a trick of the camera and special effects work on-screen, but people really suffered and died during the war.

Mou pulls no punches with his film, even having an argument with the Chinese government over its production due to better relations with Japan at the time of the film's release. He's been accused by critics of making nothing more than an exploitation film. *Men Behind the Sun* was banned in some countries and censored with editing in others. In Japan, Mou's life was threatened due to the extreme nature of the film and accused of being a sensationalist and a liar. Mou himself has claimed that the scenes of a young boy's autopsy to harvest organs was actual footage from the camp. History has shown, however, that Unit 731 did exist and that anywhere between 3,000 and 250,000 people died there, men women, and children, mostly Chinese nationals, though the usual estimate cited is 10,000. And Unit 731 was not the only facility of its kind.

We also know that Lt. General Shiro Ishii was a real person, a microbiologist, having been the Chief of the Imperial Japanese Army's Medical Section and later named to Surgeon General. He had plans to launch biological weapons in California but was captured along with most of the top personnel from Unit 731 at the end of World War II. The Soviets wanted to try him for war crimes but the United States intervened and he was never charged or prosecuted. It has been rumored that some of his warfare techniques were used during the Korean War.

Men Behind the Sun is both engrossing and disturbing and is not a film for those with a weak stomach. The special effects hold up pretty well and the acting is very good making something exploitative that much more effective. It is uncomfortable to watch and is one of the most unsettling films I've ever seen. It's unrelenting in its horrors and Mou has made no apologies for his movie. There have been three sequels, but none with the historical accuracy or significance of the original film. If you can stand it, then *Men Behind the Sun* is worth seeing, just for its historical content alone. If you like pure exploitation, then even as a historical film, *Men Behind the Sun* should be on your to-view list.

◇◇◇◇◇◇◇◇◇◇◇

Snowpiercer

(Korea 2013; USA 2014)
Director: Bong Joon-ho
Runtime: 2 hours 6 minutes

Though not technically a horror film, *Snowpiercer* shares many elements you would expect to see in the horror genre. It is a fantasy/thriller/action movie set in the not-too-distant future aboard a train circumventing the world with the last remaining human life in existence. The film was directed by Bong Joon-ho (*The Host*, 2006; *Mother*, 2009) and co-written by Bong and Kelly Masterson and is loosely based on a French graphic novel series titled "Le Transperceneige" originally written by Jacques Lob, Jean-Marc Rochette, and Benjamin Legrand. At a cost of $40 million, *Snowpiercer* is the most expensive Korean film ever produced. It initially was only to have a limited release, but due to wide acclaim the film was given expanded distribution by The Weinstein Company in both theaters and digital streaming services, but has earned more than twice that amount, to date.

Snowpiercer follows the story of the last remaining human survivors of a catastrophic and unintentional consequence of an experiment meant to reverse global warming in 2014—an ice age killing every living thing on the planet except those on the train. Seventeen years later the people are living separated according to class with the poor in the rear of the train surviving on manufactured protein bars for sustenance. Curtis (Chris Evans of *Captain America* fame), along with his mentor and de-facto leader of the downtrodden in the rear cars, Gilliam (John Hurt), have been receiving messages in the government-provided food. Gilliam convinces Curtis that it is time for a revolt, especially after some more of the children from the rear are taken by Minister Mason (Tilda Swinton). Curtis makes it to the prison car where he revives the train's security designer Namgoong Minsu (Song Kang-ho who has starred in a few of Bong's films, including *The Host*, 2006 and *Memories of Murder*, 2003, as well as Park Chan-wook's *Thirst*, 2009). Gilliam's plan is to use Minsu's knowledge of the security systems to open the doors of the train cars and get the group to the water supply car which they can use to negotiate with the train's designer and engineer, Wilford (Ed Harris).

Things don't go as planned and while Curtis and a few of the rebels are distracted in a classroom car while marking the New Year—which celebrates one circumnavigation of the planet—the rest of the rebel army are ambushed and killed, including Gilliam. Curtis pushes on, determined to get to Wilford. Minsu has his own agenda, however, and it involves getting off the train with his daughter Yona (Ko Ah-sung) whose mother died some years earlier in another rebellion. They did get off the train but died almost immediately after. In the years since, Minsu has noticed a difference in the world beyond the train. The small group does finally reach Wilford, but nothing is what it seems.

Snowpiercer is a fantastic film and it's hard to believe that it almost didn't get the distribution it deserved. For years I have touted films of various genres from Southeast Asia and I can now point to a solid film that many have seen, without it having been a remake.

While the film deals with some very serious subject matter and especially in light of current events, it is not as serious as it initially seems. *Snowpiercer* is bleak and apocalyptic, but with a bit of black comedy thrown in for good measure. Tilda Swinton's Minister Mason is an obvious caricature of conservative political figures both past and present—Swinton herself has named Margaret Thatcher, Adolf Hitler, and Silvio Berlusconi among her inspirations for the role—and all of the characters at one point or another come across as caricatures though they can also be very relatable. For instance, Octavia Spencer's Tanya and Ewen Bremmer's Andrew are two frantic parents who just want to get their children back.

The train is like a microcosm of society, everyone separated by class and money with the "rabble" in the back receiving barely enough to survive and the wealthy in the front enjoying a hedonistic lifestyle. Wilford himself is a character out of an Ayn Rand novel, a wealthy industrialist who just happened to have built the one thing that could save at least some of humanity—all life—after the government screwed things up far worse than ever before. Curtis is the perfect hero on the surface and Gilliam is the perfect idealist, pushing Curtis to help make a better world for the other less fortunate ones around them. None of these people are completely who they initially appear and it makes for great storytelling. Curtis is deeply flawed with a disturbing motivation, Gilliam is not the great humanitarian, Wilford is just a greedy person with a God complex, and Mason is high on her power over the people at the back of the train.

Snowpiercer was filmed almost entirely on specially built train cars within a studio so the confining space is real. The fight scene between Wilford's guards and the rebels in a dark car seen through night-vision goggles and the quarters in which the passengers at the back of the train live are highly claustrophobic, as are the cryogenic sleep spaces that Minsu and Yona are awoken from in the prison car. Mason and Wilford are positively creepy and Minsu is stuck in his own head after becoming an addict. And when the rebels discover what their protein bars are made from, it is stomach-churning. Of course there are some very heavy dramatic moments, such as when we find out the story of Yona's mother and the other rebels, and when Curtis finally tells the horrible secret he's been holding on to and using as motivation to be a better person and do something for the betterment of others.

Bong has a history of bending and twisting the expectations of whatever genre he is working in and he has done that with *Snowpiercer* as well. The film is a mix of science fiction, action, horror, and thriller. And as with twisting genres, Bong has also included many twists within the story itself. Nothing and no one are what they might seem and the film keeps you guessing until the end, which, by the way, is as ambiguous as I would expect from an Asian film and full of both hope and despair. Bong's insistence on keeping his vision intact when the distribution company wanted the film cut down is a true testament to the man's work ethic and his love of film and what it can accomplish. *Snowpiercer* is a blockbuster of a film and if you haven't seen it yet, you must remedy that.

By RICHARD DANSKY

Photo courtesy of Adam Scott Glancy

Adam Scott Glancy was one of the small handful of game designers who revitalized Lovecraft for the modern era with the fast paced re-imagining of what adventuring in the Cthulhuverse might be: *Delta Green* (1996). Since 2001 he's headed Pagan Publishing, the home of *Delta Green* and miniatures game *The Hills Rise Wild,* among other projects. He took a few moments to sit down and discuss, among other things, mail-order machine guns, the origins of *Delta Green*, and why having a smartphone in the world of the Mythos might not be as useful as you'd think.

Richard Dansky: What was the genesis of Delta Green?

Adam Scott Glancy: The original inspiration came from John Tynes. He was looking for a way to finally bring a campaign structure to *Call of Cthulhu*. I mean, why in the world do you have a group of players that includes a gangster, a professor, a dilettante and a tribal fisherman going out to hunt down the Cthulhu Mythos? How many times can a relative you never heard of leave the creepy old mansion or the cursed book to you in his will? How many times can a decimated party recruit the hotel bellhop, who just happens to be a Great War veteran and unemployed archeologist, to join them in their quest to defeat supernatural horrors? John's idea was to create a campaign background whereby groups of player characters with widely differing backgrounds would have a reason to work together and a reason to constantly have new supernatural threats to

investigate and defeat.

The thing he wanted to avoid was making the players the members of a secret government agency with virtually unlimited resources and powers to deal with the threat. One of the things that always made *Call of Cthulhu* fun was the struggle against huge odds. This was never a game that was supposed to be about getting piles of gold and cool toys. It was about taking on evil that completely outclasses you and defeating them using brains and brawn in the right amounts.

Since a government agency would ruin that balance, John Tynes came up with the brilliant idea that Delta Green would not be an agency, but rather a broad conspiracy throughout federal law enforcement and intelligence agencies. As an illegal conspiracy, the members of Delta Green wouldn't be able to call in the paratroops or airstrikes, but would have access to information, a certain amount of public deference to their credentials and with a command structure above them, there would always be a conduit for more missions being sent their way. Also, if the players are part of an organization, that provides a mechanism for replacing the inevitable casualties the investigators will suffer.

RD: What were some of the inspirations?

ASG: For me, the original inspiration for mixing the government and modern conspiracy into the Cthulhu Mythos

DELTA GREEN

A CALL OF CTHULHU SOURCEBOOK OF
MODERN HORROR AND CONSPIRACY
FROM PAGAN PUBLISHING

"This is like nothing anyone has ever understood. This is pure evil, pure destruction. This is the apocalypse."

written by
DENNIS DETWILLER
ADAM SCOTT GLANCY
JOHN TYNES

illustrated by
TOREN G. ATKINSON
DENNIS DETWILLER
HEATHER HUDSON
JOHN T. SNYDER

ASG: Fewer than most people imagine. For the Delta Green design team (John Tynes, Dennis Detwiller and myself), Lovecraft's stories were always modern techno-thrillers, stories about science revealing new and uncomfortable truths about man's place in the cosmos. Sure, the stories were set in the 1920s and 1930s, but they were meant to be modern stories, not period pieces. Lovecraft's scientific horrors slide very handily into the modern era.

RD: It was fairly easy to say that weapons from Lovecraft's time were just going to bounce off shoggoths and nightgaunts.

ASG: I would deny this assertion. In Lovecraft's time you could order Thompson submachine guns via mail order. There's no end to the amount of high powered weapons available between the wars, including Great War anti-tank rifles like the Mauser 1918 T-Gewehr. Let's not forget the flame-throwers, white phosphorus grenades, rifle grenades and a variety of light machine guns. The Browning .50 caliber machine gun made its debut in 1921 and is still in use today. It's not the stopping power of weapons that has necessarily increased since Lovecraft's time, but rather the accuracy and magazine capacities.

RD: But how do you assess what modern arms are going to do against nameless horrors, and how do you put that into a combat system?

was the Lovecraft story *The Shadow Over Innsmouth*. The narrator recounts that the town of Innsmouth, which had been corrupted by a Mythos cult, had been raised by the Federal agents and the military and the population imprisoned. From that story we know that in the world of Lovecraft, the Federal Government has some small idea that supernatural threats to national security exist. So, before I started working with John Tynes, I had been working on my own material parallel to Delta Green about the US Government's interest in the Mythos. I was proposing an agency that had gotten things wrong. They think they understand the Cthulhu Mythos, but they really don't have a clue, thus making them dangerously misinformed. A lot of this material was incorporated into the Majestic-12 section of the *Delta Green* book.

The other big inspiration was, of course, the conspiracy theories and UFO-ology that was all the rage in the 1990s. There seemed to be a proliferation of conspiracy theories once the Cold War ended. Dennis Detwiller was, and indeed still is, adept at seamlessly grafting elements of Lovecraftian fiction onto modern conspiracy theories.

RD: What were the biggest challenges in bringing Lovecraft into the modern era?

ASG: There is a fair amount you can ascertain about the ability of kinetic energy to damage Mythos horrors based on what the stories tell us. The fact that Mi-go are killed by weapons and drowned in floods suggests that they have some vulnerabilities. On the other hand, things composed of "non-terrene matter" won't necessarily obey the same laws of physics that terrestrial life does. So that gives designers a lot of wiggle room to justify how, and to what degree, various critters are immune to human-designed firepower. For me, it's less about making Mythos critters invulnerable to bullets as it is about making the Mythos creatures fight smart, on their home turf, using every advantage to strike from ambush, and retreat before they can be targeted.

RD: One of the central tenets of Lovecraft's fiction is that too much knowledge is dangerous. But in our modern age, we're living in an information-driven society, where if you've got an iPhone you've got most of the recorded knowledge of humanity sitting in the palm of your hand. How do you reconcile those two for the game setting?

ASG: First of all, the dangerous knowledge of Lovecraft's world isn't going to be found on Wikipedia. As much as I enjoy shows like *Buffy* or *Supernatural*, it always drove me nuts when they look up how to stop the Monster of the Week on the internet. Presuming the information about the Mythos was even on the internet, how can the investigators (or even the cultists) sort out the truth from the dross that clutters up the internet? Do you really want to take on a vampire armed with the nonsense you read on some blog? The unintentional disinformation is going to be quite thick.

The thing about iPhones is that their ubiquity doesn't guarantee that the data they collect will be accepted as genuine. Today everyone who can afford to do so carries a high tech surveillance device on their person. Their smart phone stands ready to record any supernatural event and upload it to the internet so that the truth can be seen by everyone... and be immediately denied, debunked, argued over, re-edited and subjected to DRM takedowns. Not by any secretive government agency, but just by the trolls on the internet.

RD: And for the hardcore fans, I have to ask: Where did the Clockwork Child end up after Pagan Farm sank into the Tarn?

ASG: Well for one thing, Pagan Farm, or "Pagan Haus" as we called it, still stands. I still live in the house that Kenneth Hite once called a "Frat house for serial killers," however the decor has improved slightly as the other Paganistas moved on to new domiciles. As for the Clockwork Child, no one has seen it since 1999. I suspect you'll hear the squeak of its wheels any minute now. ◆

DELTA GREEN
EXTRAORDINARY
RENDITIONS

CTHULHU MYTHOS
STORIES OF
MODERN HORROR
AND CONSPIRACY

CARTER   DETWILLER
FARNELL   FIELDING
GLANCY   GOODFELLOW
HALBANY   HANRAHAN
HARMS   HITE
IVEY   LOWDER
MANA   MICAL
STOLZE   TYNES
WINNINGER

WAR STORY

A. SCOTT GLANCY

It was the first time Agent Ross had killed monsters, and he wasn't enjoying it.

"Jesus, this is bad. This is *really* bad."

Ross kept repeating the phrase, like a mantra. The rest of the team ignored it and just let him process what he'd seen and done. Of course it was bad. What the fuck else was it going to be?

Ross's team leader, Agent Reynolds, ordered Ross to keep watch while he, Agent Rita, and Agent Rick set to policing up the four bodies and sanitizing the crime scene. The .22 caliber holes Rick and Rita had put in their heads didn't leak much once their hearts stopped, but just to keep things tidy Rita sealed the entry wounds with duct tape. What blood did hit the floor and walls had to be wiped up and sprayed down with bleach. They'd brought enough body bags so nobody had to share. The rest of the Skoptsi never made it to the trap door in the floor of the garden shed that covered the entrance to their escape tunnel. If they survived the concussion from the Semtex detonating in such a confined space, then they would die smothered under an avalanche of dirt instead.

The Maryland State Police had unwittingly done their job perfectly, flushing the Skoptsi out of their secret temple beneath the Our Lady of the Virgin Birth Basilica. When the Skoptsi were good and bunched up in their escape tunnels, the explosive charges Reynold's team had set detonated in sequence, dropping tons of earth on top of the fleeing Skoptsi. With any luck, and without survivors to contradict the assumption, the Maryland Criminal Investigations Bureau would presume the explosives were planted by the Skoptsi to cut off pursuit and that they simply misstimed the fuse, burying themselves. State law enforcement budgets being what they were, Reynolds doubted the tunnel would ever be fully excavated or that a complete body count would ever be made.

An accurate body count was the least of the things the Maryland cops would never know about. They'd never know about the four Skoptsi Reynold's team had double-tapped as they emerged out of the tunnel, coughing and gagging on the dust and carbon monoxide. They'd never know about the three other escape tunnels, each with its own team of Delta Green agents waiting to execute any people who made it past the cave-ins.

Not that Reynolds would have called the Skoptsi 'people.' With the Skoptsi it was less a matter of their biology than it was their behavior, though not for lack of trying. Fortunately Delta Green had acted before the physical transformations had begun in earnest. There had only been one Gof'nn Hupadgh Shub-Niggurath rebirthed by the Magna Mater in the last couple of centuries, but that was one too many by their reckoning. Now it, along with its faithful, were dead and buried. Saving the public from shit they would never believe in even if they were allowed to know about it—that's what Delta Green had been doing since before the Second World War. Didn't make it any less illegal, however.

"Agent Ross, give a hand with the bags," Reynolds called once Rick and Rita had zipped the last body bag closed. Ross slung his M-4 and dutifully took one end while Agent Rick took the other as they carried them

through the back yard and tossed them into the rear of the van. All eight passengers were in the van and heading east in just a few minutes. There weren't any seats in the back, so Rick and Ross squatted on the wheel wells while the four cadavers stretched out luxuriously on the floor. Nobody spoke much. Every so often the police scanner would announce a new horror back at the site of the raid, and Ross would whisper something about how bad it was.

It didn't sound so bad to Reynolds. Every emergency service in the state was converging on the Skoptsi's unincorporated village. It sounded like their basilica had caught on fire and was well on its way to being reduced to ashes. The simultaneous raid on the Families Without Frontiers adoption center had netted four "killed while resisting arrests" and twenty-three live but most-likely psychologically perma-fucked kids. The kids had been brought to Maryland from various eastern European shitholes to be adopted and indoctrinated into the cult of the Magna Mater, which is what you do to make a new generation when your cult practices castration and genital mutilation. At least now they wouldn't have their privates hacked off to honor a prehistoric fertility goddess. This "night at the opera" was the most agents Delta Green had put on the ground since New Orleans, and so far they were getting away with it.

Dawn was still three hours off when they arrived at the rusty industrial site just inside Pocomoke City. The sign on the outskirts of town declared Pocomoke to be "The Friendliest Town on the Eastern Shore." Nothing about that statement appeared to be correct, apart from it being located on the eastern side of the Chesapeake Bay. At this time of night, no lights burned. Nothing stirred. Which was just the way Delta Green liked it.

Rita jumped down from the van and unlocked the padlock chaining the gate shut. Once the van was through she closed and chained it again and unlocked the roll-down garage door on the side of the warehouse. Once the van was inside, and the roll-down door padlocked, the van doors were thrown open and the body bags unceremoniously hauled out. It made Ross's stomach flop to hear the sound of the cadavers' heads strike the cement floor. No one else seemed to flinch. Rita flipped the breakers. Florescent lights shivered to life, revealing the tools they would be using to complete the mission.

In the middle of the concrete floor squatted an eight-foot long, three-foot wide, stainless steel cylinder, set into an equally shiny and sturdy-looking frame that gave the contraption the appearance of some kind of massive telescope for observing the heavens. The insulated cables that connected it to the power supply, and the thick hose that ran from it to a drain set in the floor, belied that function. Next to the devices 5-gallon tubs of Potassium Hydroxide were stacked, marked with labels warning of their corrosive effects. A nearby table was stacked with respirators, rubberized gloves, boots, and other personal protective equipment that looked like something a fisherman would wear while trawling off the coast of Labrador.

"We lucked out, kids," Reynolds said as he checked the device's connections. "First ones in, so we'll be the first ones out."

"Three hours per body still means we're going to be here until sundown," Rick grumbled as he tugged another body bag out of the back of the van.

"Just be glad we don't have to wait in line for the other teams to cook theirs," Rita said as she began checking the PPE for cracks or tears. "We got a count yet on the other teams?"

Reynolds checked his burner phone. He'd already sent his text out. Just 'R4.' The other three cells had answered similarly. K1. O3. P2.

"Yup. They bagged six total. They are going to hate that we got here with four in front of them."

Ross looked sick at the prospect. "Shouldn't we have a special unit to do this kind of work?"

"No, we shouldn't," Rick said straining to drag the body bag across the floor. "First of all, who'd want to be in that unit? It'd be punishment detail for fuck ups. And you really don't want certified fuck-ups in charge of making all the evidence of your murders go away, right?" He dropped the end of the bag he was dragging. The contents sounded like boots when they struck the ground. "Second, A-Cell prefers it if we have to wash our own dishes. Makes you think twice before you dirty up a plate, don't it?"

"What the fuck are you talking about?"

"He means A-Cell doesn't want to make it too easy for us to kill our way out of a situation," Rita said, unzipping the first bag. Dead guy. Wispy beard. Blood dried in his hair. She slid open the blade on a box-cutter and began cutting off the corpse's bootlaces. "Make the option too painless, and you'll default to it. Overuse it. Take out a bystander because you pulled the trigger before you confirmed the target. You think it's no fun rendering a bunch of fucking sadistic psychopaths who brutalized children? Now imagine having to put someone through the resomator who didn't deserve it?" She tossed the boots into a plastic 55 gallon drum.

"Overuse it? At what point have we overused the option? I mean do we even know how many people we killed tonight?"

"All of them, I hope," said Rick.

"No. I'm serious," Ross pressed. "Do we even know how many were in there when we set off the explosives?"

"No, we don't," Reynolds said. "And it's best not to start counting. That can get… unhealthy."

"It's gotta be over three hundred," Ross continued. "I mean that was the number of attendants at their last ritual, right? Like three-hundred and sixty-four men, women and children."

Reynolds didn't sugarcoat it. "Yeah, that'd be the number if we got every last one of them."

"Let's hope so," said Rick, dragging another body to the resomator.

"Jesus," Ross said to no one and everyone. "This is bad. This is so fucking bad."

"No one's disagreeing," Rita said as she cut the pants off the first corpse. "So come over here and give me a hand. The sooner we get started the sooner we're done. Then I can get drunk."

"And I can get laid," said Rick, dragging the last body.

"You never get laid," Rita said, smiling as she cut the sleeves off the cadaver's shirt.

"I never get laid," Rick huffed theatrically. "Speaking of which… Ross? How about you come over here and get a good look at what someone's junk looks like after they've hacked it off and fed it to an extradimensional life form masquerading as a fertility goddess?"

"Fuck no."

"Too bad," Reynolds said. "Get over there and help Rita get the clothes and I.D. off them. Rick? Get suited up in the PPG. You get to cook the first one. I'll help you load."

Nobody hesitated, but nobody moved with much enthusiasm. The others had done this before, and Ross had been briefed on the ugly process. The four bodies, three men and a woman, were cut from their clothes inside their body bags, the shreds of clothing and shoes dropped into a 55 gallon drum to be filled with bleach. The wallets were emptied and all the money and plastic inside fed through a crosscut shredder that reduced them to mulch. Any info on driver's licenses and credit cards were copied by hand onto flash paper for later analysis. Wedding bands and jewelry weren't removed. The resonation machine had a trap that would catch any surgical implants, fillings and jewelry once the bodies were liquefied. Likewise the body bags were designed to dissolve in the same process of alkaline hydrolysis that liquefied the bodies. Only the zippers would survive. Once the cylinder was sealed, the mixture of lime and water inside would be heated to over 300 degrees, and pressurize to ten atmospheres to prevent the water from boiling away. In just three hours the process of "aquamation" would reduce the body to a thin, DNA-free liquid composed of amino acids, peptides, sugars and salts. The bones could be crushed with bare hands, but they'd brought a cremulator to grind them into a fine, ash-like substance that could be disposed of, along with the liquid remnants, right down a regular drain. Or in this case the big industrial drain right in the middle of the warehouse floor. The operation manual said you could use it to fertilize a garden or green area, but that seemed like too much of a risk.

When Rick and Reynolds had their personal protection gear on, they zipped up the body bag and hefted onto the roll-out rack that extended from the stainless steel resomator like the open breach of a cannon. A cylindrical cage surrounded the rack to catch all the "bones' shadows" and other indigestibles that the process couldn't reduce.

When the tank was closed and the mixture of water and potash lye began to fill the tank, Ross excused himself to get some air.

"It doesn't really smell," Rick called after him. "Even when you open the drain."

"That's not the kind of air I need."

"Leave the rifle," Reynolds said. "The locals are going to be up soon."

Ross unslung the weapon and placed it by the door before going out, throwing the bolt and stepping outside. Reynolds walked over and picked up the weapon. He hadn't stopped thinking about it since Ross had started twitching. Ross hadn't made a move to unsling it despite the way he was talking, but it had hung there reminding everyone that when someone with an automatic weapon is unhappy, things can get big in a hurry.

Reynolds had two choices. Secure the weapon in the van or leave it by the door. If he moved it, Ross might think they didn't trust him, which, in fact, they didn't. This was Ross's first Opera with R-Cell. Normally they wouldn't have brought an F.N.G. out on something this heavy, except manpower levels were desperately low. Reynold's other option was to leave the weapon there by the door. Where Agent Ross could snatch it up on his way back in and…

Reynolds crossed the warehouse, picked up the weapon, checked to see that it was on safe, then walked back to the van and stuck it in the front passenger seat. If Ross didn't like it, he'd just tell him that only an idiot leaves a fully automatic weapon right next to an open door. Rick and Rita watched his every step. They seemed relieved.

Of course that didn't do anything about the Ruger Mk III pistol Ross had in a shoulder holster under his jacket. They all had one. Each pistol was constructed with an integral silencer. So, silver lining, if things devolved into a firefight, the noise wouldn't disturb "The Friendliest Town on the Eastern Shore."

Reynolds stripped off his PPE gear and tossed it aside. He pulled his pistol, made sure the safety was off and pulled the bolt back to charge the weapon and cock the hammer. He slipped it back into his shoulder holster and looked over at Rick and Rita. Both looked pale, like they expected Reynolds to walk out the door and put two rounds into the back of Ross's skull. Reynolds met their worried gaze, shook his head 'no' and went out the door after Ross.

"Just as well," Rick said to Rita. "I'd rather not be stuck here for an extra three hours."

Out in the parking lot Reynolds saw Ross standing by the chain-link gate, smoking and pacing. There wasn't anything in the training manual for how to handle an agent who was looking shaky, mostly because there wasn't a training manual for Delta Green. There wasn't an operations manual either. Or case files. When everything you do is illegal, you just don't generate as much paperwork.

Reynolds scraped his feet on the wet asphalt to make sure Ross didn't think he was sneaking up on him. He wished he had something to do with his hands, like a cigarette to smoke, or a flask to offer, anything to show he wasn't reaching for a weapon. But he hadn't smoked since lung cancer got his parents, and drinking during an Opera… a field operation, was not to be encouraged.

"You got one of those for me," Reynolds began awkwardly.

"Sure." Ross popped a smoke out of the end of his pack, offered it to Reynolds and lit it with practiced ease.

Shit, thought Reynolds. *Fucking menthols.* He did a poor job pretending to smoke. Ross could see it.

"You come out here to get me to buck up? Maybe tell me some feel-good war story to help get my head on straight?"

"Not really," Reynolds said. "This isn't the sort of work where you pass the bottle and reminisce about that time when Agent Terry got bitten in half and wouldn't stop screaming until I shot her in the head. Or that time when

we had to sanitize Agent Peter's apartment after he took a bottle of sleeping pills and tied a plastic bag over his head. This job doesn't come with war stories anyone wants to hear. Or a gold watch for that matter."

"Well you better come up with something to say, because when I signed on I was told that we were going to be protecting people. Saving lives. But right now, from where I'm standing, it looks like I've joined a fucking death squad. Is that what we're doing? Building a better future one dead body at a time?"

"Ross, we've both seen the things no one believes in,"

Reynolds said. "That's why A-Cell headhunted us for Delta Green. And we wouldn't have joined if we thought the rules of evidence could apply to the shit we've seen. Courts haven't been in the habit of accepting spectral evidence since Salem Village. How the hell do we build a prosecutable case against someone whose means are physically impossible to demonstrate? And even if we managed a successful prosecution, a prison is just a larder or a recruiting ground. They'd feed and grow behind those walls until the walls can't contain them anymore. We tried mass incarceration after Innsmouth and it was a cluster fuck."

"So the solution is mass murder?"

"Fuck no. Not every night at the opera is going to be like this."

"But was this the worst?" asked Ross.

"The worst what? The worst thing I've ever seen working for Delta Green, or the worst thing I've ever done for Delta Green?"

"I just need to know if this is as bad as it gets."

Reynolds thought for a few seconds, then flicked the cherry off the end of his cigarette and put the butt into his jacket pocket. "Okay, war story time. You listening?"

Ross nodded.

"I've been at this a long time," Reynolds began. "Back before Alphonse and the whole mid-Nineties reorganization. Back then it was just a bunch of guys ad hocking. Very informal. No money. Fewer resources. Most of the time we found ourselves chasing down stuff long after the

situation had resolved itself. Too much time spent mopping up the toxic piss-stains left in the wake of whatever really bad shit had just happened. Day late. Dollar short. Super-fucking frustrating. Got it?"

Ross nodded as if that was important.

"So this was back in '94. We were still nursing New Year's hangovers when Romeo Dallaire's 'Genocide Fax' hit the UN. Kofi Annan wasn't interested, but a colleague of mine, let's call him Caleb, Caleb was fucking interested. He'd been with Delta Green since in the '60s, back when there were budgets and manpower and a license to kill issued right from Pennsylvania Avenue. Caleb had seen some shit. He'd been in the Congo in '64 when the Bloody Tongue feasted and fucked its way across a river of blood. That's something else you don't want to hear about.

"By '94 Caleb was out of the Company, but still active in Delta Green. He'd been my recruiting officer, so when he called me and said he had to get to Rwanda fast I didn't ask. I just made it happen. Caleb would have gone in alone, despite his age, but I wasn't going to allow that. I burned a not-inconsiderable number of favors getting us into Kigali by April Fool's Day. Our UN documents held up, but I suspect Dallaire only tolerated us because he thought we were CIA and was hoping we'd report something horrible back to D.C. and spur some action. That wasn't going to happen, of course, not after that black eye in Mogadishu. We didn't stay long regardless.

"See, we arrived less than a week before the two Hutu presidents got blown out of the sky. Then it was on. Radio Hutu was bellowing about Tutsi cockroaches and how the time had come to 'cut the tall trees' and suddenly every scruffy looking Hutu rummy had a cheap, stamped machete in his hand and was drenched in blood."

Reynolds took a moment to find his words. The first word out of his mouth was, "Blood, Ross. You can't even imagine the amount of blood. This wasn't Katyn Forrest or Auschwitz or Phnom Penh. This was nearly a million people hacked to bits by shitty Chinese machetes that bent and dulled after the first few blows. Didn't slow them down though. Those *Interahamwe* fucks would just keep hacking away, unable or unwilling to make a killing blow. And the rapes… they raped 'em before they killed 'em. Raped 'em after they killed 'em. Raped 'em while they killed 'em. They used their cocks like knives and their knives like cocks.

"Caleb was convinced. I was convinced. Everything in front of our eyes was right out the Castro debrief. People were 'free and wild and beyond good and evil, with laws and morals thrown aside and all men shouting and killing and reveling in joy.' Right? So Caleb and I weren't going to wait around for the Old Ones to teach them new ways to shout and kill and revel and enjoy themselves. We were going to shut this shit down or die trying.

"We dumped our UN cover, bought a bush pilot with a fistful of Krugerrands, and flew into Byumba Province to hook up with the RPF. Those were the Tutsi rebels in the north. The moment the killings started the RPF had gone on the offensive. They blew across that DMZ like fucking berserkers because well, what the fuck other option did they have? We knew they were the only folks in the theater who'd spill blood to stop this… Caleb called it a baptism; sometimes he called it an offering. Whatever it was, we needed to find a way to aim this RPF sledgehammer at the things that needed smashing before the overture ended.

"Caleb had the coordinates for some old weapon caches that the Company had forgotten about. It was all '60s surplus, but enough of it was sufficiently intact to buy us front row seats with the RPF. We stayed right on the RPF's heels. Once they saw the massacre sites and the little girls raped until they prolapsed, they went insane. I can't say Caleb and I did anything to restrain them either. The only way Hutu men were spared was if there were surviving Tutsis around to speak in their defense.

"But we weren't looking for revenge. What we needed was intel. We needed to know about the secret agenda behind the Interahamwe. Who were the real masters of the Impuzamugambi? Had anyone been talking about old gods? Had anyone seen a special grove or garden being built in the last year? What about unusual lights in the forest? Is there anyone new in Col. Bagosora's entourage? Anyone vaguely Egyptian? Who told Kabuga to name his radio station 'Thousand Hills Free Radio?' Thousand Hills? Fuck! Thousand Young of Shub-Niggurath, right? How could that be a coincidence in the middle of all this shit!"

The look of alarm on Ross's face told Reynolds he'd been getting progressively louder. He looked around guiltily. There was no one to hear.

"Yeah," he nearly whispered. "After five weeks of this we were fucking crazy. But at least we were in good company. The RPF guys were pretty pleased that the prisoners couldn't answer our questions. What with all the rapes, the RPF guys pretty much always wanted to start at the genitals. Some of the Hutus tried to make something up to stop the pain, but they only had to lose one eye to get them to stop lying.

"Thing was, we were getting nowhere. Nothing was turning up. The Hutu provisional government had been running the genocide from the town of Gitarama. Caleb was convinced the proof we needed would be there. After the RPF captured Gitarama we spent a week tossing the place and found absolutely nothing. Without skipping a beat, Caleb switched his certainty to the capital, Kigali. I followed him, but I was beginning to wake up to what was happening. For the next three weeks we went neighborhood by neighborhood, anyplace the RPF had secured, and a couple they hadn't. We tossed abandoned offices of the Interahamwe and the Impuzamugambi. We searched the Presidential Guard barracks, the offices and broadcast stations of Thousand Hills Free Radio, the homes and offices of guys like Bagosora, Bizimungu, the widowed First Lady, and anyone else in the *le clan de madame* political clique. And by this point in the story, I'm betting you can guess what we found."

"Nothing," Ross answered.

"Nothing to do with Delta Green's remit. No sacred groves. No hidden temples. No non-terrene artifacts. No hypergeometry. No Aklo. No sign of alien intelligences or any human collaboration with them. Nothing.

"We were in one of Kabuga's villas and Caleb was trying to talk the rebels into tearing the place down to the studs. He tried selling them on the idea that Kabuga had a secret treasure stash or some shit like that, but our reputation as the two crazy Americans had already preceded us. When I tried to get Caleb to face the situation, that there was nothing here, he completely lost his shit. Called me a disloyal coward. Said I never had what it took to be Delta Green and that he was a fool for recruiting me. Seventy-four years old and he just grabbed an axe and started swinging on the walls. All the while he's screaming stuff like he'd seen the signs, that we would know the time of their return. Over and over he said he had to save the world for this. That this wasn't us. That it couldn't be us. That this had to be Them.

"I let him go at it until he couldn't lift the axe anymore. I thought that the exertion took the fight out of him, but I was wrong. He only stopped swinging when he was in full cardiac arrest. He died before we could get him back in the truck. He couldn't speak, so I just kept telling him I'd stay. I'd keep looking. I'd stop it. When he was gone I paid the RPF guys to drive me north to get out through Uganda. When Caleb was too ripe to move we pulled over and found a place to plant him. I doubt I could find the spot again even if I wanted to."

Reynolds trailed off so suddenly that Ross couldn't believe the story was over. He waited for more, but it didn't come. Then the forgotten cigarette he'd left burning blistered the webbing between his fingers and he dropped it onto the asphalt. "So that's it? That's as bad as it's ever gotten for you?" Ross said, rubbing the burn.

"For fuck's sake, Ross. The lesson of Rwanda wasn't about how bad things can get. After Rwanda I finally knew what the best-case scenario was going to look like. Even if we locked up this world tight, if we threw away the key and the gate, if we exterminated every unnatural thing on the Earth, we won't create a fort. We'll create a prison. At the end of the day we'll all still be locked up in here with us."

"Humanity as blood-soaked rapists?" Ross sputtered. "If that's really how you see it, then why the fuck do you even bother? Why fight at all?"

"Because here's the alternative. The Great Old Ones wake and walk the earth again. Then there won't be room in this world for us and our Rwandans. There won't be room for anything recognizable as human. Our story will be over. Individually. Collectively. Done.

"You asked if Delta Green were murderous fanatics killing our way to a better tomorrow. Well, we're not. Because it doesn't take long doing this job before you realize it's never going to get any better. Not ever. What we're killing our way towards isn't a better tomorrow. It's any kind of tomorrow.

"So, are you going to help," Reynolds finished, "or are you going to leave it for someone else to do?"

Ross said nothing for a long time. Neither did Reynolds.

"A tomorrow where another Rwanda could happen," Ross said steadily, "still sounds better than the alternative."

"Just barely," said Reynolds, "but I'll take it. C'mon back inside. I'll walk you through how to run the resomator."

Murmurs in the Dark

THE MAGIC OF THE SWORD

BY DONALD TYSON

As the Apocalypse gallops ever nearer to us on its sixteen hooves, it seems an appropriate moment to reflect on the preeminent symbol of war that has endured throughout human history undiminished—the sword.

No other weapon has held such profound symbolic significance. There are other ancient symbols of war, each with its own set of meanings—the axe, the hammer, the spear, the bow—but none of these has achieved the stature of the sword in our collective awareness. The sword is somehow more personal and intimate, yet at the same time more potent.

What is a sword, in its bare essence? It is an instrument for killing human beings face to face. That is its only dedicated function. It was not designed for hunting purposes. It was not used to execute common criminals or slaughter livestock. Of all humanity's weapons it is the most pure, in the sense that it is designed and intended only to kill men.

The spear and bow were both used for hunting. The hammer and axe were common in medieval warfare, but the axe was also used to cut trees, and the hammer to break stones—neither is martial to its core, but both were subverted to martial uses. Even the gun was used from its earliest evolution to hunt for both meat and sport.

In modern times, the gun has achieved a status as a martial symbol that rivals the sword, but the gun has existed for less than a five centuries as an effective personal weapon, whereas the sword has impressed itself upon the consciousness of mankind since before the beginning of recorded history. Little wonder it remains the more potent of the two symbols.

Sword Symbolism

The sword derives its potency as a symbol from its essential shape. When we look at swords in a general sense—one might say when we look at the archetype of the sword—what do we see? We see a long tapering blade that extends straight away from a blunt hilt, to which there is usually affixed a cross guard.

The straightness of the blade represents extended force, and the tapering of the blade to a sharp point focuses that force and makes it piercing. This piercing, extended force of the sword projects in only one direction, from the cross of the hilt to the point. The cross guard and the bluntness of the pommel at the end of the hilt prevent the force from rebounding in the opposite direction.

The sword is usually held in the right hand, which is esoterically the side of the body that projects, and it forms an extension of the right arm. Of course in actual warfare swords were sometimes held in the left hand by left-handed soldiers, but we are here considering the archetypal sword, and that projects force from the right hand. The right side esoterically stands for consciousness. It is the solar side of the body.

Swords also cut with their sharpened edges. They can slay by cutting in either direction, to the left or to the right. From this arises the symbolism of the sword as an instrument of justice and of judgment. The judge who holds the sword of justice may use it to deal out either punishment or mercy. Two individuals engaged in a legal dispute sit one on the right hand of the judge and the other on his left. The sword will strike the guilty and spare the innocent.

Atop the courthouse known as the Old Bailey in London is a statue of the goddess of justice, who holds in her left hand a set of scales, the pans of which are level, and in her right hand a naked sword that is perfectly vertical.

In this context it is worth mentioning that whereas common criminals in England were usually hanged, or if they were of a somewhat higher social class, decapitated with an axe, nobles of the highest birth were given the honor of decapitation by the sword. It was viewed as a more honorable way to die. Why? Because the sword was a weapon of war, and to die in war was an honorable death. There are replicas of executioners' swords in the Tower of London on display for visitors. They are enormous, two-handed weapons to insure that no more than one stroke of the blade was needed.

Muslim Swords

Of course not all swords are straight, but the majority of the oldest swords had a straight blade with two edges. The Muslims who fought the Christian knights during the Crusades are shown with curved blades, but a little know fact is that in the earliest centuries of Islam, Muslims used straight swords.

The Islamic curved sword has its own essential symbolism which differs in some respects from that of the Christian straight sword. The curved swords of Islam express the power of the moon, and reflect the crescent of the moon in their shape. The straight swords of Christendom express the power of the sun in their shape—the sun casts down straight beams of fiery light upon the earth. The sun is constant, the moon mutable.

The curved shape of the Muslim sword blade is more feminine in a symbolic sense, and more partial than the straight, masculine, impartial shape of the Christian blade. It leans to one side. This makes it less an instrument for dealing impartial justice, and more an instrument of predetermined punishment. We see its use in this sense in the beheadings by sword carried out by terrorists with regularity across the Middle East.

There persists a belief that the curved blade of the Islamic sword, or the curved tip of the Japanese katana, make them better cutting instruments than the straight European sword. Historians of medieval history who have run practical tests on the straight and curved swords using sides of beef and pork report that this is not the case. The straight sword cuts with its edge as well as a curved sword—or at least, the difference if there is any is not noticeable.

Magic Swords

It is not surprising that given the long history in the West of the sword as a weapon of war, and its symbolism as both an instrument of conquest and of justice, that a mythology grew up around it. There were fabled to exist certain swords that were magic, and possessed of various extraordinary properties.

One of the earliest magic swords mentioned in literature is the sword that God set before the Tree of Life after the expulsion of Adam and Eve for disobedience. It is evident that it was a straight sword with two edges from the description of it in the biblical book Genesis 3:24: *"So he drove out the man; and he placed at the east of the garden of Eden Cherubims, and a flaming sword which turned every way, to keep the way of the tree of life."* The point of this flaming sword turns both to the left and the right to guard the approach to the Tree of Life. From the wording it appears that Eden as a whole was guarded by the angels known as Cherubims, but the Tree received a special guardian in the form of a flaming sword.

Another magic sword that appears near the end of the Bible, in Revelation 1:16, is the sword that extends from the mouth of Christ on his second coming: *"and out of his mouth went a sharp two-edged sword."* It is obvious that this sword is symbolic, not actual. It is the sword of truth, the sword of justice, the sword of divine judgment. Concerning the use of this sword, Revelation 19:15 states: *"And out of his mouth goeth a sharp sword, that with it he should smite the nations: and he shall rule them with a rod of iron."*

Notice in this second quotation that it is the sword that smites and divides, but the rod that rules and unites. This is the difference, at the symbolic level, between the sword and the scepter.

We see this difference expressed in the deck of 78 cards known as the Tarot. One of the four suits is the suit of Swords, and another is the suit of Wands. In the practice of Tarot divination, the suit of Swords is generally an unfortunate suit pertaining to loss, separation, sorrow, and discord, but the suit of Wands is largely benevolent and has to do with leadership, governance, union, and order.

The sword is one of the four great elemental symbols in the Tarot. The other three are the wand, the disk and the cup. Each symbol has its own numbered suit. The masculine suit of Swords is generally understood by Western occultists to represent elemental air. The masculine suit of Wands is understood to represent elemental fire. The other two feminine suits of Cups and Disks stand, respectively, for water and earth.

Why is the symbol of the sword considered airy in Western magic? Well, consider its appearance in use. The naked sword blade cuts through the air, dividing it, whirling, flashing, arcing, flying like a living thing. As the tongue of the judge divides the breath in pronouncing judgment, so the blade of the sword divides the air in the administration of that judgment.

The first among archangels, Michael, is usually depicted with a sword as a weapon (although sometimes he is shown with a lance or spear, which is symbolically incorrect). He is a warrior angel, best remembered for casting the Dragon down from heaven to the earth. We read in Revelation 12:7-9: *"And there was war in heaven, Michael and his angels waging war with the dragon. The dragon and his angels waged war, and they were not strong enough, and there was no longer a place found for them in heaven. And the great dragon was thrown down, the serpent of old who is called the devil and Satan, who deceives the whole world; he was thrown down to the earth, and his angels were thrown down with him."*

The Christian church of Seventh Day Adventists believes that there is only one archangel, Michael, and that Michael and Christ are really the same being under different names. The symbol of the sword unites these two figures. Michael is the only angel strongly identified in Christian legend with the sword.

Viking Swords

The Vikings placed great value on their swords, which won the reputation in battle of being almost unbreakable. This was achieved by a method of forging known as pattern welding, in which a bundle of rods of steel were heated until they were soft, then twisted in a vise so that they overlapped each other. The twisted bundle was then reheated and hammered into a sword blade. The pattern of the twisted steel rods remained visible in the blade after it was polished, and resembled the scales of a dragon. This gave rise to the name "dragon blades" for these swords.

In the Viking sagas there are a number of famous magic swords mentioned by name. It was the custom of the Vikings to name their swords. Often, the name of the sword conveyed a sense of its magic power. The greatest swords were either forged by dwarfs or other magic beings, made from metal that fell from the heavens (meteoric iron), or were found in the ancient burial places of great warriors.

In the last case, it is the age of the sword that lends it special value because it was a widespread belief in ancient times that the men at the dawn of history were wiser and greater than the generations of men who came after them. They were closer in time to the perfect nature of man at his creation, and hence closer to the gods.

The common view, expressed by the Roman poet Ovid (d. first century AD) in his famous poem, *The Metamorphoses*, was that the world was in decay. A Golden Age of great heroes in the distant past had given way to a Silver Age, and this to a Bronze Age, and finally to the Iron Age of the present, where men were flawed and easily corrupted. The same opinion was conveyed by the earlier Greek poet Hesiod (7th century BC) in his poem *Works and Days*, but Hesiod inserts a fifth age of man between the Bronze Age and the Iron Age, and calls this the Heroic Age.

In the *Volsunga Saga*, the magic sword Gram is thrust deep into a tree in the mead hall of the Volsungs by the god Odin. Only the great hero Sigmund is able to draw the sword from the tree. His possession of this magic blade causes envy and unrest, until finally Odin battles Sigmund and shatters the blade of the sword. Sigmund's son, Sigurd, reforges the pieces of the blade into a new sword and uses it to slay the great dragon, Fafner.

You will note in this legend the close parallels to the story of King Arthur, who as a boy was said to have pulled a sword out of a stone and thereby become a king, and also the portion of J.R.R. Tolkien's *Lord of the Rings*, where the magic sword, Narsil, that was shattered in battle with Sauron, is later reforged by the elves and renamed Andúril by Aragorn to represent his rightful kingship of Gondor. The musician Richard Wagner (1813-1883) also drew upon this Viking saga for inspiration when composing his *Nibelungenlied*.

In the Hervarer Saga, King Svafrlami, who is a grandson of Odin, compels the dwarves Durin and Dvalin to fashion for him the magic sword Tyrfing, which is able to cut through rock and iron and never misses its stroke. Out of resentment the dwarves curse the sword so that it must kill each time it is drawn from its sheath, and also that it must cause three great evils, and that its owner Svafrlami will be slain by it.

Again, we have very popular sword lore appearing in this saga. It was a common belief of warriors that when a sword was drawn, it must shed blood or misfortune would occur. When its owner happened to draw the sword by accident, he would use it to cut himself so that

his own blood stained the blade, thereby turning away the bad luck. Even down to our own time, house carpenters held the folk belief that it was lucky when you cut yourself on your own chisel. I remember my father telling me this when I was around eight years old, and cut myself while playing with his chisel, which as was sharp as a razor.

The fantasy writer Michael Moorcock wrote a series of novels concerning Elric of Melniboné and his enchanted sword Stormbringer, which can cut through almost any substance. The sword is a chaos demon in the shape of a sword that seeks a life each time it is drawn from its sheath. Even a small scratch from the great black blade is fatal, because the sword has the property of drinking the souls of those it slays. A portion of this vital energy flows to Elric, which is why he is unable to abandon the accursed blade—without the strength it gives him, he is virtually an invalid. Over the course of his possession of the malicious blade, it manages to trick him into killing several of his friends. In the end of the series, the sword kills Elric himself, transforms into a demon, and flies up into the sky laughing.

Viking swords were made magic not only by age, their place of origin, and their makers, but by the addition of runes to their blades. Several Viking blades have been found adorned with rune symbols. The runes are both a system of writing, and a system of magic. In their beginning, magic was their primary function, but in later centuries their magical use was gradually forgotten.

One Viking sword recovered from the River Thames, known as the Thames scramasax, bears the entire runic alphabet, on the principle that if one rune confers power or protection, all the runes will be even better. This was not really the case. There were rules for how the runes were to be used magically. One of them involved repetition. Repeating a single rune a significant number of times empowered it and the weapon on which it was incised. We often see ancient Viking blades on which are scratched groups of the same rune, alongside obscure words in runes that may be words of power. Exactly how this system of repetition was used is not known. What did four repetitions of a rune mean, as opposed to seven repetitions? We don't know.

Two individual runes often inscribed on swords by their owners are the Teiwaz rune and the Algiz rune. The first in shaped like an arrow point, and confers courage and protection. The second is shaped like a cross with the arms raised at an angle. It wards off danger and harm from the person who carries it.

The runes inscribed on various weapons such as swords, axes, shields, and helmets are often very crudely made, indicating that they were probably put their by the warriors who owned and used the weapons, but who had little or no knowledge of the use of runes for magic. When used in this simple way, they represent a kind of good-luck talisman.

Sometimes the person inscribing runes onto the blade called upon the help and protection of one of the gods, and wrote the name of the god in runes. The names Tyr and Thor commonly appear on rune relics. Tyr was known for his honor and courage, and Thor for his might in battle.

In Norse mythology it was believed that the rune symbols were a gift of Odin, the All-Father, to the human race. Odin was said to have hung upside down, tied to the trunk of Yggdrasil, the tree that is the axis of the universe, for nine days and nights without either food or water. At the end of his shamanic ordeal he saw the runes glowing in fire among the roots of the tree. He reached down and snatched them up before they could vanish away. The runes and their magic are his legacy to us, his mortal children.

Wayland the Smith

In Norse, English and German folklore, magic swords were sometimes fashioned, not by druids, but by Wayland the Smith, a curious character in northern mythology. He is a blacksmith with the power to forge magic weapons, including magic swords. In this respect he resembles the Greek god Hephaestus. In one myth, Wayland was captured in his sleep, hamstrung, and imprisoned on an island, where he was forced to fashion precious items for the king who captured him. This parallels the myth of Hephaestus, who is lame, and who dwells in Mount Aetna on the island of Sicily. Like Wayland, Hephaestus is a master blacksmith who can create magic weapons.

Wayland is the reputed maker of numerous magic swords, in addition to Gram, the sword given to Sigmund by Odin. Among them are Curtana, sword of Ogier the Dane; Mimung, which Wayland forged to battle a rival smith; Almace, the sword of Archbishop Turpin; and Durendal, the sword of Roland, paladin of the Emperor Charlemagne.

Durendal was the sharpest sword ever made and had the property of being unbreakable. It was empowered by the relics of various Christian saints, including a bit of cloth from the hem of the Virgin Mary's skirt. At his death Roland feared it would fall into the hands of the Saracens and tried to destroy it, but could not, so he concealed it beneath his corpse.

Beowulf

In the Old English poem *Beowulf*, the hero of the same name is gifted with a magic sword named Hrunting ("Thruster") by a fellow warrior and hero named Unferth. Concerning the sword, the poet says:

> the brehon handed him a hilted weapon,
> a rare and ancient sword named Hrunting.
> The iron blade with its ill-boding patterns
> had been tempered in blood. It had never failed
> the hand of anyone who hefted it in battle,
> (*Beowulf*, line 1456 et al.)

From the wording of the poem we can see that the magic aspect of the sword resulted from its great antiquity, but also from the "ill-boding patterns" on its blade. These patterns were probably runes. It is also said to have been tempered in blood. This practice was believed to make the steel of the sword harder. In a more mystical sense, it constituted a blood sacrifice to the sword, or rather to whatever spirit was induced to occupy it and empower it.

Beowulf used the sword to kill the monster Grendel, but as it fell out, Hrunting failed Beowulf in his moment of need, when he fought Grendel's more powerful mother. Fortunately, Beowulf found another magic sword in the monster's treasure hoard. This one had been crafted by giants, and with it he was able to slay Grendel's monstrous mother.

The reference to giants may refer to the antediluvian giants of Genesis 6:4: *"There were giants in the earth in those days."* If so, this association would lend the sword the might of a vast antiquity; but its power also derives from its forging by creatures other than humans. Giants are magical beings of enormous strength.

Excalibur

No examination of the magic sword could exclude the most famous of them all, Excalibur, the blade wielded by King Arthur of Britain when, as his legend tells us, he freed the island from the yoke of the Saxons and united it as a single kingdom. The sword first appears in early Welsh poetical works under the name Caledwich ("Hard-cutter"). Geoffrey of Monmouth in his *Historia Regum Britanniae*, which was written in Latin, called the sword Caliburnus. When the myth of the sword descended to the Old French romances, the name became Excalibur, the name by which we know the sword today.

The twelfth century French poet Chrétien de Troyes wrote that the sword had the power to cut through iron as easily as it cut through wood. Sir Thomas Mallory (c. 1415-1471), who finalized the myths surrounding King Arthur and his sword in his *Le Morte d'Arthur*, wrote that the name of the sword meant "Steel Cutter."

In the legends of Arthur there are two magic swords, which are sometimes represented as the same sword. There is the sword in the stone that Arthur pulls forth to demonstrate his right to rule his kingdom, as the true heir of Uther Pendragon. As I mentioned above, this story is suspiciously similar to the *Volsunga Saga* story of the magic sword Gram, which Sigmund pulls from the tree Barnstokkr. In the saga the sword is shattered by Odin, but later reforged. There is also the sword that is given to Arthur by the Lady of the Lake, a spiritual being who in my opinion represents the soul of Britain.

A way to reconcile these two swords is to have the first Excalibur broken, cast into the waters by Arthur, and then renewed by the Lady of the Lake. This was the approach adopted by John Boorman in his 1981 movie *Excalibur*.

It's impossible to know what the actual Excalibur might have looked like, if there ever was a sword that gave rise to all the legends we know today. Arthur is believed by some to have lived around the early 6th century. Pictish swords from that period somewhat resemble the later Viking swords. They have heavy straight blades, blunt points, and heavy pommels, with cross guards that are sometimes crescent-shaped.

In the Arthurian legends, possession of the sword gives Arthur the divine right to unite and rule over Britain. Its magic power lies not so much in its ability to cut through steel, but in its divine authority. During the final, fateful confrontation with the traitor, Mordred, who in modern versions of the legend is Arthur's own illegitimate son, Arthur is wounded and orders that the sword be cast back into the waters and in this way returned to the Lady of the Lake. The sword is very much Arthur's personal weapon, and can be legitimately wielded by no other hand.

Light Sabers

The power of the sword's iconic symbolism is very clearly displayed by its presence in the *Star Wars* series of movies. The Jedi Knights of these movies are motivated by honor and a sense of justice. Their personal weapon is the sword reduced to its primary, essential symbolic form—a beam of force that extends from the hand. The magic of the light saber is its ability to cut through any substance as easily as it cuts through the air. It also serves as an impenetrable shield, when the knight wielding it uses it to block

and deflect offensive projectiles or laser beams.

Why did George Lucas choose to showcase something so archaic as the sword in his futuristic space saga? He wanted to represent in the Jedi Knights the honor, duty, and loyalty of the medieval knights of French Romance.

If the Jedi Knights have an analog in European history, it would be the Knights Templar. These holy red-cross knights devoted their lives to helping and guarding pilgrims on the road to Jerusalem. Their weapon was the single-handed straight sword, which appears in many illustrations of the Templar knights. The hilt of these swords served the pious Templar knights as a holy cross. When they knelt to pray, they rested their swords upright in the earth before them, so that the sword hilt came level with their faces.

The Templars became corrupted by wealth in their later evolution, and when their order was destroyed by the French king Philip IV in 1307 in order that he might seize their wealth for himself, their spotless reputation was soiled by numerous tales of blasphemy, sodomy and devil worship. It is likely that most of these stories were false. They were extracted under torture for the sole purpose of destroying the reputation of the holy order.

The corruption of the Templars has a parallel in the Jedi Knights who are drawn to the Dark Side of the Force in the *Star Wars* saga. It is worth noting that the light saber is a magic weapon that can be used either for good or for evil. A light saber can be used just as effectively by a Darth Vader as by a Luke Skywalker.

When I say the light saber is magic, I mean it in the sense of Arthur C. Clark, when he wrote in his Third Law that *"Any sufficiently advanced technology is indistinguishable from magic."*

Conclusion

Even though the sword has not been a useful weapon of war for several centuries, the symbol continues to dominate the collective consciousness of humanity. We dream about it. We see it everywhere around us, in video games, in comic books, in fantasy novels and movies. The unprecedentedly popular television series *Game of Thrones* features the sword prominently. It shows no sign of dimming in our awareness.

The sword may be regarded as the symbol of war itself. Until very recently, military officers wore them at their sides even though it was expected that they would never actually use them. Even so, they were used by soldiers of Japan during World War Two, and by Korean soldiers during the Korean War. Those who used them were slaughtered by soldiers with guns, but it is noteworthy that anyone would even think to use a sword in modern combat. The Armistice that ended the Korean War was signed in 1953—within the living memory of many people. And at that time, men were still dying with swords in their hands.

In Ronald Reagan's address before the 42nd session of the United Nations General Assembly, he posed the question, *"Cannot swords be turned to plowshares? Can we and all nations not live in peace?"* The imagery is drawn from Isaiah 2:4—*"and they shall beat their swords into plowshares, and their spears into pruning hooks: nation shall not lift up sword against nation, neither shall they learn war any more."*

Well, it was a nice idea in the time of Isaiah, who is said to have lived during the 8th century BC, and still a nice idea in the decade of Ronald Reagan, but during the intervening period there was no sign that it would ever come to pass. As long as there is cruelty and injustice, there will be men who seek to deal out justice with the sword, or its modern replacement, the gun. There is every reason to believe that the symbol of the sword will live as long as war itself, and war is eternal.

◇◇◇◇◇◇◇◇◇ ◇ ◇◇◇◇◇◇◇

DARK POETRY:

BRYAN THAO WORRA

Bryan Thao Worra is an award-winning Lao American writer. His work has appeared widely, including Innsmouth Free Press, The Book of Dark Wisdom, Mad Poets of Terra, Illumen, and Strange Horizons, He holds a Fellowship in Literature from the National Endowment for the Arts, and his work is included in the Smithsonian Asian Pacific American Center's traveling exhibit "I Want the Wide American Earth." He's been featured internationally in Australia, Canada, England, Scotland, Germany, France, Singapore, Hong Kong, Korea, Chile, Pakistan, and across the United States. His collection of Lao American Lovecraftian poetry, *Demonstra*, received the 2014 Elgin Award for Book of the Year from the Science Fiction Poetry Association. You can learn more about his work at http://thaoworrablogspot.com.

BRYAN THAO WORRA
DEMONSTRA

A POETRY COLLECTION

A DISTANT SOUND OF WAR

It took half a forever to hammer out
The uneasy New Vientiane Accords,
Ratifying them with the authorized
Delegates of the United Multiverses,
Navigating ten thousand protocols.

When the sanguine Truth at last was known,
Less mortal powers snickered that it took
Humans so long to recognize our Deep Wars
across weird eons of warp and wound,

Our laughable cosmic quagmires
Where we fought blind, uncertain,
Unsure we were in a war at all,
And not merely

Some perverse natural order.

Before the higher celestials,
How crude our mere weapons
Of "destruction" and "conquest"
Among demigods and demons.

The Nyak Kings laughed raucously
At human ingenuity.

For all our efforts, at best we could end
One lifetime at a time.

"What might was THIS?
You squandered MILLENNIA
Obsessed with bone and tissue?
Obscene!"

Even our greatest stars,
Harnessed for destruction,
Were catastrophes for a single plane,
One brief incarnation at best,

Two, if we were astronomically lucky.

They believed us humored
With elaborate vows and verse among
Cosmic serpents, winged beauties,
Living planets and jovial warbeasts,

Vows to eventually forego
Their mechanisms of indiscriminate
Multiversal havoc and mayhem,
Their screaming soul-smelters of
Interdimensional terror.

Future carnage, they assured us,
Would be more precise, deliberate,
And conclusive, if that comforted us.

Our generals and sages knew.
Ultimately, we were all lying,
Buying time between smiles,

Awaiting an advantageous kalpa
To use our preferred engines of polycide.

We hid this secret plan in a poem in the past,
A time the others still think never happened.

CHIMARINE

Cut apart tomorrow's cattle
You'll find a "human" within,
Or at least enough compatible bits to replace
Most of what gets blown away
> In some plasma-flinging brouhaha
> Over contested territory on our poisoned Earth.
Once we overcame our grotesque attachment
To bilateral symmetry in favor of social utility,
We FINALLY moved beyond "the Draft" to "the Graft"
> A purple heart just one of many varieties now available,
> Combined arms just the beginning.
A brain, properly reanimated, we learned,
Can store more than one soul, even a whole squad,
If some green butter bar fouls up enough.
> At least, the obedient scraps.
> The rest is debatable and suspected superfluous.
Give a Chimarine a modification, it kills for you for a lifetime.
Teach that Chimarine it was "human,"
Well, you get what you've got coming.

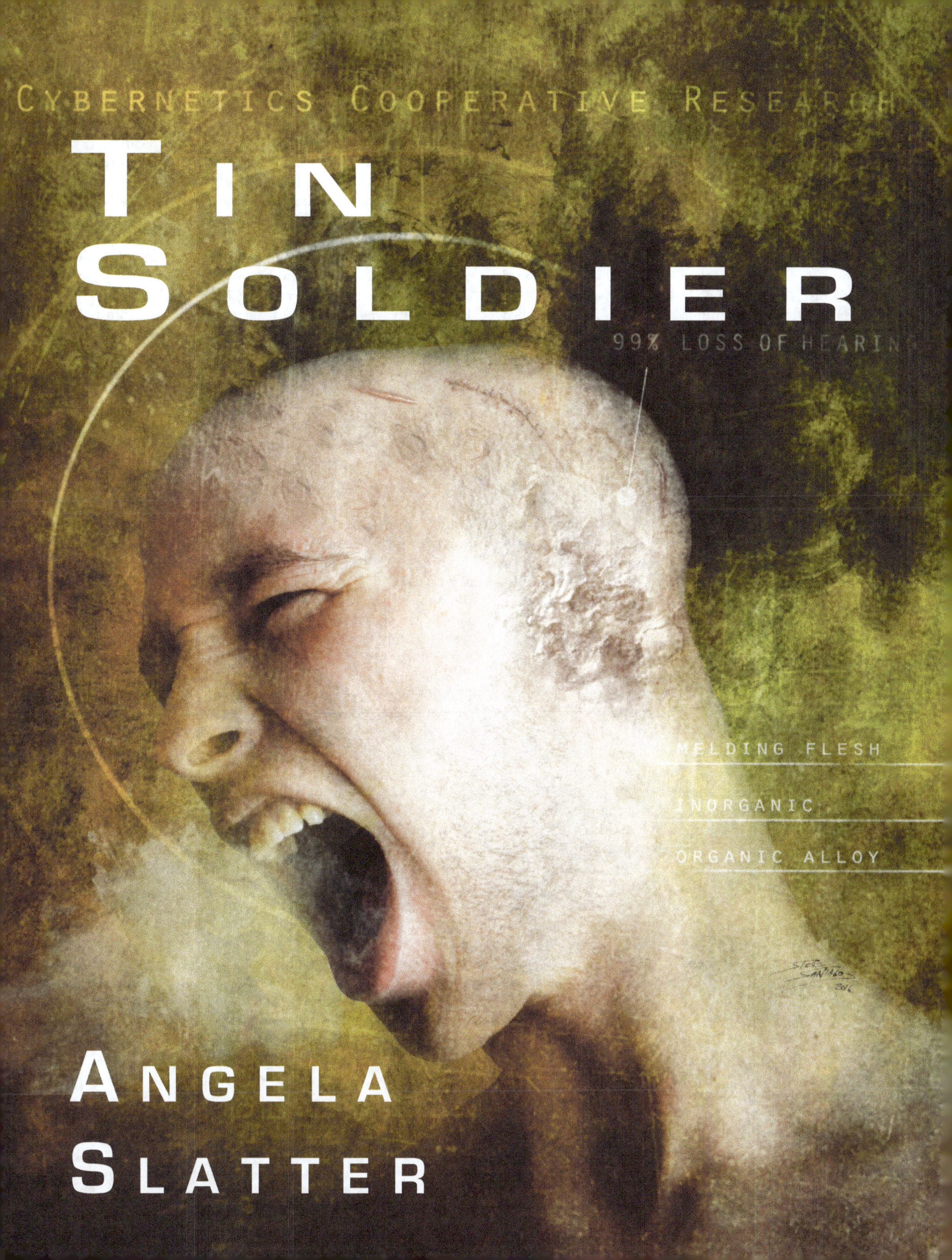
CYBERNETICS COOPERATIVE RESEARCH
TIN SOLDIER
99% LOSS OF HEARING
MELDING FLESH
INORGANIC
ORGANIC ALLOY
ANGELA SLATTER

'He asked for you.'

I hadn't set foot in Tenby Hall for six years, I hadn't seen Harry Vander in seven, and I'd neither seen nor spoken to Worth de Havilland in nine. All in all, it was a bit of a shock to the system, with so many ghosts floating around me. The Hall hadn't changed, its interior was the same not-quite-right white, the lights a bit too bright, a preponderance of shiny metal and tasteful furniture, milque-toast artworks, the strange slippery carpet they'd created so that gurneys and wheelchairs could run along it but footsteps would still be muffled. And it strictly speaking wasn't a Hall—it was a tower, but just about everything was a tower nowadays and the CCR Board wanted a name that stood out. Tenby Hall was a cross between a hospital, a research facility and a guinea pig hutch, no matter how much money they threw at it or what the nameplate said. Situated in the middle of a field in Hampshire, it stuck up like a big finger directed at the sky.

Harry was greyer, in both hair and face. Looking at him made me glad I'd gotten out when I did. His eyes were tired and sad, a bit suspicious. He'd put on a some weight—he'd once been greyhound thin, now there was just a little paunch billowing under his suit, and the lab coat looked tight across the shoulders. Was the tarnished gold band on his left hand a sign that his wife or husband could cook, or that there were too many takeaway meals on his dance card? I wondered if there were any little Harrys running around, and calculated how old he was: ten years older than me, so nudging fifty-two, fifty-three. I'd been thirty when I'd first started at Tenby, the baby, the prodigy, the enfant terrible—no one else had been under forty. I was a girl to boot. Imagine the fun.

'He asked for you,' Harry repeated. 'We suggested his family but he got very agitated. It wasn't worth having him hurt himself.'

'Did he say why? Why me?'

Harry shook his head, shaggy hair needing a cut. 'He was adamant. And he's still important. It took us a while to find you. You did a good job of disappearing.'

'Bollocks, Harry, you searched the iDirectory and had my number in about 2.5 seconds. Only the poor have any real chance of disappearing in today's world.'

'Well, you took a long time about returning my call,' he grumbled, and I had. Two weeks in fact. I could tell from his expression that he thought I might have bothered to dress up a little, too, something better than jeans and a t-shirt, leather jacket and boots. Instead he said, 'You need to prepare yourself, Faith. He's... well, not to put too fine a point on it, he's a fucking mess.'

I nodded, said nothing, felt the sense of unease that had been steadily building since I got Harry's message throb and expand. It sat at the back of my throat, malignant, making it hard to swallow. We stopped outside a frosted glass door and Harry pulled a swipe card from his pocket, ran it through the reader, then pressed his thumb deeply into a gel pad beneath. The lock clicked and the door slid aside.

We stepped into a vestibule, empty but for a long bench running along the floor-to-ceiling glass wall in front of us. On the bench, stainless steel, were bottles of pills, paper towels, syringes, antiseptics, bandages, white towels, bags of saline, kidney trays, all manner of medical paraphernalia. Through the glass, though, that's what caught my eye, the man in the wheelchair.

If Harry hadn't told me who he was, I wouldn't have recognised him. Even then I was prepared to call Harry a liar and walk out, not look back. In the end the only thing that convinced me were the eyes, when he seemed to sense us and turn around. It had to be the eyes, because nothing else was the same, nothing else was right.

There were no legs below the knees, just rough red-looking stumps; only one arm remained, the right, the other ended just above the elbow. His left ear was gone, sheared off at the skull, making his head look lopsided. The mouth was crooked, lips strangely thin, and a nerve ticked irregularly just above his left temple. Under the white hospital gown, he seemed smaller, thinner, his muscle mass wasted. Shaved off, his hair was a black shadow across the skull broken only by scars, some long, some jagged, some simply dots, one almost a perfect square; his face was clean-shaven too, but the blue stain of a beard darkened his chin and thin cheeks.

It was the eyes, though, so blue, so large, with lashes like an alpaca and brows straight and fierce. The expression in them was the same, as if something always vaguely amused him. And when he smiled, or gave an approximation of one, the lift at the corner of his mouth was identical, the little quirk that said *Well, you and I are okay, but the rest of this world? Fucking nuts!* And it made you think you were the only two who counted, that it was your little club. His face lit up and he knew it was me, so I guessed his brain was intact even if the rest of him looked like Picasso had taken to an Action Jackson doll with a hatchet.

The lump in my throat flipped over and over. I felt sick. I wanted to run.

All these years and he asked for me, no one else.

'What have you told his family?'

'That he's still on a black op, linked with the American forces in Saudi.'

'Why did he ask for me?'

'Ask him yourself.' He pressed his thumb into another gel pad and the door to the inner room gaped like a chasm. 'We fitted him with a temporary voice box when we knew he was going to live. It's just a stop-gap measure until we could get you... get a specialist to step up.'

That should have made me nervous but I wasn't really listening. All I was thinking about was fleeing. I took four steps backwards, stopped, tried to make myself move in the opposite direction, couldn't, looked at Harry, shook my head. 'I can't. I can't, Harry. It's too much, too long ago. I...' I didn't bother to finish the sentence, turned on my heel and walked as fast as I could without actually breaking into a run.

❧

Once I got on the M3 I set the car on auto and slept most of the way back to London. Sleep, though, was no escape. I dreamt of Oxford back in 2195, and of Worth de Havilland the first time I saw him.

There'd always been a university regiment and an Officers Training Corps, but for a long while that had mostly been about students playing at soldiers. Only some of them took it seriously as a career move, most were just marking time until their degrees were done and they could join Daddy or Mummy's firm in the city, or wait for an inevitable inheritance as soon as some rich uncle or aunt dropped off the twig. They were never *real*, not in those days; at least not until a nifty Act of Parliament had decreed Oxford not merely to be a place of higher learning, but also a military academy. The never-ending road show of wars the government subscribed to needed not just new flesh, but new training grounds. New College was colonised by men and women who took their service seriously; now soldiers played at being students.

They weren't all moneyed thugs, but that was a large chunk of their population. They acted as though they owned the place, played rugby on the quadrangle, hassled students both male and female, and God help you if you weren't white. For fun and practise, they abseiled down the facades of buildings that had resisted the depredations of Henry VIII, the Roundheads, World War II bombing raids, the Irish-Islamic bombing campaigns of 2070 and 2080. They dislodged medieval gargoyles, broke stone rosettes, scrawled graffiti on the walls of the All Souls, and in the chapels broke stained glass windows older than their family names. Those without a bloodline, but the right degree of aggression went along for the ride.

The curious anarchy of an undercooked, undisciplined military held sway until the Vice-Chancellor had had enough. He called a general strike and was supported not just by his crusty old dons, but also by the majority of students, who'd found their studies interrupted and made damned-near impossible by the tramp of jackboots and general thuggery.

My family was incredibly poor, so poor, we still lived in a house. Well, a shack, still one step up from the camps on the Welsh Border; only the truly indigent couldn't afford a place in one of the meanest tower blocks. My older sisters married as soon as they were legally able, just to get out, not caring that they left us behind, just to be able to move into one of the tower blocks at the very outskirts of London. I was an accident, ten years after my parents thought they were done, and I had a brain, a fierce, questing mutant of a brain that dragged me upwards. It pulled me through scholarship exam after scholarship exam, it got me into Oxford. Eventually it got me to Tenby Hall where, due to the new, freer laws about work done by individuals for corporations, I was able to patent my research and trademark my designs. Tenby Hall still has to pay me for anything they do using technology I created. My parents and Gran live now in a penthouse apartment atop one of the towers on the site of Old Buckingham Palace. My sisters don't starve or want for anything, but they live where they married; I'm petty like that.

An education was the only way out for me and, in the early days, the military bloc was playing havoc with that. Like a lot of other students I was pissed off and we were spoiling for a fight. I was one of a group who wrote and circulated a protest flyer. Nothing quite says "civil disobedience student-style" like a scrappy yellow piece of paper. Rather than risk detection by using electronic means of communication and dispersal, we'd typeset it every Friday afternoon, then four or five of us would wander the campus, looking for unattended copy machines, then bang off as many prints as we could. We'd pass them along to other students who acted as couriers, walking streets after dark, slipping the roughly folded pages into mailboxes, under windshields, hastily taping them to poles and pub doors, and trying like hell not to get discovered.

If you *were* caught, the least you had to fear was a beating; the worst was expulsion, loss of scholarship, blacklisting for the rest of your life so you could never, ever expect a job better than that of a mudlark. Not as a result of university action, but of the influence of rich and powerful parents of military gorillas pretending to be students. Though rumours had begun circulating that the Home Secretary was going to intervene, we'd believe when we actually saw it; too many promises like that had disappeared like smoke on the breeze. We kept writing, kept printing, kept dissenting.

I got caught. Of course I did.

I'd left the Bodleian with a couple of hundred yellow sheets buried at the bottom of my satchel. Someone had either seen me making copies, or they'd been suspicious for a while, and watched me. At any rate, I found myself dragged into the space between two buildings by three men in camouflage-patterned clothing, who proceeded to empty the contents of my bag into a puddle of muddy water. When they found the flyers I was slapped until my ears rang, was spun around and had my face pushed against the rough brick of the wall so blood seeped from abrasions. I stayed quiet, determined not to show fear, until busy, greedy hands began to pull at my belt; then I started to scream.

Which was when it all stopped.

He was beautiful: raven's wing black hair, dark blue eyes, long lashes, full lips, olive skin, broad cheekbones, square jaw, broad shoulders, deep chest, wearing army greens. Tall and straight. Powerful. He pulled the ringleader away from me and threw him down, giving him a kick so vicious that I heard ribs break. The other two dispersed, dragging the injured one with them. They all seemed afraid of him and it made me glad.

He helped me back to my college room, washed the blood off my face and sprayed an antiseptic bandage over the seeping graze.

'Okay?' he asked.

I nodded. 'Okay. Thanks.'

He was gone, then, no names exchanged, nothing. And it took a while before I worked out he was the one sent in by the Home Secretary—Edward de Havilland's own son—but he found me again and again. In the library, at lunch, in the pub, at my lectures, in my favourite spot by the river. Somehow, he was always there.

'Are you following me?' I demanded one afternoon as I sat propped against a tree, and heard the soft footfall of boots.

'Yes. I was wondering when you'd notice.'

'I'm teaching you a valuable lesson.'

'Which is?'

'Anything you get too easily, you don't appreciate.'

That was the first time he kissed me, there by the river, with the warmth of the sun on our skins, the lap of the water, the murmur of passing students. He was loyal and funny and smart. He was steadfast.

And I'd run from him.

In my Hampton Tower apartment, the phone kept ringing: I recognised Harry's number and ignored it. For a while he kept hanging up, trying again, but he should have remembered that I could always out-stubborn him. Eventually he left a message, saying my name had been left at the Hall security desk along with a temporary swipe card and he'd arranged for my old security clearance to be resurrected; a dorm room would be set aside for my use if required. Just in case.

Just in case.

It was three am by the time I got back to Tenby. I was beyond sleep. Driven to return.

I stepped through the vestibule into Worth's room which, now that I was paying attention, was more than comfortable: still white with a state-of-the-art hospital bed, but otherwise furnished a bit like a drawing room, two over-stuffed chairs, a bookshelf, a table with impossibly carved legs, a chaise longue worth more than my watch (a Vintage twentieth century Rolex). It was a little cold, but they'd drawn the blankets up over him. The pale yellow of a nightlight glowed in a corner.

In his sleep, he looked almost as I remembered, as if slumber smoothed away the aches of waking hours. The long lashes resting on his olive cheek, the lips fuller in repose, his lack of limbs hidden. I sat gently on the edge of the bed, reached out to touch his face. His right hand snaked up to grab my wrist, still dangerously fast. In the weak light we stared at each other. I leaned in and kissed him and found that I still responded to the touch of him as I always had. My eyes stung. I wanted to talk, to tell him I was sorry, but if I had tried I knew the only thing that would come out of my mouth would be a long, low howl of grief that would remind him of all he'd lost, of all that was gone. So, instead, I filled my mouth with the taste of him so that we might both forget for a time.

The War on Terror was entering its one hundred and ninety-ninth year; big celebrations were planned for the bicentennial. They couldn't make any more soldiers than they already had—military programs had sprung up across the Western world sponsored by the so-called allied powers, those on the side of good. At least, they were allies as long as they toed the line—in the past, alliances and allegiances had shifted—if a nation disagreed with the US-led, British-backed coalition, there was a good chance said nation would find itself added to the blacklist of "evil" nations. New Zealand had gone that way—only the North Island remained, the South had the consistency of charcoaled toast. Similarly, Tasmania (with the consent of the Australian Mainland Parliament) had been flattened; as had Japan, the Netherlands, a large chunk of Indonesia, Switzerland (greatly affecting the world's supply of watches and chocolate); Belgium got lightly fried and the Court of International Justice in the Hague was the target of a surgical strike on Valentine's Day in 2085.

The military had always promised those at the bottom of life's ladder—orphans, kids from poor families, the uneducated, the poor—a chance to improve their lives. If they didn't get killed, then once they'd served their tours, they could make a fresh start with more money than they otherwise might have ever seen. Some people figure it's worth it, the PTSD, the insomnia, the strange illnesses and rashes, the suicidal urges, the marriage breakups. And just like the soldiers, the terrorists—or freedom fighters, depending on who you spoke to—didn't disappear. They kept breeding, they had belief, they had faith, they had nothing else to lose.

So in Britain, the government decided that if we

couldn't breed more and we couldn't make more, then we had to be able to repair very effectively and very efficiently the ones we did have. Hence, the Cybernetics Cooperative Research program at Tenby Hall, which had always been the site of some military hospital or other. During World War One, it was those affected by mustard gas; in World War Two those suffering shell shock; after the first Gulf War it took care of those with the strange diseases no one could account for, from medical experiments neither the Americans nor the British would admit to carrying out; the second Gulf War—which basically had never really ended—saw Tenby enlarged and turned into a plastic surgery facility, specialising in replacing amputated limbs. Cybernetics was the next step in the medical evolutionary chain.

I started working on my specialty at Oxford, did my PhD on melding flesh and bone with inorganic materials, on getting the atomic structures to mesh together meat and metal. I created an organic alloy that mimicked the growth of a living being. Harry developed an artificial skin that would work with my cybernetic limbs. They sent us the worst injured soldiers, those taken apart by mines and explosions and guns and weapons that should never have been turned against human flesh. They sent us those who should not have lived, who had nothing to lose and who didn't care whether we put them back together or not. We called it the Humpty Dumpty Ward, between ourselves and our patients. The first year, we lost fifty percent of our intake. By the third year, we saved ninety-five percent. We were drunk on achievement; *I* was drunk on playing God. I'd patented all my creations and it made me rich, sickeningly, petrifyingly rich. Almost as rich as the bastards that kept sending us to war.

I thought I was sending those soldiers home to new lives, to a rest they'd earned by the sacrifice of their limbs, of their peace of mind. But after a while I started recognising faces, scars; I found men and women I'd already put back together coming across the table again and again,

torn and ruined over and over.

I left Tenby Hall when I realised they were using my work to *recycle* humans so they could be sent back into war zones to be broken again. All that work, all that pain and sorrow, and they would simply keep sending them back until their bodies couldn't be patched up anymore, and they had to be scrap-heaped. They still haven't managed to make robot soldiers—of all things, that still eludes us, robots are no more than toys, laughable things that kids play with—we've never managed to make robot servants or robot hookers or a robot that thinks independently. We've never made a facsimile of a human that presents a greater danger to us than we do to ourselves. But the cybernetics? That's where we've excelled ourselves. The melding of injured flesh with a living, healing metal, with networks of artificial neurones that can imitate the workings of a human body, replace what's been lost. Even the skin, though it doesn't feel quite like the real thing—there's

a smoothness to it that's almost plastic-y—but it doesn't feel awful, not totally wrong.

And here was this man, who'd once been everything to me, waiting, wanting me to put him back together again.

'Worth, I don't do this anymore. I haven't done it for years. There are people here who *can*, I trained them.' We both lay on the bed, he under the covers, I on top, shivering a little.

'I don't want them,' the voice was not just metallic, it was *metal*, hard and cold. 'No one else knew me—before.'

So there was the heart of it: I was to rebuild my lover, from remembrance, on his hope that *my* memory of him would match *his* memory of himself. Memory: the worst thing in the world, an unreliable tool and he wanted me to remake him in the image in my head.

❧

'Why did you leave?' Three months down the track and his robotic voice box had been replaced by a new organo-cyber one that Harry and I had created between us. 'Why did we break up?'

I looked at him, confused.

He shook his head. 'Only I can't remember. I can't remember anything about that part of us. I have blank spots, that's one of them.'

I was working on an ankle joint, checking the connections before I spliced the nerves with those of the foot we were going to attach and let grow. The left leg had been working perfectly for a couple of weeks, so it was time to finish the right. Worth's left arm was a little stiff, but with the exercises we had him do it was loosening up nicely. Harry had him on a course of fish oil, of all things, but it seemed to be doing the trick. I stayed bent over the limb, not wanting to answer him. My eyes burned.

'Faith, look at me.'

I did, blinking.

'Whatever it was, it doesn't matter now.' He smiled. 'I'll forgive you anything.'

'That's big of you, Worth, but I'm not the one needs forgiving.' My voice was rough, a film coated the back of my throat, acrid and stubborn. His face clouded. It hadn't occurred to him that *he* might have been the one in the wrong.

'What did I do?'

'Worth, trust me, some things are best forgotten.' I stood up. 'I can attach the foot today; I'll tell Harry to prep for surgery this afternoon.'

I turned away. He grabbed at my wrist: he had regained his strength, in fact, his right arm had become stronger after we'd augmented the musculature. I could feel the circulation slowing in my forearm. I wiggled my fingers to show he was hurting me. He loosened his grip but didn't let me go.

'Tell me what I did.'

I sat next to him, took a deep breath. 'You remember how we met?'

He smiled, nodded.

'Two years after that, there was the Siege of Magdalen College. In spite of what your father did, in spite of your work there, the military still wasn't popular. There were more and more student protests against the war. Magdalene was the centre of it all, where they gathered, discussed, dissented. The university's governing body tolerated it, encouraged it quietly. The government was getting tired of it. You and I—it was the only thing we used to fight about; it was the reason we broke up. There was a protest, a huge protest march from Oxford to London. Got so much attention, the world saw it wasn't just lazy hippies, grubby students or the rent-a-mob protesting; it really stirred things up.

'So they sent in soldiers against Magdalen—students barricaded themselves in. We were there for a week—I was with them. You were brought in as a negotiator. There were more important people than me there but none of them could be risked. I agreed to talk to you outside, thought you might stay your hand because of our relationship.' I swallowed hard.

'What did I do, Faith?' He was desperate now.

'I went to talk to you, and you hit me. You knocked me out and from what I heard later you carried me behind the barricades and left me safe with a doctor. Then you went back and led the attack.' I leaned forward, elbows on knees, head in hands, feeling waves of nausea break over me. 'One hundred and forty-seven students were killed. Anyone not taken out in the rocket attack was shot when they tried to crawl from of the wreckage and look for help. That's what you did. That's why I left.'

He was silent for so long that I wondered if time had stopped around us, but when I looked up he was examining his left hand, staring at the places where the skin was still a little thin, where he could still see the workings of the things I'd made for him, grown for him. The things that would see him walk free, into a life of privilege once more: Worth de Havilland wouldn't go back to the fighting, not this time. His father, Prime Minister now, had finally been advised of his location, of his condition, and he was determined his only son would never be at risk again.

'Worth?' I said. How much difference would this knowledge make to him? He'd lived with what he'd done for nine years. How much had it bothered him then? Or was he comfortable with the idea he'd just done his duty? Now that this memory had been returned to him, would it matter at all?

'I would give anything,' he said, meeting my eyes at last, 'to make it up, to pay for all those lives I don't remember.'

❧

He looked as good as new. I think maybe he was a little taller and he joked about that. The scars were mostly gone. His hair had grown back, wild and curly and I hadn't let them cut it.

'How do I look?'

'Perfect. No one would know you're a tin soldier.'

We stood on Westminster Bridge, ignoring the House of Parliament and Big Ben, hunched and leaning into each other to try to ward off the cold breath of the coming winter.

He was warm and tender and there had been moments in the past eight months when I forgot everything bad that had ever happened between us. When I could ignore the remembrance of rebuilding him, of having so much of his blood on me that my scrubs turned dark, of reconstructing him like he was a doll I'd taken apart to play with. There were times when I could forget who he was and what he came from and everything he had done.

When he'd knocked me down and kept me safe behind the barricades, he'd given me the worst nightmare I would ever have: the thought that I survived just because he loved me, and in that one afternoon he had helped to murder almost all of my friends. Sometimes I still dreamt of him walking the bloodied halls of Magdalen, pistol in hand, pumping a teflon-jacketed bullet into brains that should have been used to help heal the world, not to decorate a wall. I wondered if he'd remembered other things about that day, although we'd not spoken of it since I gave that part of his memory back.

'The old man's trying to pass an Act today. No one knows about it so far, he's kept it very quiet.'

My heart beat with an irregular rhythm for a few painful moments. I *knew*. I had overheard Worth's father on one of his visits. 'Oh?'

'He wants to extend the Tenby program—replicate it across the country. More Tenbys, more soldiers back to the field. It's all about the bodies,' he said bitterly. 'I'm going to meet him for lunch. I don't think you should come, Faith.'

He moved his hands across my belly. Even though it was still flat, somehow he knew. And somehow he knew something else. 'I don't know how else to stop them. They'll never stop, Faith.'

'I love you.'

'I love you. I never stopped.' His face against mine, my hands in his, I could feel the subtle difference between the real skin and the false. He kissed me slowly, sadly. 'For what it's worth, Faith, I'm so sorry.'

He didn't even give me time to say that I was sorry, too; he turned and walked away, across the bridge towards the House of Parliament, a tall, dark figure in the crowd, his coat billowing around him in the wind, people stepping out of his way.

In my handbag was a small black metal box, an old fashioned key safe, which now seemed impossibly heavy. Inside was a detonator, only two inches long by half an inch wide. It was keyed to the system I'd planted inside Worth—all the components, all the cybernetics to make him walk and work were also a small integrated bomb. I knew enough people who remembered the Siege of Magdalen, who'd lost children and friends, siblings and lovers. People who could make or get me what I'd asked for when I made my decision.

I would give him ten minutes, let him walk into the House of Lords, time to get inside, time to sit down with his father, with all the lords of destruction within range as they sat down to their meals. Then, with my hand on my belly, I would press the switch.

My tin solider would be steadfast to the last.

Weird Reflections

By Mike Davis

Photo courtesy of Mike Davis

What actually happens when the stars are right and the Old Ones return? When Cthulhu awakes from his slumber? Most Lovecraftian stories do no more than hint at this, but since one of the themes of this issue is apocalyptic fiction, I thought it would be good to list a few anthologies that actually let you find out:

Cthulhu's Reign, edited by Darrell Schweitzer. I read this when it was published in 2010, and it is an anthology that I really enjoyed. Well, I suppose "enjoyed" is one way to put it—some of these stories really disturbed me. Not surprising, since there are tales here by such luminaries as Richard Lupoff, John Langan, and Laird Barron. "What happens when the other Old Ones, long since banished from our universe, break through and descend from the stars? What would the reign of Cthulhu be like on a totally transformed planet where mankind is no longer the master? Find out in these exciting, brand-new stories."

Apotheosis: Stories of Human Survival After The Rise of The Elder Gods, edited by Jason Andrew. A recent anthology with stories by Cody Goodfellow, Pete Rawlik, and others. "Lovecraft Mythos

stories often climax at the moment of the fateful return of the Elder Gods and the audience is left to ponder what might happen next. This anthology features stories about humanity under the reign of the Elder Gods and ancient terrors."

Tomorrow's Cthulhu: Stories at the Dawn of Posthumanity, edited by Scott Gable and C. Dombrowski. Stories by Molly Tanzer, Darrell Schweitzer, Damien Angelica Walters, Cody Goodfellow,

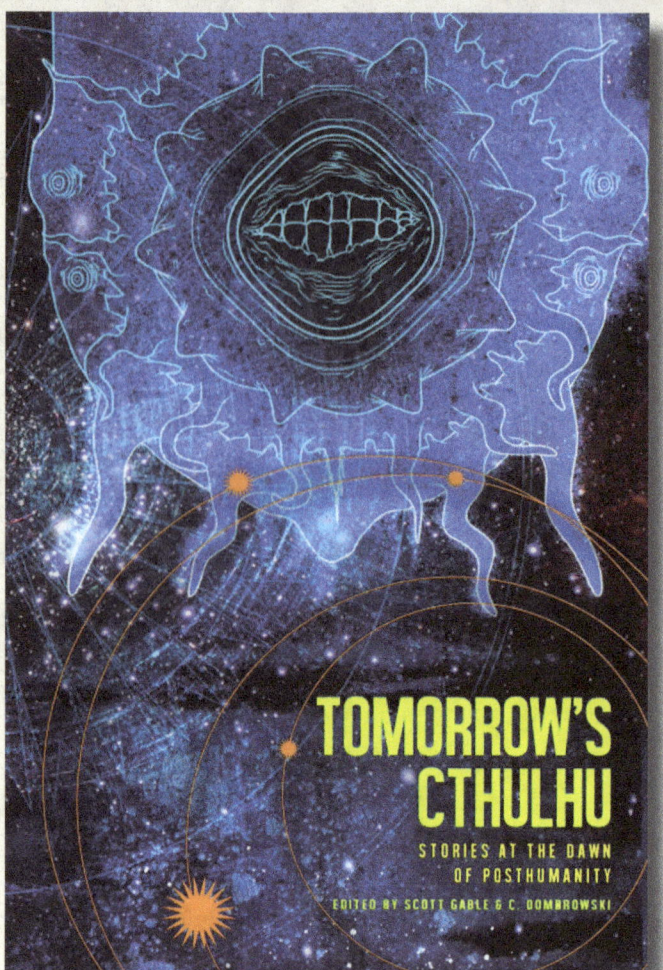

Also be sure to check out Autumn Cthulhu, a collection of 19 Lovecraftian stories edited by Mike Davis and based on the theme of the autumnal season. Featuring such awesome authors as Daniel Mills, Richard Gavin, Laird Barron, Joseph S. Pulver Sr., Gemma Files, and Ann K. Schwader, plus many more, you simply must check this one out.

—Ed.

and others. "These are transhumanist, near-future science fiction tales of the Cthulhu Mythos. These are tales of more than merely cosmic dread. They exist in our world of the coming decades."

There aren't many, as you can see. Most mythos fiction takes place before the Cthulhuian Apocalypse. But if you're a fan of Lovecraftian fiction and you're looking for something different, try these three books.

THE JACK SIGLER THRILLERS:

An Interview with Jeremy Robinson and Kane Gilmour

BY WILLIAM SIMMONS

William Simmons: Thanks for taking the time to sit down with *Dark Discoveries*, you guys. Your thrillers tend to combine myth, science and action. Are these natural bedfellows, and how difficult is it to create a novel incorporating them?

Jeremy Robinson: I think they are. Throughout history the human race goes through shifts of understanding, where what was once myth or magic becomes science. Exploring ancient myths with modern eyes is often exciting, and when applied to creatures like the Hydra, action is inevitable. Of course, we're still human, and still haven't really figured out the universe, not to mention our own planet, so I also enjoy creating modern myths based on fringe science or subjects still beyond our understanding.

Kane Gilmour: I think they're bedfellows, too, if for no other reason than all of those things are interesting to me as an author. Writing a novel takes a while. You could conceivably bang one out in a few weeks, but it can't be accomplished in a single day. No matter what, you are thinking about the story for a while. And during that time, all of the things that influence and interest you are vying for your mind's attention. They naturally wind up in the story, even if you didn't set out to incorporate them consciously. With the Jack Sigler stories, we are actively trying to incorporate

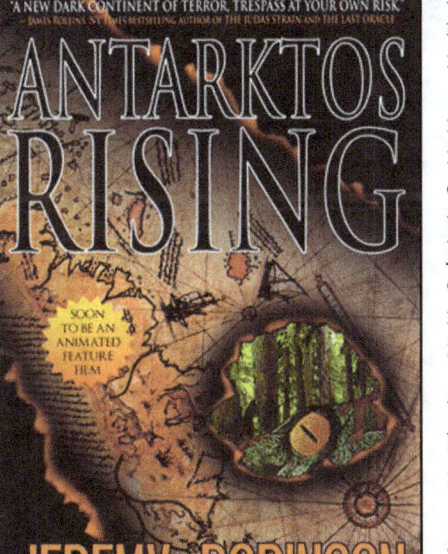

'A NEW DARK CONTINENT OF TERROR. TRESPASS AT YOUR OWN RISK.'
— JAMES ROLLINS, *NY TIMES* BESTSELLING AUTHOR OF *THE JUDAS STRAIN* AND *THE LAST ORACLE*

ANTARKTOS RISING

SOON TO BE AN ANIMATED FEATURE FILM

JEREMY ROBINSON

AUTHOR OF *RAISING THE PAST* AND *THE DIDYMUS CONTINGENCY*

myth and action. The science comes more from a need to keep things as realistic and believable as possible.

For me, I normally start with a story idea and action. If the story doesn't incorporate the mythology, it usually comes when I try to add some danger to the plot or creatures to a story like a Jack Sigler story. I don't think it's difficult at all to incorporate those elements, really. The one flows into the next during the process.

WS: How valuable are ancient religions, belief systems, and mythologies to your fiction? For humankind in general?

JR: Nearly all of my books (except those with co-authors) have some kind of connection to religious beliefs, whether they be modern day or ancient myth. I've explored the mythos of most ancient civilizations (The Jack Sigler Thrillers), and frequently use the Bible as a source for monsters (The Antarktos Saga). I also use Biblical stories as a source for developing flawed heroes. In terms of humanity as a whole, I think ancient religions and myths are like family trees. They're humanity's roots, going back to when we first started trying to figure things out, and they still provide us with sustenance today.

KG: I think the answer to both questions is that these things

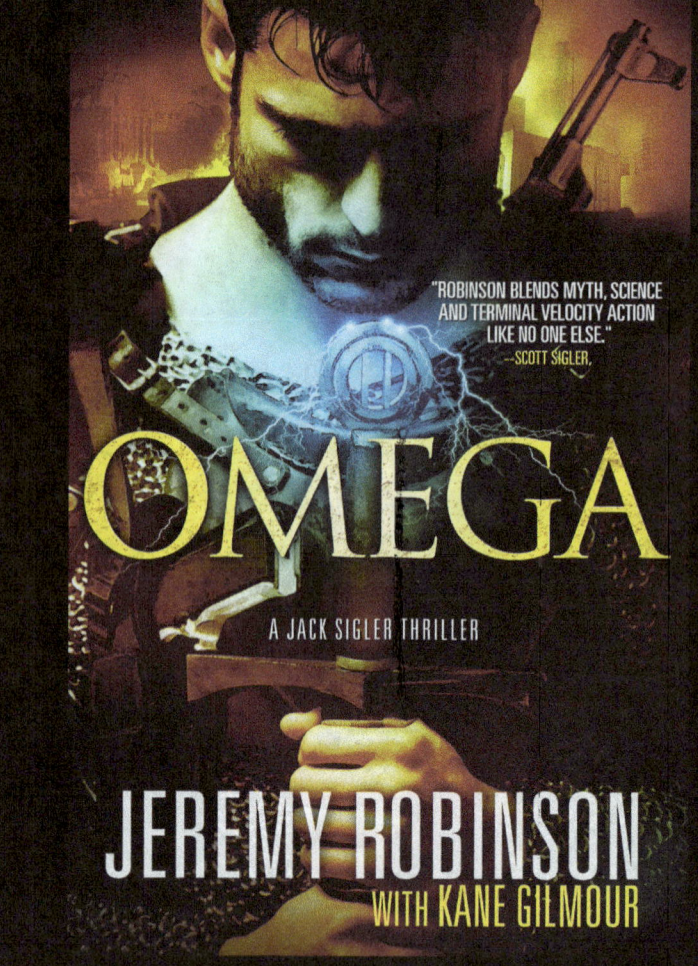

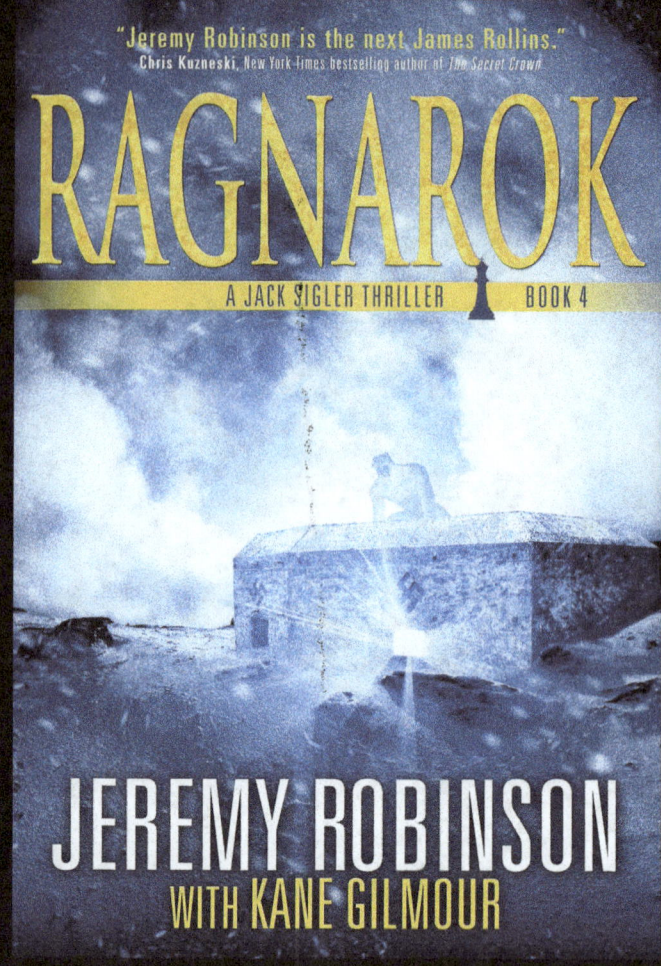

can provide a historical legitimacy to current beliefs, and those current beliefs yield the same crop: *hope*. For humankind in general or for characters in a story, hope is a powerful elixir. Ancient religions can tie into plot elements or exotic locales, and they feed into the mythology and beliefs that form a backdrop to a culture, allowing readers from a variety of backgrounds to connect with the ancient or modern peoples from far-flung locations. Without that context, it's difficult for someone who hasn't travelled to identify with different cultures. Having that kind of background showcases similarities in belief, and that can often be the lynchpin to compassion. If I set a story in Korea and bring in some of the religion or mythological beliefs, it helps a reader from the UK who has never been to the Far East, to get a better understanding of the setting and the people in the story.

On another level, these kinds of things add some nice historical authenticity to an adventure story set in the present. If I say there's a weapon that can blow up the moon, people will be skeptical. But if I say there was a gold and gem-encrusted chest from 4000BC in a cavern in modern-day Tibet, and that it was placed there because of the havoc it had wreaked on ancient civilizations and that the people of the time believed the chest contained a dwarf goddess—and that this chest is what can obliterate the moon today—readers are more likely to buy into it for some reason. Their own beliefs about ancient culture will likely contain many mysteries that cannot be explained, and so the leap in their imagination seems easier.

WS: Hmm, interesting. But do you find intriguing paradoxes or juxtapositions between the supernatural and scientific? How do you exploit these in fiction, in particular, the Jack Sigler novels?

JR: There is a lot that we consider supernatural that falls into the category of "we haven't figured this out yet." Things like OBEs (out of body experiences) or ESP (extra sensory perception). Even the UFO phenomenon falls into this category. I also think there are some things that will probably remain beyond the limits of human understanding, like the spiritual realm, if there is such a thing. The balance of these two seemingly opposing subjects, and figuring out which side story elements fall on, is exciting... even when they're not part of a story.

KG: Certainly there can be both paradoxes and juxtapositions or alignments between the supernatural and the scientific. A lot of that in fiction occurs when a writer asks "what if" questions, and then tries to find the science that can rationally explain those questions. In *Omega* we wanted King to travel back in time almost three millennia to suit the needs of the story. The next trick was finding a way for that to happen, and using enough science to plausibly explain the concept, as well as tying it into the internal logic of the Jack Sigler series. I think the way we exploit things is when we then say: "Right, what cool, well-known things can we incorporate from history and mythology or the supernatural that would fit here?"

In the case of *Omega*, it was the Colossus of Rhodes and Cerberus. So that was a case of exploitation rather than discovery, where juxtaposition was concerned. We did the things necessary to make things fit. Other times, like with the Chess Team novelette "Show of Force" in the *SNAFU: Survival of the Fittest* anthology, the science comes first. I had heard about the Siberian Anticyclone weather pattern and suggested to Jeremy we use that for the story setting, regardless of whatever creatures it contained.

WS: In *Ragnarok*, the fourth Jack Sigler novel, you focus on universal apocalypse. In fact, mass destruction of cultures and societies appears in much of your fiction. For what personal or aesthetic purposes do you focus on such apocalyptic elements?

JR: I've been trying to figure that out for a while, too. I dream about the end of the world, and I'm drawn to novels, movies and TV shows where humanity is on the brink of extinction. I think it's because, when you peel away governments, politics, and all the trappings of the modern world, you're left with characters who are truly vulnerable and desperate, whose psyches are ready to be explored. I also think it's powerful to take that most bleak of situations and still manage to find hope. There's just something about that approach that resonates with me, and maybe with anyone else who has, at some point in their life, felt hopeless.

KG: In *Ragnarok*, Jeremy had encouraged me to "go nuts" on my parts of the story, and I went down the path of the epic destruction to be found in things like *Dragonball Z*. I think we might have even gone too far, from a continuity editor's perspective, as it's a frequent occurrence now when Sean Ellis is working on a new Chess Team adventure—like *Empire*, which should be out now—that he has to ask me if a given city was decimated by the events in *Ragnarok*. For me personally, with that story, I wanted to bring in a lot of international locales that I had travelled to (like Namsan Tower in Seoul) or bring in little details I knew about (like the McDonald's across from Karachi

International Airport). Other than those aspects, I really think that bringing the danger up to apocalyptic levels might cause a reader to lose all hope that the characters *can* find a way to safety and success. So when they do, and it's done in a (mostly) believable way against the context of the story, I think most readers are very pleased with the outcome. As a writer, I also think it's a lot of fun to utilize landscapes and problems that wouldn't be present in a typical reality-based scenario. Right now, a character has a wealth of technology available to them. But what happens when you take that away? And then throw in monsters that can move almost faster than you can see? What do you do against a giant lightning-spitting sphere of energy that eats whole cities?

WS: Any other ideas about why readers enjoy immersing themselves in tales of wholesale destruction?

JR: I suppose there are two types of people enjoying mass destruction: those who take pleasure in watching the world burn, and those who identify with the dire situation and are encouraged when characters manage to overcome the odds. I think most people fall into the second category, and those are the people I'm writing for. I occasionally get a negative review stating that the whole book should have been unending carnage, so the first category definitely exists. But I think most people want to know that the worst life has to offer (the horrible deaths of those we love) can be surmounted.

WS: What was the creative impetus for Jack Sigler and crew? What did you base the premise and/or characters on?

JR: The creation of Jack Sigler is an interesting combination of inspiration and publisher direction. Thomas Dunne, an imprint of St. Martin's Press, had read my novel *Antarktos Rising* and loved it. But *Antarktos* features the giant, half-human, half-demon Nephilim from the Bible, so Thomas Dunne basically made this offer: "Can you give us something like *Antarktos Rising*, but without the Biblical stuff?" I had written a screenplay titled *Hydra*, and the subject matter fit what they were looking for, so that story's main character, George Pierce, became a secondary character, and I created the Chess Team to fill the military role the publisher was looking for.

WS: How did you come to write together? Could you describe your collaborative process? Particularly the challenges of merging two distinct voices/approaches?

KG: We met through e-mails and I became his editor. The co-writing started with the 'Chesspocalypse' novellas, when Jeremy invited me to co-write a novella for the Deep Blue character. Our collaborative process often starts with me hanging out at his home in New Hampshire for a day,

and we bat story ideas around. By the end, the story is nearly 50% from each of us. Then I get back to my home in Vermont and write up the ideas as a loose outline, only to see that we usually only have 2/3rds of a story. Through e-mails we flesh a few more things out. Next, I write a first draft of the story. These are usually missing a few chapters' worth of the final product, that Jeremy either adds or asks me to add. He'll go over the whole story then, sometimes re-writing an entire chapter's worth of writing when it's filled with passive voice or clunky wording. Happens to all of us, even those of us who are editors and can spot that in other people's writing. He makes sure the story aligns with his internal vision of the characters and streamlines some scenes. Then the story comes back to me after his pass, and I give it an edit.

As far as merging voices and approach, I've been editing Jeremy's work for several years now. Between that

and some explicit instruction from him, I've learned a lot of things about writing. But I've also played a part in shaping his voice through edits. So there's probably not as much distinction between voices as there might be with another co-author. Where we probably differ more is with approach, with him needing to reign me in when I want scale on set pieces to get too big. On the other side of that, sometimes I think the direction Jeremy wants to go in might be too far out, and I pull him in a little. Recently we collaborated on a post-apocalyptic novel not yet released, called *Viking Tomorrow*. With that story I think we reached a more evolved state in our collaborations, with both of us throwing out ideas of our own to better serve the story.

WS: Where is the Jack Sigler/Chess Team series headed?

KG: Well, *Empire* (Book 8) should have just come out at the time this goes to print. In it, Jeremy and Sean Ellis have crafted a tale that delves into the Dyatlov Pass incident and ties into another well-known character from history, while following Jack Sigler's obsessive quest for answers about his long-lost sister, Julie. All of that is set against the backdrop of an impending war with a major superpower, and the team's current status as outlaws. Plus, there's the mystery of where Tom Duncan has been taken and held. Sean and Jeremy already have ideas for Book 9, and the resolution to several dangling story threads. Then J. Kent Holloway and Jeremy have cooked up another tale of King's time in the past for the Jack Sigler Continuum series, called *Centurion*. That will be coming later in the year. Finally, last year, supporting cast member George Pierce led a team of his own, with some very familiar faces from the Jack Sigler Thrillers in *Herculean*. Now running the Herculean Society under the guise of the "Cerberus Group," George and his compatriots are set for another adventure later this year, in *Helios*, again by Jeremy and

the character, and then pull back to see how the two things come together. The character developing personal stakes raises the tension for the bigger picture. One without the other lacks the same kind of punch.

KG: I find that the personal dreads come up more when I'm inside the head of a given character. If I don't have any action at that moment, more often the character is facing something unknown, and that's the perfect time to slip into their fears, or make them deal with something personally gruesome—like Rook in the pit, during *Ragnarok*. Tapping into these things for me is more a question of "What can I do now to make things terrible for this character?" Sometimes that's as simple as having them stranded in the dark with something slithering nearby. Other times

Sean. Maybe at some time in the future, I'll dive back into the fray as well. I've long had an idea for a story with Anna Beck, who sometimes works with the team as callsign: Pawn, and I have an idea for a WWII-era Continuum story.

WS: Your work probes into both intimate and cosmic fears. How do you tap into these terrors, and when do you know when to fluctuate between universal terrors and the very personal dreads of single characters?

JR: As a person with an out of control imagination, I'm always picturing worst case scenarios, when I'm writing and when I'm doing anything else. As a result, I have an easy time coming up with horrible scenarios for my characters. The question of when to switch between universal terrors and the personal variety has solely to do with whether the story calls for exciting action, or character development. And I find it works best to launch into things in a big way, zoom into the personal level, building

the sky needs to be falling. I have no idea where these things come from. I'm not especially afraid of cosmic starbirds descending from the skies or vertigo, but I can imagine these fears for the characters.

WS: So what are you afraid of?

JR: Everything. I wish that were an exaggeration, but like I said, with an unhinged imagination, I see danger everywhere. As a writer, it's a blessing. As someone who would like to sleep occasionally, it's a curse. In terms of personal phobias, I'd say... sharks, flying and spiders. They're not enough to keep me out of the ocean, or a plane (if there is a really good reason), but I wage wars on spiders that dare to take up residence in my office. And, like most people, my biggest fear is death. I wrote a whole book about it (*Torment*) posing the simple question: "Are you ready to die?" People who answer in the affirmative tend to like the book, those who are unsure tend to get really angry about it. I flip-flop on the subject.

KG: Nothing. Hah. No really, very few things. I feel put out by the difficulties of things, but I'll jump off a cliff, or eat something nasty. I don't have phobias, per se. I used to be claustrophobic, but not anymore. I think I tend to steadily plow into my fears and expect them to give way. Like Jeremy, I see danger in things everywhere, but that just makes me plan for ways to defeat that danger. If there are sharks, I'm thinking of what I can clobber them with in the nose. If I'm in a plane, I'm imagining it *can't* crash—or if it can, that I'm indestructible and will somehow survive the crash. I'm more concerned about drowning in a sinking aircraft that's crashed into the sea than dying from impact. Probably because it's something I can fight. I'm instead coming up with plans for how to get out of the liquid-filling tube, and how many people I can save along the way. Spiders I catch under glass and escort from the house. I'm not really afraid of anything anymore. I used to fear snakes, but I was around a lot of them overseas and in the American Southwest. I have anxieties, for sure, but like typical fear-inducing things, I just see them as challenges to be overcome. Everything can be defeated. (I'll probably be that guy who dies because he tried to fight a bear instead of running from it.)

WS: Do you find catharsis for some of these anxieties in writing?

JR: Absolutely. I actually sleep a lot better when I'm writing, exorcising my personal demons all day goes a long way to freeing my mind to focus on happy things later on. But that never lasts long.

KG: I find catharsis for my anger in writing. Things irritate me and I work that out in my writing. And similar to what Jeremy said, when I'm writing, I'm thinking about the story instead of personal demons, so that's welcome.

WS: What emotional, psychological, or aesthetic benefits do you feel that dark and fantastic fiction offers readers?

KG: Stephen King said we make up horrors to help us cope with real ones, or something to that effect. I agree. I think readers like to gravitate toward the dark and fantasy sides of fiction for pure escapism, catharsis, or even wish fulfilment. There's something comforting about watching characters battle the supernatural and come out on top. It allows us to remind ourselves that we can face anything life really throws at us. That covers emotional and psychological, but aesthetic is an interesting question. Sometimes we crave that dark aesthetic, don't we? It was the primary reason I wrote *The Crypt of Dracula*. I missed the spooky old castles, dark craggy cliffs, and claustrophobic villages of the old Hammer style horror films, and I wanted to use those kinds of settings in a horror-adventure story. There's something about those settings and the dread they infuse us with, if we grew up with those stories. We are attracted to them while at the same time repelled. Like a particularly gory car crash, we know we don't want to see, but we need to look to satisfy that morbid curiosity. I think what makes dark and fantastic fiction so appealing is that it satisfies that need, while providing us the safety of retreat from it when we need to escape. We can watch the zombies on *The Walking Dead*, but when the show is over, if we're really creeped out, all we need to do is leave the light on when we go to bed. The next day, it's life as usual.

WS: How challenging is it to make the impossible believable… to evoke realism from the supernatural in an age increasingly isolated from faith and completely immersed in technology?

JR: In most instances it depends on the personal beliefs of the readers. Those inclined to believe in the strange, supernatural or spiritual can more quickly suspend their disbelief. So the trick is to include enough science to make wacky story elements plausible to those unwilling to consider realms beyond their understanding. Sometimes that just means finding a scientific theory that fits, or basing the story on science already in progress and taking it to the next level. Sometimes that means twisting real science into something that sounds real. A knack for writing convincing B.S. got me through college. It works in novels, too.

WS: Do you feel you belong to a particular genre? Why or why not? If so, is this limiting or helpful when writing?

JR: This is one of the biggest challenges of my writing career. Most authors are very easy to pin down genre-wise. But I not only write sci-fi, thrillers, fantasy, horror, and action-adventure, I often mash the genres together and sometimes come up with my own sub-genre: like the Kaiju Thriller. People who might really enjoy the post-apocalyptic robots of *Xom-B* might not enjoy the pure action-adventure of *Herculean*. So reaching these different audiences is a challenge. Some have asked why I don't just pick a genre and stick with it. But that feels too creatively stifling. I'm not writing purely for the money. Never have. If I had, I wouldn't have kept writing for the 13 years I wasn't being paid at all. If I narrowed my vision to a single genre, I'd get bored, my books would get boring, and I'd end up hating my job instead of loving it. So it's helpful in terms of writing. But for marketing, it's a challenge.

KG: I absolutely *started* in a genre. I was going to write action-adventure exclusively. Hence my first novel, which is still waiting for a sequel. But along the way I got pulled into the Chess Team universe, a horror author pseudonym, and several sci-fi/bio-horror short stories. People keep asking me for fiction with monsters and science fiction, and I keep doing it because it's fun and it pays well. Then along the way I had ideas for epic fantasy and mystery, "New Pulp" and full-on horror novels. So now I'm absolutely multi-genre. I read a lot of genres, so I think it's probably natural that I want to write stories across those boundaries. I don't know that it's limiting or helpful, per se, when writing. But the diffusion across those boundaries isn't helping me create a brand, with regard to marketing. That's for sure. But I keep on doing the next thing that sounds fun, and hoping that will work out. No regrets yet.

WS: Is there anything in particular you would like to share

BOOK 1 OF THE BERSERKER SAGA

VIKING TOMORROW

JEREMIAH KNIGHT

BESTSELLING AUTHOR OF *HUNGER*

with your readers before we leave?

JR: A ton of works are in the pipe. There are a slew of novels coming out in 2016. *Empire* (the 9th Jack Sigler Thriller) should be out when this magazine goes to press. Also this year will be *Feast* (the sequel to *Hunger*), *Unity* (a new Kaiju Thriller series) and *Project Legion* (the final installment of the Nemesis Saga). There are also the *Project Nemesis* and *Island 731* comic books, and other cool news I hope to be able to share soon. To stay on top of all the things in development, you can visit www.bewareof-monsters.com, sign up for the newsletter, visit the Facebook fan page, and listen to the Beware of Monsters podcast.

KG: Ragnarok Publications is running a Kickstarter right now for their anthology *MECH: Age of Steel* (https://www.kick-starter.com/projects/jmmartin/mech-age-of-steel-anthology).

Both Jeremy and I have exclusive short stories in that book, and we're joined by a host of other great writers and artists. I'm co-author with Jeremy on the *Island 731* comic book, the first issue of which should be out from American Gothic Press, the comics imprint of *Famous Monsters of Filmland* magazine, in August. Later this year, Prime Books will release the US edition of their reprint anthology, *The Mammoth Book of Kaiju*, which also features one of my short stories (for those who can't wait, the UK edition is available now). The above mentioned *Viking Tomorrow* novel might see the light of day in late 2016 also. Scott Vaughn and I will be wrapping up our New Pulp/Sci-Fi webcomic, *Warbirds of Mars*, this year. And finally, this issue of *Dark Discoveries* features a brand new short story of mine called "One Hundred Chances for Glory." Thanks for having us both!

◇◇◇◆◇◇◇

A SPECTRA FILES NOVEL

BLACK JANUARY

DOUGLAS WYNNE

WELCOME TO THE WADE HOUSE WHERE THE DOORS OPEN YOU

Two years after the Starry Wisdom Church unleashed their dark gods in Boston, Becca Philips is trying to put the events of the Red Equinox behind her when Agent Brooks tracks her down in Brazil. Becca has been summoned back to Massachusetts by SPECTRA, the covert agency entrusted with keeping cosmic horrors at bay. Her special perception and skills are requested at the Wade House—a transfiguring mansion of portals to malevolent dimensions.

Becca would like to refuse, but Brooks believes her estranged father may be lost between worlds at the abandoned estate. As Becca struggles with grief and forgiveness, she joins a team of explorers uniquely suited to decode the secrets of the strange house in the black snow. But what secrets do her companions harbor? And who among them will take theirs to the grave?

Own both of these titles from Douglas Wynne

"Douglas Wynne has done what countless authors have tried—and most have failed—to do; he's brought Lovecraft into the modern world. And he's done it in such a plausible and unsettling way, you'll wonder what lurks just beyond the understanding of man and you'll fear the coming of darkness. A love letter to Lovecraft, no fan of the Mythos should let this one pass them by."

— Brett J. Talley, author of *That Which Should Not Be* and *The Biters*

RED EQUINOX

DOUGLAS WYNNE

ONE HUNDRED CHANCES FOR GLORY

KANE GILMOUR

Thick mist rose from the damp black mud, turning the infantry trench into the mouth of a sinister passage into the Earth's dark heart. Visibility was nil beyond a few meters, and Sergeant Matt 'Professor' Brady scowled at the thought of entering the moist tunnel. Still, he was about to take a step forward, the tip of his M-4 raised. He had to be an example for his men. However before his booted foot moved, Corporal David 'Butch' Leighfield started howling from behind.

"Oh, mother of fucks! Get it off! Get it off of me!" Butch screamed and thrashed, throwing his body down into the mud and rolling, as the others all jumped back in shock. Clad in a nearly black pattern of combat camouflage uniform, his torso was almost invisible in the gloom as it rolled and bucked in the squelching dark mud. Until he finally ripped the jacket and underlying t-shirt up and away, to reveal his savaged flesh.

"Holy crapsticks!" PFC Christopher 'Quick-Clot' Ouellette, the team's medic, leapt forward to help the wounded corporal. All around Butch's torso were tracks of tiny puncture wounds, in twisting, waving patterns. But the medic didn't reach Butch before the man bucked over onto his back, exposing the front of his torso and the creature responsible for the chaotic damage.

A shiny black centipede skittered across Butch's tattooed chest. Its tubular body's diameter was as wide as a man's forearm, and the thing was easily two feet long. The creature's sides were festooned with frantic limbs that propelled it off Butch and into the mud, where it tried to burrow into the ground.

Private Jennifer 'Specks' Ravenswood lunged after it, her black-coated machete in hand. In one swipe she sliced through the beast. The blade bit into the soft mud under the centipede with hardly a whisper, as the two halves of the creature wriggled before coming to a halt. Greenish-yellow fluid leaked from the wounds, and the wicked pincers at the creature's head oozed a bluish river into the moist ground. Specks reached down with the tip of her blade to poke the seemingly dead beast, and the pincers twitched. She stabbed the blade down into the head and the appendages froze.

"Damn it, he's going into shock," Quick-Clot said, cutting the remains of the fabric away from Butch's neck. The wounds were all a raised vivid pink, and Butch's eyes rolled upward into his head.

"What do you need?" Professor asked, leaning down on one knee next to the medic.

"What the hell?" the medic said, recoiling.

Butch's mouth was opened in a perfect O as milky green foam bubbled up out of his throat.

"What is that?" The sergeant was disoriented. The mission was about to go off the rails before it had really begun, and he couldn't make sense of it.

"It's venom," a new voice called from the edge of the group. Private Andrew 'Punster' Scully was on the fringe, watching their rear. He was also the team's tactical communications officer. While they were out of contact with command due to massive storms over this part of southern Burma, he had researched the landing zone extensively before they had arrived. That included all the information about wildlife he could find. "Those pincers at the head are called forcipules, and they're filled with venom."

"Deadly venom," Quick-Clot said, pulling his hand from Butch's wrist and the man's absent pulse. "He's gone."

"Son of a bitch." The sixth and final member of the team, José 'Slicer' Elizondo, was the team's sniper, and he was currently ahead of the group in the mist somewhere, lying face down in the mud. He spoke to them through their communications gear, on a direct line-of-sight channel, so he couldn't have been too far away. "Are we aborting?"

Professor thought for just a moment before replying, his answer beyond reproach. "Negative. But watch the fuck out for poisonous centipedes."

"Oh, sure," Slicer replied. "Now you tell me. I'm up to my neck in mud here, and I can't see a thing because of this mist. An army of centipedes could be coming my way and I wouldn't know it."

"Pull back, Slicer," the sergeant said. "You're no good if you can't see, and who knows how many more of these things are out there. Listen up. We were sent here to do a job. We knew there would be dangers. We'll mourn Butch when the mission is over. Right now, we keep heads on swivels and get on with it."

Within minutes the team had pulled Butch's body into the mouth of the trench. There he would be obscured by the mist and hidden from sight by anyone on the beach, where they had made their landing. Slicer rejoined them, coated from head to toe in the ever-present mud. After quickly tucking their combat jackets into their trousers and cinching their belts tight to ward off any further incidents with creepy crawlies, Professor sent Specks down the trench, roughly ten feet ahead of the rest.

An African-American woman with the body of an East German wrestler, Specks was happy to take the lead. The barrel of her weapon raised, she slipped into the mist without a word. The mission was simple: somewhere ahead in the dense fog was a small command center. The Junta had nearly been vanquished by the excessive flooding the previous year. Most of Myanmar had been turned into sucking mud flats from the mountains to the sea. But a few remnants of the old guard had held fast. Here in the Ayeyarwady Region in the south, the sky was perpetually shrouded in mist, as the weather patterns on the fringes and over the mountains clashed and collided, like they did everywhere these days. Satellite intelligence had been minimal, but occasional murky shots of the infantry trenches in the mud had been gathered, though no one had been able to pinpoint the location of the command bunker. Still, it was a simple operation: send in a small team, find the building, and blow it up, ending the last outpost of the former regime. While the United States and the rest of the world had grudgingly tolerated the humanitarian abuses by military dictatorships in Myanmar, once Mother Nature had deemed the country null and void, sweeping away recent democratic reforms and most of the population into the Bay of Bengal or into the depths of the earth under successive waves of mud, the rest of the world had determined it was time to sweep out the totalitarians, too, before sending in the development aid money.

Professor tried to keep his head out of politics and focus on the task at hand. Keep his people alive. Find the objective. Reduce it to rubble. Get out with his remaining four soldiers alive. Simple goals. Laser-like focus. But it all slipped his mind when he heard Punster whisper:

"I've got movement. A whole damn lot of movement."

2

The team had travelled no more than a half a mile into the twisting, turning trenches through the mud, when Punster's warning brought them to a halt. Professor's head snapped back and forth as he tried to peer into the dense mist at either end of the trench. As it was when they had entered after Butch's death, the visibility was only a few meters in each direction.

"Which end?" Professor asked.

"Which end what?" Punster replied.

"Which end of the trench are they coming from, dammit." The trench was a meter wide and two tall in places, but of uneven height. The mist loped across the top, as if it were the ceiling of a tunnel. Along the base of the walls, there were irregular lumps and pockets of mud about the diameter of a basketball, but Specks had kicked one, and it had collapsed. They were nothing but more dirt and mud.

Punster was monitoring for enemy movement on a device he wore strapped to one forearm. Professor didn't understand all the science behind it, but he knew it tracked sonic vibrations and air pressure, resulting in a kind of localized radar for the team, as they moved blindly through hostile environments. So even without Slicer on overwatch, Punster could alert the team of enemy advances.

"They're not *in* the trench," Punster said. "They're coming over the mud flats. Twenty meters out."

The others all raised their carbines in the direction the tech expert pointed, holding their breath and listening hard for sounds. But other than the damp tick of water and mud, dripping over the top edge of the trench and down to their boots, Professor could hear nothing but the beat of his own heart in his ears.

It sounded irregular and loud.

"How many?"

"Hard to tell. They're massed together." Punster tapped quickly at the device on his arm, and then frowned.

"What is it, *esé*?" Slicer hissed, looking over his shoulder.

Punster tapped again at the touchscreen, then looked up to Professor's expectant face opposite him. "Sarge, the signal stopped. Or they all disappeared."

Professor frowned and glanced at the lip of the trench. "They know we're here."

"No," Punster whispered. "If they stopped moving, this would still pick them up. It's like they stopped moving *and breathing*. No vibrations at all. But it's still picking us up, so I know it's working."

"What does that mean?" Professor asked.

Punster shrugged. "No idea. It's like they're just dead. Just like that. Or gone."

"Fuckin' tech, man," Specks said to herself.

"Quick and Slicer, over the top. Slow and steady. Give me real eyes on the situation."

Punster dropped his forearm in frustration, clearly upset that his technology had failed the team in their moment of need. The young medic rushed over against the wall and made a step with his linked hands. The Hispanic sniper popped his muddy boot into the man's hands and vaulted up over the lip of the trench. A second later, he dropped an arm down, and Quick-Clot grabbed the phantom limb extending from the white haze. He was hoisted up as rapidly as the sniper had scaled the slick surface.

Punster, Specks, and Professor closed ranks, the woman's weapon aimed upward, while the two men faced opposite directions, covering both ends of the trench.

"Thought it was supposed to rain all the damn time here now," Specks muttered.

Professor knew the rain would be a hassle, and possibly even a danger to them with the unstable mud, but it would clear away the hazy white mist, and they would be able to see.

At least a little.

Even though the enemy contact was only twenty meters out, Professor knew it would take some time for the two men to belly-crawl at sniper-speed toward the site. Slicer was slow and cautious at all times, and it was one of the reasons Professor had chosen him for the mission. They had worked together before, and the sergeant liked to have people he knew he could count on. The medic was the team's only new member this time, and so far the kid from New Hampshire was proving himself just fine.

Professor breathed in through his nose and let the damp air out his mouth. The loamy smell was even more acrid than it had been at the beach when they had entered the trench, but his nose could detect nothing else.

No smells. Can't see anything. Only sound is dripping water. Tech is useless. No wonder these bastards dug in here. It's a perfect camouflage.

"Bossman, we got a problem." Slicer's voice was soft, but came in clearly through their headsets. "Ain't no one here."

"What?"

"Only little swish marks in the mud. No footprints. No body marks. Me and homes are covered in sticky here, and we're leaving huge tracks. Nobody but us been through this mud, I'm tellin' you."

Professor turned to the tech expert. "Punster, that thing was reading us, you say?"

"Perfectly. It still is." He held up his arm, and the device showed three red blobs, indicating the three of them, and twenty meters across the mud there were two more red blobs, which would be Slicer and Quick-Clot.

"How many red dots were there before?" Professor asked, turning his attention back to his end of the trench. His weapon was still up, and he tried to peer into the impenetrable mist.

"Too many to count. They were all over each other." Punster lowered his arm and resumed his own watch for the far end of the trench.

Silence filled the air as the tension grew, each team member tense and ready for something—anything—to happen.

"Describe the swishes." Specks's voice was louder than the others, and startled and confused Professor.

"The what—?" he started to ask.

Specks was all business though, and she spoke over him. "Punster, what's the tolerance on that thing? Could it have registered something smaller than human?"

Before the tech expert could respond, Slicer's voice came over their headsets. "How big was that centipede, man?"

The medic replied quickly but with a quiver in his voice. "Exactly that size."

"Oh shit," Slicer said. "We got maybe a dozen or more of these tracks in the mud. I'm thinkin' there's a lot of bugs out here, Sarge."

Before Professor could reply, the ground began to thrum and quiver, as if the mud flats were experiencing an earthquake. He looked up and the side wall of the trench fell over on them.

3

Darkness filled Professor's sight, and an intense pressure pounded on his eardrums, against the long droning strain of the noise he had heard… seconds before… seconds before…

Before what? he thought, struggling to bring his mind into focus.

The mud, he remembered. *The mud wall collapsed on us.*

Lunatic panic set in as he realized he had been buried under an avalanche of sloppy earth. Adrenaline flooded his system, and he began to flail and thrash, not knowing which way was up or how long it would take to get to a fresh breath of air. He could feel the slimy mud plugged up into his nostrils, as his lungs screamed for oxygen. His ears were filled with deep brown sludge, and even through his panic he realized he was only 'hearing' the droning sound because of its vibration against his skin.

He struggled back and forth, his limbs held fast by the sheer weight of the damp muck. It was like squirming to be set free from his older brother Bill's chokehold when they were kids. Professor worked his shoulders and elbows and then, with a slow tug, his right forearm slipped free from the resistance and met only air.

He began clawing back toward himself, pulling mud from where he thought his face might be in the absolute darkness. Though he could see nothing, he felt a deep blackness nibbling and scrabbling its way inward from the edges of his shadow vision.

I'm blacking out. I can't. Not yet—

Then soft yielding flesh touched his manic arm, and he recoiled, first thinking he'd grabbed hold of one of the centipedes, but his arm was quickly grasped again and squeezed, and then he could feel at least two or three hands digging the mud away from the top of his head. In a minute his face was free, and he sucked in a huge breath, the thick mud coating his tongue as he did.

Specks and Punster were still pawing at him, tearing away great wet globs of clay-like earth and wiping at his face.

"Enough," he sputtered. "I've got it."

He heard a mumbled reply and then realized, as he wiped a slice of wet slop from his eyelid and flicked it away, that he wasn't hearing them clearly because of the mud in his ears. The droning noise was gone now. All he

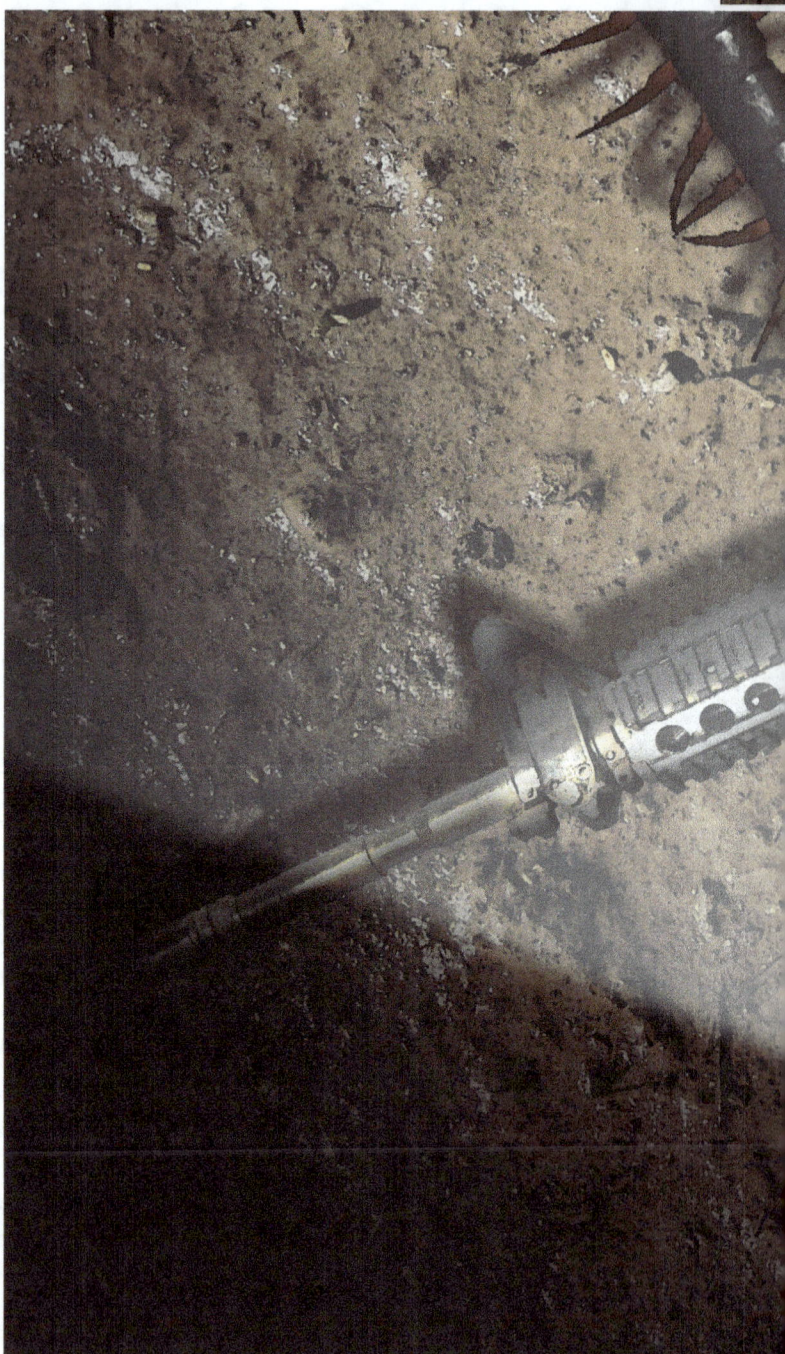

could hear was his own heartbeat in his head, echoing and hyper.

He grabbed for his canteen at his belt, unscrewed the lid, and doused his right ear with a huge splash, digging in with his fingernail until sound came back to him like a popped eardrum after a long airplane flight.

Specks looked as if she'd barely been covered by the

mudslide. Punster was as bad off as he was, his face and goatee coated in thick black muck. The only part of him not covered in brown was a coiled loop of coaxial cable tied down on his shoulder. As the resident tech guy on the team, Punster came prepared for any eventuality, and his personal kit was different from everyone else's, including odd electrical plugs and converters, cables, collapsible and rollable keyboards and monitor screens, and even a

strange sprayable can of goop that could solar charge portable electronics.

Professor was about to ask after the others when the normally passive look on Specks's face shifted to a frown. Before he could turn, she lunged toward him, the long black machete slipping from its sheath on her back. He dodged left and she continued past him, swiping the blade laterally and severing yet another of the deadly centipedes. This one was smaller than the first, but still easily a foot and a half in length. She had spotted it coming across the mud slope that now led to where there should have been a trench wall. It was coming from the direction in which he had sent Slicer and the medic.

He keyed his comm, and spoke softly. "Slicer? Quick-Clot? Sitrep?"

There was no answer, but as he waited in silence, he could see movement across the field of mud. But it was the wrong kind of movement. Low to the ground and wriggling. Zipping left and right. Dark, but reflecting the faint misty light off their shiny surfaces.

Centipedes.

Probably fifty or more.

We must have uncovered a nest, he thought.

As the tidal wave of shimmering black squiggles surged forward down the slope, Professor could hear distant screaming. Then he heard a warning shout from Punster. He turned his head, still covered from the waist down in mud, and looked back down the partially collapsed trench.

Hundreds more. Maybe thousands. They were boiling over each other in a torrent, like water forced through a sluice.

He tried to move and found he couldn't.

The weight of the mud on his legs had him trapped.

Right in the path of doom.

4

Professor struggled to free his legs as the waves of creatures came at him from both sides. He couldn't reach his knife, and he wasn't sure he could wield it the way Specks was using her machete anyway. By the time he sliced through one of the wriggling creatures, a hundred more would be on him. Instead he scooped and tore at the mud binding his legs, while Specks advanced down the trench with her M-4 raised. She started firing small bursts, splattering creatures the length of children, their greenish guts flecking the mud walls of the trench.

Punster came to Professor's aid, digging with both hands and flinging the mud between his wide stance and behind him like a dog. Globs of heavy earth buried the leading edge of the horde approaching down the slope behind him. Professor saw the strategy and flung his own scooped mud up the slope, creating a tiny retaining wall. He didn't know how much good it would do, but it was all he had.

As he pulled a leg free, his other boot still stubbornly locked in place in the deep mud, two things happened. He heard Specks shout and switch to full auto, depressing her trigger and blasting a spray of bullets down the length of the trench. He also heard the thunderous roaring drone noise again, and this time he could feel the ground under his booted foot shiver with the vibration. Punster still scraped at his trapped leg, as Professor pulled his sidearm and began blasting individual centipedes that made it over the improvised wall of muck.

The droning noise shifted and grew louder, pulsing against his brain. He still fired the pistol one handed, hardly aiming now at the tumult of creatures cresting the wall. He grabbed his skull with the other hand, begging the vibration to cease.

Specks ran out of ammunition, and Professor heard her over the freight train drone, shouting profanities, followed by, "Fuck this shit. Frag out!"

Wait, what? Professor had time only to turn his head and realize he was still stuck in place and unable to dive for cover from the grenade Specks had thrown. She leapt in front of his body to shield him from the blast. *Aww, hell no…*

He could just see the lobbed projectile clear some of the incursion wave of twisting black bodies and embed itself in the soft, sucking side wall of the trench. Then Specks was obscuring his view. The drone increased in pitch and tone, growing louder, like an airplane coming in for a landing.

The grenade detonated, smothering the drone with its own devastating thunder. Specks slammed backward, her web-belt and ammo pouches smashing into his face, breaking his nose, and filling his eyes with bleary tears.

As he rubbed the moisture from his face, Specks took a step forward, and he felt his left leg finally come free from the squelching mud. Specks took another two steps down the trench, tentative, as if she were afraid to step on any of the centipedes. As she moved, Professor could see that her ploy—assuming she'd thought it through—had worked. The explosive had collapsed the opposite wall, burying the tidal wave of squirming beasts in a second landslide of sloppy brown and black soil.

A glance behind him and Professor could see that Punster was still flinging gobs of the stuff up the first collapsed slope. Parts of the centipedes were exposed, still wriggling madly. Then as Professor watched, the remaining creatures burrowed down into the goopy ground, disappearing from sight. The idea that they could tunnel had not really occurred to him yet. As the notion sank in, and he realized the extent of the mud flats in the delta, he understood that their chances of getting out alive were practically zero, especially if the creatures continued to attack. But instead they had turned and run. He wondered if it had to do with the monotonous roar of whatever was causing the droning noise.

It's almost like an army marching across the field, he thought, but he knew the Burmese force they were to attack couldn't have numbered more than two dozen. Then his own observation sank in, and the thought of what might be making the onrushing noise crashed through his head.

Oh no, it can't be.

He whipped around to speak to Specks just in time to see her stagger and turn back toward him. The sight stole his voice from his throat, leaving just a dry gurgle. The woman was lurching like a drunk, and her arms hung listless at her sides. Her flak jacket was speckled with glittering metal fragments, and blood gushed down from where her chin should have been. Her face was completely gone, a mask of blood and bone, but beyond her savaged visage—a crater instead of a face—she appeared unharmed. She took another two steps, like a toddler making its first attempt at locomotion.

Professor felt his gorge rising, as the disoriented woman wobbled and tottered along the sloping crest of mud, until she seemingly lost her balance and began to tilt toward the trench wall that was still intact. He felt an overwhelming cascade of sadness sweep over him as he prepared to watch her plummet to the ground. She would die here. In the ooze.

But she never fell.

The penetrating buzz of the droning noise reached a crescendo, and the mud wall she was falling toward exploded outward at her. Antennae, the length of a truck, burst forth from the mire, entwining around her, as the giant centipede body attached to them plowed into her like a runaway bullet train.

Train.

It was the only word Matt 'Professor' Brady could think, as the enormous centipede barreled across the trench, taking the savaged soldier with it as it burrowed into the mud field. Hundreds of legs, each larger around than Professor, and twice as long, propelled the creature along. The sergeant stared, his mouth open, as the seemingly unending parade of segments continued across his vision.

5

When the massive centipede had passed by, leaving in its wake a new trench perpendicular to the last, Professor simply gaped in awe and dawning understanding. Several thoughts hit him at once, and he was paralyzed by the raw quantity of data. The trenches in the delta were not manmade at all. The basketball-sized holes along the foot of the walls were indents from that gigantic creature's legs propelling it through the muck. And if the intelligence could be trusted, and there really was a Burmese stronghold here in the muddy fields, then they had to *know* about the massive beast. Had to be controlling it somehow…

The small ones. Its babies. They sent its children after us first… They can control it with its children somehow.

Professor turned back to find Punster keeled over on his side, dead, his eyes rolled up and the thick viscous foam that had choked Butch spilling out of his throat and down his chest. The sergeant glanced down and saw one sluggish centipede moving toward him. It looked like its back half had been stamped on, the trailing legs useless and being pulled by the front half. It was a few inches from his foot, and he considered for a second letting it live, if it was the enormous one's offspring. But then he realized he'd get no such return favor from its mother. He strained his brutalized hearing and could detect the distant drone of the giant creature. As he listened, the sound seemed to get closer.

His boot came up without a thought and he rammed the heel down, mashing the attacking creature into the soft silt. His team was dead. He was going to die. His brain ran through the possibility of making it back to the beach, but he dismissed it instantly. There was just no way. The enemy had thrown nature at him, had somehow harnessed or created this aberration, this monstrosity. They had killed his entire team without a shot fired, without dirtying their hands.

The injustice of it galled him. He tried Slicer and Quick-Clot on the comm, one more time, just to be sure. The panic of his isolation threatened to extinguish his anger, until he looked back to Punster's body and saw half a dozen of the younger creatures burrowing into the soft, exposed parts of the technician's flesh.

Then an unholy rage consumed him, and he marched forward, snatching up the thick black coil of cable on the dead man's shoulder. He used it like a whip, slashing and tearing at the burrowing animals, until they were in pieces or fully inside the corpse. He tugged a grenade from Punster's chest, pulled the pin and let the spoon fly. He tossed the device at the dead man and ran down the murderous alley, toward the newly formed side trench.

He made it around the corner just as the explosive device erupted with fire and death, spewing mud and thousands of tiny limbs into the air. When the ringing in his ears abated, he heard what he had hoped to hear—the droning noise—approaching. He was furious, and now, so was Mama.

His fury brought him insight, and it also gave him clarity. The thought that had come to him when he'd seen the giant centipede was *Train*, but now that he thought more about it, he realized that the beast had really only been the height and width of a twin-sized bed. It might have been as long as an actual train, but its diameter was not *that* big. He understood that the creature probably used and reused the trenches it created, because they were two to three times as deep as the beast was tall. They would only be that way if the massive thing had travelled these paths multiple times.

It was coming back, and it was probably coming along one of the pre-made trenches. If he was wrong, and it burst from underground again, it would mash him into a paste. He would be dead instantly, just as Specks had died. But if he was right, then there was one final opportunity for him to make something out of this whole mess. One thing he could do to deliver hell to those who had it coming.

The enemy had used this thing's babies. As weapons. So maybe, just maybe, he could enact that old adage about the enemy of my enemy…

Professor raced down the trench and then skidded to a stop at a place where the walls looked somewhat low and dry. He kicked the toes of his boots into the soft ground, like an ice climber front-pointing with crampons. The heavy steel-toed combat boots were just as good. He reached up with one hand, grasping the lip of the trench, and with the other, still holding the thick black TV cable, he scrabbled and clawed and grabbed until he was on top of the muddy field. The droning noise was reaching an earsplitting level, but he couldn't see more than a dozen meters into the white misty gloom. He glanced at his watch, the liquid compass pointing north. Then he looked up and smiled.

Perfect.

The enemy lay in that direction, and the rampaging beast was tearing toward him from the south. He quickly stood up and unfurled the length of cable, then tossed it across the trench as far as it would go, the middle of it dipping down to the floor of the trench. He laid back down in the mud, wrapping one wrist around the end of his improvised garrote, and hiding from the potential sight of the mega-centipede. He didn't know what their eyesight was like, but he didn't want to take the chance the thing would divert its course from the trench and off-road right into him.

The sonic roar increased, and he could feel the mud beneath him vibrate and hum. He worried for a second that the tremors would collapse the wall he laid upon, burying him once again. Panic gripped his heart at the thought of being re-submerged in muck. But he rolled just a bit and could see the massive creature barreling toward him—right at his cable.

Then it was there, moving fast, completely unaware of him or the cable.

Professor rolled hard, taking the cord wrapped around his arm with him. He landed on top of the huge creature's neck, just as the other end of his cable flipped up and around the top of the hurtling centipede. The metal screw on the end slashed across his face, filling the left half of his vision with a red blur. His hand snaked out though, and his fingers felt the thick black plastic sheath try to pull away. He pulled hard and wrapped the cord around his other wrist, rolling, and twisting his hand until he had taken in all the slack.

The massive creature bucked its head upward, and then slammed back down into the trench. With the coaxial cable as a rein, Professor held fast. The centipede continued its mad dash through the trench, its sole upward lurch seemingly its only protest to the unwanted hitchhiker.

Professor got one of his knees up to his chest and leaned backward, loosening his cable just enough to get a boot on the animal's slick back. He allowed another coil of cable to loosen, and like a surfer catching a wave, he snapped to his feet, arms outstretched against the cable for balance.

The mist swept past his face, and he realized that only his right eye was sending any information to his brain. The entire left half of his face had simply gone numb. But that was okay. He could balance on the hurtling force of nature that was the centipede, and as it approached a Y-shaped fork in the mud, he threw his weight to the right, tugging on the cable. The massive centipede took the right-most passage—heading north, toward the enemy.

Matt 'Professor' Brady held fast to his steed. The team was gone, and his life was most likely forfeit. But the mission was still viable. He could take out the enemy force using their own devastating weapon against them. Propelled at some insane speed by the gigantic creature's multitude of legs, he relished the madness of his centipede mount. He knew very little about centipedes, but he did know that they rarely had exactly one hundred legs. Still, that was the common perception. One hundred legs. And they were working for him now.

Riding into a hostile entrenched force, he still had one hundred chances for glory.

JOE DONNELLY

BY ROBERT MORRISH

Photo courtesy of Joe Donnelly

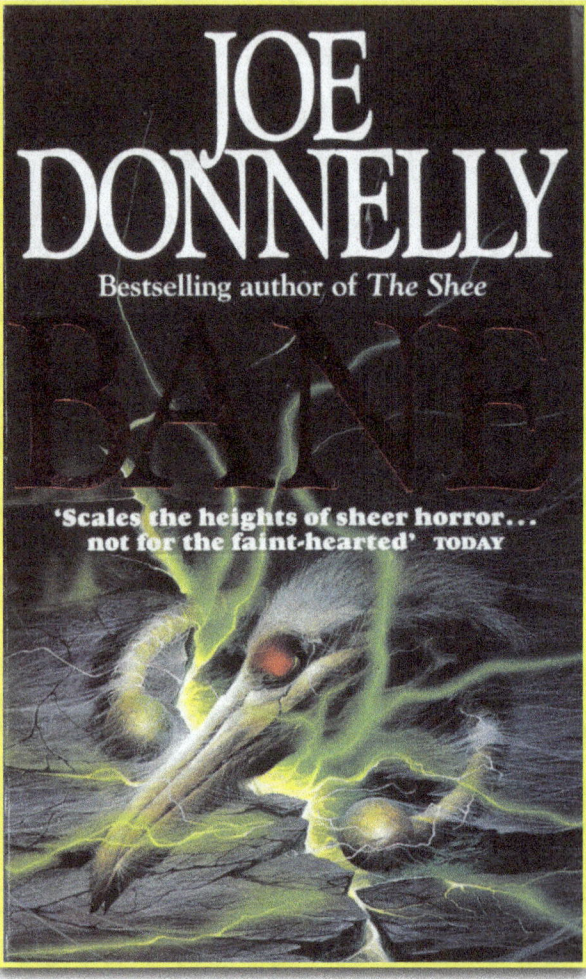

JOE DONNELLY

Bestselling author of *The Shee*

BANE

'Scales the heights of sheer horror...
not for the faint-hearted' TODAY

During the horror boom of the 1980s and '90s, many UK authors were able to make the leap across the pond, obtain U.S. publishers for their work, and achieve varying degrees of success. Authors such as Clive Barker, Ramsey Campbell, Stephen Laws, and Phil Rickman fall into this category. But there were also several UK horror writers who were quite successful in their own country but whose work was only briefly, or never, picked up for American publication—writers such as Steve Harris, Mark Chadbourn… and Joe Donnelly, who I interviewed for this installment of "What The Hell Ever Happened To…?"

Donnelly was born in Glasgow in 1950, and has lived most of his life in Dumbarton, Scotland, about 20 miles northwest of Glasgow. He holds an advanced postgraduate research degree in American Studies from the University of Glasgow, and worked as an investigative journalist for a variety of Scottish newspapers between 1968 and 1998, receiving Reporter of the Year, and Consumer Journalist awards. He began publishing fiction in 1989, and published eight horror novels in the next eight years before his horror career came to a halt, at least temporarily. In the following interview, an occasionally cranky and idiosyncratic Donnelly talks about the inspiration for his work, and what he's been up to since 1997...

DD: You began publishing with the 1989 novel *Bane*, in which a journalist returns to his childhood hometown in the Scottish hills, where he discovers that an ancient evil has awoken beneath the dark rock that looms over the

local estuary. What prompted the idea for *Bane?* Which horror authors inspired you at the time? And how did you place the book with Hutchinson?

JD: I had a nightmare one night and woke up and wrote down the details (as a journalist, I always had a notebook handy). Some time later, I read the notes and it all came back to me and it started to form the idea of a story. I started it as a hobby, but it soon became a book. I contacted an agent and she sold it within weeks.

DD: Your next novel, *Stone* (1990), is also set in rural Scotland, where a family of five moves into the grand old Cromwath House, only to find that the house's walls hide an elder evil. Described as a "chilling blend of Celtic legend and contemporary life," *Stone* received praise from the likes of *Fear* magazine ("A magnificent book hiding the type of horrific secrets I adore") and *Observer* ("Fans of Clive Barker should be sufficiently harrowed"). Could you describe the genesis of this novel?

JD: I have always been fascinated by ancient standing stones, which in Scotland go back 7000 years. I just imagined that a house made from standing stones might contain some old powers that could be awakened. I always wonder... what if?

DD: *The Shee* followed in 1992, centering on a photographer and a writer who are marooned in a cottage in the west of Ireland during a storm, while nearby archeologists uncover a mysterious site and unwittingly unlock the tomb of a 5,000-year-old goddess of destruction, the Shee, who has the power to assume any shape. Again, please tell us how this idea came about. Also, I believe this is your only horror novel to use a setting outside of Scotland—why the change in venue?

JD: I was a journalist for much of my life and I was often in Ulster covering the Troubles. I also have a great interest in Celtic mythology, and as I witnessed some atrocities in Northern Ireland, I was moved to show comparisons between myth and reality.

DD: *Kirkus*'s review of the book was generally favorable, although critical of the explicit gruesomeness ("...Donnelly soon slips into a rotting and drippingly pustuled ghoulishness, a picnic of diseased, grabbing, pullulating vulvas… Well written, yes—if you like lapping up pus and maggots for fun")—do you think that was a fair criticism?

JD: Never read this review. Sounds a bit over the top to me. But if I ever see a pullulating vulva, I will probably agree with him. Assuming there is such a thing.

DD: 1993 saw the publication of *Still Life*, in which the recently-paralyzed Caitlin Brook has moved back to her childhood village overlooking the Fasach Wood, where she and her romantic suitor encounter a local healer who styles her potions after those used thousands of years earlier by Druidic shamans to summon a stag-antlered demon. You clearly have a strong interest in combining ancient evils with contemporary settings... does that combination reflect what you liked to read at that time, or were you plotting with more commercial interests in mind?

JD: I have never plotted with commercial interests in mind. I just loved the idea. *Still Life* is one of my favorite stories, because I loved the characters, and the very

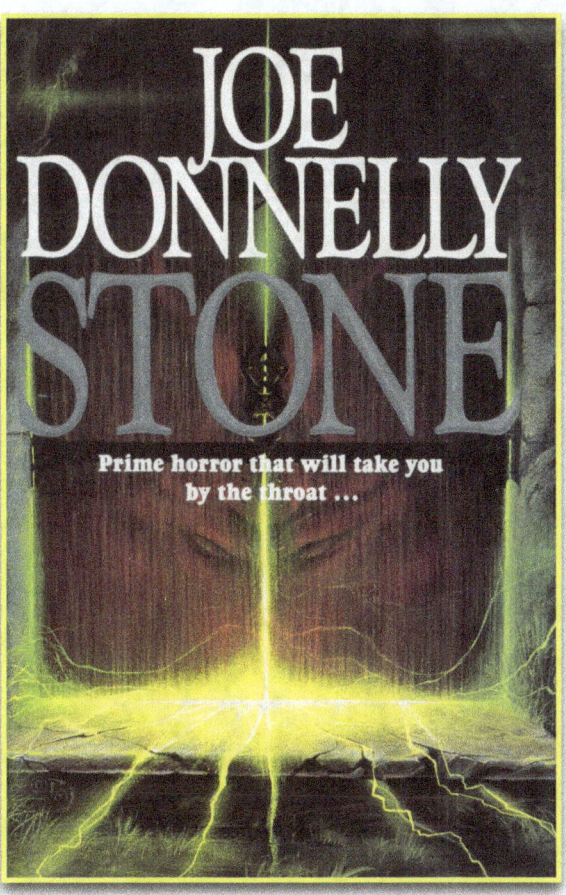

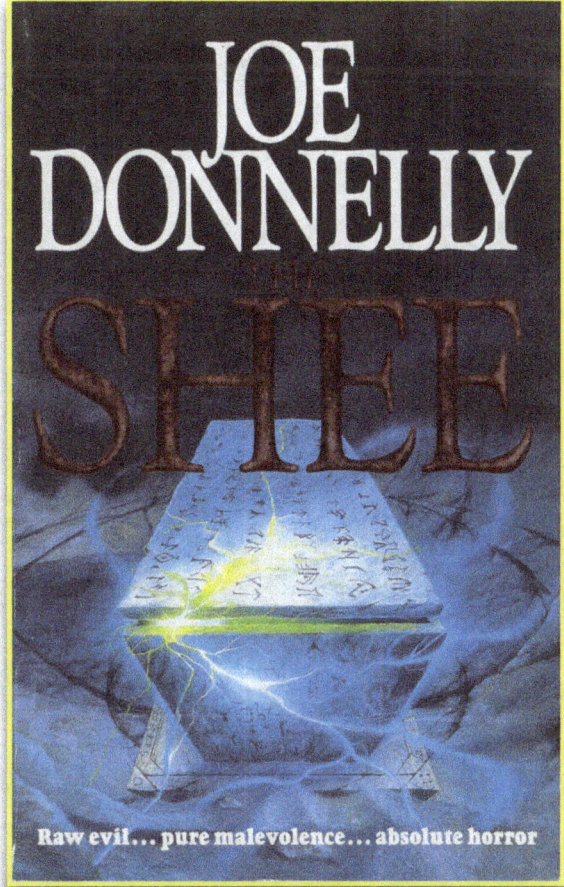

idea of a forest that comes alive. I have renamed the book *Nightshade* as an ebook… check out joedonnellybooks.com!

DD: Reviews of *Still Life* were again sometimes a mix of positive comments along with warnings about gore, as in the case of *Publishers Weekly*, who said: "Donnelly strikes at the gag reflex in this gruesome, harrowingly suspenseful offering set in Scotland… Interesting Druidic lore augments this well-written romp, but it's only for those who can stomach blood-filled horrors described in precise detail." Do you feel like *Still Life* and your other novels were notably more bloody and violent than other horror novels being published at the same time?

JD: Not at all. When the story develops, you can't imagine what will scare people... only what might scare yourself. I tend to describe in detail, because I am living the story as I write. I visualize what is happening and imagine it's *me* that's going though it. If you write paranormal horror, it's not all pancakes and lemonade. Read Stephen King's *IT*—he's a master of detail… gory, gruesome, but he's also a master of relationships and emotions.

DD: In *Shrike* (1994), the evil entity is released by a séance, dreams play a pivotal role in the proceedings, and the protagonist is a policeman seeking to catch the brutal killer who has filled the town of Levenford with an overwhelming sense of dread. You had frequently used journalists as protagonists in previous books… was the use of a policeman in this book a deliberate move away from that model? Also, dreams often play an important role in your stories—is there any particular story behind that?

JD: Levenford is my hometown of Dumbarton, through which the River Leven flows. I chose a policeman because he fit better into the story, not being a smartass journo like me! Dreams do play an important part, because I dream a lot, and I remember them. Mostly I dream about flying, or solving major problems in the world, but some are darker and wake me up needing a strong drink.

DD: *Havock Junction* (1995) centers on a mother who has rescued her daughter from a creature that needs ritual sacrifice to perpetuate its youthful existence, and now the creature and her forces are in hot pursuit. This novel seems like more of a classic chase story—was that an intentional choice, or was that just how the story "wrote itself?" It also seems like this book has the strongest female protagonist of any of your books—again, was that an intentional choice?

JD: *All* of my books have a strong female protagonist. Every single one! What they all have is a bonding of female and male protagonists. Maybe I like feisty women. But Patsy Havelin is a *mother*. And I think there is no stronger urge in the world than the maternal instinct.

DD: The monster in *Incubus* (1996) is not drawn from Celtic mythology, but *is* ancient, featuring a creature with a very long period of development, appearing as a baby and forcing various women to undergo extended periods of lactation in order to feed the creature. Once the creature begins its rapid maturation, the death count begins to rise in tandem. As in *Shrike*, the lead characters are police, but unlike most of your other work, the threat is not completely removed/resolved by the end of the book… any particular reason for that?

Also, with this book, I believe you changed publishers to Michael Joseph. How did that change come about?

JD: The publisher change came about because we had a recession and I was dumped, along with other authors. The story came about when I was a journalist, writing about a woman (with severe emotional problems) who had stolen a baby. For

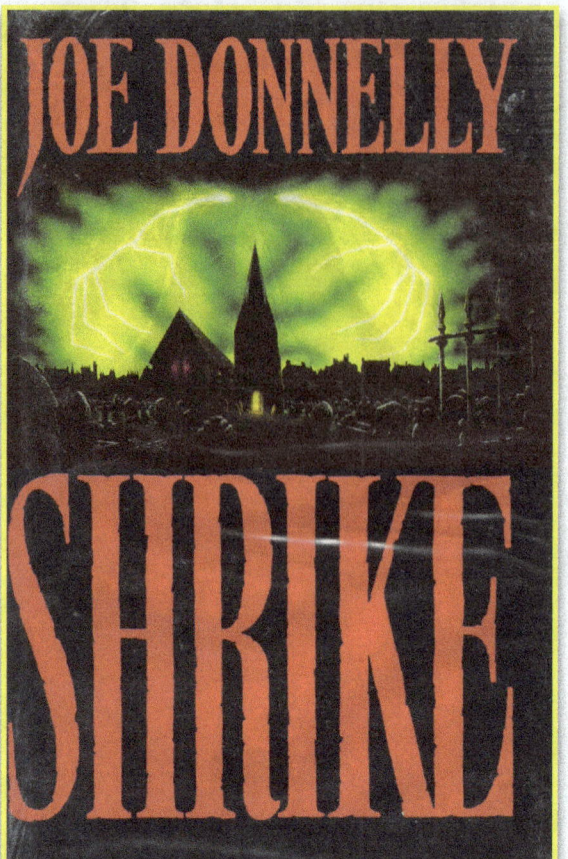

some reason, I just wondered in reverse... what kind of baby would steal a mother. Also, I have a great interest in nature, and I am familiar with all sorts of parasites... I left the ending unresolved because if such things exist, you never know.

DD: *Twitchy Eyes* (1997; reprinted as *Dark Valley*) is set in the late 1960s on the West coast of Scotland, where a stranger's arrival in town coincides with the murder of two children. Five boys soon embark on an adventure in the hills outside of town, unwittingly putting themselves in the killer's cross-hairs. Is this the only one of your horror novels to feature a non-contemporary setting? And is the only one to feature a non-supernatural threat?

JD: This book takes me back to my younger years when a strange man—described by people as having "twitchy eyes"—molested a number of people in my town, at a time when there were a number of unexplained killings. Much of the book is a true account.

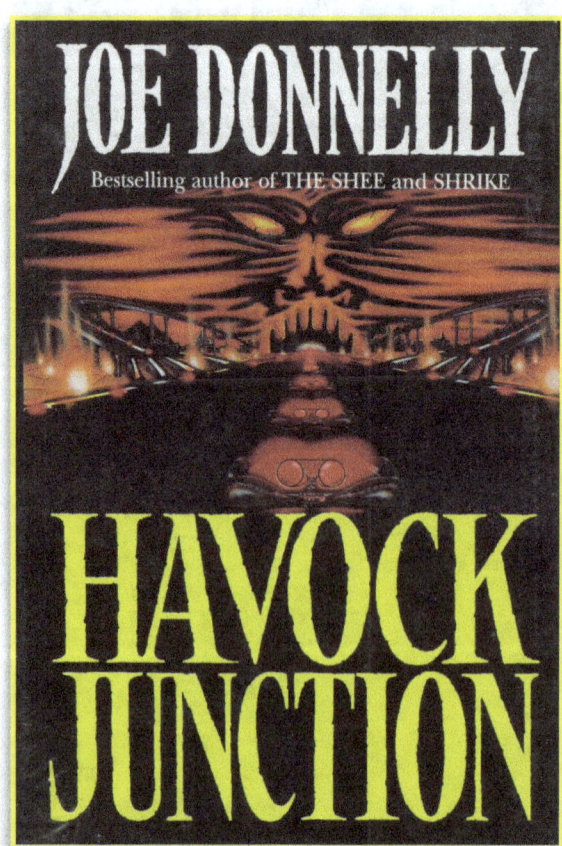

DD: Several of your horror novels employ brief, oblique references to earlier novels. Were those references sort of "insider remarks" for your more loyal readers, or were you beginning to try to stitch together a larger canvas?

JD: Only *Dark Valley* and *Shrike*, as I recall.

DD: None of your horror novels were published in the US. Did you ever come close to getting an American publisher? Do you think your career in horror might have been longer if you did get a publisher across the pond?

JD: Couldn't care less.

DD: Between 2007 and 2010, Orion published your Jack Flint series, a trilogy involving Celtic mythology that was geared for younger readers. Were these written primarily in response to market opportunities, or did you have a specific interest in YA books? Also, I've seen mention that you were working on another YA novel, based on Nordic mythology. Is that book still slated to appear at some point?

JD: I know and care little about market opportunities. The Jack Flint books had been on my mind for years and I loved writing them. I am working on another novel, provisionally titled *Thunderhammer*. I never liked the titles, Jack Flint and the _____, because Harry Potter was such a big deal, and mine are nothing like Harry Potter. So now on Kindle, they are *Mythlands*, *Spellbinder* and *Shadowmaster*.

DD: You had a ten-year break in publishing between *Twitchy Eyes* and the first Jack Flint book—what were you up to during those years? Did you stop writing for a while?

JD: I had personal stuff that needed my attention.

DD: In recent years, you've also published the crime novels *Risk* and *Full Proof*. I believe these were both published solely in e-book form by Impera Media. Do you have more work planned in the crime/thriller category?

JD: You can't stop having ideas for stories. I'm a compulsive storyteller. I love both books. One is a romp and one more heavy, but both set in my home town!

DD: I believe you're in the midst of trying to make all of your titles available in e-book format... do you have the rights to all of them, and how is that effort going?

JD: I have all the rights to all my books. I don't really care. I write, I fish. I collect fossils and rocks.

DD: With your most recent books being the three YA fantasy novels and the two thrillers, you've clearly moved away from writing horror. Was that primarily due to the downturn in the horror fiction market, a lessening of personal interest in the genre, or…?

JD: I never look at markets. Don't care. Read my books or don't.

DD: Has any of your work been optioned for film or television? Have you done any dabbling in script work?

JD: I have had a number of offers, but I'm an investigative journalist and I can tell bullshit.

DD: Have you ever written any short fiction, or have you worked solely at novel length?

JD: I have a stack of short fiction. I'm a compulsive writer!!!

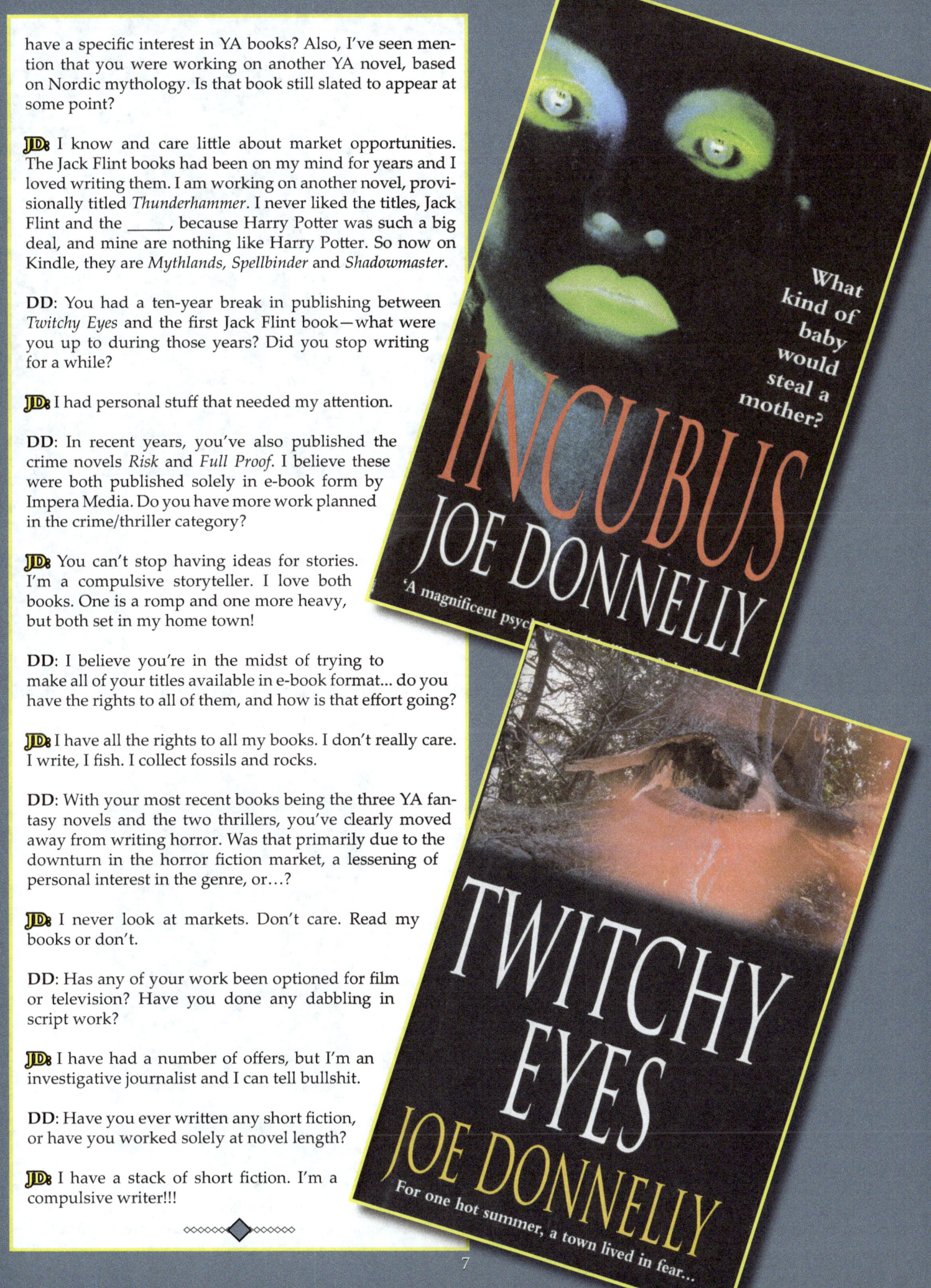

What kind of baby would steal a mother?

INCUBUS
JOE DONNELLY
'A magnificent psych

TWITCHY EYES
JOE DONNELLY
For one hot summer, a town lived in fear...

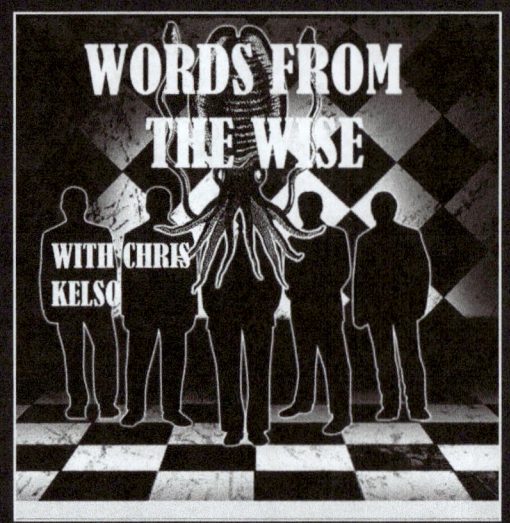

WORDS FROM THE WISE

BY CHRIS KELSO

Photo courtesy of Colin Dunsmuir

(Chris Kelso is a writer, editor and illustrator from Scotland. His books include The Dissolving Zinc Theatre, The Black Dog Eats the City and many more.)

WORDS FROM THE WISE – Nick Antosca
(Take it seriously but have a back-up)
Nick Antosca

Making a living off of your writing is going to be a long shot – unless you're willing to sacrifice all artistic integrity by making Xerox models of *50 Shades of Grey* or *Twilight* just to make a buck (it can be awfully tempting). Even the best writers had day jobs. Burroughs worked as an exterminator, Bukowski as a mail carrier in a post office…even Agatha Christie was an Apothecaries' assistant by day!

Nick Antosca has five books to his name and has written teleplays for shows such as *Hannibal* and *Teen Wolf.* Today he kindly bestows some of his infallible wisdom.

___

The question posed to each author is – *"A young author comes to you seeking advice. They're riddled with insecurities and completely overwhelmed by the publishing industry. What are your Words from the Wise?"*

NA – Have a backup plan or a day job so you can write what you want. Otherwise (unless you have money in the bank or family that will support you) you will always be chasing the next freelance paycheck or notion of what publishers will be looking

for… *No one* really makes a living just from being a fiction writer or journalist. I mean, a few people do — literally a few hundred

Photo courtesy of Nick Antosca

in the entire world. The rest teach or have day jobs.

Zadie Smith teaches. Jonathan Lethem teaches. They all

teach for extra money. Treat writing like a hobby even if you are earning money at it — do it because you love it.

And AT THE SAME TIME treat it like a job and take it very seriously. Treat it like a job where you are both the boss and the employee. Write every day, ideally in the morning when your brain is fresh, before the day gets screwed up. Your most productive hours are almost certainly going to be the first two hours after you wake up. Also, read a lot.

It provides nourishment and makes the writing come more easily.

Write with an outline. Writing the outline counts as writing. A lot of the most important creative work is done before the writing begins.

If you have no plan and don't know how the pieces fit together, you will run into trouble. You will find interesting surprises, but you are undermining yourself by embarking without a map. You don't have to stick exactly to the map if you find yourself disliking the route, but you're in better shape if you have it.

WORDS FROM THE WISE – John Shirley

(Be prepared/Learn to write)
John Shirley

Now…it might sound like an obvious piece of advice, but knowing how to write is one of the most crucial parts of getting your stuff picked up. It doesn't always have to be flowery or convoluted – but it does have to be mindful of pace, structure and, of course, the flow of the prose. John Shirley is the Bram Stoker Award winning author of Black Butterflies, Demons, City Come A-Walkin', the A Song Called Youth cyberpunk trilogy, Doyle After Death, Wyatt in Wichita, Bleak History, and many other books. He was co-screenwriter of THE CROW and has written for television. Here's his Words from the Wise…

The question posed to each author is – "A young author comes to you seeking advice. They're riddled with insecurities and completely overwhelmed by the publishing industry. What are your Words from the Wise?"

JS – *In answer to your question re the young writers*

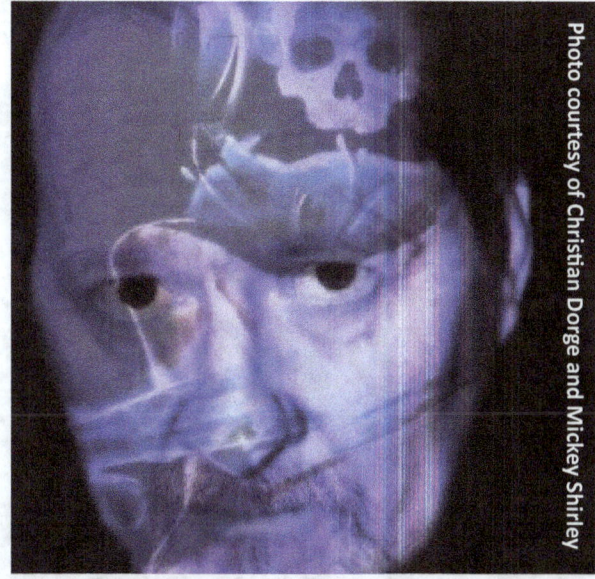

tormented by uncertainty about the publishing industry and what to do…that's funny, so am I. That's because everything has changed. The industry is both vaster–and more selective. It's both larger and more restricted. It's huger–and more specialized. The peculiar truth that has always been true, however, is that on the one hand, it's hard to break in; on the other, they are always looking for new, fresh talents. They do ask themselves who will write the new Hunger Games, and so on. So while it's hard to break through, weirdly–they're always looking for people. Persistence helps. But you've got to have a good product too.

Something that's quite new is the fact that people occasionally do, now, jump from general self publishing and ebook self publishing, to successful book publishing. The extreme case of this was The Martian–the novel was self published. It sold enough that it was picked up by a major. I haven't read the book–my wife has and assures me it's very enjoyable and intriguing and generally well researched. Well written. So you see, you can't just spout some new story idea you have–"zombie children that you adopt and turn vegetarian!"–and because it's a new variation, really have hope that it's going to break through. Just a variation is not enough-cultivate originality and strong, gripping writing, based on being steeped in the strong gripping writing….It really has to be well written. And it has to be fairly literate–that is, the writer reads, and absorbs more than comics and books based on anime, or comics and books based on their favorite movie or television series. They don't do most of their reading online, either. They read a lot of successful books, and classic books. They read books of short stories of all kinds. They get a feel for voices and language and sentences and paragraphs and pacing and chapters and, especially, characters. They get a sense of what good, fun to

read but realistic dialogue is…from reading. I mention this because it seems to be lacking in lots of new writers.

When you read, read as if interrogating the writing. Enjoy it, but also notice how it's put together. Some people do this more naturally than others. I absorbed it like a sponge; some people have to work at it. They have to notice what makes one writer's voice, their style, different than another's. This may mean reading the same text two or three times. Once for enjoyment, later for analysis.

The markets out there seem to me to be less penetrable than they used to be–there are fewer companies reading manuscripts that come in unsolicited. So, this means, you can 1) try and make a name with yourself with short fiction in magazines that consider fiction from unknowns and 2) Try to get a literary agent. You can try to meet an agent (and editors) at a convention for the kind of writing you like. Science fiction, mystery conventions, whatever. You can finish an entire novel–typed according to the formats you can find described in books and articles–and one with an interesting title and simple but fairly original concept, then find places to pitch it to an agent. Research that. It happens…

Go to readings and literary events. Follow journals that describe the publications and markets for the genre you like, if you're writing genre (and know what genre means–look it up if you don't know). Locus Magazine is a good one to start at for science fiction or fantasy. Google these things.

But most of all, write–to learn to write, write. Write what you would want to read…and try to be original enough that you're going to grab people's attention…

An Interview with Geoff Brown of Cohesion Press
By Chris Kelso

CHRIS KELSO: What made you want to pursue another military themed horror anthology? Why do you think there has been a resurgence in the genre (I'm thinking Weston Ochse and Jonathan Maberry in particular, both of whom you have a strong association with already)? Do you think one reason it's become so resonant is because it reflects the current landscape in America?

GEOFF BROWN: I know what I like to read, and I couldn't find much of it around at the time. There were a few authors putting out things like that, but they were few and far between apart from some of the classics. Wes and Jonathan are both giants in the scene, so I'm very happy to have a strong working relationship with both which has resulted in multiple stories in *SNAFU*s from each of them. I think the current world situation, while not too different in regard to constant warfare and tension in world politics, is more obviously a real powderkeg with all the different fights and wars going on, along with the newer threat of global ideological terrorism—a constant spectre hanging over us. This overwhelming tension has brought to us in the Western world a new fear and a new desire for our own military to save us from the big bad beast overseas. This ties in nicely with military horror and military sci-fi. We all know that some genres, especially speculative fiction in the form of horror and sci-fi, tend to echo and represent the current trend in human fear of the times. This surge of military and action-based horror is maybe a sign of what we fear in the 2010s.

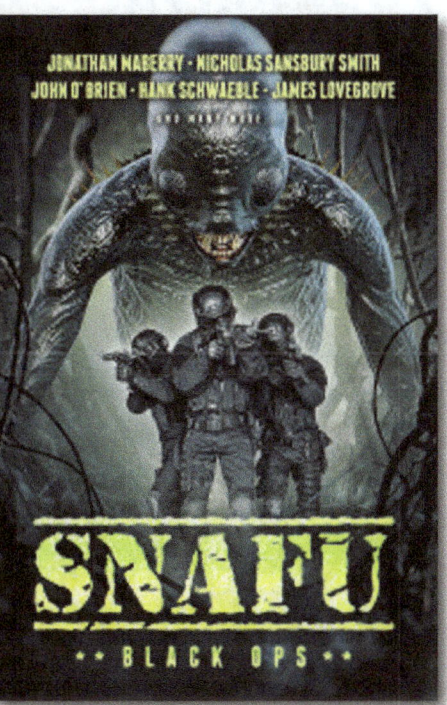

CK: There are a lot of established writers in *SNAFU*, did you solicit these people or was it an open call?

GB: I solicited some of the major-league writers, and the rest of the TOC were made up from the open call. I decided early on in the creation of the *SNAFU* concept that I would make sure I had some name authors with established fans in each of the anthology releases, to ensure a base of readers would sit up and take notice. This would go a long way toward guaranteeing sales and ensuring the lesser-known writers had a chance of being read by people who might take notice of them and help their careers along a little bit.

CK: What's next for you? I read that you want *SNAFU* to be a big series, one encompassing gunslingers and ninjas. I know you were also once editor at *Midnight Echo* magazine and President of the Australian Horror Writers Association, do you plan on getting involved in an editorial capacity with another magazine or are you enjoying spearheading anthologies?

GB: I am so overwhelmed with work these days (I now own a haunted lunatic asylum and run ghost tours through there 364 days/nights a week) that I have taken on an editor-in-chief for Cohesion Press and for the *SNAFU* series as well. I love reading the solicited and open call stories, so I'll never take a full backseat in the *SNAFU* series,

but my trusty sidekick, Amanda J. Spedding, has taken the driver's seat for most of the things we put out these days. I'm happy to be a front-seat passenger.

The Gods of
H.P. Lovecraft

James A. Moore
Donald Tyson   Jonathan Maberry
Christopher Golden   Adam Nevill
Martha Wells
Seanan McGuire   Joe Lansdale
Brett Talley   Laird Barron
Douglas Wynne   Rachel Caine
David Liss   Bentley Little

Edited by Aaron J. French

Writing Conflict: A Lament with Lisa L. Hannett

BY AARON J. FRENCH

Aaron J. French: Thank you for taking the time to sit down and talk with *Dark Discoveries* about your recent book, *Lament for the Afterlife*. But before we get to the novel, could you tell us a little about your biography, where you grew up, what inspired you to write short fiction, etc.?

Lisa L. Hannett: Born and raised in Canada, I now live in Adelaide, South Australia—city of churches, festivals, bizarre murders, and pie floaters. I've had over 60 short stories published, some of which appeared in my first collection, *Bluegrass Symphony*, which was nominated for a World Fantasy Award and won the Aurealis Award for Best Collection; two other collections co-authored with fellow Australian and award-winning author, Angela Slatter; and my debut novel, *Lament for the Afterlife*, won the Ditmar for Best Novel this year. I've got a PhD in Old Norse-Icelandic literature, an Honours degree in medieval lit and fantasy fiction, and a Fine Arts degree in painting and photography. When I'm not writing, I'm a Lecturer in English and Creative Writing here in Adelaide, a gym junkie, and an Instagram devotee.

My somewhat glib, but nevertheless honest, answer to what inspired me to write short fiction is that I (foolishly) thought writing short pieces would be easier than writing novels. Ha! Novels, I thought, were so much harder because there were more characters involved, more complicated plots, bigger and more detailed worlds… but of course, that's not necessarily accurate. Short stories have their own challenges: for example, saying only what needs saying and not a word more; evoking place and character without over-explaining; staying focused on the single effect, seeing it through to the end, and resisting the temptation to embellish it. Why I continue to write short fiction is because I love refining stories, paring them back to the essentials, being forced to choose the perfect phrase instead of the long (potentially flabby) sentence, and being restricted in terms of scope. Short stories always leave me wanting more, which is a good thing.

LAMENT

FOR

THE

AFTERLIFE

LISA L. HANNETT

AJF: Tell us about your writing schedule, how do you get the work done on your short fiction? Do you ever draw on dreams for your ideas? Life experiences?

LH: You know how lots of writing gurus tell people to "Write every day?" Well, I took that idea, scrunched it up, and chucked it in the garbage years ago. Like so many writers (of short or long fiction), I've got a fulltime day job that can often be demanding and draining. As a Lecturer in Creative Writing, I spend a lot of time reading, editing, critiquing other people's work—so, every so often, I get home in the evening and the *last* thing I want to do is look at another draft, even if it's my own. So I write what I can, when I can; sometimes this means I write every day, other times this means I write three times a week. It always varies, and this is something I've learned to recognise and work around—but in order for this approach to work, in order for stories to be finished and sent out into the world, I am strict and also honest with myself. There is *always* time to write, if you want to do it badly enough. So I'm anal-retentive when it comes to scheduling my time. Using a paper diary-calendar, I plot out my work time, my writing time, my admin time, my "fun" time (this last is as important as the rest) and then I stick to this schedule. I write in the evenings and on weekends, and snatch time during weekdays when I can. I'm lucky in that I've got a lovely support network of friends here, all of whom understand when I ditch them to become a writing hermit. This understanding helps so much!

As for inspiration: I rarely draw on dreams for fiction because dream logic is not story logic. Dreams are bursts of strong emotion but, by and large, they're nonsense. They need reworking if they're going to make good stories in the waking world. I've sometimes translated a striking dream image into a story, but it usually is a *translation*: how it appears in the written piece often looks nothing like how it was in the dream. However, I've *definitely* drawn on life experiences in my stories—little details about character's appearances or the things they have in their houses, their motivations, the jokes they make and/or the horrible things they say to one another, their hopes and their disappointments, wonderful and awful events in their lives—so much of it comes from things I've done or remember from my childhood. So many of the characters are pieces of me. Even the horrid ones. But, having said that, these versions

are also *translations* from life, not accurate or objective or realistic representations. The best fiction, in my opinion, is derived from what's personal—what's important to us, and thus might be the hardest and scariest to write about.

AJF: Your stories encompass many genres. How do you navigate that, marketing yourself in a specific genre as it were, and what do you prefer to write?

LH: Again, I feel really glib saying this, but: most of the time, I tend to write first, then worry about stuff like marketing afterwards. And by "worry about" I really mean "make sure I send my story to the appropriate market" and that's about it. Knowing which market is the right one takes some research—I'll read the magazines to which I intend to submit work, to make sure my style of story is aligned with their guidelines and tastes; I'll read anthology guidelines carefully; I'll read lively discussions about "genre"—so that I can add genre labels to my work, if necessary. But one of the most beautiful things about "speculative fiction" is that it's an all-encompassing term: it can mean fantasy, SF, horror, science-horror, adventure-fantasy, magical realism, and so on and so forth. So I figure as long as I'm writing stories with elements that bend or take a step away from reality, that use uncanny or unsettling images, that ask "What if?" and reply with magical, weird, or horrifying answers, then I'm in the right zone.

AJF: *Lament for the Afterlife* is your first full-length novel, published by ChiZine. How did this book begin, and what was it like making the transition from short fiction to a novel? Difficult?

LH: *Lament* began as a story ("The Good Window,"

published in *Fantasy* magazine in 2009) that dealt with concepts and a world I wasn't quite finished exploring. Ideas percolated in the back of my mind for a few years, expanding and becoming more complex over time, until I had Peytr's narrative figured out; he's the lynchpin of the book, so once I knew what he was like, what troubles he had and was going to face (basically, once I'd nutted out the first chapter) I had a pretty good idea what the novel as a whole was going to encompass. So, in a way, this novel wouldn't exist if it wasn't for the short fiction that preceded it.

Something that made the transition between short fiction and novel-length story a bit easier, in this particular work, is the narrative structure. The story unfolds chronologically (Peytr ages as the chapters progress and, in general, event C follows event B follows event A) but the narrative isn't exactly linear: it is told from various angles, all of which come from or lead to Peytr, and these different perspectives allowed me to use many of the same tools I employ when writing short stories. Working on my next novel, the biggest challenge I've confronted in transitioning between short and long forms is the daunting luxury of

leave these extra bits in.)

AJF: The book deals with many very intense themes. There's a lot we could touch on. But one thing in particular that stood out was the present tense prose. What made you choose the present tense? There is a definite immediacy, is this deliberate to evoke the confused atmosphere of war?

LH: The short answer is: yes. The longer answer is that, yes, immediacy in this particular story was *really* important. Peytr is a soldier, a civilian, a boy embroiled in a never-ending war: it's a daunting and hopeless situation he's in, and the present tense helps to capture the uncertainty, intensity, the brief "now-ness" of everything he's going through. It's off-putting and unsettling, reading a war story in the present tense, because you aren't afforded the comfort of the "ed" at the end of verbs, grammatical signs which let you know, however subtly, that either Peytr has survived and is now reflecting on the past, or at the very least *someone* has survived to narrate this tale retrospectively. Present tense robs readers of this certainty, which, in my mind, replicates the characters' precarious positions in life.

AJF: Tell us about Peyt and Dake. How did you approach character development for a story like this?

LH: Although many characters get airtime in this novel, Peytr's character and experiences are what drive it. In chapter one, he's a scrawny, insecure, poetic guy of sixteen, living in a world where men are either soldiers or veterans (and where many women are, too). My academic research focuses on Old Norse-Icelandic literature—sagas about Vikings and war bands and honour-based cultures—so I've got an enduring fascination with societies that revolve around these concepts, which has undoubtedly influenced my approach to character development. But Peytr doesn't fit into a traditional model of "masculinity," which instantly makes him vulnerable, confused, and (in my mind anyway) interesting.

space—there's so much room to breathe in novels, to flesh out worlds and characters just for the sake of fleshing them out, that my short story-writing brain rebels against all of these "wasted" words. (I know they're not really wasted, of course—these meanderings and insights into characters are things that make novels wonderful!—but after years of trimming fat out of my stories, it's often a challenge to

At the beginning of the book, he's stuck sharing a suburban bungalow with another family (many habitable places have been bombed out of existence)—one of whom is Daken, a confident, macho guy of eighteen. Dake is everything Peyt isn't, everything Peyt wishes he *could* be. But Daken is more than just Peyt's foil; it's not as easy as "Peyt is not a stereotypical 'guy' but Dake pretty much is—let's see how these characters clash." Instead, I tried to approach them as characters who love and hate each other, who are selfish and generous, who are where they are because of things they've done to each other (not always good things, of course), and who are the most important people in each other's lives—even if many years pass in which they don't make contact. So, basically, they're brothers. Enemies. Friends.

AJF: One main theme of the novel that comes across for me as well in the novel is trauma. And the way the wartime scenes unfold almost makes it feel like you're in the trauma with the characters. Could you expand on the idea of war and trauma in creation of the scenes?

LH: There are as many ways to tell stories about war as there are people who have been involved or affected by it; the tone that dominates in this novel is, as the title suggests, a lament. I'm fascinated and perplexed and horrified by wars that seem to drag on long after any hope of "winning" (however such a thing can be quantified) has passed—the Vietnam War, the Gulf War, the Israeli-Palestinian conflict, the ongoing devastation in the Middle East, and elements of World War I—and these feelings are dramatized in *Lament for the Afterlife*. This isn't a story about heroes and conquerors, but about regular people being forced into extraordinary and often terrifying circumstances. These aren't superheroes, but average Joes being uprooted, displaced, and yet fighting on because that's what's expected, because there's no other real option. It's my job as a storyteller to plunge readers into the characters' worlds and thoughts and emotions; given the parameters I've just described, this means keeping a close-third perspective, not letting readers know anything the character him/herself doesn't know, and allowing my poor characters (and possibly readers' sensibilities) to get hurt. People are remarkably resilient, but at the same time we're pretty darned fragile. I wanted to capture this paradox—survival and trauma—not just in the battle scenes (of which there are few, really) but in the after-effects, the PTSD, the onslaught of memories each

character has to cope with as the war continues to play out around them. There are moments of joy and love and calm in the narrative as well, of course! But being brief and bright, these moments can make readers feel even greater loss (along with the characters) once they're gone.

AJF: Sorry to stay on the downturn here, but what about torture? There is a nice use of the withholding of information in particularly intense scenes. Tell us about that.

LH: From my (subjective) perspective, there's only one real instance of torture in the book—it's the catalyst that sets Peytr's life onto its downward spiral, right from the get-go in chapter one. However, I do take your point: lots of terrible things happen to people throughout the novel, sometimes intensely awful things. When it came to writing these scenes, I didn't want to shy away from what was happening. Fading to black, as far as I'm concerned, is not usually the most effective or best or *fair* option—especially in dark fantasy and horror. It can be a cheat or a cop-out. It can demonstrate a lack of trust in your readers. At the same time, though, I didn't want to bludgeon readers with explicit details or splatter-porn or gore. That wasn't the point in this story. So I tried to strike a balance between ruthlessly leading readers into dark places, but then providing only crucial details once we got there—enough so that when they started to get that bad feeling in their guts, when they started to ask themselves *is this awful thing really happening to this not-necessarily-awful character*, they'd clearly see that, *yes indeed it is*, but they'd fill in the blanks as extensively or as sparsely as they saw fit. Monsters—and things like torture—are most chilling when we *don't* get to see them in excruciating detail.

AJF: What was it like working with ChiZine? Do you work with an editor, an agent?

LH: Working with CZP is awesome. They publish incredible, award-winning books, and with their focus on dark, genre-bending literature, they are the perfect publishing house for *Lament for the Afterlife*. CZP books are top quality—from the stories, to the interior design and details, to the gorgeous Erik Mohr artwork—and I'm always delighted to work with them. They went above and beyond in their production of *Lament*, giving the book a stunning cover and also an interior illustration midway through that I *adore*. As for working with an editor—yes, I absolutely do! Any writer working as a professional will work with the publisher's editing team—and this always improves the final product. My editor at CZP, Samantha Beiko, was (and continues to be) fantastic—she got what I was trying to do, and she wielded her editing knife with a light, precise touch. Couldn't ask for more, really.

AJF: Where do you see horror fiction and dark fantasy fitting into the overall scheme of popular literature at the moment? Where do you see it going?

LH: This is a huge question, so I'm only going to take a nibble at its corner and focus on the horror side of things. And even then I'm going to narrow my focus to one area of horror writing, which I think is thriving—and will continue to thrive— and that's short fiction. Of course, there are some brilliant horror novels out at the moment (Gemma Files's *Experimental Film*, for example) but if we're looking at the overall scheme of things, then short horror stories are where exciting things are and will continue to be happening. British horror is booming, there are great horror magazines in the US, great anthologies and single-author collections coming out of Australia and Canada, all of which make for a lively international scene. TV is doing wonders for the genre, in terms of getting horror and dark fantasy into more mainstream avenues. The Polly-Anna side of me likes to think that shows like *Game of Thrones*, *American Horror Story*, *Hannibal*, and the forthcoming production of Stephen King's *Dark Tower* series (just to name a few) will allow for cross-pollination: viewers may become readers, readers may become viewers, and living rooms worldwide will have a little more darkness on their bookshelves and entertainment systems as a happy consequence.

AJF: Who are some of your most favorite and influential authors and books that have helped shape you into the writer you are today?

LH: I've said it elsewhere, but it bears repeating: pretty much everything I've read, even the crap, has had some sort of influence on my writing. Since that's impossible to narrow down, I'll focus instead on some of my absolute favourites: Michael Crummey, Margaret Atwood, Margaret Laurence, Timothy Findley, Patrick DeWitt, Shirley Jackson, E. Annie Proulx, David Malouf, Robert Shearman, Kirstyn McDermott, Angela Slatter, Helen Marshall, Lavie Tidhar.

AJF: And finally, what new projects do you have on the horizon—also where can our readers find out more about you?

LH: As we speak, I'm finishing up my next collection: *The Homesteaders* is another book of short stories set in the world of *Bluegrass Symphony*. Backwoods witches, immortal soothsayers, bear-shaped child-stealers, raven-shaped miners, and lots of ghosts make up some of the characters in these tales, all tinged with a down-home country twang. I'm also in the process of editing/doing rewrites on my next novel, *Ketill's Daughter*, which is the first in a two-book series, *The Invisible Woman*. Set in Viking Age Norway, this book tells the early story of Unn the Deep-Minded—wife of one king, mother to a second, and eventually a famous Viking herself—as she struggles to find her own fame and fate in this warrior world, all while her shape-shifting time-travelling *fylgja* (a kind of spirit guide) keeps butting in to mess things up for her… The second book in the series (called *Deep-Minded*) will follow Unn out of Norway into medieval Ireland, Scotland, and finally Iceland. She was quite the world-traveller! While working on these novels, I'll also be fleshing out another short story collection: this one is a cycle of tales set in the same seaside world as "A Shot of Salt Water" (published in *The Dark* last year). Anyone keen to stay in touch can find me on Facebook (Lisa L. Hannett), on Twitter @lisalhannet, or on my website: lisahannett. com.

The last in a long decadent line of piratical Spanish eccentrics, Bartleby Cadiz grows up in isolation to be as mad, bad and metaphysical as his ancestors. But he feels there is something different about him. What can it be?

JournalStone – Bizarro Pulp Press

Bram Stoker nominated author Peter Adam Salomon has laid bare the intricate horrors of the human condition in this poetic compilation; PseudoPsalms: Saints v. Sinners. Exploring the eternal human struggle for salvation, where the light and the dark create shadows, shrouding poetry.

Captain Bernice Wygone watched as the last of the repaired Valkyrie robots exited the well-deck, the water churning into a greenish-blue foam as the hovercraft cleared the ship. Her ship, *Horizon,* was playing guard today, watching for trouble as the big amphib launched air and sea platforms like a dog shaking off fleas.

It was awesome.

"Captain, the engineer is onboard," called the executive officer—the XO—as he entered the ship's bridge.

The XO was still fairly new, but she liked Commander Belsik and trusted him from the moment she'd seen him work a bridge during their first hectic underway period together.

"Is this one cleared?" she asked.

Belsik shook his head and handed the captain a file, then deftly took over the binoculars and her place at the window. Yes, there was a watch—excellent sailors and junior officers to run the bridge—but that extra set of experienced eyes when the gator launched was standard practice. As a cruiser, the *Horizon* didn't have the crew numbers to simply double up watches. Everyone had to do a little more sometimes. Lately, that meant twenty-hour days instead of sixteen.

"Great. Another one I have to keep in the dark and still get work out of." Wygone checked the file quickly. There were no surprises except one. "He has nanites?" she asked in disbelief. "Are you kidding me?"

The XO gave her a look, then raised the binos to watch a big-bellied vertical launch plane rise from the gator's deck. "Look again. He has four kinds."

"Shit," the captain said, flipping to the medical clearance page. The big red stamp on the front page only told her that he had them, not the details. "*Sugar Wash, Insulin-Up, Cholest-erase,* and *Heart Assure. Is he eighty?*"

Belsik only shrugged. Of course, the engineer—Albert Stevens—wasn't eighty. He wasn't even forty, but he was a Type 1 diabetic and that told the whole story. Or rather, he *had* been a diabetic. Now, he wasn't.

And those with replicating nanites weren't allowed on Navy ships during deployments into a war zone. There were simply too many potential problems. Anything can be weaponized and any tech can be disrupted. And the ship itself was a giant disruption.

Of course, there were exceptions, the captain included, since she'd been shot full of *First Responders* after a car accident. But the accident was over and her injuries healed, so hers were no longer needed. If they went kaput, no one cared.

Actually, the captain wished hers would stop working. The entire concept was too freaky for her, like she had some sort of man-made parasite inside her body.

She'd taken to standing at a particular spot on the bridge wing because of the radar. It made the hair on people's arms stand on end, so she bathed in whatever slight rays she might get there, hoping to fry the remaining nanites.

Slamming the file shut and tossing it onto the shelf by the captain's seat, she put the problem out of her mind while she listened to the bridge crew decode a maneuvering message from the gator and plot a course to their next station. She smiled as the reports and commands flowed smoothly.

The XO put down the binos as the gator ended flight quarters and well-deck operations. "Well, what do we do about him, ma'am?" he asked.

"Just make sure the doc gets insulin or whatever from the gator hospital. If his quit on him, then we'll medivac him. It's the best we can do."

***

"I'm not sure I understand," the engineer said, eyes on the curtain that separated him from his drones. "Why can't I see what they're being loaded with?"

Wygone kept a neutral look on her face, trying hard to suppress her impatience. This would be the third explanation, first with the payload boss, then the XO, and now it was her turn. "Albert, as explained before, you're not cleared for this program. You're not 'read in' for the mission, and currently there's no valid need-to-know for you. I'm very sorry."

The buzz of another drone passing into the landing zone drew Albert's attention, his expression going almost slack with nerdy pleasure. Wygone found it hard not to smile at the abrupt change, like a switch had flipped inside his brain.

"Albert?" she prompted.

He shook his head a little, then gave her an embarrassed smile. "Sorry. I've only gotten to watch them at sea a couple of times and only for tests. Never like this." The smile dropped and he scowled at the curtain again. "I thought we were just doing medical nanite distribution, with the Valkyries doing the same in the cities. We're not?"

"Oh we are, but the payload is classified. It's not a matter of changing the mission to something nefarious," Wygone said, watching for his reaction.

He made a face. "Proprietary information? I get it. They have to get their profit, right?"

The heavy curtain slid back to reveal the next two drones, both now loaded and ready to launch. The payload chief dropped a pair of medical gloves into a red bag, then smiled at the engineer. "Sir, all ready for launch. Would you like to monitor from here? I never know when that weird fault will happen."

Albert was clearly ready to forget his concerns and eager to see the drones launch, to do some engineer stuff. He started forward, then abruptly halted and turned back to the captain. "I'm good. I won't try to peek."

With a little head shake, she waved him on and said, "I hope you can figure out the problem for us."

Making her way back up the bridge, she watched as the two drones launched without a hitch, then headed north, ready to spray their payload into the air above the target area.

"Everything okay, ma'am?" the XO asked, coming to stand next to her on the bridge wing.

The breeze was up and the ship was altering course to keep the wind direction and speed optimal for launching. The sound of the crew preparing their turns to capture the wind filtered out of the open bridge wing door.

Captain Wygone loved it when the wind changed like that. She was created for the sea and was lucky she'd realized it early enough to forge a life tied to the open water. There were many sacrifices, but each one was worth it. The ship shifted beneath her and white water foamed away from the hull as the ship changed course, leaving a curved blue and white wake behind her.

She took a deep breath and then glanced up at her XO. He had that look as well, the dreamy gaze of someone who understood the magic of the sea.

"It never gets old, does it?" he asked.

"Never."

"And Albert?"

Wygone nodded and glanced up at the windbirds as the ship completed her turn. Perfect. The officer on watch was young, but very good. "He thinks it's just proprietary information. He's fine."

"And how are we doing? With the dispersal?" he asked. He'd been handling the bridge for her during the morning briefing, so he'd missed it and they'd not yet had time to talk.

"Eighty percent in our theater. Two hits so far. Other theaters have more. Brazil has seventeen, believe it or not."

The XO looked as surprised as she'd been, and possibly as envious. Their theater was the hub—the source—of the terrorist organization that had set off two dirty bombs. There was credible evidence that they were behind the release of a weaponized Zika virus recently discovered in Europe and Asia. Mosquitoes bearing the new version had recently been isolated as far away as India.

Of course, the mosquitoes skipped this dry part of the world. It was the perfect weapon for a quasi-terrorist bunch of governments to use. The fifth Gulf War was turning into a very dirty one, and it wasn't even officially a war. *Yet.*

It was a stroke of genius to piggyback this operation onto a worldwide effort to distribute medical nanites. Urged on by the United Nations and governments alike, it was intended to close the growing gap in medical care between the first world and the third.

And it had been a note-taker inside a classified meeting who had thought of it. A twenty-year-old kid with no operational experience. It was brilliant.

All the way back to Bin Laden decades ago, terrorist leaders received the very best medical care while their soldiers and believers suffered and died from medieval diseases. And once medical nanites hit the scene, there was no way they'd ignore those little miracles of science.

While a vial of knock-off *Cholest-erase®* could be had for the price of a few good dinners, every high-ranking terrorist snagged in the last couple years had been filled to the gills with premium-grade medical nanites. And many different types of them too. From *Heart Assure* to improve heart function and prevent heart attacks, to *Air Plus* to counteract the effects of smoking or pollution, they had them all.

And no one else in these backwater hellholes had them. Not after sixty years of warring with the West and among themselves. But how could the U.S. spot that difference from a lot farther away than the end of a hypo? More nanites, of course. Well, that and plain old nanoparticles.

The drones and Valkyrie robots were distributing nanites to everyone in a massive, worldwide campaign to end chronic disease. So were tent hospitals and field workers on every continent.

It was a real program and would bring real results. *Rounders* for those with sickle-cell, *Mal-Gone* for those in areas where malaria still ran rampant, and more. Even the weaponized Zika had a nanite-based prevention—though cloaked as a nanite for regular Zika, which was bad enough.

But for a few select task forces, that was just a cover. The real targets were individuals. While the United States might light up like an over-decorated Christmas tree if nanite-carrying citizens were tallied, here in these war-torn countries where terror is born, that was not the case.

Valkyries collected DNA surreptitiously to identify known players or relatives, while the drone payloads allowed the force to isolate certain kinds of premium nanites. If the sensor nanites the drones sprayed encountered target nanites—the replicating kind that produced heart and lung nanites—they would stand out like a beacon. Many of the nanoparticles in the drone payloads had just one function: attach to a target nanite and shine their unique signature.

And of course, the nanites they were seeking were exactly the ones not being distributed in this operation.

The XO cleared his throat, bringing Wygone back to the present. She waved out at the brown haze above the horizon. Even this far out, the dirty coast ruined the blue view. "We know they're there somewhere, maybe right in the middle of that craphole they call a city. It's possible they've gone to ground in the mountains. It's just a matter of time."

***

Wygone burst into the briefing room like her hair was on fire. She hated not having anyone except the normal bridge crew up during flight quarters, but at least the Officer of the Deck was one of her best.

"Show me," she commanded even as the door shut behind her.

The intelligence specialist started the replay on her biggest screen, while live footage continued rolling on the others. A drone view began, complete with data fields. Craggy hills, squat and ugly buildings inside walled compounds, farm animals.

"It's coming, ma'am," the specialist said, then pointed to a spot on the screen. "Along the right side."

The captain sucked in a sharp breath when a cluster of bright spots populated the otherwise dark sensor image. No one could miss that. A concentration of at least a few dozen individuals, some so close together that they made a larger blob of light.

"And here. Watch." The specialist moved her finger to the line of road the drone flew along. Sure enough, the dark spot of a vehicle stood out because of the bright glow inside.

Then it was past and gone.

"When do we get another flyby? How many? What's the location? And we're sure those weren't members of the royal family or government exiles?" the captain asked, her fingers almost itching in readiness.

The XO put up a hand and said, "Excellent work, Petty Officer Simmons. You do your thing and I'll brief the captain."

Wygone narrowed her eyes at Belsik, but he only motioned her to the other side of the room. She followed, but glanced back at the screens as the specialist began her work. Lines for measurements immediately began crossing the screen.

"Sorry about that, ma'am. She got pretty tongue-tied

with me, so I thought I'd let her do what she's good at. Also, we don't know much yet. That footage is ten minutes old."

She nodded, taking a deep breath. In the past week, more than sixty signatures had been picked up, but extractions were being delayed or done only under exacting conditions to avoid tipping their hand. While more than one terror network was involved, some of them were global and as sophisticated as governments. Disappearances would be noted.

This was where the leadership of the worst network held sway. They had even taken over whole cities and territories to appear legitimate. There were no Valkyries giving injections in areas of ongoing conflict, but the drones and their payloads still filled the air.

"I want to brief the admiral as soon as possible. He'll get the satellites on that area."

The XO nodded and said, "I already called down. They've got the secure room comms up and ready for you."

Wygone smiled like a kid getting a snow day off school. "This could be it."

Belsik's return smile was just as big. "Finally."

***

Satellite confirmation, intelligence sources, and even post-analysis of old footage showing construction at the site made it official. This was the location of the primary mover, the ace of spades in the terror card deck. And he was surrounded by his closest advisors in that ugly rural compound. A whole crowd of bad people to capture and interrogate was living right under their satellite noses.

As a cruiser, the *Horizon* would play no active part in the capture. That was for special ops on the amphibious craft. Even so, the wickedly armed warship would have a key role in the air defense portion and they would play escort. They would also be the intermediate flight deck for the transfer of prisoners.

Assuming there were prisoners.

Wygone hoped that there were, sincerely and with all her heart. Now that the terror networks had acquired and were beginning to use bioweapons with increasingly horrific results, it was more important than ever to get information. Where were the labs? Who were the specialists? Or even worse… what legitimate governments or spies were selling the lethal germs and viral agents?

Weaponized Zika was a terrifying new development. With a twelve-percent rate of disastrous fetal impacts, the lid wouldn't stay on the secret forever. Eventually, it would become common knowledge. It was spring now and summer's mosquitoes would expose the truth.

And it was only a matter of time before it hit the United States. It might already be happening.

They needed information and badly. And nothing was too extreme when it came to stopping terror now. Nothing was too drastic or too expensive.

As the Chief of Naval Operations had announced in his fleet brief, "A reset—a complete and total elimination of threats to worldwide safety—is all that will suffice."

Those had been strong words, but ones that Wygone agreed with. They were just putting small fingers into leaking dams and hoping for the best. Now was the time to strike and do it right… and to find the sources of the bioweapons and eliminate those too.

So yes, Captain Wygone wanted prisoners in the worst way possible. Someday, she wanted to be a grandmother.

Glancing down at the display, she saw her ship positioned inside their maneuvering box. With a nod, she listened as her deck officer passed a signal and then waited as the Command and Information Center—CIC—forwarded it to the admiral's ship via secure communications. It was unwieldy, but it was imperative that the ship remain quiet and unnoticed.

And everything was going swimmingly, almost textbook. The first stages of the operation had been near-perfect.

The harsh buzz of her comms line broke the spell and she yanked up the receiver. "Captain speaking."

The XO's voice was strained and tight, very unlike him. "Ma'am, we've got a problem. Can you come down to CIC?"

"Now? They're extracting. Why are you in CIC?"

"It's urgent, Captain," he said, his voice artificially calm. If he wasn't watching the extraction, then she already knew it had to be urgent. That fake calm just reinforced it and made the hair on the back of her neck stand on end.

"On my way," she said. Her bridge officer was looking at her while trying not to let on she'd been listening. "Don't screw up. I'll be down in CIC."

Wygone barely touched the treads as she hurried down the ladders toward the protected spaces of the CIC. The XO stood ready at the hatch, holding it open—also unusual—as she jumped off the final ladder.

"What happened?" she asked.

The XO's eyes were a little too wide, his mouth a little too tense… and he radiated fear. Wygone scoped out the CIC, half-expecting some sort of dangerous disruption like a sailor going bonkers from the stress. There was nothing out of the ordinary—well, ordinary for a tense operation like their current one—save that the CIC Officer and Chief were at the comms station and crowding the tech. Both leaned over the tech's shoulders, intent on the screens.

The XO put a hand to her arm to stop her from moving in that direction, something he'd never done before. He was also sweating in the too-cool air. "Ma'am, wait. This way," he said, swallowing hard and motioning her toward a rear compartment in the CIC away from the watch floor.

As soon as the hatch opened, Wygone saw for herself—in vivid color—what had made the XO so pale. The Global Broadcast Service feeds filled the screens, a half-dozen channels interspersed by Command Chat thrown up on the other screens.

"What the hell?" she murmured, looking up at the feeds.

One of the great ironies of deployment was that the ship could get television feeds direct from the states faster than they could get command information. It was simply the nature of the world that made it so. Television channels didn't need security or verification. They simply flowed in a one-way stream of information toward any receiver that could pick it up.

And now it was streaming chaos. Four different news channels were filled with moving figures, a riot or massive battle on each. Red was the dominant color of those on the ground.

"It just started coming in. It supposedly began an hour or more before that, but it's spreading." He took the keyboard for a command chat window and scrolled it back. "This is from Cyber Command. Something happened, starting somewhere near Portsmouth Naval Hospital. I'm trying to get Third Fleet up, but if you look, that channel is covering San Diego, so it's clearly there too."

While he spoke, Wygone scanned each of the screens, her mouth open and her mind racing. The scrolling headlines told a confusing tale. Ordinary people all over the United States were simply going insane and attacking each other.

A bouncing camera feed from a helicopter showed the familiar lines of the San Diego Naval Hospital. The wide lots around the loose connection of buildings were filled with people, many of them wearing the blue and green gowns of hospital patients.

The image shifted to the hospital roof where Life Flights normally landed. Almost as if the landing pad were a fighting ring, a huddled group of people was backing away from two people in hospital gowns. Butts in clear view as the gowns gaped, one of the attackers circled like an animal, while the other shuffled forward. A respirator hose hung out of his mouth and waved back and forth like an elephant's trunk.

"What the hell?" Wygone repeated.

The volume of the feed came up and a breathless voice-over began. "…appears to have no effect on them. Police are overwhelmed and in some cases are joining the stricken. There's been no official word yet, but other news sources are reporting the same scene all over the U.S. We're just getting word from Canada and Hawaii."

Wygone tapped the volume controls and looked at the XO, his eyes wide and shocked as they scanned the screens. "Military concentration areas. All of those places are military concentration areas. What's going on?"

The XO shook his head and then pointed to one of the screens, a shouting newscaster inset into the scene of chaos. "They said it started in Portsmouth, or maybe Fort Bragg. Something about medical nanites."

Wygone's stomach dropped into her toes and for whatever reason, the words of the CNO came back to her. *A complete reset.*

"Get—" Her words were cut off by the hatch banging open and the CIC Chief bursting in.

"Captain, secure call from the *Pretoria! Pretoria* actual."

That meant it was Frank, the captain of the gator they were assigned to. He had a crew of a few thousand sailors and marines. His vessel was also the flagship, so he carried the admiral's staff and the special operations staff. If anyone knew what was going on, it would be him.

Wygone pushed past and saw too many necks craning to look at the comms desk. There was an operation going on and each of the watch-standers had a job to do. Their eyes needed to be on their jobs.

"Mind your stations!" she shouted. Heads whipped around and returned to their screens. At the comms station, she accepted the receiver and tried to ignore the rapid scrolling of the chat windows dividing the screen. "Captain Wygone."

"Bernice, this is Frank. Everything is tits up. The freaking admiral's staff are acting like they've got all day to figure shit out, so I called you. The extraction team is running for the hills right now and the helo is down. They frigging *ate* the pilot. Freaking *ate* him!"

Wygone's mind was in a terrible high gear, the whining kind that preceded an engine spinning apart and shooting shrapnel everywhere. A single clanging alarm kept repeating in her brain. *Nanites. Nanites.* Her skin started to itch at the thought of all those millions of tiny machines inside her.

"Frank, who ate the pilot? Was it our troops or the targets? *Who?*"

He was crying. She could hear it over the line, that thickness in his voice. Frank was the most level-headed person she'd ever met. They'd known each other since the Academy and grew close during the third Gulf War. If he was crying, then she probably wasn't ready for whatever she was going to hear. He was also her best friend and she wished she could comfort him.

"We're not sure exactly, but the helmet cams made it look like locals. They never even made it to the target, just the landing site. But one of the team started screaming before then, even while they were landing. He kept screaming that something was in his head and then he took off. Jumped right out of the helo!"

"Frank, did it start when they got close to land? Did it start there or at altitude?"

Shouting interrupted the line and Wygone flinched as the receiver hit something hard. Listening, she heard the faint words, "…rendezvous is overrun… they had to launch the boats… returning to mother."

Her mind was moving almost too fast. She gave it a few seconds, but she knew that Frank wasn't going to pick up the phone again. Looking up at the main display, the big range circles off the coast pulsed in orange light. And her ship… her ship acting as the lily pad for the helo… her ship stationed close to land.

Wygone practically tripped over the comms tech to reach for the CIC Officer's station and flipped the switch for the speaker to the bridge. "Officer of the Deck, this is the Captain. Turn the ship. Don't set a course, just turn us directly away from land at full speed. I'll be right up. Acknowledge!"

The XO was right behind her. "What are you doing, Captain? We're not secured from operations!"

She waved a hand back for him to be quiet and shouted, "Acknowledge!"

"Turn the ship away from land at full speed, aye!" The voice of the officer was firm, but the confusion that laced the statement was evident.

"I'll be on the bridge in a moment. Everything is alright. Just do it," she said in a more normal tone. The last thing Wygone needed was for her to do the wrong thing out of fear or uncertainty. She was good, but she was young.

Turning to the XO, she said, "I don't know for sure what's going on, but the operation is pretty much DOA. *Pretoria* just told me that this thing is here too, not in so many words, but a local ate his helo pilot, so I'm connecting the dots."

Belsik's mouth dropped open at her words and he swallowed. "Here?"

"I've got to get on the bridge. I'm getting away from land. I don't know anything for sure, but I'm not taking chances." What she didn't say was that her cynical side felt this was more than an accident.

"*Gataby* is in distress!" shouted the comms tech, waving for the CIC officer between typing frantically into her terminal.

Wygone grabbed the XO's arm in tight fingers and practically dragged him to the comms station with her. She had a feeling she already knew what she would see.

The *Gataby*—a new destroyer with the best passive sensors in the world and the electronic profile of a rowboat—was even closer to shore than the *Horizon*. Acting as information collector, the *Gataby* was also the emergency rendezvous for the operation if the extraction had to proceed by sea rather than air. The tiny blinking icon of the ship was nine miles closer to land than the *Horizon*.

"Put that channel on speaker," Wygone ordered. It was a risk. Keeping the chaos confined to headsets might be better, but this was happening and the better her sailors understood the stakes, the more diligently they would work. The mushroom philosophy—keep them in the dark and feed them shit—had never set well with her.

Heavy breathing and screaming punctuated by static filled the CIC from the speakers. "…secure inside the CIC. The bridge is secure. Engine room is not secure. Chief Engineer is tearing it up and… and… he's killing them! Repair lockers…" On the screens, the chat window scrolled past, partial entries filled with fear and misspellings.

Twisting the knob to lower the volume, Wygone looked from the XO to the CIC officer. "We have to get far from land. Everyone with nanites needs a minder or needs to be secured someplace safe. Put them in the fo'c'sle. Let's hope we don't need to man the anchors anytime soon."

The XO's expression changed and he straightened slowly, his gaze fixed on her. "Ma'am."

It was all he needed to say. They both knew it.

She nodded, "Me too. But I've got work, so you get me a minder. You and me, we can't be in the same place at the same time. You need to be ready to take over. Get me a gunner and make sure he's armed."

"Are you sure?" he asked.

"Very."

***

Whatever it was, it took the gator next. One minute the *Pretoria* was in command, the admiral's staff bouncing orders for rendezvous to the ships in their task force and the flight deck busy recovering drones. The next minute, there was screaming and chaos. Within moments, bodies were flying over the side of the ship, some of them running, some of them thrown.

The ship was still afloat and moving, but anyone alive was trapped in whatever space they found to hide in and the howls leaking through the comms made it clear they wouldn't be going anywhere. Wygone stopped listening after Frank tried to make a break for the bridge and never arrived.

That's also when Wygone gave orders to shoot down any drone within range.

Their ship, designed to suppress enemy air power, was now being used to shoot down their own craft before those could get anywhere near. And because they were no longer transmitting their position and had left the task force—at high speed—she hoped no more would come. After all, someone had to tell them to land on her ship. They didn't just do it themselves.

She pointed to the little box of chips and wires on the bridge's chart table. It looked no different than any other busted piece of electronics. "And you're sure that's it?" she asked, looking at Albert and the drone mechanic who had brought the piece up.

Both men nodded, but they were not super-confident nods. Albert said, "It's the only thing it could be. It's a transmitter, but it relays data rather than holding data to transmit. In short, it's used to broadcast data we send it."

"Or someone else sends," she said. He nodded at that, his lips pursed and his face grim.

It had been four days since things went south. The ship was on her own, using a fuel-conserving speed that kept them alone and away from land. Or air routes. Everyone on the ship knew the score and the Global Broadcast played continuously on the mess decks and in the wardroom.

The world was unraveling before their eyes. Newscasters still wore too much makeup and the electricity was on, but the infested were roaming the streets and no one was safe. Even worse, those who were attacked joined the fray.

Even the ones who looked half-eaten.

Nanites were the cause, that much was known. Medical nanites. *Heart Assure* banged damaged hearts back into action. *Grafters* and vanity-assuaging *Scar-Gone* nanites knitted together pebbly skin over wounds. *First Responders* jolted the still forms back to life.

And they were all replicating nanites, the kind that made more of themselves when a new person was bitten and clean blood met nanite-infested blood. Or they were factory-nanite types, the kind that reconfigured based on chemical needs inside the body, the kinds for diabetes, for cancer, for cholesterol. And somehow they were reconfiguring to take the humanity out of humans, creating animals filled with aggression and anger and unceasing hunger.

Ominously, the relay system to make satellite phone calls back to the U.S. was no longer working, so no one had been able to reach family. Even the email system wasn't cooperating. They were cut off from civilian methods of communication and Wygone was unwilling to use the military systems and give away their position.

She was unwilling because their task force was effectively gone, and each of those ships had remained connected to the military communications grid. Maybe it came via drones or through regular communications, but this thing was coming for everyone who stayed connected.

Wygone watched Albert leave the bridge, a sailor strapped with a gun two steps behind him. Her gunner watched her every move, so she knew how he felt.

Her walkie crackled and the XO's tired voice came through. "Captain, we picked up a subfeed embedded inside the Global Broadcast. It's for you."

Suspicion and fear made goosebumps stand on her arms. "You have someone clear listen yet? Signal analysis?"

Now that the crew knew the stakes, sailors had come forward confessing to black-market or off-the-books nanites from private doctors. Everything from blood cleaners for those who smoked a little wacky weed to cholesterol eaters for the paranoid. There was even one who had loaded up on unnecessary anti-cancer nanites after her grandmother died of breast cancer.

A full twenty percent of the crew was infested and there wasn't a thing they could do about it.

But those clear of infestation had stepped up to the plate. They handled all communications and, in this case, checked the signals for anything odd.

"It's clear as far as we can tell, Captain. It's full of noise so there's only so much we can do."

Wygone looked at the gunner and he nodded to let her know he was ready. She clicked the button and said, "I'll be right down."

The gunner hot on her heels, she hurried toward the secure comms room. The passageway had been cleared of infested crew just to be safe. There could be no mistakes or they would be another New York City… or another *USS Pretoria*.

At her nod, the comms tech flipped the switch and the space filled with the electronic bounces of a hidden sound feed.

"*Horizon, Simpson,* and *Herald*—and any other ships in the Fifth Fleet who may pick up this broadcast—this is Admiral Grant, Assistant Chief of Naval Operations. Stay strong, stay firm, but stay away. Do not approach within twenty miles of any landmass. Do not communicate with any device. Turn off all receivers—including the one carrying this broadcast—the moment this message is received.

"The CNO is dead and he took the secret of this horror with him. We do not know how to stop the broadcast that is destroying our world. We cannot find the source. We won't stop trying, but it is everywhere and we are dying.

"Whatever beliefs you may hold, I hope that power is with you this day and for all the dark days to come. I have no relief to send you, no fuel, no food, no ships. You are on your own for now, but I will not stop trying. Any ship that is safe should raise the Tango signal flag to any other ship they approach. Do not approach any ship that does not signal Tango.

"God—or whatever higher power may exist—be with you. Admiral Grant, out."

Her heart nearly frozen by the gravity of those words, Wygone said, "Pull the feed. Pull all the feeds. Cut all communications. No receivers at all. I want them physically disabled."

The comms tech immediately turned away to begin coordinating the process. It would take time. This ship was a modern one, designed for rapid and heavy communication needs. Communications lines ran through its frame like blood vessels in a body. She and the XO shared a look, because they didn't need words. They both knew the questions and they both knew the answers.

How much fuel? How much food? How much time?

The answers were all the same: not enough.

With a little shrug, the XO said, "There are merchant ships, cruise ships. Even our Navy ships once…" He paused to lick his lips, glancing up at the gunner. "Once everyone on board is gone. We could use our helo to ferry supplies, maybe."

Wygone's laugh was short and bitter. "And carry two hundred thousand gallons of fuel in milk jugs maybe?"

Again, he shrugged.

The gunner cleared his throat to get their attention, his expression a little embarrassed when they looked at him. "Ma'am, we're very good at boarding and seizure. Our team is good. All we need is one replenishment ship. The *Trundle* was with our fleet. It's out there."

The XO and Wygone faced the gunner. The best ideas always seemed to come from the sidelines. And this was a good idea.

The XO said, "*Trundle* has a crew of ninety. If it went like the others…"

"Then half of them went over the side and the uninfected might be hiding," Wygone finished for him.

The air in the tiny comms room changed, the atmosphere suddenly sparking with that small glimmer of hope. Wygone grabbed at that hope. "It's something. This can't last forever."

Belsik clapped the gunner on the shoulder and smiled. "Good thinking, sailor. We'll start small, rescue who we can, take the ships and disable their comms. Make them safe. We'll reassemble the fleet and ride this out. You're right. The oiler is the first one we need."

Wygone watched as the fire inside the XO lit once more, the plans forming in his head and hope once again alive. He left the space with a spring in his step that Wygone hadn't seen since this began.

As the hatch closed behind Belsik, the comms tech jolted up from her seat and flung her headphones onto the desk. A shrill shrieking noise erupted from the walkie on Wygone's belt at the same time. "Ma'am, we've got a signal—"

Whatever she might have said was lost in the haze of red that fell over Wygone's eyes, the buzz of a thousand bees in her head filling her ears with indescribable noise. And anger. And hunger. The smell of the gunner was like the promise of peace after war.

If only she could get to him.

The gun raised as she turned, her teeth on his wrist and her fingers digging into his face. Her final coherent thought was a wish.

Please kill me.

But not until I finish eating.

TENTACLE DOWN!
MILITARY HORROR AND VIDEO GAMES

BY RICHARD DANSKY

There are a lot of horror video games, and there are a lot of military themed ones. What there isn't a lot of, however, is overlap between the two styles, far less than one would think. In part this is due to genre convention and game design elements—military games, particularly first person shooters, are about projecting force at a distance, and zombies get a whole lot less interesting as enemies if you're dropping them a half a kilometer out with a scoped sniper rifle. Furthermore, the core fantasy of most military-themed games—especially shooters—is a power fantasy, while horror is often predicated on a certain level of powerlessness. With the mechanics of these games geared toward supporting the fantasy, horror gets squeezed out.

To be sure, many horror games have tried to give their protagonists military backgrounds, but the genre demands of horror—isolation, locked camera angles, forced up-close encounters and suchlike—don't always work with the hallmarks of the military.

There are those who would argue that the omnipresent "space marines" would qualify is at least a nod toward the military, but by and large there's little about their approach, tactics, or portrayal that definitively identifies them as part of an organized, tactical military.

With these obstacles in place, it would seem difficult to generate any sort of military horror in a game setting. Fortunately, there are two successful approaches to the problem.

The first is simply amping up the horror elements. Dropping a zombie at half a kilometer is one thing; dropping one while hundreds more rush at you and you don't have enough rounds for them all is entirely another. Such is the premise of Call of Duty's intensely popular "zombie mods." First introduced in *Call of Duty: World at War*, the zombie mode was unlocked by completing the single player campaign and then watching the credits all the way through. This in turn started a new campaign called *Night of the Undead*. Set at various sites in Europe and the Pacific theater during World War II, the "Night of the Undead" campaign proved hugely popular. The first mission involved fending off a swarm of Nazi zombies intent on attacking an abandoned bunker, and other spaces included a research facility, an asylum and a swamp. This step into the fantastic also allowed the developers to get a little frisky with the weapons available to the player, supplementing the standard World War II arsenal with working "Wunderwaffe" like electricity projectors and teleporters.

The mode worked, in part because of the well-polished gameplay, in part because of the immense popularity of zombies, and in part because the zombie aspect was framed within the game's standard military conceit. Once it was postulated that the zombie outbreak had been created in a secret Nazi lab, one that could be infiltrated in a mission akin to other missions in the game, then the military approach to the zombie infestation worked within the game's context. The content in zombie mode wasn't canonical for the larger Call of Duty universe, but it did mesh with the game's aesthetic beautifully. Ultimately, the mode was so successful it led to the continuation of the mode in followup titles in the *Call of Duty: Black Ops* series, as well as Ideaworks' two standalone spinoffs.

Taking a different tack is the *F.E.A.R.* franchise, originated by Monolith and continued by Day One Studios. The setting for the game isn't military, but the title of the gam refers to an elite Special Forces unit, the leader of which the player portrays. The game doesn't skimp on its horror bona fides—the main antagonist of the first entry in the series is a ghostly girl named Alma, whose name is a shoutout to a character in Peter Straub's classic *Ghost Story.* Simultaneously, the series' look is informed by the J-horror aesthetic, and this hybrid mashup of Eastern and Western influences produces a deeply creepy setting.

As for the military aspect, *F.E.A.R.*'s advanced AI for its day allowed computer-controlled squadmates to behave tactically, giving the idea that these were in fact Special Forces operators called on to face a supernatural threat much more credence. It was one thing to call your AI buddies "Special Forces" back in 2005, quite another to see them behave tactically and react to enemy action in what felt like an authentic and appropriate way.

The series concluded with *F.3.A.R* in 2011. The last entry featured contributions from horror luminaries John Carpenter and Steve Niles, further cementing the series' unimpeachable horror cred.

A different choice is to abandon the shooter model entirely and instead go for a more strategic, turn-based setting. That was the tack followed by Red Wasp Design with *Call of Cthulhu: The Wasted Land.* A turn-based game set during World War I, *The Wasted Land* picked up dark hints from several Mythos stories and fleshed them out, putting cthulhoid horrors on the battlefields of the Western Front. Designed for mobile platforms in conjunction with the Lovecraft experts at RPG publishers Chaosium, *The Wasted Land* puts the player into conflict with enemy soldiers, Dark Young, and other horrors as they trace a deranged scientist who has learned forbidden knowledge (of course) and seeks to exterminate humanity. With a play aesthetic of the classic *X-Com* games, *The Wasted Land* swaps out fast-twitch combat for turn-based strategy and patience. As for the military aspect, much of the game takes place on the battlefields of World War I, with the horrors of indescribable monstrosities from the stars mixing seamlessly with the horrors of trench warfare. The result is an engrossing, visually appealing game that leverages its military setting to contextualize and heighten the horror of the main plot and antagonists.

While military-themed horror video games are relatively rare, those examples that do make it through production are often standouts. As difficult as successfully meshing the demands of horror with the necessities of game production might be, those who have succeeded at it have reaped both financial and critical rewards.

And of course, scared the hell out of a whole new generation while they were at it.

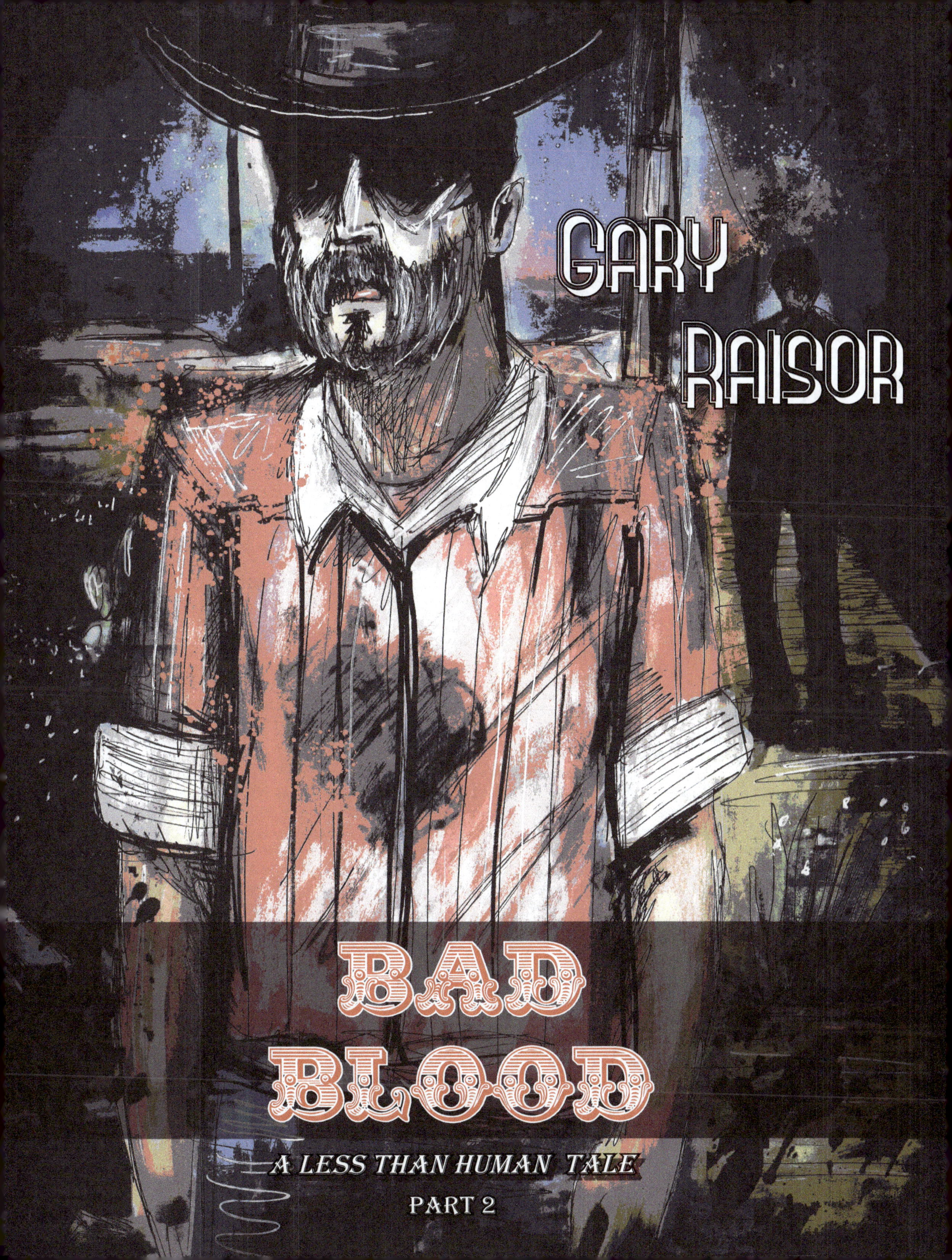

GARY RAISOR

BAD BLOOD

A LESS THAN HUMAN TALE

PART 2

The woman pointed at the gas gauge. "Is that right? That can't be right."

Earl's lips thinned as he followed her finger. He couldn't slide an ace between the needle and the E. "That blonde bastard chewed my ear off about how much this car cost. And he couldn't put in a dollar's worth of gas?"

The woman looked him over, stopping at his bare feet. "That toe looks sore."

"I think it's broken."

"Well, thank you, Mister Broken Toe, whoever you are."

"No thanks necessary. I was just stealing a car." He tipped his hat. "Name's Earl." He wrestled the Caddy around a corner, pointed it away from town. "Who the hell are you two and, more importantly, who's that crazy son of a bitch back there?"

"I'm Phoebe Ann. That's Janey." The woman dabbed at her bleeding nose. "That crazy son of a bitch back there goes by the name of Autie."

Earl smiled at Janey, pointed at her teddy bear. "Who's your friend?"

The little girl smiled back, signed something at Earl.

"What'd she say?"

"Said his name is *Pooh*, and he needs a *Bandaid*."

"We all do. We get shed of this mess, you think maybe *Pooh* would like a milkshake?"

Janey's smile grew to a giggle as she signed.

Phoebe Ann translated. "She says you're silly. *Pooh* only eats honey."

They drove in silence for a few seconds. "I ask you a question, Earl? Where's your boots?"

"I lost them in a creek. Chasing after a wolf. Long story." Earl wanted to give her a dirty look, but her nose was still leaking red. "You mind doing something about the blood on your face?"

"Why?"

"I've got kind of a thing about blood."

"What kind of thing?"

"A bad thing." He looked at her evenly. "Trust me, you don't want to know."

She grabbed a couple of cigarette butts from the ashtray and jammed them up her nostrils. Her fix looked kind of comical, but it stopped the bleeding.

"The nearest gas station is Lucky's," Earl said. "That's about twenty miles from here. I doubt we got the gas for that."

"So what's the plan, Wolf Man Broken Toe?"

"I've got a car. Broke down. If I can get us to it, I can siphon out some gas."

"You don't sound too sure."

"We'd have to go off road. I don't know this old Caddy'll make the trip. There's a storm coming, too. It catches us…"

Before Earl could say more, Phoebe Ann yanked the steering wheel. The car shot off the road and made for the open scrub-land.

Earl battled the car, trying to keep it pointed in a straight line. "You trying to get us killed?"

"We run out of gas on the highway, it's a done deal. Autie's pissed. He'll drive up and shoot you. Might scalp you, too."

"We don't want that. I'm kinda particular about my hair. What about you and the kid?" Earl kept wrestling with the steering wheel.

"He won't do anything to us, not until he gets what he wants."

"What's that?"

"Long story. I'll tell you later. If there is a later."

Earl didn't have time to argue. The Caddy's suspension was 1959 and it lost traction in the loose, powdery dirt every time he made any sudden turns.

Before long, headlights appeared in the rearview.

Earl adjusted the mirror. "Uh oh, looks like your boyfriend spotted us."

The pursuing headlights in the rearview were doing a lot of bouncing. But they drew steadily closer.

"What the hell is he driving?" Phoebe Ann asked, looking back.

"Looks like a *Winnebago*."

"No shit." A few seconds later. "Can you tell what model?"

Earl waited for a flash of lightning. "I can't say for sure, but if I had to guess, I'd say it's the *Chieftain*."

Earl grinned. Phoebe Ann busted out laughing.

"What's so funny?"

"Is that an Atlanta Braves pennant on his antenna?"

"I believe it is."

The *Winnebago* grew closer in the rearview. Bouncing over the rough patches, the RV was an elephant in a steeplechase. Earl's only consolation was that every time the cowboy popped up off the seat, the son of a bitch winced. Probably had some busted ribs. To go with those busted balls.

"Earl, you packing by any chance?"

"No ma'am, lost my piece in a creek."

"Knowing Autie, he's got a backup piece around here somewhere." She reached under her seat, felt around, and came up with an old hogleg *Colt*. "Yep. He keeps this one for sentimental reasons."

"Yeah, sentimental, that's what I said first time I seen him. Probably cries over sick puppies and such." Earl eyed the beat-up pistol. "Will that thing even shoot?"

"Yeah, I fired it one time. It shoots a little to the left…"

"Like an inch or two?"

"More like a foot." Phoebe Ann cleared her throat. "Or two."

"Is it even loaded?"

"No."

"Well, I reckon we can always throw it at him," Earl said, "if we want to get that close."

While Earl did his best to avoid wrapping the car around the rock formations rushing up out of the dark, the woman jimmied open the glovebox with a screwdriver she found on the floorboard. She pulled out the contents.

Earl shot her a glance. "Any cartridges?"

"About half a box," Phoebe Ann replied. "Along with—" she finished counting "—seventy-three cents, a comb, and a *Trojan* still in the pack."

Earl's eyebrows shot up.

"That's odd, the *Trojan*'s got corn stuck to it." Phoebe Ann glanced at Earl. "Wolf Man, you okay? You look like

somebody just stepped on your pecker."

"I'm fine," Earl stammered. He regained his voice. "You gonna shoot Autie in front of the kid?"

"I'm thinking yeah. Insults don't seem to be doing the job." Phoebe Ann loaded the *Colt* like she knew what she was doing. "Close your eyes, Janey."

Snapping the cylinder into place, she turned and put three slugs in the *Winnebago*. The radiator began spewing steam.

"That's some pretty decent shooting." Earl cast a sideways glance at the woman holding the pistol. "Where'd you learn to handle a gun like that?"

"I used to do a little rabbit hunting back in Ohio when I was a kid."

The RV was starting to look a little winded. It dropped back.

Earl studied her for a second. "I ask you something?"

"If I'm such a good shot, why don't I shoot the guy chasing us? You wouldn't believe me if I told you."

"Try me," Earl said.

"Bullets won't stop him. Even if I could hit him."

Earl, without batting an eye: "Not even silver ones?"

"Yeah, those would do the job. Got any?"

"Nope."

Phoebe Ann's features filled with grim determination as she turned and fired three more times. Looking grim with cigarette butts poking out of one's nose wasn't easy, but she managed. Little stars dotted the *Winnebago* windshield in a fistful of seconds. Two bullets went wide of the driver. The last one caught him in the forehead. There was a flutter of fake blonde curls and Autie slumped over the steering wheel. The RV coasted to a halt.

Earl stopped the car. "You sure that bullet didn't work? He looks deader than disco to me."

"Wait for it," Phoebe Ann replied.

The cowboy sat up, shook his head. The RV resumed moving.

"Something's starting to bother me, Earl." Phoebe Ann shook the spent casings onto the floorboard. "You just saw me shoot a guy in the head, and that guy shakes it off like it was a bad day at work. You didn't bat an eye. I ask you a question, Earl?"

"How come I'm not filling my drawers?"

"You're a mind reader." She put more bullets in the gun, snapped the cylinder closed. "If I was to put one of these in your head, what would happen?"

"Well, let's say I might forget what I had for breakfast. Also it wouldn't do much for these seat covers."

Phoebe Ann cocked the pistol. "What are you?"

"Nothing special, just your everyday, run of the mill parasitic vampire. Kinda like you and ol' Autie back there. I figure my partner made both you guys. Same as he did me."

"Your partner is a sadistic monster."

Earl sighed. "Yes ma'am, the west is overrun with undead sons of bitches. No offense, ma'am."

She leaned over and sniffed him. "Got a news flash for you, Wolfman Earl. You're human."

"That can't be. I haven't been human in a hundred years."

"Yeah? Then why's the toe not healing?"

"Son of a bitch."

Less than a minute later, the *Winnebago* shuddered to a halt in a cloud of steam. The stuff was pouring out the front. The blonde dandy jumped out of the RV and ran around to the back.

"What the hell is he doing now?"

A few seconds later, the cowboy came around riding something with two wheels.

"Is that what I think it is?" Earl said.

"Only if you think it's a *Vespa*."

"Are you goddamned kidding me? We're being chased by a son of a bitch on a *Vespa*. This guy's really starting to piss me off." Earl wheeled the Caddy around. "Alright, new plan."

"What's on your mind, Earl?"

"We need gas." Earl squared up his hat. "Only one place to get it. From the *Winnebago*. Tell Janey to get low. You 'bout got that *Colt* loaded?"

"Yep. We going True Grit on Autie?"

"You got it, sister."

Phoebe Ann signed to Janey. The kid dove into the backseat and disappeared from sight.

"Phoebe Ann, would you mind feeling around under the seats?"

"What are we looking for? More bullets?"

"Nope. Garden hose. I got a feeling this guy doesn't spend much time at the pump."

"You looking for something like this?" Phoebe Ann held up a five-foot coil of green.

"Yep. I knew this guy was a gas thief."

"That's your plan? Siphoning gas from the RV?" Phoebe Ann shook her head. "He'll never let you get that close."

"Maybe he will. If I can piss him off a little more. Got an idea. Hand me that comb." With those words, Earl took off his Stetson, stood up in the seat and started combing his hair. "Ow! Think I hit a tangle. Better hand me the brush, honey!"

The *Vespa* sounded like an angry hornet as it launched.

Still raised up above the windshield, Earl called out to the *Vespa*. "Fill your hands, you son of a bitch."

"I think his hands are already full," Phoebe Ann pointed out. "And I'm pretty sure he already knows he's a son of a bitch. Also I don't think he can hear you."

"You always talk this much?"

"Only at the wrong times. Mostly when I'm scared. He's going to fill your radiator full of holes, you know."

"We'll see." With that, Earl dropped back into his seat and punched the gas.

The Caddy and the *Vespa* rushed each other. Bullet holes dotted the windshield on Earl's side.

"He really doesn't like you."

"Counting on it." Earl peeked over the dashboard. "Get a man pissed enough, he don't think straight. Right now, all this guy wants to do is to kill me."

"Which he can, since you're human."

"Thanks for reminding me." More holes appeared in the Caddy windshield.

Phoebe Ann raised up and snapped off a shot. The

cowboy anticipated her and laid the *Vespa* over on its side. The shot went wide. Phoebe Ann fired again. That one sparked the scooter's gas tank. Gas began spraying from a hole.

"Damn, he's fast," Earl said.

"Yeah, but he's not fireproof." Phoebe Ann snapped off another shot. A spark and the scooter sprouted flames. The flames turned into a fireball.

"Everybody hang on." Earl spun the steering wheel. The car began swapping ends. Spinning like a top, the Caddy's rear-end smacked the *Vespa*. The two-wheeler and its flaming passenger went airborne.

Earl slammed on the brakes. The Caddy stopped spinning, righted itself like a barge in rough waters. It was now pointed toward the *Winnebago*.

The *Vespa* came down hard and did somersaults for a good twenty or thirty yards, kicking up dust along the way. Somehow it was still burning when it came to rest.

"Everyone stay down." Earl threw the Caddy into reverse.

Autie struggled up next to the pile of burning metal and fired at the Caddy backing his way. His aim was shaky, and still bullets splatted into the trunk.

Still firing, the cowboy scrambled up into a pile of boulders. Suddenly he turned and began shooting at something else.

Earl felt a thump as he backed over the scooter. "He won't be chasing us on that thing." He paused. In the rearview, he'd caught a glimpse of coyotes boiling over a rise.

"This has been one strange night." He threw the car in drive. "Let's see if we can round up some go-juice."

***

Earl smiled at Janey as he siphoned gas from the *Winnebago* into the Caddy. "How long she been a deaf mute?"

"Since three," Phoebe Ann said.

In the distance, they could see the cowboy running toward them. More like a rapid hobble. A long way off, he fired. His bullet fell short.

"Sweetheart, you take off those high heels," Earl shouted at the cowboy, "you'll be able to run faster." He turned back to Phoebe Ann. "What happened to Janey, a fever?"

"No, I think our blonde friend there killed everyone in her house, right in front of her. She hasn't spoken a word since."

The cowboy's next bullet was closer. "Alright, we gotta go." Earl yanked out the hose and tossed it in the backseat. He vaulted in, hit the gas, bounced the car over some ruts. The old Caddy squealed like something in pain.

"How'd the kid get away?"

"Nobody knows. A biker found her wandering along I-90 over by Sturgis. She was by herself. Whenever anyone asks her what happened, all she does is make the sign for wolf."

"Really." Earl glanced back at the kid. The hair on the back of his neck was standing up again. He managed to keep his voice casual. "A wolf saved her. That musta been one special wolf?"

"Yeah, when anybody asks her about it, she makes the sign for white. I've never even seen a white wolf, have you?"

Earl didn't answer. A few minutes later, he looked over, saw something cutting through the tall buffalo grass off to their left. Whatever it was, it was gaining steadily on their floundering Caddy. A pennant for *Red Man* chewing tobacco on an antenna poked out above the sea of green like the fin of a shark cruising in for the kill.

A *Vespa* slipped out of the grass behind them. The scooter was pink. The rider was the cowboy.

"Son of a bitch! His and her *Vespas*. I should've checked the *Winnebago*."

The cowboy tipped his hat at them, revealed a wig so curled from being singed in the fire it looked like a bad perm.

Phoebe Ann raised up, took a shot at the scooter, but it had dropped back out of range. Earl spun the Caddy around and made for the cowboy. Their pursuer made no move to escape. Instead he stopped out in the open. Grinning, he calmly unstrapped something from his back.

"Oh shit, get down," Earl yelled.

A flash and the lobe of Phoebe Ann's ear disappeared in a spray of red.

She dropped back into her seat, clutching the side of her head. "He's got a rifle?"

"Yep. Came with that ugly ass scooter I'm guessing." Earl spun the Caddy around and tried to put some distance between them and their pursuer. He wasn't having any success. The *Vespa* maintained its distance.

"What year is that half-dollar you pulled out of the glovebox?"

Phoebe Ann peered at the coin. "Says '63 on it."

"You know what that means, don't you?"

Her face went blank for a second. "Holy shit, it's silver."

"Yep. Up to '64, they made 'em out of mostly silver. We need to find someplace where we can get a fire going."

Up ahead was something that sort of resembled a giant *Chia Pet,* and Earl made for it. As he drew closer, he could see an old Chevy truck that had once been green. Now it was worn down by sand and weather and it had a couple of pine trees growing out of its skeleton. There must have been twenty more cars and trucks scattered about that had outlived their usefulness.

Scraping up against the trees, Earl fought the steering wheel, as he managed to wrestle the car around. He left the shaggy bark streaked with candy-apple red.

"You could've missed that tree," Phoebe Ann commented.

"Yeah, I could have. But I want to keep Autie pissed."

The Caddy threaded its way through the graveyard of bleached-out steel and busted glass.

The *Vespa* edged a little closer. That was when Phoebe Ann raised up and started shooting again. She fanned the *Colt* like she'd done before and bullets sprayed the scooter. Glass shattered. Paint chips flew. One slug found a front tire, causing the scooter to wobble. It began bouncing on the rough ground, then weaving, then flipping, kicking up gouts of dust before ending up on its back next to a 1960 *Nash Rambler* that had been cut in two. Someone had planted flowers in the back half, Earl noticed. Looked like Black-eyed Susans.

"I don't care how many times that son of a bitch gets airborne, it never gets old." Her hands a blur, Phoebe Ann reloaded. This time the bullets bit into the *Vespa's* exposed gas tank. The sound reminded Earl of BBs plinking a tin can.

The two-wheeler coughed once, as though it needed to be excused, then disappeared behind a curtain of flame.

The driver was on fire when he stood up. It looked to be another four alarmer.

Apparently oil and gas *was* hard to get out of suede. The rider rolled around on the ground, first one direction then the other, until the flames were all out. He stood up, smoking. A second later, he popped right back into flames, like one of those trick candles on a birthday cake. He hit the dirt again. This time it took a while before the cowboy climbed to his feet, and Earl felt his sphincter unclench a little… until the hatchet-faced rider grabbed something off the ground. The man who favored yellow settled his hat on his head, which still had little wisps of smoke curling upward.

"Get down," Phoebe Ann yelled, "he's found the rifle."

A bullet punched into the Caddy's rear end. The car jerked. Whatever the blonde killer was shooting at them with, it damned sure didn't sound like no BB gun plinking a tin can this time.

"That rifle sounds big, like maybe a .243." Earl snuck a peek back. A flash and his hat was pinned to the windshield for a second. He grabbed the Stetson when it dropped to the dash and returned it to his head.

Earl put the hammer down and the powerful V-8 surged forward, fishtailing in the loose dirt. Suddenly he found himself trying to turn the corner by a windmill. The junkyard made sense now. All the vehicles back there must belong to whoever owned this windmill.

There was a sign on the windmill: a happy little buckaroo sitting on a pony. It was a sign that promised the adventure of a lifetime.

At the moment, Earl was having the adventure of a lifetime as he clipped the windmill, tearing out the supports and sending the happy little buckaroo and his pony crashing to earth.

Earl barely steered the Caddy out from under.

They'd stumbled onto a dude ranch, a place that took tourists for trailrides in the badlands.

Behind them, their pursuer squeezed off another shot. A back tire began unraveling.

Earl plowed through a corral fence, taking down the resale value of the car some more. Wood splintered, a steer horn snapped off. His forehead smacked the steering wheel and the horn began playing *Yellow Rose of Texas* as the car swapped ends. There wasn't much Earl could do except hit the brakes and hold on while horse after horse was mowed down in a tangle of flailing limbs. Luckily, most were knocked to the side. One went over the hood. Another almost ended up in the backseat with the kid. Still, it appeared the car was going to make it through without killing any of the animals.

That was, until Earl saw the kiddy pony. The one

pictured on the windmill. Old and fat, it didn't move. Maybe it was asleep. Maybe it was stupid. Or maybe it would rather commit suicide than let another fat-assed tourist kid ride it. Anyway they hit the pony head on with a squishy thud and it went down like a duck at a shooting gallery, lodging under the car and lifting the Caddy's front end completely off the ground.

Earl tried to back up. No luck. He even tried to force the car over the pony. No luck. The pony was simply too fat, the traction too poor. They were stuck.

Up at the ranchhouse, the porch began squeezing out barking dogs. Lights popped on. Earl had a feeling the cavalry was about to ride over the hill and he grinned. These ranchers were a tough lot. They'd shoot on sight, ask questions later.

The ranchhouse door creaked open and Earl got his first look at the cavalry. His grin faded. His reinforcements consisted of an old man in pee-stained longjohns, with a rifle and a kerosene lantern. The old man looked to be about eighty and seemed less than eager to pry his scrawny ass out of the doorway, but he had an old woman close behind, who kept pushing him. She had on some kind of face cream that Earl had seen on TV one time. It was green and was supposed to lift your face. Take years off your appearance. Earl decided she needed at least another quart of the stuff.

After a little more prodding, the man raised his kerosene lantern, fired the rifle into the air and yelled, "Who's out there?"

There was sour look on his face when he turned back to the old woman to see if he'd done good. His answer was a bullet through his lantern, then his skull, setting his head on fire. He fell back against the old woman, dead before he hit the ground. She leaned down to look at him, unsure of what had happened. That move proved tragic.

Within seconds, her head was ablaze, too. Apparently that face cream not only made a person younger looking, it could be used to start a fire.

Several of the ranch hands had raced to the bunkhouse door to see what all the commotion was about. They were gunned down where they stood. None of them caught on fire, though.

The cowboy slapped another clip into his rifle, began walking toward the Cadillac. It was a leisurely walk and yet it covered the distance quickly.

"He's coming. I need more shells," Phoebe Ann yelled over the screams of the burning woman.

Earl fumbled around under the seats, came up with an empty *Jack Daniels* bottle and three lone bullets that had somehow escaped their brethren. Phoebe Ann snatched them from his hand. While she was reloading, the old woman streaked past their car. The next shot from the dark kicked Earl's Stetson into the air before he even heard the rifle's flat crack bounce off the barn. The echo was still dancing in his ears when he watched his hat light in the water trough. It appeared his hat was fonder of water than a Mallard.

Punching the gas, Earl shifted between reverse and drive, still trying to rock the car off the pony. The car wouldn't budge. He could hear the pony's hooves beating a tattoo against the undercarriage, though.

Earl eased up on the gas pedal. He was only burying the back wheels, anyway. A few more inches and the rear-end would be sitting flat on the ground.

Another chunk of lead nicked Earl's right ear, punched through the windshield and scattered the dust ahead of them.

All the animals, except for the trapped pony, were hopping and bucking as more shots came from the darkness and smacked into the car. It was the damndest thing Earl had ever seen; the horses were too terrified to leave the corner of the corral they had crowded into. He'd seen horses run back into a burning barn. So what the hell could scare them so much they stayed in one spot?

Finally, the cloud of dust Earl had kicked up drifted over them. He grabbed his ear, realized it was bleeding. Green around the gills, he thought about looking at it in the rearview. Then thought better of it.

They still needed cover. The problem with the dust, it was thin, and the cowboy's next shot barely missed the little girl, who had popped up to see what was going on. Yanking her down by the straps of her overalls, Earl floored the gas, throwing up heavy roostertails of dust that finally hid them. He knew their cover wouldn't last long, but it was all he could do at the moment.

Throwing open the car door, Earl took another look at the back axle. It was barely an inch off the ground now. Once it touched, the Caddy wasn't going anywhere, even if they could get free of the pony. He heard the other door open.

"Where you going?" he whispered as Phoebe Ann slipped from the car and crawled to edge of the dust cloud.

"To give our blonde friend a shooting lesson."

At the edge of the dust cloud, she stretched out on the ground and took aim at the impossibly distant target. Taking a breath, she held it, steadied her hands, squeezed off a shot. A heartbeat later, the approaching figure was flung up and backward, landing in a loose-limbed sprawl. His boots twitched like lazy dogs trying to scratch.

Behind Earl, the kid popped up. He pushed her down and she popped right back up. After several more tries he realized he'd have better luck shoving toothpaste back in the tube, so he hung her from the headrest by her overall straps. Dangling several inches above the floorboard, her feet began kicking as she worked on getting loose.

When Earl turned back, he saw the lanky cowboy had gotten right back up and was continuing toward them.

"Shit, need to shoot him in the head." Phoebe Ann steadied the large caliber pistol in hands that didn't seem large enough to hold it.

The *Colt* jumped.

Blond curls fluttered in the distance, and, this time, the cowboy clutched his face and dropped to his knees, as though he'd suddenly decided he needed to stop right where he was and pray for forgiveness.

She put another bullet into the figure, again knocking him down.

A few seconds later, he climbed right back to his feet.

Phoebe Ann looked over at Earl, desperation in her eyes. "I couldn't gauge the wind. It kept changing."

There was nothing Earl could do about the fat pony lodged under the car, either. There was a pickup on jacks parked over by the ranchhouse. "Can you check out the truck?" he asked.

Keeping low, Phoebe Ann detoured by the burning rancher and grabbed his rifle. She took a look at the truck before she crept back to the Caddy.

"What's that truck look like?" Earl stared at his foot. A piece of broken glass protruded next to his broken toe.

"Looks good. Probably runs like a top. Soon as they get the transmission back in."

"Shit." Earl could only watch wistfully while the fire consumed it. No help there. The old woman, now fully engulfed in flames and shrieking at the top of her lungs, was hopping around like a demented firefly. She'd already run into the house several times already, setting it on fire, too. Probably just a matter of time till she hit the bunk-house and then the barn.

A bullet came from the dark and hit the old woman. Instead of going down, her shrieks grew louder. Became ear shattering. The bullet had only wounded her in the leg and she was running around in circles. The cowboy fired again. He hit her in her good leg.

She stood still and continued screaming.

Finally a third shot came from the dark, blowing the comb on the back of her head into the barn and cutting her bubbling shrieks off.

A "You're welcome" followed by laughter floated out of the distance.

Ignoring the laughter, Earl looked around, noticed the dust had about settled. They were going to have to make a run for it on foot. In his case, a hobble. His little toe was as big as a full-grown rattler's head.

Gritting his teeth, he reached for the little girl.

But she wasn't where he'd left her. She'd wriggled loose. Before Earl could lay his hands on her, she scrambled out and took off across the corral like greased lightning, pig-tails flying as she wove in and out of the milling horses. She was quick. There was no way he could catch her.

Earl saw what she was after—his *Stetson*. He yelled at her to let it be, even though he knew she couldn't hear him.

Fishing the hat out of the water-trough, Janey began working her way back to the car. The frightened horses bore down on her, then, a second before they'd trample her, the herd split suddenly, flowing around her like creek water around a boulder.

For some reason Earl had the impression the horses were trying to avoid hitting her. Even though they smelled blood and fire. Before that thought could take serious root, another shot came from out of the dark. The blonde killer had spotted the kid and was shooting into the herd, drop-ping horse after horse, trying to make one fall on her.

A white gelding sprouted a wound in its neck. Spewing gouts of red into the dust, it reared and pitched sideways, barely missing the child.

Before it died, it spasmed, catching the little girl in the face with a hoof, sending her rolling end over end. She fetched up against a fence post, covered with blood. Not moving.

Earl was convinced her skull was crushed.

Phoebe Ann let go with a strangled scream and started toward the kid, and it took all of Earl's strength to hold her back.

From the darkness, they could hear the sound of laughing.

Clutching the Stetson and *Pooh Bear* in a headlock, the child popped up, a little pigtailed jack-in-the-box, and gamely continued toward the car. The cowboy stopped laughing and began shooting, kicking up dust all around her.

"Don't fall for it," Earl said. "He's not going to shoot the kid. He's only trying to get you out in the open."

Phoebe Ann started shooting back, forcing the cowboy to take cover.

The kid's steps were wobbly, but she made it over to them.

Dabbing at the kid's bloody face as she leaned against the car, Phoebe Ann realized most of the red belonged to the horse. There was definitely going to be a good sized knot on her forehead.

"That kid's got sand," Earl said to Phoebe Ann.

Sand or not, Earl was about to give the kid what for as he grabbed for his hat. But instead of handing it over, she dropped to her knees, wedged it beneath the remaining back tire. She jumped back in and, this time, when Earl stamped the gas, the Caddy rolled free with a spine-crushing jolt.

Earl saw the little pony's head was resting at an unnatural angle. No more fat-assed, spoiled tourist brats yelling giddyup and digging their heels into its ribs. It was dead.

"Sorry, little buddy." To Earl's amazement, the pony climbed to its feet. Nope, it wasn't dead. Just skinned up bad. The Shetland hauled ass to the other side of the corral.

There it stood trembling while Earl did a U-turn, throwing up a ton of dust to cover them.

He leaned out to scoop up his hat.

With the blown tire slapping, they put some distance between themselves and the unstoppable cowboy.

***

A quarter of a mile later, they were flying.

Earl was using his battered Stetson to wave *adios* to the walking man. He slapped his hat on, punched the lighter about to light up a smoke, when they popped over a hill. That was when he heard Phoebe Ann scream.

He could only watch as a sea of green and brown rushed at them. The old couple from the ranch were into more than putting tourists in touch with nature and saddle sores—they were into organic gardening. The calming herb. Weed to be exact. The organic part was horse manure. In abundance. There must have been tons of the stuff covering the field, stinking to high heaven.

The car coasted to a halt.

After some wheel spinning, Earl climbed out to push the mired-down Caddy. The first thing he succeeded in doing was falling face first into the manure. He managed to find some that was fresh.

Spitting, he dug the slightly used grass out from between his teeth. "I don't think those horses are getting enough oats." The manure was packed in there good. He had to take out his teeth and beat them against the car.

The kid looked over at Earl and began doing something with her hands.

A pissed-off Earl asked Phoebe Ann if the kid was having some kind of fit from that kick in the head.

"She's never seen false teeth before," Phoebe Ann answered, fighting back a laugh. "She says your face is all green."

"Yeah, what's so damned funny about that?"

"She says without your teeth you look like *Kermit*, the frog."

"*Kermit* eats flies. Guess what I eat?" Earl snapped his false teeth closed an inch from the kid's nose.

While she was busy picking herself off the floorboard, he went back to pushing. He slipped, hit his chin on the car's door frame, and this time his teeth flew from his shirt pocket and scooted across the hood, fetching up against the one steer horn that remained.

"Serves you right for scaring a child," Phoebe Ann said.

"What about all the times she scared me?" Earl said, retrieving his teeth while surveying the car. He moved to the back, began pushing. No good. Without his teeth, he couldn't get his back into it. Gritting your gums wasn't the same.

The only part moving was the back wheels, and all they were doing was slinging more manure on him.

Only after Earl was thoroughly caked with horse biscuits did the kid jump from the backseat.

She walked over and stared up at him solemnly. Even on her tiptoes, she was still an inch shy of his belt buckle. Motioning for the smelly Earl to bend over, she gently removed his Stetson and again stuffed it beneath the back tire. Then she gave it a solid kick with her size-two *Pooh Bear* sandals, wedged it under there good.

"Why do you hate my hat?" Earl gave her a hurt look. "It never did anything to you."

***

Once they were free of the compost heap, they decided they'd better stop and dig out the spare. They couldn't risk getting stuck again. Earl put Phoebe Ann behind the wheel and hobbled around to the back of the car.

Popping the trunk lid, Earl was in for a shock; inside were two men. And one of them had a pistol pointed right at his face.

The old hustler half dove, half fell to the ground, slipping in something. No time to examine it closely, but the substance looked suspiciously like more horse shit.

Scrambling to the side of the car, he waited for the men to come after him.

After a few seconds, Earl edged closer to the trunk, wondering why nobody had made a move yet. By now he had a pretty good idea. He bounced a couple of rocks off the men just to be sure. Still nobody moving. That was good.

The guy who had scared Earl was a hugely overweight Cheyenne in chinos and a blue work shirt that had barbecue sauce on it. He had a rabbit's foot tied on a leather thong around his neck for luck. From under a mane of black hair, he was staring straight at Earl with a fierce expression, a cocked pistol in one hand and a half-eaten bag of *Doritos* in the other. From his lip the blackened remains of a joint still clung. His companion was a skinny old man in jeans and a suit coat. He had no right hand, but he held a can of dried-up bean dip in his left.

As Earl crept closer, his earlier suspicions were confirmed; both men had been murdered, shot through the head. Earl hated that they had been killed, even as he breathed a sigh of relief and hoped nobody had seen his one-and-a-half gainer. He wasn't that lucky.

The kid was grinning at him from the backseat. Tugging at Phoebe Ann, she again signed something.

"She says you hop a lot higher than *Kermit*," Phoebe Ann interpreted.

Earl did some signing of his own; a pantomime of a spanking. The little moon-face popped out of sight.

The old hustler decided they needed the dead man's pistol. Only problem was, he couldn't seem to get the dead man to turn loose of it. Apparently rigor mortis had set in. He and the dead man were making quite a racket struggling over the weapon.

Phoebe Ann heard and asked what he was doing back there.

"Just rootin' around for the jack," Earl answered with as much dignity as he could muster. "You two stay where you are. I got everything under control." He grabbed a canteen, rinsed off his false-teeth and popped them in. Munching a handful of *Doritos* from the bag, picking out the ones that weren't splattered with brains, he went to digging for the jack for real. As he went to turn away, he thought he saw something move. He froze. For an instant, Earl could swear the dead man's eyes had been following him.

Earl realized his nerves were getting the best of him. He grabbed another handful of *Doritos,* began munching while he set about changing the tire. Still, he couldn't shake the feeling that eyes were on him and he looked up—

—saw the kid staring hungrily at his *Doritos*. He ate a couple slowly before giving some to her. That callous treatment of his hat still had him bothered.

After the tire was changed, Earl yelled at Phoebe Ann to keep the kid down while he pulled the dead bodies out of the trunk.

When they drove off, Earl caught a glimpse of something moving in the rearview. A pack of coyotes were surrounding the bodies. No white wolf, though.

***

As Earl and Phoebe Ann topped a switchback, they heard a tire slapping. Earl threw his hat on the floorboard, then his teeth. Stopping, he climbed out, sure the spare had gone bad.

Except it wasn't the spare he'd heard…

…it was galloping horses.

They looked back, saw Autie had saddled a cow pony from the corral and was now riding hell-bent-for-leather after them.

That wasn't the worst of it. In his hand, he was holding the lead rope of another three horses, strung out behind him in a flat-out run.

"My God, what's he doing with all those horses?" Phoebe Ann stared at them with open-mouthed wonder.

"It's an old cavalry trick." Earl, too, watched the horses snake their way across the moonlit scrub. "I've done it myself, I'm ashamed to say. He'll ride that horse he's on to death, then he'll switch over to a fresher one. It's a mean-ass way to get someplace quick."

"Can he catch us like that?"

"In country like this, oh yeah."

Phoebe Ann tried to draw a bead on the rider. There wasn't much to shoot at, he was crouched low over his mount.

She lowered her rifle.

Earl's graveled voice was matter of fact. "It won't do you any good to shoot him. You've got to put him afoot. That means you shoot his horses, Phoebe Ann. Every damn last one of them."

"I don't know if I can do that." She sounded shocked at the idea.

"Here, let me to take a crack at it." Earl reached for the rifle.

She snatched it away. "I'll do it, alright." She adjusted the rifle sights, raising them as high as they would go. At eight hundred yards, the horse Autie rode wasn't even the size of a thumbnail. And it was moving. Taking a deep breath and holding it, Phoebe Ann squeezed the trigger.

Two seconds later, the bullet skinned the animal's hindquarters, and it squealed, a high-pitched, almost human sound of pain that carried across the distance. The animal began bucking, throwing its rider.

"He's airborne again." Phoebe Ann cocked the rifle. "You figure there's still some gas soaked in that jacket of his? Let's see." She sparked a shot off a boulder inches from the rider. In seconds, he was on fire again.

The other horses bolted, dragging along the rider who clung to the lead rope.

After a bit, the fire spread to the rope, and rider was left holding a rope to nothing. He once more managed to put out the fire and get one of the horse stopped. He remounted. Within seconds, he was riding straight at them. The rider was closing the distance fast.

"Keep shooting," Earl shouted at her.

Slowly, reluctantly, Phoebe Ann put the rifle to her shoulder and fired again. Despite her reluctance, the 30-30 smacked the horse to earth. The rider followed, ass over elbows.

A moment later, the animal scrambled up, its heaving, sweat-covered flanks caked with dust. Blood poured from the horse's mouth.

"I was trying to nick his ear," Phoebe Ann said. "Make him stumble."

"You shot my horse," Autie shouted at her. "I didn't think you had it in you."

To her horror, the rider pulled his pistol and shot the animal in the head. The horse crumpled. He laid down behind the dead animal, rested his rifle on the saddle and began firing.

"When I get my hands on the kid, I'm going to skin her alive," the rider called out. "I've got a hundred bucks says she finds her voice."

Phoebe Ann fired twice more, puffs of dust flying up at the points of impact. "Can we go after him?"

"That's what he wants. He's got something up his sleeve."

A few minutes passed. "Alright, I'm getting bored." Autie whistled and the horses that had ran off appeared. "Back to Plan B."

"I knew it!"

"What?" Phoebe Ann said.

"He's put some of his blood in those horses. They'll do whatever he wants."

"Then what was the rope for?"

"To fool us."

Earl wasn't prepared for Phoebe Ann's next shots. The first horse, a small Pinto fell immediately as though the pins in its legs had been yanked out, while the other one, a beautiful medicine-hat stallion, staggered a couple of trembling steps before dropping. Even then, the animal didn't die right away. Earl could see its head jerking feebly while it struggled over and over to get to its feet. She fired again and the horse became still.

Tears were streaming down Phoebe Ann's face.

The rider was now left with one mount. The one he was riding. He and the horse hightailed it into the high grass.

"Let's go." Earl started the Caddy and eased out onto the plain.

10 minutes later

Autie was coming for them. He dug his spurs in, savagely forcing the animal past all endurance. Strings of saliva hung from its straining mouth as it tried to suck in air.

As it tried to keep going.

Something inside the animal ruptured. Blood colored the saliva.

Unable to stand such suffering, Phoebe Ann put a bullet between the wild, pain-filled eyes and it collapsed in a boneless heap.

But that wasn't the end of it. A second later, Earl saw something that made his own blood run cold—another string of red passed from the rider and entered the horse. It was something Earl had seen Steven Adler do, infest an animal with his own blood so he could make it do whatever he wanted.

Within seconds the horse lurched upright and the rider jumped back aboard. Even though the horse was missing an eye and about half its brain was poking out, it was still coming after them.

Earl hit the gas.

And immediately slammed on the brakes. They had come to the mouth of a dried-up arroyo. If he took the car in there, they'd be sitting ducks. Autie would get above them and pick them off at his leisure. Earl had no choice, he had to turn the Caddy around and head back the way they came. Straight at the blonde rider.

Earl motioned at Phoebe Ann to get ready.

But Autie had already jumped from his horse. He laid

down a hail of bullets, punching more stars in the windshield. Under this new barrage, the glass finally gave up the ghost. Peeling away, it flapped off into the night.

More muzzle flashes came from up ahead.

They ducked. Not fast enough, though. Earl's already shot-to-hell Stetson was a casualty. This time was a little different, though. This time a good chunk of his hair was plastered to the sweatband along with his blood. The hat was pinned to the backseat, creeping up, an ungainly bird that wanted nothing more than to fly away from all this noise. Just as the hat was about to get airborne, the kid pounced on it. But in doing so, her head had popped up above the seat.

Earl saw in the rearview and made a grab for her.

She dodged him. She probably thought she was going to be strung up from the headrest again.

Autie saw and lined Earl up in the rifle sights. He had Earl dead to rights.

Yanking the car to one side, Earl caused the bullet meant for him to clip the headrest.

Two things happened almost simultaneously:

First, the two sets of fuzzy dice rolled onto the back floorboard along with the kid and his hat. Second, the ricochet caught Earl in the meaty part of his arm, causing him to jerk the Caddy off course.

Earl risked a quick look back to make sure the kid was okay. She was. As he grabbed for his hat, he couldn't resist looking to see what the dice had rolled. He wished he hadn't. The first set showed snake eyes—two aces. The second set was an eight. For some reason those numbers meant something to him...

He looked over, saw Phoebe Ann wasn't doing so hot; her forehead had been split open by glass slivers from the shattered rearview. Still trying to return Autie's fire, she poked the rifle out the window. That was a mistake. A bullet hit the *Winchester* and ricocheted into the dash. Glass and plastic exploded. Earl caught most of it in the face. The bridge of his nose snapped.

Earl was swallowing blood and his eyes were filled with tears while he tried to run Autie down. Barely able to see, all he managed to do was sideswipe the animal, setting it back on its haunches.

The Caddy made it past, but not before a bullet found the front passenger tire. Bad as that was, one found the radiator, too. There was a hissing sound and the odor of antifreeze was suddenly in the air, sweet and metallic.

Autie remounted and started after them, his smiling teeth startlingly white in his dust-covered face.

***

With a growing sense of dread, Earl watched the needle on the heat gauge creep into the red while he nursed the car along. The old hustler was hurting bad. "I can't decide which hurts more, my toe, my ear, my scalp, my nose, or my leg. Which now has glass buried in it."

"I always heard that two injuries were supposed to cancel each other out."

"That might be true. Even on four. The trouble is I got five. It's not an even number. Nothing is canceling out. I wish whoever told me that shit was here right now. I'd be more than glad to show them it's a bald-faced lie."

Trailing the car, Autie stayed just out of range.

Finally the Caddy's overheated motor began stuttering, and Earl had no choice but to stop and let it cool.

That was when the rider made another charge.

Spurring his heavily lathered mount, he made straight for them. The sound of the horse's hooves echoed off the hills. It sounded as though an entire regiment was bearing down on them.

"I'm going to see if I can hit his horse," Phoebe Ann told Earl. "We've got to get that son of a bitch on foot. Otherwise, he's just going to shoot us to pieces."

"We don't have too many pieces left."

Leveling the 30-30, Phoebe Ann wiped blood from her eyes and shot at the animal. Dust flew up several yards behind it. She shot again.

And missed.

"Start the car," she shouted at Earl, "something's wrong with the rifle."

After several anxious moments, Earl managed to fire up the big V-8 and they lurched off.

He had no idea how far they'd get. The gas hand, the heat gauge needle, weren't even quivering now but lay there like something dead, and the radiator was only hissing softly, nearly empty, as it leaked a trail of thin white vapor into the night. But what truly scared Earl was the sound the overheated motor was making. It was knocking something fierce, on the verge of locking up. It sounded like someone was under there with a big old sledge-hammer, trying to break something. There were smells coming from up there, too. Not just fried antifreeze. Plastic and rubber. Even the paint on the hood was beginning to blister. It was just a matter of time till the old Caddy quit.

Up ahead, next to a couple of granite spires, Earl spotted a pack of coyotes milling about. They looked like the same ones he'd seen in the garage. No way to be sure, though.

Next to them were the murdered Indians who were in the trunk earlier.

"Do we have any more ammo?" Phoebe Ann asked, throwing down the rifle and grabbing the pistol.

"No, but I think I know where we can get some. Hang on."

Jamming on the brakes, Earl skidded to a halt next to the dead Cheyenne with the pistol that he'd hauled out of the trunk earlier. The dust continued on, a fast-moving train that blew past. Earl jumped out, put his foot on the man's arm and prepared to wrench the weapon loose. That was when the Indian winked at him and whispered, "Got any *Tums* on you, brother? That bean dip's got me all bloated."

Spooked, Earl jumped back and fell on his ass. Caked horse shit fell off.

"You folks'd better get going," the Indian said. "Or you'll spoil the surprise."

Earl needed no encouragement—he clambered in and hit the gas. The car sputtered away trying to catch the dust train.

As Autie's horse drew within range, the dead Cheyenne jumped up, let go with a fart, a blood-curdling war cry, and started shooting. Feet planted, shoulders squared, gun cupped in both hands, it was an awesome display of shooting prowess…

…except for one tiny little thing.

Every single one of the bullets missed their target. They sparked off the loose rocks behind the horse.

In front of the horse.

Beside the horse.

One bullet didn't hit anything at all.

"You never could shoot worth a shit," the one-handed Indian told his companion with a sneer, as he threw the can of bean-dip. "If you could, we wouldn't be dead now. Way you shoot, you'd better hope they got food-stamps in the Happy Hunting Ground, else you're gonna be one hungry motherfucker."

"If you hadn't fell asleep, that white devil wouldn't have got the jump on us. So shut up, you're messing up my aim."

"What aim?"

The overweight Cheyenne shot again, his last shot, and it hit a bush, causing a couple of quail to take flight. They startled the horse.

The animal stepped wrong and there was a pop, loud as a pistol shot. The animal's leg broke but it didn't go down right away. It tried to keep running, even though its shattered leg was coming apart, flopping like a wet rag as the hoof smacked the ground. A few more strides and the leg folded into an impossible angle, causing the cow pony to pitch forward in a clatter of rocks, throwing the rider and rolling over him.

While the rider climbed to his feet, slowly this time, the Indians did something that made Earl grin—the hugely overweight Cheyenne and his one-handed companion mooned Autie. The moons were full-out moons, too. Pants to the ankles. Pimply butts in the wind.

The sight of the naked red butts waggling back and forth on the hill enraged the blonde rider so much he began pumping bullet after bullet into the dead men. A slug caught the big one in the arm and he dropped the bean dip. It began its erratic trip down the hill, bouncing from rock to rock.

Both men jerked when the bullets punched through them, then they fell forward with their pants still down around their ankles.

A series of war whoops erupted from them, followed by high cackling laughter that floated out across the hills. The sound was picked up by the coyotes who joined in. It was an eerie serenade. The hair on the back of Earl's neck stood up for the second time tonight.

While Custer was busy reloading, a couple of the coyotes ran over and touched noses with the dead men on the ground. Something red passed between them. It looked like blood.

Before the rider could raise his rifle, the entire coyote pack scattered into the night. Within seconds, it was as though they'd never been.

The bean dip finished its trip down the hill and ended up at Autie's boots. He ground it underfoot.

Earl decided he'd seen enough and he floored the gas

pedal, risking a broken axle as he sent the car rocketing across the prairie floor. A flat ricochet reached his ears a second after a puff of dust kicked up off to one side. The dead Indians had bought them some time. The two men had obviously been infested by a blood-eater, and that brought up two questions. Which one was it? And why was it helping them?

Questions that couldn't be answered at this time.

Earl stood on the gas until he was sure they were out of range. He noticed the chilly air was forcing the heat gauge down a notch. It was their first real break, but they weren't out of the woods yet.

Once they were safe, Earl took a deep breath, pushed his own punctured, dust-covered, smelly Stetson back on his head and looked over at Phoebe Ann.

She was quietly crying.

"That was some pretty fair shooting you done back there," Earl said, trying to cheer her up. "You made that son of a bitch eat a lot of sand."

"All I'm doing is pissing him off," Phoebe Ann answered.

"Pissed off don't even come close."

Phoebe Ann wiped the tears out of her eyes, leaving a patch of clean on her bloody, dust-covered face. "Sorry, I'm very upset at having to shoot so many horses. I can't stop him," she said, "no matter what I do."

Squirming in his seat, Earl had no idea what to say to that. He reached in his pocket, handed over his handkerchief. It was the only thing of his that wasn't covered with either blood or horse manure. "Your shooting saved our asses back there… ain't nobody but Annie Oakley can shoot like that," he finally said.

"It's been a long time since anybody called me by that name." Her hands were shaking now and she leaned out of the car to throw up.

"How long has it been?" he asked when she pulled her head back in.

"I figure better than fifty years." Reaching in her pocket she produced a piece of laminated newspaper.

"What you go there?"

"My obit."

GREENVILLE DAILY ADVOCATE
Annie Oakley died in Greenville, Ohio, November 3rd, 1926, after an eight-week bout with pernicious anemia.

"Sounds to me like Annie Oakley might have had a blood-parasite." Earl cast a quick look over his shoulder. Framed against the moon, he caught a dwindling glimpse of Autie walking after them, rifle slung over one shoulder, munching on a bag of *Doritos*. The bean dip must have been too dry.

"Not to be nosy or nothin', Annie," Earl asked, "but how come old George Armstrong Custer is after you?"

"Not me. The girl here," Annie answered, fighting to get herself under control. "I just keep getting in the way." She handed Earl a *Bandaid*. "Found this in the glovebox."

"I wouldn't know where to put it," he answered. "Give it to Janey for *Pooh*."

After they'd been driving for a few minutes, Earl hit a patch of rough ground, forcing him to slow down. That caused the car to begin overheating again and he had to stop to let it cool. Over the ticking, popping engine noises, he asked, "So you going to tell me why Custer wants to kill the girl?"

Annie looked away. "Money. George'll do anything for a dollar. If you don't have a dollar, he'll do it for free. Long as he gets to kill an Indian."

Earl wasn't buying. "Now, why would Custer come all the way to Deadwood to kill one little Indian girl?"

"I guess you don't know about the war going on?"

"Hell, there's always a war going on somewheres. People don't need much of a reason to kill each other." Earl studied the solemn little girl in the backseat. Something about her face was familiar.

"This one's not somewhere. This one's right here." Annie reached out a shaking hand to the little girl, who took it.

The child wiped away Annie's tears with a grubby little paw, leaving behind more dirt streaks.

"The Indian casinos have been taking a bite out of Vegas business," Annie said, "and there's certain folks who don't cotton to that." She stared out into the night, her dark eyes filled with anger. "They don't want Indians to have a piece of the pie, so they put out some contracts. I guess they figure a few killings and the hard-line Indians'll see reason."

Earl was fidgeting with his Stetson, trying to get it to set on his head right. That last bullet had really put a hurt on it. "I'm guessin' the kid belongs to one of the tribal elders who needs some persuading? Somebody's granddaughter?"

"You might say that. Her name's Janey. Janey Tatanka-Iyotanka." She pulled the small girl close, began rocking her.

"Her last name is *Sitting Bull*?" Earl's eyes grew wide. "As in the Sitting Bull who kicked Custer's ass at Little Bighorn?"

"That's right."

"Holy shit." Earl was starting to get the picture and he shook his head in disbelief. "No wonder he wants her so bad. How long you been watchin' over Sitting Bull's people now?" He did some quick arithmetic, answered his own question. "Damn, girl, I calculate a hundred years. Don't you think that's long enough?"

"Long enough'll be when Custer's dead. Really dead."

"I got news for you, Custer was rotting meat when one of those blood eatin' things got up inside him at Little Bighorn. I heard it crawled up his ass. Course that's probably just a story. You know how those things get started." A disgusted Earl was about ready to give up on his hat. It was a shapeless mess, filled with holes, caked with horse manure.

Earl threw the battered Stetson down on the seat. "Anyway, Custer's crazy mean on account of that scalping he got. It won't never heal. That blood eater inside him won't let it. They say it hurts all the time, like a bad tooth. That'll put a man in a bad mood."

Earl couldn't stand to let his hat go. He reached for it.

A grubby little paw snaked out, grabbed it before he

could.

Earl fixed the kid with a jaundiced eye when she began poking at it. "You do one more bad thing to my hat, little lady, I'm gonna personally hand you over to Custer. He'll probably make you into house slippers."

She merely grinned at his bluster and signed something back.

"What did she say?"

"If he can catch me," Phoebe Ann interpreted. "She reads lips, too."

After about a minute, she had the hat poked into shape, sprinkled with baby powder from her pocket, and handed back.

"She's got a chafing problem," Phoebe Ann explained.

Earl sniffed his hat. It smelled like baby powder and horse shit. "Even Steven Adler doesn't like that son of a bitch, Custer." Earl cocked his hat at a precise angle, wishing he could check it in the rearview. But that baby had eloped with the windshield. A horse biscuit dropped from the brim, landed in his lap. "There ain't no way you can stop him."

"I didn't say I could do it by myself," she countered. Tears began welling up again.

"Oh, no you don't, Missy. Count me out. I'm not gettin' mixed up in no crusade. You never seen how I handle a gun." Earl looked at the kid, made a shaking motion. "Could I see that baby powder for a minute?" She handed it over and Earl sprinkled it all over himself.

"You're already mixed up in it." Annie's blue-gray eyes fixed on Earl's face. "Custer's seen you, and he's not one to forget." She fought back a grin. "Especially since you put that steer horn up his ass."

"You don't worry none about old Earl. Cause tonight I'm makin' like a tumbleweed and puttin' *my* ass in the wind." Earl handed the battered old *Colt* back to Annie. "Here, you take this, cause soon as we come to the first sign of civilization, I'm stealin' you a car. You and that kid have got to get out of here."

With those words, their car ran out of gas.

***

A little later, the storm that had been threatening finally arrived. The rain was cold and it didn't do much to wash off the horse manure, but it did wash away their tracks.

***

The first sign of civilization turned out to be a truck stop just off the reservation, a place called MOM'S. "*Top off your tanks, have some pie,*" the sign said. The place was quiet, that three-in-the-morning quiet, even though there were cars and trucks all over the parking lot. Earl sat the kid down, tried to get some feeling back in his arms. He hoped the toe stayed numb.

When Earl and Annie limped inside the diner to get little Janey something to eat, they soon learned why it was so quiet. Everyone in the place was dead, shot where they sat, and five of the bodies had been mutilated. An Arapaho man, his wife, and their three children had all been scalped

and were sitting lined up with cigars in their hands.

Above the glistening heads of the dead family, their blood was splattered on the wall in a dripping sign three-feet tall.

It said simply, *GOOD INJUNS. TWO FOR A DOLLAR.*

Annie pulled the little girl close, burying her face so she couldn't see.

"I gotta say one thing for old George, subtlety ain't never been his strong point." Earl grabbed the first set of car keys he saw off the counter and backed away. Bolting to the parking lot with their small charge in tow, they heard singing. They couldn't tell where it was coming from, though, not until the tall, lantern-jawed colonel stepped from the shadows.

It took a moment for the words to register with Annie and Earl.

"*Ten little, nine little, eight little Indians,*" Colonel Custer sang in a surprisingly good baritone while poking at the scalps on the antenna of a pickup. In the faint light, the clumps of hair looked like bats hanging from a skinny tree limb.

"Well, well, well, I was beginning to wonder if you two were ever going to show up." The colonel took a final puff on his cigarette, ground the red butt underfoot.

Annie grabbed for her pistol and Custer casually raised his own gun, which he'd hidden beneath his jacket the whole time, and calmly shot her. Right above her belt buckle. She grunted, slammed back against a beat-up old Ford, hung there for a second, then slid down on her knees. Blood began pouring from her mouth.

"I shot you with a silver bullet. Had an A on it. Or was it a C, as in c u next Tuesday." Custer studied her for signs of further danger. "Thought that bullet was going to be in my pocket until the end of time." He didn't see any threat left in Annie and put his gun away. "I was getting bored sitting around here, so I had to entertain myself." Waving a hand languidly, he pointed at his newly decorated pickup. "It's not as good as my old Caddy, but it's coming along. I couldn't find any fuzzy dice for the rearview, so I thought maybe some baby shoes. You think they're too much?" He giggled. "Yeah, you're right, I guess I should've taken the feet out first."

The dandified colonel straightened his jacket, which was burned through in places. "I must apologize for my appearance, I haven't had a chance to call on my tailor." Still smiling, he walked over, kicked Annie onto her side and snagged the blood-covered pistol from her belt. Then he put a couple of bullets in Earl's legs before attaching the last scalp to the antenna and dragging Annie to her feet by her hair. He turned to Earl. "You look like shit, mister."

Earl struggled to his knees, pulled the little girl behind him. His toe no longer hurt.

Still holding Annie by her hair, Custer slammed her into a camper face first and re-busted her already busted nose. Blood poured. "That's for shooting me earlier." He dabbed his face with a crusty yellow handkerchief knotted around his neck, fighting for calm. The colonel's nose had been blown off. Where it used to be was just a whistling, snot-filled hole. The rest of his face didn't look much better.

Earl realized what Custer was about to do. He swallowed the lump of ice in his throat, found his voice. "Why don't you try me first, baby killer?"

The colonel turned, took in Earl's words. "Whoa there, old timer. You find yourself some backbone. You'll get your chance at me, soon as I'm done with her." He stopped, a look of puzzlement crossing his face. "What the hell have you got all over you there, Hop Along? It smells like a baby crawled into some horse-shit."

"It's baby powder. Good for chafing."

"Really."

"Yeah, you put it on your ass. Want some?"

Custer's eyes narrowed as he finally got a good look at Earl. "Don't I know you from somewhere, maybe a long time ago?"

"Not likely," the man on the ground said. "I don't kill Indian women and children for money."

"Now there goes that mouth again." Custer shook his head, dabbed at his runny nose-hole. "I don't always charge. Sometimes I do it for free…" He took another sniff with his ruined nose and a smile of sudden and absolute delight tugged at his lips. "What should I do with you, Earl?" The blonde colonel pondered for a moment before snapping his fingers. "I know, you and me can go kill us some Indian babies. I know where there's one we can start with. She's right behind you. How's that sound, Earl?"

Earl didn't answer.

"Of course I'd have to cut my rates on this one," Custer said. "I'd only charge half-price, since she's a half-breed."

"Are you going to bore me to death," Earl answered, "or are we going to settle this like men?" His tough talk didn't hide his fear, though. His voice had quavered a little there at the end. It took away from the effect he'd been trying to achieve.

"Hey, Annie," Custer said softly, "can you smell all that testosterone in the air? Is it making you moist? I think I'm getting a little moist."

The only moistness Annie felt was leaking from her nose and stomach. "Earl, you can't go up against Custer. You wouldn't have a chance." Pulling herself up next to the camper by the side mirror, she spat blood on the tarmac and forced her tortured body to stand up straight. The effort made her feel like someone was dragging something cold and sharp through her insides.

Showing a red, gap-toothed smile, she stared straight at Custer. "That's a pretty nice rag-top Caddy you had back there, George. Of course, it's a trashed piece of shit, now. But I've got to know one thing, you ever put the top down? And, you know, just let the wind blow through your… scalp?"

Custer's cold, lifeless eyes fixed on her. "You think that's funny?"

"Oh yeah," she replied. "But not as funny as that tube of hair restorer I found in the glove-box."

Custer studied her from beneath his hat brim while he continued dabbing at his oozing nose hole. His smile widened past human, but there was no laughter in his voice. "Alright, you win, Annie, you get to die first. Don't disappoint me, draw fast, shoot straight, Indian-lover." He loaded the old *Colt* and tossed it at her feet where it landed with a clatter. "You don't, you get to watch me put your little friend's scalp on that antenna there. She'll get to watch, too." He grinned at the little girl with his broken teeth. "Then you'll both get to let the wind blow through your scalps."

His smile fading, he took a few steps back and tossed a silver bullet on the asphalt between them.

"You've got three shots in your pistol, Annie. You put me down, you can finish me off with that silver bullet."

They faced off in the parking lot beneath the glow of flickering green neon that popped and sputtered, advertising *"DIESEL. EAT AT MOM'S."* Custer slowly circled her, and his spurs, caked with bits of horse blood and hair, made little jingling noises.

Somewhere in the distance, a pack of coyotes began howling, the sound rising to a fever pitch.

Earl couldn't make out their problem, only that they were agitated. That was understandable. He was feeling a little agitated himself.

Then there was only silence while Custer lit a cigarette, stuck it between jagged lips. He looked like the *Marlboro Man* in the final stages of cancer. "I hear you shot one of these out of Kaiser Wilhelm's mouth once upon a time. Maybe you'd like to shoot one out of mine." Licking the blood of the Arapaho scalps from his fingers, he shoved his pistol in his belt. But only after Annie did it first.

"Anytime you're ready, Little Sure Shot," Custer said with a wink. The colonel settled his hat on his head while he waited for Annie to draw. He puffed on his cigarette, watching her with the same flat-eyed intensity of a snake watching a bird.

Annie was game, she got to her pistol first, but she hemorrhaged blood at the crucial moment and Custer easily outdrew her.

"Well, well, well. I guess the Kaiser wasn't shooting back at you," Custer drawled, covering her. "It's time for you to take your medicine, little lady. You proved you shoot like a man." He cocked his .45. "Let's see if you die like a man." Without changing expression, Custer put another bullet in her stomach, sending her smashing into the base of the neon sign. "That one was silver. Stings, doesn't it?"

Earl made a move for the truck, shielding the little girl with his body. He managed a few steps on his blood-soaked knees before Custer put a bullet in the door.

"Hey, don't leave yet, old timer, we're just getting started."

While Custer was looking at Earl, Annie tried to cock her pistol. She was weak, shaking badly, the pool of blood beneath her growing deeper by the second. Her face had grown white as chalk.

Before she could pull the hammer back, Custer walked over and kicked her in the face, then savagely brought his boot-heel down on the *Colt,* breaking several of her fingers. That didn't quite satisfy him so he sliced off her trigger finger, used it to pick a bloody scab out of his nose-hole.

Sticking the finger in the band of his hat, he gazed down dispassionately where she lay at his feet, watching her struggle to breathe.

Her chest was rising and falling in ragged gasps from the pain and she had grown even whiter.

"Looks like you're dead, Annie," Custer said. "Just like your husband, Frank. I didn't want to tell you this, but we might not get another chance to talk. Old Frank cried like a little schoolgirl while I was killing him. Of course, I'd cut off his manhood by that time. Even then, he wanted to live. He offered to tell me where you were if I'd spare his life, did you know that?"

"I don't believe that." Annie tried to summon the strength to lift the pistol. "Not for a second." She didn't have it in her.

Smiling, Custer hunkered down so they were at eye level, as he gently took her mutilated hand in his and raised her pistol to his own head. "Your shooting days are over, Annie. You might as well be dead." Puffing on his cigarette, he blew a huge lazy smoke ring that hovered above her head like a halo.

Annie spat in his face.

Wiping the blood and saliva off, he tasted it. "Well, I was going to tell you what else I did to old Frank, but I don't think we have that kind of time. You're bleeding out fast." He caressed her face with his blood-smeared fingers. "Such a pretty girl. I recommend a closed casket, Annie— since you're not going to look so pretty without hair and a nose."

pistol was busted or he was out of ammunition.

Custer saw Earl's gun was useless and turned back to the coyote before it could run away.

The coyote had other plans. It lunged, sinking its needle-sharp teeth to the bone in Custer's wrist, and the pain caused the colonel to drop his gun as though scalded.

Before Custer could recover, the animal grabbed up the fallen pistol in its teeth, squirted like quicksilver between the Colonel's legs and deposited it in Earl's lap. Staring at the saliva-covered *Colt*, Earl couldn't quite believe his eyes. He tossed the old gun, picked up the new one and pointed it at Custer's head.

"Well, this is a surprise."

"Not your first, I bet."

"Make your cruel jest." Custer reached for his hat. Squinched his eyes closed. He looked like a teenaged girl waiting for her first kiss.

Thumbing back the hammer, Earl squeezed the trigger and the pistol spat out its payload of silver.

Only problem was, Custer jerked his head to one side at the last second. The shot went wide.

It hit Custer's other ear.

The ear hung there for a second, rocking back and forth like a license plate with one screw in it. Then it dropped.

He deliberately raised his pistol, leveled it at her face… and shot out the *SEL* in *DIESEL*. The sign now said *DIE. EAT AT MOM'S*.

Laughing at his own cleverness, he put his pistol away, pulled out his blood-stained skinning knife and sauntered back across the parking lot, intending to scalp the little girl right in front of Annie and Earl. "Sorry, cowboy, I know I promised you this one. But don't you worry none, pard, there's plenty more where she came from."

The colonel grabbed the kid by the arm, but before he could make the first cut, a coyote sprang out from behind the camper and launched itself into the air. When it came down, it had Custer's ear in its mouth. The coyote dropped the piece of gristle and howled in triumph.

A surprised Custer also howled. With wordless, incoherent rage. His voice rose in pitch until it matched that of the coyote.

Fumbling for his gun, he started to shoot the animal that mocked him.

Earl scrambled across the parking lot, grabbed the pistol from Annie's hand and pointed it at the vain blonde Indian killer. A squeeze of the trigger and the gun jumped in his hand, the bullet hitting Custer in the ass, sending dust flying. Earl tried to fire again, but the hammer struck a dead cartridge.

Custer hobbled around to face his attacker. "Damn, Earl, I'm beginning to think you got a thing for my ass. You one of those side-saddle cowboys?"

Quickly Earl recocked the *Colt*, squeezed the trigger. Nothing. He did it again. Nothing. Either the damned

The colonel opened his eyes and stared at the lump of flesh on the pavement, nestled between his ruined three-thousand-dollar black rhino boots. Without ears and a nose, his head seemed somehow smaller—kind of like a ferret in a hat. "Looks like you might have pulled that shot a tad to the left." He raised a hand when Earl recocked the pistol—"If you'd be gentleman enough to give me a second—" Custer picked up the ear and tucked it into his jacket pocket. "I'd like to hold onto this. Little Bighorn, you know."

The coyote reared up on Earl. Something red trickled from its nose and found the wounds on Earl's legs.

***

Suddenly Earl is seeing himself facing down men in a saloon. They're Seventh Cavalry, he can smell the stink of violence on them. They draw guns and he shoots them both. Over and over. They call him by name, but it's not his name. He staggers out into the dirt street. Coyotes wait there. Even stranger, the coyotes are accompanied by an old Indian man in tattered gray buckskins and a stovepipe hat. The old Indian munches on Doritos *and stares at Earl for a moment, before turning and walking away, his steps covering an incredible distance until finally he's gone from sight.*

Earl came back to himself.

When he tried to shoot Custer again, he found the gun was empty.

A couple of clicks later, Custer cracked open his eyes. "Out of ammo? Well, now, ain't that a shame. In all the excitement I guess I forgot to reload my gun." The colonel was grinning from ear-hole to ear-hole, like a man who'd just filled an inside straight. "Whew, that was a close one, Earl. Thought I might've been in trouble, there for a second." The grin faded and something shifted behind Custer's eyes as he reached around behind his back. "One time I got shot in the head, I couldn't find my car for a week."

Earl kept squeezing the trigger even though he was only getting empty clicks.

"Something's bothering me, pard," Custer said. "Why on god's green earth would a coyote risk its ass for you? Or anybody, for that matter? Last time I checked, coyotes aren't in the Good Samaritan business."

"Maybe it's not me he's interested in," Earl answered, stalling, searching his pockets for one more shell. "Maybe you remind him of something he buried."

Before Custer could answer, the coyote sprang, all four feet leaving the asphalt. This time, though, the colonel was ready. He threw up an arm, stopping the animal's teeth inches from his noseless face, and came out with his skinning knife. He plunged the serrated blade all the way to the hilt in the animal's soft, vulnerable stomach and twisted. The animal, caught on the steel, emitted a strangled yelp, tried to push away.

Its efforts to escape were useless.

Custer held the animal close, ripping upward, his eyes glazing with pleasure when the pink and gray entrails spilled onto the asphalt with a wet rush. "There. I guess that'll be enough of that." He reached in, pulled out the animal's still beating heart and tossed it in Earl's lap. "Seen that in a movie, one time. Always wanted to do it."

Earl scrambled back.

"What, nothing to say now, Earl?" Custer pulled his severed ear from his jacket pocket, the one Earl had shot off earlier, and held it up to Earl's face, pretended to listen. "All out of witty repartee? All out of smart mouth? I thought so." Still looking pleased with himself, Custer wrenched his knife free and hobbled toward Earl, the blood-covered blade steaming in the chill night air.

"How about a little off the top, Earl? Gotta look sharp when we go calling." The glowing tip of the colonel's cigarette illuminated his lifeless eyes as he moved closer.

"Don't you want to know why this coyote's helping me?" Earl asked, still playing for time. He seemed to remember that he used to have a cartridge and that it had slipped through a hole in the coat pocket into the lining. The only reason he ever kept a cartridge was the powder could be used to start a campfire on wet nights.

Custer tested the edge on his knife. He seemed happy with it.

"Or why the coyotes were chasing the white wolf?" Earl blurted out, quickly patting his pockets.

This time, a look of true annoyance passed over the colonel's ravaged face. "I'm not even going to ask what you know about a white wolf. I've wasted too much time here as it is." He looked at Earl and his eyes turned blood red for a moment as the creature inside him swirled in anger. "I'll get the answer when I eat your blood."

Earl felt something that might have been a cartridge.

He slid his hand into his pocket, searching for the hole it had slipped through.

As Custer approached, the little girl darted out from behind Earl and placed herself in front of the old hustler.

"Well now, isn't this sweet." Custer studied her like she was ice cream that had unexpectedly come with his pie.

Earl couldn't get his hand through the hole in his pocket.

"When I was a youngster," Custer informed him, "back in Monroe, Michigan, we had a saying. You might remember this one, Earl. Children should be seen, and not heard." The colonel patted the little head. "And that's what I love about this one, she can't be heard." He grabbed the child by a pigtail, yanked her away from Earl, and placed his blade at her hairline. "You might want to close your eyes, sweetheart. This is going to sting a little. Believe me, I know."

From out of the darkness, a flat crack. At first Earl thought a car had backfired. Until the glowing tip of the colonel's cigarette winked out with a wet sizzle. A second later, a puff of white drifted from his suddenly enlarged nose-hole, and floated upward, as though the colonel was sending up smoke signals.

The former lieutenant-colonel of the Seventh Cavalry appeared so surprised it was almost comical as he looked over at Annie in disbelief.

It appeared Annie's shooting days weren't quite over. She was holding the pistol in her other hand.

Earl dragged out the bullet he'd found in the lining of his jacket. Loading the pistol, he swung it in Custer's direction.

Annie called out to Earl. "Nineteen sixty-three." She dug the silver half-dollar from her pocket and flipped it spinning toward Custer's face. Earl fired. Driven by the bullet, the silver coin smashed into the Colonel's head with deadly force. Smoke poured from the hole. Annie shot again, striking the fifty cent piece. She tried to fire again, but she was too weak to hold up the *Colt* any longer. The effort had taken the last of her strength. The gun fell to the pavement, a second ahead of Custer.

When the Colonel pitched backward, his hat sailed to the pavement, revealing the horrible scars of his scalping at Little Bighorn. He pulled up his burned suede jacket, trying to hide from their eyes.

From the dark, a white wolf loped up. It touched noses with Annie. Blood passed from Annie to the creature. "I'm going with Frank." With those words she died. The wolf stared at Annie's disfigured killer for a moment, then turned and loped off into the night. The coyotes followed.

Crawling across the parking lot on his stomach, Custer was doing his best to retrieve his hat while Earl walked after him. Earl bent down, retrieved the silver bullet Custer had tossed down earlier. He put it in the *Colt's* chamber and turned Custer over. "Hide your eyes, Janey."

"Who are you?" Custer said.

"My friends call me Bill. Some call me Wild Bill. You can call me Mr. Hickock."

The sound of the pistol was loud in the parking lot.

Laird Barron's fourth collection of macabre stories continues his inquiry into the darkness of the human heart. Herein, a teen party presages an extinction event; professional final girl Jessica Mace investigates a cursed carnival; the wild hunt pursues a broken-down outdoorsman and his loyal hound.

SWIFT
to
CHASE

LAIRD
BARRON

HELLNOTES

THE HORROR REVIEW

HORROR, SCIENCE FICTION
& FANTASY REVIEWS

FICTION, MOVIES, AND ART
DEDICATED TO THE HORROR GENRE

JOURNALSTONE
YOUR LINK TO ARTISTIC TALENT

The Conveyance
Brian W. Matthews
JournalStone
June, 2016
Reviewed by Michael R. Collings

Brian W. Matthews' *The Conveyance* is one of those rare books that is extremely difficult to review. Everything about it—setting, characters, plot, language—is perfectly suited to embrace readers and carry them along to a startling yet fully logical and coherent conclusion. The most trivial-seeming elements are introduced, almost unnoticed, yet ultimately play key roles in plot development, making readers—at least *this* reader—think, "Of course. Why didn't I see that before?" Yet to point to those bits, or those that more clearly relate directly to what happens in the novel, runs the risk of spoiling moments of surprise, incredulity, horror, suspense, and outright emotional upheaval.

As a psychologist, Dr. Brad Jordan is used to keeping secrets, including potentially devastating secrets. *The Conveyance* begins with him approaching one such secret, closely harbored by twelve-year-old Doug Belle. Following a near-fatal accident on the way home, he confronts another when he realizes that his wife, Toni, is behaving oddly; and yet another that night, at the home of his best friend, Frank Swinicki.

Gradually, he and Frank unravel a complex web of deeper, darker, and deadlier secrets involving bizarre dolls, their maker, and the tiny town of Emersville. This last level proves the most dangerous of all and—through Matthews' deft mastery—encompasses all the secrets that have gone before, binding them into a massive, long-lived conspiracy that alters Brad's essential understanding of reality and threatens the existence of humanity itself.

Matthews does a sterling job of uniting individual elements into a seamless narrative. With bits reminiscent of such disparate novels as Stephen King's *Needful Things,* Dean R. Koontz's wonderfully comic horror tale, *Ticktock,* and Ira Levin's *Rosemary's Baby, The Conveyance* remains a highly original story, captivating from its earliest moments and simultaneously compelling and impelling. Highly recommended.

The Cold Embrace: Weird Stories by Women
Edited by S.T. Joshi
Dover Publications
May 18, 2016
Reviewed by Elaine Pascale

The Cold Embrace features tales of dark fiction written by women over nearly a one hundred year time span. The collection is bookended by Mary Shelley (1830) and May Sinclair (1922), and contains names that would be familiar to any Gothic fan. These were women who wrote without the benefit of Women in Horror Month; women who made supernatural tales popular, and in so doing, created the opportunities that exist for women writers today.

The anthology contains both recognizable and rare offerings. Standouts include the titular story by Mary Elizabeth Braddon — it holds no surprising twists, but the writing is taut and peculiarly efficient. The same can be said for Gertrude Atherton's "Death and the Woman." There is also Charlotte Perkins Gilman's "The Yellow Wallpaper," which is often pressed upon college students — a misfortune, as it assigns labor to an experience that should be amazing. A curious soul, discovering Gilman's story, will delight in its alarming take on female hysteria, as opposed to wondering how long of a paper he or she must write about it. Edna Underwood's "The Painter of Dead Women" twists the romantic trope of an American abroad, marveling in the malevolence that lurked beneath the gilded age. Also enjoyable are the two haunting tales of revenge: Ellen Glasgow's "The Shadowy Third" and Marjorie Bowen's "Scoured Silk."

Joshi crafts an insightful introduction and includes tales that are as literary as they are disturbing. *The Cold Embrace* is not an easy summer read, but it should be a requirement for all who are interested in Gothic literature, as well as for those who celebrate our contemporary women in horror.

Ghost Heart
John Palisano
Samhain Publishing
February 2, 2016
Reviewed by Marvin P. Vernon

Rick is a young mechanic in the small New England "bedroom community" of Whistleville. Things are pretty laid back for Rick – aside from having a girlfriend that he's not quite sure of in the fidelity department, there have been some new arrivals in town who are causing serious problems for him and his friends. These people are infested with a disease called the Ghost Heart; the condition make them strong and invincible as long as they drink human blood, but eventually they fall victim to the disease as they turn pale and fade away. Rick is unfortunate enough to fall in love with one of them.

When reading the summary of John Palisano's *Ghost Heart*, it is impossible not to think "vampire" (and it would be fair to call this a variant of the vampire mystique) but Palisano's vampires are not eternal – they are sick. The condition brings lots of perks to it provided you have a fresh supply of blood, yet there is a price to be paid. Rick is at first an innocent spectator to this new affliction; he is targeted by the Ghost Heart-inflicted gang led by a rather vicious man named Damien, but he has also met Minarette, a devastatingly beautiful girl who seems lost in her own way. The heart of the tale lies in Rick's inability to avoid misfortune, the penalty his friends pay, and the inevitability of a doomed love. Think *Romeo and Juliet* with vampire thingies.

That is the crux of what makes this novel so interesting – it isn't really a horror story as much as a love story. But wait horror fans, it should be mentioned that this is indeed a scary book. There is a lot of eerie atmosphere building throughout the pages and even though Whistleville is a small town just outside the cities, there is a feeling of isolation in which the town appears powerless against the Ghost Heart carriers, and the police are less than competent. As we find out more about the Ghost Heart and its victims, there are some incredibly tense scenes that should satisfy most horror aficionados. Yet it is the relationship between Rick and Minarette that fuel the tale – Rick is young and insecure, whereas Minarette is irresistible and at first seems sure of herself. She is also doomed, and her vulnerability starts to come through as the story develops. The author ties this relationship in neatly with the horror plot and it works quite well. This dark resemblance of a romance is a nice deviation from the "scare them and scare them some more" habit of many recent books where human emotions are secondary.

I would recommend *Ghost Heart* to someone who likes a good horror novel yet wants something that also features important human interactions and issues or someone looking for a novel that is vampire yet not really vampire. It is always nice to see a new bent on the old warhorse and doubly nice to read a book that is able to add some real human dilemmas to its story.

Paper Tigers
Damien Angelica Walters
Dark House Press
February, 2016
Reviewed by Josh Black

With only one novel and one collection to her name before this, Damien Angelica Walters has nonetheless garnered quite the following in genre circles, and with good reason.

In *Paper Tigers* we meet Alison, a young woman bearing the scars – physically and emotionally – of a fire that stopped her former life in its tracks. Once well on her way to becoming a teacher, she now lives a life of isolation, afraid to set foot outside of the house. Her body is unrecognizable, her fiancé is gone, her hopes and dreams seem a distant memory. Her mother and physical therapist are trying in earnest to help, but things are moving much too fast for her to handle. She hasn't lost hope, but she's stuck in a sort of limbo.

One day, having summoned the courage to get out for a walk, she comes across an antique shop wherein she finds a curious photo album which might be just the thing she needed. The photographs are like doorways to the past, to a house inhabited by a man who has the power to take away her scars. It's an incredible offer, but of course there's a price to be paid.

From here on out, as Alison moves between past and present, her internal plight and the things happening to and around her are masterfully intertwined. In some passages *Paper Tigers* reads like a psychedelic, classically gothic fever dream, while in others it becomes a quiet rumination on the way past scars can transmute and take on an internal life of their own. The whole of it is wrapped in purposeful, delicate prose. Upon rereading, it reveals multiple layers, both of Alison's psyche and the nearsighted way our society often views the contrast between beauty and ugliness.

The novel's structure lends itself to a sort of vicariousness that has to be difficult to pull off, and it's testament to Walters' skill as a storyteller that everything here comes together as well as it does. As Alison drifts in and out of the album, the reader becomes drawn into the book she inhabits. Sometimes gentle, sometimes harsh, the way these pages flow is like the breathing of a living thing. It doesn't quite cross the line into metafiction, but it's fitting that the last part of it is called "The Final Page".

This isn't just a great novel – it's one of the best horror novels in recent memory. If you're a fan of the genre at all, you owe it to yourself to read *Paper Tigers*.

With a Voice that is Often Still Confused But is Becoming Ever Louder and Clearer
J.R. Hamantaschen
West Pigeon Press
September, 2015
Reviewed by Josh Black

J.R. Hamantaschen's debut collection, *You Shall Never Know Security*, was a very well-regarded one in the horror and weird fiction communities. The followup, *With a Voice that is Often Still Confused But is Becoming Ever Louder and Clearer*, further proves that Hamantaschen is the real deal. Hopefully he'll bring us many more stories.

"Vernichtungsschmerz" shifts between dreams and consciousness, the crux of the plot hinging on a literal life or death decision. Julia, a high school junior, is visited in a dream by a being that offers her a choice: live out the rest of her life knowing the truth about death, or follow the being into death, voiding her existence painlessly and immediately. The truth, as it turns out, is that death is a subjectively eternal agony, "… every nerve and molecule of your being, flayed, in perpetuity." After Julia makes her choice, the gauntlet is passed to her three closest friends, and the rest of the story follows them as their own choices play out.

The glimpse into depression offered in "A Related Corollary" is painful, but primal in its honesty. It's a scant few pages describing, ostensibly, a couple of friends sharing drinks. What it really defines is the bleak interior landscape of a woman caught in an ineffable blackness. The sadness, hopelessness, and alienation of depression are painstakingly described, and likewise the paradox of being simultaneously engaged with the world and seeing reality for what it truly is.

In "The Gulf of Responsibility", a social worker who's mildly disillusioned with the mundanity of his life draws himself unwittingly into what may or may not be a grand conspiracy involving some sort of death cult (it's essentially a mystery story, so the less said here, the better.) As it turns out, sometimes when you're paranoid, they *are* out to get you. The conclusion works as well as it does partly because the main character is more or less an everyman who makes the simple decision to live a little. As he says, "I made myself care. I should have just minded my business, like everyone else. No one really cares. I just wanted something to do. I wanted to feel like I was doing something, well, like I was doing something productive. I'm so stupid." A later story in the collection, "Oh Abel, Oh Absalom", expands on this one with a different main character.

In "Big with the Past, Pregnant with the Future", the accidental leak of the admissions materials of roughly half the first-year students at Yale Law School dredges up an otherworldly, traumatic event from one student's past. The politics of academia meet personal horror, and if anything is certain, it's that nothing ever can be.

"Soon Enough This Will Essentially Be a True Story" begins innocently enough and becomes the literary equivalent of a book reviewer's worst nightmare. Karen, a top Goodreads reviewer (and fervent entrant of contests) wins a book in a giveaway. Five minutes later she gets an email stating the book has been sent. After reading some of the book, she realizes she doesn't like it and decides not to leave a review. From here on the author makes himself known in an increasingly disturbing manner, and it's clear he's a volatile individual. Murderous, even. As all of the stories in the collection do, this one works on multiple levels. There's the sheer terror of being stalked and threatened, and the eventual gore factor. Beneath the lurid surface it looks at the precarious balance between validation-seeking and the importance of privacy in the digital age.

While the previous story had some nasty gore, "I'm A Good Person, I Mean Well and I Deserve Better" has it by the bucket-load. In a considerable change of pace from the previous stories, this one is set up as a standard revenge tale and ends up being a blood-drenched, riotous love letter to horror b-movies and retro video games, with a side of laugh-out-loud scatological glee. The strains of ineffectuality and estrangement that mark the collection as a whole are still at play here, but "play" is the operative word.

"Cthulhu, Zombies, Ninjas and Robots!; or, a Special Snowflake in an Endless Scorching Universe" takes a scathing look at a Cthulhu convention. Explored here is the absurdity of reducing Lovecraft's mythos to a series of trinkets, clothing, and pornography, the lauding of his work despite his personal beliefs, and the paradox of capitalizing on his philosophy in fiction while avoiding it in everyday life.

Depression is the focal point once more in the final story, "It's Not Feelings of Anxiety; It's One, Constant Feeling: Anxiety". Here we have a man who seems happy enough with his lot in life, but scratch the surface and we find he's merely going through the motions. There's something to be said about *caring* enough to go through the motions, of course, but this too can fall apart under the right circumstances. These circumstances are front and center here, as the main character's feelings of despair and futility are given tangible form. The end result is far from pleasant.

Put simply, *With a Voice that is Often Still Confused But is Becoming Ever Louder and Clearer* is a brilliant and vital addition to the landscape of dark fiction. Hamantaschen has an impressive eye for detail, for the absurdities, imperfections, grit, and so often unvoiced thoughts, gestures, and actions that mark us as human. There's a pitch-perfect balance here between emotional depth and philosophical questioning. The supernatural is deftly combined with urban malaise, personalized fears and anxieties, and an undefined, deeper darkness encroaching from all corners. It's not often a collection of this caliber comes around.

Highly recommended.

Scar City
Joel Lane
Eibonvale Press
October, 2015
Reviewed by Mario Guslandi

A posthumous short story collection by the late Joel Lane (whose untimely death has deprived the literary scene of one of the best contemporary writers of dark, speculative and weird fiction), *Scar City* constitutes a well-deserved homage to the unique style of that British author.

Book-ended by an insightful Foreword by Alexander Zelenyi and a clever, affectionate commentary by Nina

Allan about Lane's "Blue" trilogy of novels, the volume assembles twenty-two stories, mostly previously appeared in print, a few apparently unpublished so far.

The collection represents a faithful, effective showcase of Lane's fictional world, a world imbued with gloom, unemployment, loneliness, desperate search for true love, booze, drugs and sex (mostly gay). An explosive mix of urban horror, a bit depressing yet fascinating, told by Lane in his inimitable narrative style — detached, sometimes flat, but able to create unforgettable pictures of human life with its frailties and its hopeless need to find a meaning for our existence.

Among the included tales, I'd like to single out those which especially impressed me: "A Faraway City" is a beautiful yarn suspended between dream and reality, while "The Night Last Woman" is a sad, bleak tale depicting a one-night stand of a loner and a gorgeous woman. In the nightmarish "Echoland," drugs open the way to a lost world from another dimension, and in the dark "By Night He Could Not See," revenge proves to date back to a long gone past. The disquieting "Feels Like Underground" (with Chris Morgan) is a kind of Aickmanesque story taking place in a hotel during a business convention, while the bitter "Internal Colonies" is a graphic tale of urban horror featuring a gang of youngsters devoted to vice and depravity.

Finally, "Winter Song" is a very short piece full of lyricism and melancholy, the beginning paragraphs of which are pure Lane: *"The start of winter is always fucking miserable. A sudden chill burns up the dead leaves with fever, the naked trees are wreathed in mist, and the four horsemen of seasonal disease – influenza, bronchitis, gonorrhea and depression – ride into town on their rachitic horses. The game is up."* Indeed.

◇◇

Into the Mist
Lee Murray
Cohesion Press
April 13, 2016
Reviewed by Michael R. Collings

Reading Lee Murray's *Into the Mist* is like watching *Jurassic Park* again for the first time. From Dean Samed's highly evocative cover, you know that there will eventually be a dinosaur—or something very like it—followed by oohs and ahhhs and then running and screaming…and dying. You just don't know when or how or who.

Then there is the added bonus of another filmic reference, this time to the *Lord of the Rings* films by Peter Jackson, with their exploration of the exotic mountain wilderness of what is in the real world New Zealand. Gorgeous…and deadly.

But what is perhaps most important about *Into the Mist* is that it manages to capture many of the stock images and motifs of creature-features—on the screen or in books—and combines those elements that trigger almost automatic responses of awe and horror and fear and adrenaline-fueled excitement into a single, coherent,

highly imaginative and ultimately impressive narrative. The characters, for example, at first seem fairly standard: the self-involved scientist who thinks it is a good idea to capture a creature that has already killed twenty or so people; the plucky female willing to undergo a personal hell in order to save the day; the stolid military guy, muscles on muscles, who nevertheless sacrifices all for his companions and those under his protection; the canny native whose knowledge of myth and legend become far more important than at first seems possible. But Murray gives each sufficient individuation that they become more than merely ciphers to be moved around as the plot demands. They become intriguing personalities that either grow or diminish through their abrupt exposure to the unknown.

The story begins in New Zealand's Te Urewera National Park as two hikers first discover what they assume to be fossil moa eggs in a recent landslide…and soon thereafter discover how mistaken they are. Several months—and a dozen more deaths—later, James Arnold of the New Zealand Defence Force Army base in Waiouru orders Sergeant Taine McKenna and his men to accompany a small group of scientists and civilians into the Te Urewera wilderness, ostensibly to protect them from possible attack by Tūhoe separatists. In fact, they are to search for an earlier group of soldiers and find out what is going on. But even Arnold and McKenna know nothing about clandestine plans to force the government to open the wilderness to gold mining. Or the hidden marijuana farm. Or the self-appointed guardian trying to keep outsiders away. Wheels within wheels within wheels.

Lest this sound as if Murray has simply thrown everything into the mix, there is one more ingredient that almost miraculously holds the story together: Rawiri Temera, an eighty-three-year-old makakite, a seer, who has been dreaming of the coming of the Taniwha, a monster from Maori legend. His insights guide the story through the collision of science and myth, of the possible and the impossible, ultimately providing the key to the sole means of destroying not only the Taniwha but the evil within it.

Murray makes effective use of her sources. There are frequent references to horror films at key moments, accentuating her narrative with readers' memories of other monsters. She develops the native mythologies well, weaving them through the story rather than simply overlaying them and asserting the supernatural. In the New Zealand of *Into the Mist*, there are monsters; there are lands that should remain untouched; there are secrets that should not be investigated; and there are constant reminders that, as one character says, "Stories exist for a reason."

◇◇

The Complete John Silence Stories
Algernon Blackwood
Dover Publications
November 2, 2011
Reviewed by Marvin P. Vernon

Of the traditional British writers of supernatural and ghost tales, I've always felt a kinship with Algernon Blackwood. He not only wrote some of the best supernatural fiction of the early 20th century but he wrote it like he "meant it." It is a cliché to say his fiction did not evoke horror as much as awe, but it is a remarkably accurate description of the power of his writings. Blackwood was quite knowledgeable about the many mystic organizations and practices that were popular from the Victorian Age on and used that knowledge prodigiously. He had a great love and respect for the outdoors and appeared to have regarded the earth and its mysteries in an almost pantheistic way at times. He could also, when he wanted to, make the wonders of earth and the cosmos most terrifying. It is that mix of wonder and terror that made Blackwood one of the most unique of the early 20th century horror writers.

Of his many short stories, the two most influential were "The Wendigo" and "The Willows" and for good reason – they evoke the very mix of awe and terror I mentioned above. However, the author was also influential in presenting the idea of the psychic detective or, in John Silence's case, the "Psychic Doctor," into the modern horror repertoire. There is no doubt the character of Dr. John Silence owes some debt to an earlier and more famous non-psychic colleague, Sherlock Holmes. He bears some of the same attributes; a keen sense of observation, an obsession to detail, a somewhat haughty but caring attitude toward his clients and a few other traits, yet Silence has distinctive differences. He is a medical doctor that, due to his amassing of a fortune, devotes his time to his interest in psychic mysteries and often helps those in need. He seems to have an unlimited knowledge of the most esoteric and dangerous phenomena. Of the six tales he is featured in, there is an unusual amount of variety in the types of threats. Even the most known terrors to the horror reader, such as the werewolf in "The Camp of Dogs," takes on a more metaphysical element.

Each story has a slightly different narrative and theme. The first one is "A Psychical Invasion" in which Silence fights off a psychic haunting brought on by cannabis use (I think there may be a hidden and outdated warning about Marijuana use here). The intriguing thing in this story is the doctor's helpful assistants: his dog and cat! Unfortunately this is the only tale in which these two clever animals are featured. "Ancient Sorceries" is the least interesting story primarily because John Silence takes a passive role by simply being the listener while the narrator tells his tale. His "helpful" comments at the end seem a bit unnecessary for the narration. In "The Nemesis of Fire," we meet the doctor's assistant, Hubbard, who narrates two of the six tales. "The Nemesis of Fire" is an involved piece regarding a string of fires and unusual happenings around an old plantation. Not only is it my pick for the best John Silence story but ranks high in all of Blackwood's fiction.

"Secret Worship" takes on a different tack as John Silence arrives late and almost as a passerby. A man is visiting his old childhood school and, fortunately for him, Silence is aware that things at the school have changed and the gentleman may be in serious trouble. The aforementioned "The Camp of the Dog" is my second favorite work in the collection and the other story narrated by the assistant Hubbard. It features a number of Blackwood's typicalities; a love for the outdoors, a view of the terrors as a mystical (if not dangerous) wonder, and optimistic hope for human nature; it is sort of a love story. Finally, "A Victim of High Space" rounds out the collection. It was the last John Silence story to be published and feels a little different. Briefly (as it is the briefest of the tales), it involves a man trapped between two dimensions which the doctor is able to help in the confines of his own consulting room. It feels a little more Hodgson than Blackwood to me.

The John Silence stories were Blackwood's first real success. Written in the first decade of the 20th century, they were followed by more atmospheric and, to me, more terrifying tales. For that reason, I find them hard to rate knowing the best is yet to come. Yet for any writer of his time, these were well developed and very entertaining works. Even in these early works, Blackwood seems already matured and set in his choice of genre and themes. For any fan of British supernatural literature, this is an essential collection.

◇◇

Pretty Little Dead Girls
Mercedes M. Yardley
Crystal Lake Publishing
March 4, 2016
Reviewed by Elaine Pascale

From the very first line of author Mercedes M. Yardley's fairy tale-esque novel, "Bryony Adams was the type of girl who got murdered," readers are beholden to care about the main character's safety. Bryony is destined to be a "pretty little dead girl," but death needs more target practice.

This was my first experience with Yardley and I was supremely impressed. Even though death lurks around every corner and every page, Yardley has created an entrancing world with warm and engaging characters. Most importantly, the language of the book is poetic and evocative and simply lovely. Her consistency of tone inspires envy and she makes use of dainty, fragile chapters that are as ephemeral as the main character.

The story is about Bryony, a magical "star girl" who is marked to die tragically and violently; a cosmic stamp that everyone who encounters her can plainly see. The narrative begins in her childhood where we are introduced to a very sweet, precocious and intelligent young girl. The young Bryony is wise beyond her years and comprehends the state of her life (that she is destined to be murdered). We follow Bryony as she tentatively accepts her early adulthood, both relishing and feeling anxiety over the fact that she is still alive. She can never rest because death is stalking her in the form of a voracious desert and a skilled serial killer. The supporting characters hold their collective breaths — awaiting some gruesome denouement — while vowing to protect Bryony with their own lives. The plot is tense, but as the subtitle denotes, the tone is very whimsical.

Pretty Little Dead Girls is a gorgeous novel, perhaps one of the most lyrical in its genre. It is charming, magical and inspiring — both as a tale and as an example of exemplary writing.

Cthulhu Lies Dreaming: Twenty-three Tales of the Weird and Cosmic
Edited by Salomé Jones
Ghostwoods Books
February 20, 2016
Reviewed by David Goudsward

In the opening of his "The Call of Cthulhu," Lovecraft famously observed that "The most merciful thing in the world, I think, is the inability of the human mind to correlate all its contents." Editor Jones takes this quote and skews it. The collected authors are asked to explore the ramifications of the human mind dealing with fragments of a great cosmic truth buried in its subconscious; still beyond the mortal mind but prone to manifestation in dreams that rapidly turn into nightmares in the waking hours.

The stories in this book explore the effect of these somnolent shards intruding into the conscious mind. Madness? Artistic temperament? Subliminal connections to the dreams from sunken R'lyeh? In *Cthulhu Lies Dreaming*, the answer is the reader's choice. There are examples of each, and other causes among the 23 tales, with dreams as both a common theme and the catalyst for a widening gyre of horror and madness.

The variety of stories is truly impressive, ranging from a new twist on the old debate between atheists and believers in "The Myth of Proof" by Greg Stolze to Cthulhian version of actual biological terrors on "Cymothoa Cthulhii" by Gethin A. Lynes. Pete Rawlik's "Notes for a Life of Nightmares" starts with the artist Wilcox, whose dream-inspired clay bas-relief began the original Lovecraft story, but as Rawlik is wont to do, he then throws sly nods to every other Lovecraft story he can casually have Wilcox passingly encounter. "Bleak Mathematics" by Brian Fatah Steele similarly introduced the mythos to the world of indie music – neither the mythos nor the art will ever be the same.

As with any good anthology, this is not to be read in one sitting. It should be stretched out over time, to savor and to avoid adding your own nightmares to the disquieting dreams within.

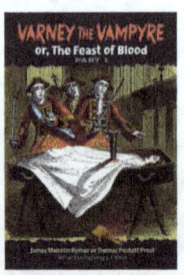

Varney the Vampire or, The Feast of Blood parts I and II
James Malcolm Rymer or Thomas Peckett Prest
Dover Publications
April 15, 2015
Reviewed by Elaine Pascale

If you haven't seen me in many moons,

it's because I have been reading the epic tome *Varney the Vampire*. E. F. Bleiler, in his introduction to the two volumes, calls *Varney*, "the most famous book that no one has read". This is entirely true: I have taught vampire seminars at the college level, have written many theses on *Dracula*, have campaigned against *Twilight* as if it were the plague, and this was my first venture into *Varney*, although I had heard it mentioned many times. After slogging through it, I now understand why it might be often overlooked.

Varney was a serialized Penny Dreadful, and it is no wonder that few have sat down to consume it as a novel or two part-novel — it was not meant to be digested that way. It contains some gothic scares and standbys — a hidden passageway, a character that resembles a long deceased man of the estate, a damsel in distress, and dark and stormy nights.

Varney is a vampire that contains some, but not all, of the vampire traits and mythology. He has fangs, bites his victims' necks, and leaves two tell-tale holes. Yet he can walk around during the day, can eat and drink. He is one of the very first sympathetic vampires, as he laments his cursed state. Varney is not really likeable or unlikeable, he is simply the central plot twist. Oddly, the other characters recognize that a vampire is in their midst early on, and then spend a lot of time remarking on how remarkable it is that a vampire is in their midst.

Scholars have argued the authorship of *Varney*; it has come down to a draw between James Malcolm Rymer and Thomas Peckett Prest. From a reader's perspective, it feels like there may be more than one author as there is very little continuity, and even Varney's history/story changes throughout. At times, he is an ancient supernatural creature, at others he is modern and human.

Tackling these two volumes feels like a herculean feat, yet *Varney the Vampire* is a story of historical significance, both in its being the first full-length vampire story, and in its original mode of distribution. If you can imagine reading it in fragments, in front of a fireplace, with likeminded "gothic soap opera" fans, it does include moments of intrigue and excitement. I recommend *Varney the Vampire* to vampire purists and fans of the historic gothic novel.

HELLNOTES

FICTION, MOVIES, AND ART
DEDICATED TO THE HORROR GENRE

The Limbus saga continues
with five more stories of horror, science fiction, and fantasy
from some of the industry's brightest stars.

JONATHAN MABERRY,
SEANAN McGUIRE, LAIRD BARRON,
DAVID LISS, and KEITH R.A. DeCANDIDO

LIMBUS
INC.

— BOOK III —

EDITED BY BRETT J. TALLEY

How lucky do you feel?

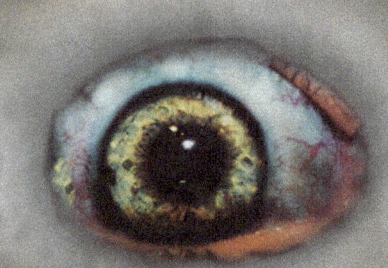

WINTER 2013
Issue Number 22
www.DarkDiscoveries.com

DARK DISCOVERIES

UNSETTLE... EDIFY... INVOLVE...

I0683848

Publisher
Journalstone Publishing, LLC

Editor-in-Chief
James R. Beach

Assistant Editors
Chuck Caruso
Aaron J. French
Jason V Brock

**Art Director,
Layout, and Design**
Cyrus Wraith Walker

Contributors
James R. Beach
Dr. Michael R. Collings
Dave Everley
F. Paul Wilson
John Palisano
Douglas Wynne
Trevor Nordgren
Brian Knight
David Agranott
Joel Kirkpatrick
Aaron J. French
Justin Giallo
Brian M. Sammons
Wayne C. Rogers
Sherri White

**Contributing
Artists/Photographers**
*Cyrus Wraith Walker (Cover and
interior artwork)*

Special Thanks
*Future Publishing/
The interview people
Rob Zombie
John Skipp
Chris Morey*

DARK DISCOVERIES
(ISSN 1548-6842) is published (Qtrly)
by JournalStone Publications, 199
State Street, San Mateo, CA. 94401

Christopher C. Payne
Dark Discoveries Publications
199 State Street, San Mateo, CA. 94401
U.S.A.
christophercpayne@journalstone.com.

Please make check or money order payable
to: JournalStone Publishing and send to the
address above.
Credit/Debit cards via Paypal at:
christophercpayne@journalstone.com.
Advertising rates available. Discounts for
bulk and standing retail orders.

Fiction

Interviews

Featrures

HOME OF
EXTRAORDINARY FICTION

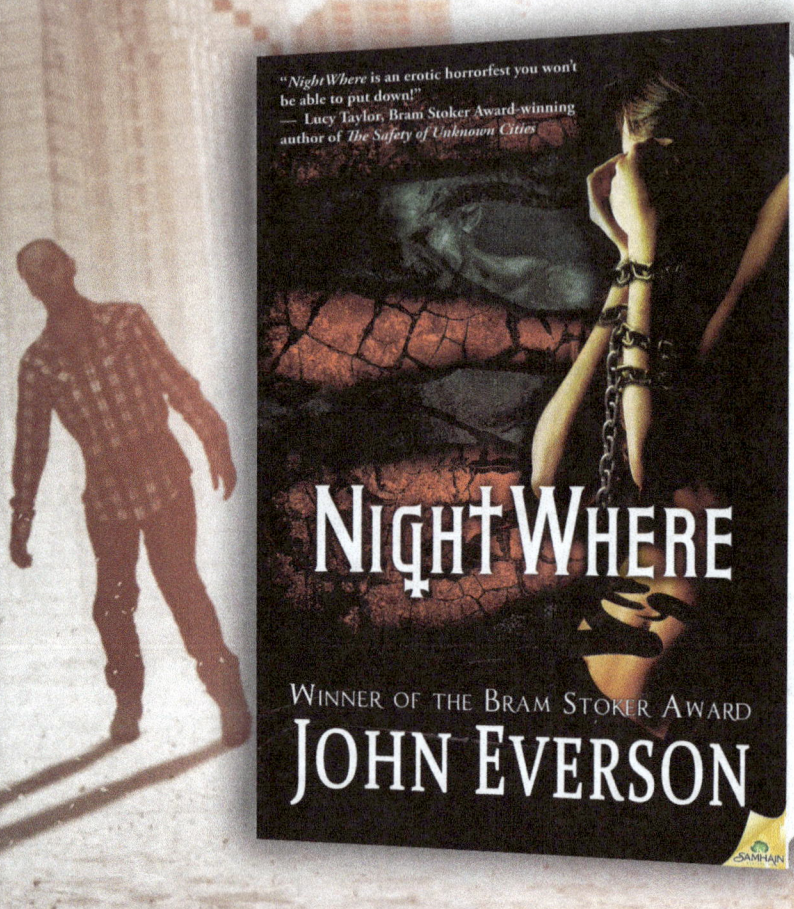

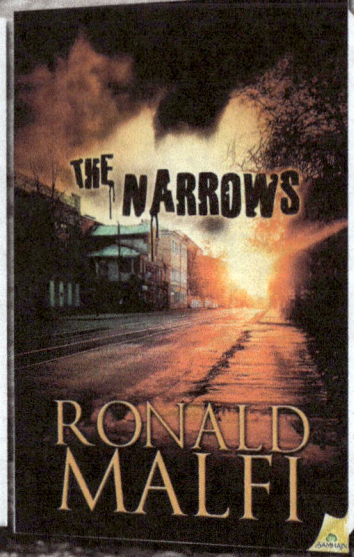

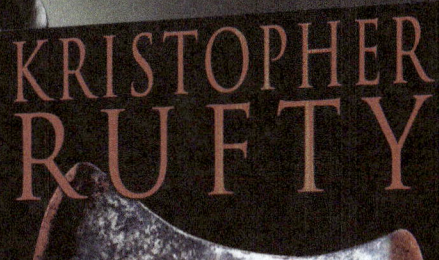

Updates
from the Dark Beach

Those of you that know me personally probably know that I have three main loves in my life: my lovely and supportive wife and three awesome kids, Horror and Science Fiction (Movies, TV, Books, Magazines, etc.) and Music (Rock and Roll primarily, and in all of its wonderful forms such as: Heavy Metal, Punk Rock, Psychedelia, Progressive Rock, Jazz Rock Fusion and more). Back in high school, I first caught the magazine publishing bug. Eventually, when I did finally start my own magazine, the Horror won out, but Rock and Roll never quite faded away.

Since we started doing the themed issues back in 2009, I've been kicking around the idea for a Horror and Rock special. Since they both have a lot in common and venture into each other's territory quite often, it seems a logical choice for a focus in *Dark Discoveries*. Many writers in the Horror and Science Fiction fields have incorporated music into their writing and many musicians have done the same with their music (the whole Shock Rock genre is a prime example of that).

In this issue, we have interviews with musicians Rob Zombie and John Skipp for you. Music-related stories by F. Paul Wilson, Brian Knight, Douglas Wynne and David Agranoff. Articles on Alice Cooper, Shock Rock musicians, Stephen King and a Top Ten Best Rock and Roll Horror movie list. On the non-music side we have an on-location article on the movie adaptation of Edward Lee's *The Bighead* and an interview with Dark Regions Press publisher Chris Morey. And reviews as well.

So there you have it. Rock and Roll and Horror movies. Crank it up!

—James R. Beach
Editor-in-Chief

COMING SOON...

A NEW NOVELLA BY
JOE R. LANSDALE

DARKREGIONS.COM/BLACKLABYRINTH

THE BLACK LABYRINTH IMPRINT   PUBLISHED BY DARK REGIONS PRESS   DARKREGIONS.COM/BLACKLABYRINTH

Knowledge: An Interview with

By Dave Everley

(Metal Hammer, Future Publishing /
The Interview People)

He's possibly the most restless man in the world of metal, and no one ever quite knows what he'll be up to next. Enter Rob Zombie, a true visionary of our time.

On his very first day in New York City, Robert Bartleh Cummings witnessed a murder. It was the early 80s and he'd escaped the clean-cut confines of Haverhill, Massachusetts and headed for the mean streets of the Big Apple with his head full of weird dreams and strange sounds. Within hours of arriving, the man who'd go on to adopt the nom de rock Rob Zombie was witnessing just how mean those streets really were.

"I was in my room, and I heard screaming," he says today. "So I looked out of the window and saw someone being killed. Day one, and I was already involved in a murder case. Welcome to New York City."

It was a fitting introduction to a world he'd only seen in films, and one that foreshadowed the music he made with both White Zombie and as a solo artist. Nearly 30 years after his baptism of blood, Rob is the undisputed ruler of that patch of land where metal meets artnoise terrorism, slasher flicks and B-movie trash culture. A dreadlocked renaissance man equally at home on stage or on a Hollywood movie lot, he's the missing link between Alice Cooper and Willy Wonka. His unique aesthetic helped drive two of the key albums of the 90s, opening the door for the likes of Marilyn Manson and Slipknot. Even when his first band collapsed in on itself, he emerged from the rubble to carve out a successful solo career.

"I've never changed what I wanted to do to meet someone else's expectations, be it the label, film studio or fans," he says. "I couldn't live with the idea of changing what I was going to do because I was advised to do it that way."

The first film the young Rob saw at the cinema was 1971's gloriously warped *Willy Wonka & The Chocolate Factory*. The first album that truly made an impact was KISS's 1976 classic *Destroyer*. While poles apart artistically, both were noisy, colourful and larger-than-life.

"Anything visual hooked me in first," he says. "I remember buying *Destroyer* without any idea of what it sounded like. I just thought, 'Wow, look at the cover, it's incredible. That must sound cool.'"

By the time he arrived in New York a few years later, his tastes had broadened to take in everything from the howling noise of Australian mentalists The Birthday Party to the gloriously trashy, mammary-heavy exploitation flicks of cult film maker Russ Meyer. When he decided to put together White Zombie in 1985, he lifted the name from a kitsch 1932 horror film starring Bela Lugosi.

"White Zombie was the first band I had," he says. "Where I grew up, nobody gave a shit about what I was interested in, whether it was music or movies. Someone like Alice Cooper seemed like they were from another planet."

By contrast, likeminded freaks and weirdos were in plentiful supply in New York in 1985. Recruiting guitarist Ena Kostabi, drummer Ivan de Prume and bassist Sean Yseult – the latter of whom would become his long-term girlfriend – he set about realising his vision.

"For me, the idea of what I wanted it to be came first and the music caught up later," he says. "White Zombie was very much the classic garage band – a bunch of people who couldn't play very well, all our equipment was crap. But I think that's what made the band unique – the limitations of your ability forces you to create something new."

The limitations were evident on the quartet's shambolic, self-financed debut EP, *Gods On Voodoo Moon*. It was a primal howl of unhinged noise that owed more to New York's nihilistic art-rock scene than the metal bands of the time. Listening back, it's virtually unrecognizable compared to the White Zombie of a decade later – not least Rob's high-pitched snarl.

"It was terrible," he laughs. "I'd hear all this stuff in my head, but then we'd make the record and it was like, 'No, that's not it!'"

The end product may have been lacking in finesse, not to mention discernible tunes, but it gave them a foothold in the New York music scene. They found themselves playing shows with the equally cacophonous likes of Sonic Youth and Pussy Galore. But while those bands over-intellectualised rock'n'roll, White Zombie's knowingly trashy racket underintellectualised it. In the smart-arse world of Downtown Manhattan, White Zombie stood out like a tramp at a funeral.

"We were everything all at once," says Rob. "I loved Nick Cave but I also loved Van Halen. I loved Sonic Youth but I also loved Sabbath. I didn't draw a distinction – I thought William Burroughs and Lemmy were equally as cool."

A string of releases followed, including raucous 1986 single "Pig Heaven" ("Terrible!"), 1987's *Psycho-Head Blow Out* EP ("The first time we sounded like we were on to something…") and the same year's debut album, *Soul Crusher*. "Soul Crusher was the pinnacle of that version of White Zombie," he says. "At the time, I liked it: 'OK, that was what we were trying to achieve.'"

Rob's musical vision was coalescing, but the lineup was less solid. In their early years, they had a steady turnover of guitarists. Sometimes this was down to musical differences, sometimes more… chemical differences.

"I was serious about what we were doing," he says. "When your guitarist shows up without a guitar and says, 'I sold it to buy drugs', that's not a good situation. Drugs were everywhere in New York. Everybody knew at least five people who had OD'd. I've always learned from others' mistakes: 'Hey, you did heroin and you're dead. Maybe that's not the best thing for me to do.'"

That may have been an unconventional outlook in art-rock circles, but it only underlined the singer's ambition. Having paid their dues on the underground, he knew it was time for White Zombie to claw their way towards the surface.

"I was never happy with just playing at CBGBs in front of 300 people for the rest of our lives. I had bigger aspirations. I thought, 'This scene has limitations. We like heavy metal, we look like a metal band, we'll just beef up our sound and start playing metal shows.'"

Replacing the tomcat-in-heat yowl of their early records with a heavier, groovier sound, their second full-length, 1989's *Make Them Die Slowly*, showed the first glimmerings of White Zombie as the wider world would know them. Most noticeably, Rob's voice had dropped an octave or two as he growled and snarled his way through the thrashy likes of Demon Speed and Disaster Blaster. There was just one problem…

"It was one of the worst-sounding records ever," says Rob. "We found out this guy Bill Laswell wanted to record it: 'Oh, he's a big-shot producer, blah blah.' So we made the record, it cost a fortune, and it sounded like it was recorded in a trash can. We all hated it."

Their next single would shake off their arty roots completely: a clattering cover of KISS's "God Of Thunder". One person who wasn't impressed was Gene Simmons, who threatened the band with a lawsuit after an image of the bassist in KISS warpaint appeared on the cover.

"Every time I see Gene, he brings it up," says Rob, laughing. "He mentions it in a fun way, but I never quite know if he thinks he's funny or if he's mad at me about it."

While "God Of Thunder" may not have set the world ablaze, it raised White Zombie's profile enough to get them noticed by the mainstream record industry. By the early 90s, many of their contemporaries had bagged major label deals. Now it was White Zombie's turn.

"We were playing a new song called Soul-Crusher live," says Rob. "An A&R guy from Geffen heard us and said, 'I love that song.

My gut feeling tells me there's something here. We're signing you guys.' We were, like, ' Whoah!'"

They may have stepped up to the big league, but success was a long way off. Their major label debut, *La Sexorcisto: Devil Music, Vol. 1*, was released in March 1992. None of the band expected it to do especially well, and in that respect, they weren't disappointed. With sales of the record hovering around the 100,000 mark, they toured America, supporting anyone who'd have them and playing to anyone who'd listen.

And then, in 1993, the band kicked off a US tour supporting Anthrax. At the start of the tour, they were selling a few t-shirts a night. By the end, they couldn't print enough to meet the demand. After eight years, White Zombie had finally become an overnight sensation.

"It happened so fast we couldn't believe it," he says. "We went from selling 10,000 copies in a week to selling 2 million copies in a week. It felt weird to go from nothing to everything."

Aptly, given Rob's love of comic books and cartoons, the album's success was largely down to a new animated TV show. Beavis & Butt-head was the creation of Mike Judge, a rock'n'roll loving animator whose cackling creations reflected his own musical tastes. When Mike featured *La Sexorcisto* track "Thunderkiss 65" in the show, the game literally changed overnight. In public, the wagon appeared to be rattling along at full pelt. In private, though, the wheels were starting to wobble. Relations within the band were becoming fraught, a situation not helped by the fact that Rob and Sean Yseult had split up after nearly a decade together. By the time they came to record 1995's thumping, widescreen masterpiece *Astrocreep 2000*, the atmosphere within had turned toxic.

"By that point, we were not getting along at all as a band," he says. "*Astrocreep* was our best record – it was the sound I'd been hearing in my head all along – but the entire record was recorded without every bandmember present at the same time. This person wasn't in then, that person was never here. It was a struggle."

Ask him what exactly caused the problems, and he's cautious. "It was a product of everything," he says diplomatically. "You spend so much time together, and people change. Money changes things. Money seems to heighten some people's personalities." He won't be drawn any further.

It was during a photoshoot just before the album was released

that Rob realised that White Zombie were rapidly approaching the end of the road.

"There was so much tension," he says. "I remember saying to the band, 'After this I'm done – I can't take this anymore.' I think certain people thought, 'Oh, whatever, he's just complaining', or maybe they just didn't hear me. But I remember thinking, 'This is it.'"

There was still a record to promote and touring commitments to honour. If Rob had any doubts about his decision, they were erased on a sold-out co-headlining tour with Pantera in 1996. *Astrocreep* had sold more than 3 million copies in America, but he knew that he had no choice but to dismantle the Frankenstein's Monster he'd spent more than a decade building up.

"It was painful," he says. "Everything I ever wanted I got, and it wasn't enjoyable. I thought, 'If I'm gonna be in a band, I want it to be fun. And if that means having to go and play smaller shows and be less popular, I'll deal with it'."

Surprisingly, when it came to the crunch, it was easier than he thought to leave behind everything he'd worked for.

"It was a relief," he says. "It had been weird for years. It was nice that it ended at its height, but what I was getting ready to do was scary."

The roll call of members of multi-platinum bands going on to equally successful solo careers is threadbare at best. Understandably, the executives at White Zombie's label, Geffen, were hardly performing backflips of joy when one of their star players informed them of his plan to strike out alone.

"I told Geffen I wanted to go solo," he laughs. "Everyone said it was a classic bad move."

For Rob, it was a leap into the unknown. "You have been in a band forever and then you're by yourself, you think, [worried voice] 'Now what?' I didn't even know who I was going to play with."

One factor he did have in his favour was that he knew exactly what he wanted to do musically. His 1998 debut solo album, *Hellbilly Deluxe*, may have streamlined some of *Astrocreep*'s more technicolour excesses, but it was effectively a White Zombie album in all but personnel.

"Musical direction was never the issue," he says. "I was never unhappy with the music, just the situation we made it in. So when I went to make my own record, it wasn't based on the idea of it being artistically freeing, it was based on the idea that I could have some fun doing it."

And did you? "It was the best!" he enthuses. "Making the record was stressful – I didn't have a band in place, so it was just me and the producer and different people coming in to play on it. But once the band was formed and we went on the road, it

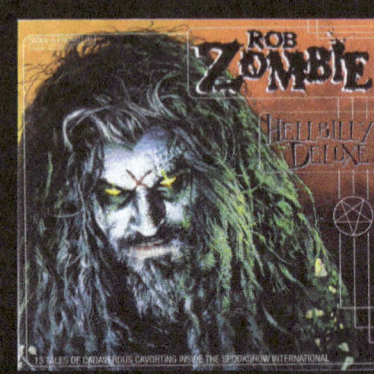

was like a revelation: 'Oh god, touring in a rock band is the greatest job in the world!'"

Three years later, he released *The Sinister Urge*, a record with even more experimental flourishes, including a brass section on one song. It came out when nu metal had run its course, and the spotlight of the press had shifted to a new wave of indie bands spearheaded by The Strokes and The White Stripes. *"Yeah, those bands got the press but they weren't doing the business,"* he sniffs dismissively. *"The Sinister Urge was a big record and a big tour."*

But once again, the internal machinery of the band was starting to jam…

"I didn't have a problem with anyone in the band, but they started having problems with each other," sighs Rob. *"It was back to White Zombie again. We were playing arena shows and no one's fucking talking to each other. I couldn't take any more drama between musicians. I thought, 'I can't do this again. I'll stop making music and start making movies."*

Which is precisely what he did. His first two films, *House Of 1000 Corpses* and its sequel *The Devil's Rejects*, were darkly schlocky tributes to the horror movies he grew up watching. As well as fulfilling a longstanding ambition to make films, it gave him the chance to work with some of his big-screen heroes, including cult actors Sid Haig and Karen Black, as well as his voluptuous wife Sheri Moon.

"House Of 1000 Corpses was like the early White Zombie records – you have something in mind but your skill level doesn't let you make what's in your head," he says. *"Whereas by The Devil's Rejects, the movie in my mind became the movie onscreen. That's really satisfying."*

While he continued to make movies, among them a remake of classic 70s slasher *Halloween* and a new sequel ("I was proud of them but they were based on someone else's idea – no matter how good your cover song, it's still a cover"), he was drawn back to music. But his 'comeback' album, 2006's *Educated Horses*, was a left-turn: the cover featured a dressed-down Zombie, and the music was schlock-free. While the package was a surprise, it remains one of his best records. But the follow-up, 2010's *Hellbilly Deluxe 2* – a Hollywood-style sequel to his solo debut – found him on more familiar ground, musically and visually. "With Educated Horses, I was forming a new band of musicians," he says.

"I didn't want to go, 'OK everybody, let's get into the crazy costume. Let's just be guys playing music.' It was like restarting. It was the beginning of building it all back up again."

His new album, the less-than-demurely titled *Mondo Sex Head*, is a remix album – the latest in a series of similar endeavours that stretches back to White Zombie's cautiously received *Super-sexy Swingin' Sounds* in 1996. Rob is the first to admit that his finger is a long way from the pulse when it comes to picking the people whose job it is to fuck around with his songs.

"We just go with the times," he says. *"We make a list of who's available, who are the remixers of the moment, and just farm it out. The only parameter is that I want them to have a sort of semblance of*

the original song. Sometimes, I've got remixes back and it's just eight minutes of a single beat."

And has Rob Zombie ever danced to a remix of one of his own songs?

"Have I what?!" he splutters. *"No, I have not. Ha ha ha! That would be foolish."*

It's understandable that Rob Zombie looks back on his long career with no small amount of pride. Few people have sustained a successful career for as long as he has, let alone one that's frankly been so bizarre. Fewer still have worked with such a head-spinning array legends as Ozzy Osbourne, iconic kids TV character Pee Wee Herman and *A Clockwork Orange* star Malcolm McDowell.

"I feel more like a peer," he says. *"I don't feel like I'm learning from these people. I don't mean that in an insulting way, but these guys aren't mentoring you. It's not like, 'Oh my god, it's Malcolm McDowell!' It's, 'Here's my friend, Malcolm McDowell, we're gonna do something together'."*

He puts his achievements down to an unswerving vision and a refusal to compromise. Which, when you consider how much he's pushed the envelope, that's some achievement.

"I wouldn't have done anything differently, because for good or for bad, I'm happy where things are at right now," he says. *"Maybe at times, things could have been done better, or more people could have liked it, or maybe not. But if you like it, it's because of me, if you hate it, it's because of me. I can live with that."*

☙ ☙ ☙

BOB DYLAN, TROY JONSON, AND THE SPEED QUEEN

By F. Paul Wilson

Dylan walks in and I almost choke.

I've known all along it had to happen. I mean, it was inevitable. But still, finding yourself in the same room with a legend will tend to dry up your saliva no matter how well prepared you think you are.

My band's been doing weeknights at the Eighth Wonder for two months now, a Tuesday-Wednesday-Thursday gig, and I've made sure there's an electrified Dylan song in every set every night we play. Reactions have been mixed. At worst hostile, at best grudging acceptance. Electric music is a touchy thing here in Greenwich Village in 1964. All these folkies who think they're so hip and radical and grassroots wise, they'll march in Selma but they'll boo and walk out on a song by a black man named Chuck Berry. Yet if you play the same chord progression and damn near the same melody and say it's by Howlin' Wolf or Muddy Waters or Sonny Boy Williamson, they'll stay. So although my band's electric, I've been showing my bona-fides by limiting the sets to blues and an occasional protest song.

Slowly but surely we've been building an audience of locals. That's what I want, figuring that the more people hear us, the sooner word will get around to Dylan that somebody's doing rocked-up versions of his songs. It has to. Greenwich Village is a tight, gossipy little community in 1964, and except maybe for the gays, the folkies are just about the tightest and gossipyest of the Village's various subcultures. I figured when he heard about us he'd have to come and listen for himself. I've been luring him. It's all part of the plan.

And tonight he's taken the bait.

So here I am in the middle of Them's version of "Baby, Please Don't Go" and my voice goes hoarse and I fumble the riff when I see him but I manage to get through the song without making a fool out of myself.

When I finish I look up and panic for an instant because I can't find him. I search the dimness. The Eighth Wonder is your typical West Village dive, little more than a long rectangular room with the band platform at one end, the bar right rear, and cocktail tables spread across the open floor. Then I catch his profile silhouetted against the bar lights. He's standing there talking to some gal with long straight dark hair who's even skinnier than he is, which isn't much of a description because in 1964 it seems all the women in Greenwich Village are skinny with long straight hair.

The band's ready to begin the next number on the set list, our Yardbirds-style "I'm a Man," but I turn and tell them we're doing "All I Really Want to Do." They nod and shrug. As long as they get paid, they don't give a damn what they play. They're not in on the plan.

I strap on the Rickenbacker twelve-string and start picking out Jim McGuinn's opening. I've got this choice figured to be a pretty safe one since my wire tells me that the Byrds aren't even a group yet.

Dylan's taken a table at the rear with the skinny brunette. He's slouched down. He's got no idea this is his song. Then we start to sing and I see him straighten up in his chair. When we hit the chorus with the two-part harmony that sounds like three-part, I see him put down his drink. It's not a big move. He's trying to be cool. But I'm watching for it and I catch it.

Contact.

Research told me that he liked the Byrds' version when he first heard it, so I know he's got to like our version because ours is a carbon copy of theirs. And naturally he hasn't heard theirs yet because they haven't recorded it. I'd love to play their version of "Mr. Tambourine Man" but he hasn't written it yet.

There's some decent applause from the crowd when we finish the number and I run right into a Byrds version of "The Times They Are A-changin'." I remind myself not to use anything later than *Another Side of Bob Dylan*. We finish the set strong in full harmony on "Chimes of Freedom" and I look straight at Dylan's dim form and give him a smile and a nod. I don't see him smile or nod back, but he does join in the applause.

Got him.

We play our break number and then I head for the back of the room. But by the time I get there his table's empty. I look around but Dylan's gone.

"Shit!" I say to myself. Missed him. I wanted a chance to talk to him.

I step over to the bar for a beer and the girl who was sitting with Dylan sidles over. She's wearing jeans and three shirts. Hardly anybody in the Village wears a coat unless it's the dead of winter. If it's cool out, you put another shirt over the one you're already wearing. And if it's even cooler, you throw an oversized work shirt over those.

"He sorta kinda liked your stuff," she says.

"Who?"

"Bob. He was impressed."

"Really?" I say, cool as the legendary cucumber on the outside but inside I want to grab her shoulders and shout *Yeah? Yeah? What did he say?* Instead I say, "What makes you think so?"

"Oh, I don't know. Maybe it's because as he was listening to you guys he turned to me and said, 'I am impressed.'"

I laugh to keep from cheering. "Yeah. I guess that'd be a pretty good indication."

I like her. And now that she's close up, I recognize her. She's Sally something. I'm not sure anybody knows her last name. People around the Village just call her the Speed Queen. And by that they don't mean she does laundry.

Sally is thin and twitchy, and has the sniffles. She's got big dark eyes and they're staring at me.

"I was pretty impressed with your stuff too," she says, smiling up at me. "I mean I don't dig rock and roll at all, man, what with all the bop-shoo-boppin' and the shoo-be-dooin'. I mean that stuff's nowhere, man. But I kinda like the Beatles. I mean a bunch of us sat around and watched them when they were on Ed Sullivan and, you know, they were kinda cool. I mean they just stood there and sang. No corny little dance steps or the like. If they'd done anything like that we would've turned them right off. But no. Oh they bounced a little to the beat maybe but mostly they just played and sang. Almost like folkies. Looked like they were having fun. We all kinda dug that."

I hold back from telling her that she and her folkie friends were watching the death of the folk music craze.

"I dig 'em too," I say, dropping into the folkster patois of the period. "And I predict they're gonna be the biggest thing ever to hit the music business. Ten times bigger than Elvis and Sinatra and the Kingston Trio put together, man."

She laughs. "Sure! And I'm going to marry Bobby Dylan!"

I could tell her that he's actually going to marry Sara Lowndes next year, but that would be stupid. And she wouldn't believe me anyway.

"I like to think of what I play as 'folk rock'," I tell her.

She nods her head and considers this. "Folk rock...that's cool. But I don't know if it'll fly around here."

"It'll fly," I tell her. "It'll fly high. I guarantee it."

She's looking at me, smiling and nodding, almost giggling.

"You're okay," she says. "Why don't we get together after your last set."

"Meet you right here," I say.

It's Wednesday morning, 3 a.m., when we wind up back at my apartment on Perry Street.

"Nice pad," Sally says. "Two bedrooms. Wow."

"The second bedroom's my music room. That's where I work out all the band's material."

"Great! Can I use your bathroom?"

I show her where it is and she takes her big shoulder bag in with her. I listen a moment and hear the clink of glass on porcelain and have a pretty good idea of what she's up to.

"You shooting up in there?" I say.

She pulls the door open. She's sitting on the edge of the tub. There's a syringe in her hand and some rubber tubing tied around her arm.

"I'm tryin' to."

"What is it?"

"Meth."

Of course. They don't call her the Speed Queen for nothing.

"Want some?"

I shake my head. "Nah. Not my brand."

She smiles. "You're pretty cool, Troy. Some guys get grossed out by needles."

"Not me."

I don't tell her that we don't even *have* needles when I come from. Of course I knew there'd be lots of shooting up in the business I was getting into, so before coming here I programmed all its myriad permutations into my wire.

"Well then maybe you can help me. I seem to be running out of veins here. And this is good stuff. Super-potent. Two grams per c-c."

I hide my revulsion and take it from her. Such a primitive-looking thing. Even though AIDS hasn't reared its ugly head yet, I find the needle point especially terrifying. I look at the barrel of the glass syringe.

"You've got half a c-c there. A gram? You're popping a whole *gram* of speed?"

"The more I use, the more I need. Check for a vein, will you?"

I rub my fingertip over the inner surface of her arm until I feel a linear swelling below the skin. My wire tells me that's the place.

I say, "I think there's one here but I can't see it."

"Feeling's better than seeing any day," she says with a smile. "Do it."

I push the needle through the skin. She doesn't even flinch.

"Pull back on the plunger a little," she says.

I do and see a tiny red plume swirl into the chamber.

"Oh you're beautiful!" she says. "Hit it!"

I push the plunger home. As soon as the chamber is empty, the Speed Queen yanks off her tourniquet and sighs.

"Oh, man! Oh, baby!"

She grabs me and pulls me to the floor.

❋❋❋

I lay in bed utterly exhausted while Sally runs around the apartment stark naked, picking up the clutter, chattering on at mach two. She is painfully thin, Dachau thin. It almost hurts to look at her. I close my eyes.

For the first time since my arrival, I feel relaxed. I feel at peace. I don't have to worry about VD because I've had the routine immunizations against syphilis and the clap and even hepatitis B and C and AIDS. About the worst I can get is a case of crabs. I can just lie here and feel good.

It wasn't easy getting here, and it's been even harder staying. I thought I'd prepared myself for everything, but I never figured I'd be lonely. I didn't count on the loneliness. That's been the toughest to handle.

The music got me into this. I've been a fan of the old music ever since I can remember – ever since my ears started to work, probably. And I've got a good ear. Perfect pitch. You sit me down in front of a new piece of music and guaranteed I'll be able to play it back to you note for note in less than half an hour – usually less than ten minutes for most things. I can sing too, imitating most voices pretty closely.

Trouble is, I don't have a creative cell in my body. I can play anything that's already been played, but I can't make up anything of my own. That's the tragedy of my life. I should be a major musical talent of my time, but I'm an also-ran, a nothing.

To tell you the truth, I don't care to be a major musical talent of my time. And that's not sour grapes. I loathe what passes for music in my time. Pushbutton music – that's what I call it. Nobody actually gets their hands on the instruments and wrings the notes from them. Nobody gets together and *cooks*. It's all so cool, so dispassionate. Leaves me cold.

So I came back here. I have a couple of relatives in the temporal sequencing lab. I got their confidence, learned the ropes, and displaced myself to the early-mid 1960s.

Not an easy decision, I can assure you. Not only have I left behind everyone and everything I know, but I'm risking death. That's the penalty for altering the past. But I was so miserable up there that I figured it was worth the risk. Better to die trying to carve out a niche for myself here than to do a slow rot where I was.

Of course there was a good chance I'd do a slow rot in the 1960s as well. I'm no fool. I had no illusions that dropping back a hundred years or so would not make me any more creative than I already wasn't. I'd be an also-ran in the Sixties too.

Unless I prepared myself.

Which I did. I did my homework on the period. I studied the way they dressed, the way they spoke. I got myself wired with a wetchip encoded with all the biographies and discographies of anyone who was anybody in music and the arts at this time. All I have to do is think of the name and suddenly I know all about him or her.

Too bad they can't do that with music. I had to bring the music with me. I wasn't stupid, though. I didn't bring a dot player with me. No technological anachronisms – that's a sure way to cause ripples in the time stream and tip your hand to the observation teams. Do that and a reclamation squad'll be knocking on your door. Not me. I spent a whole year hunting up these ancient vinyl disks–"LP's" they call them. Paid antique prices for them but it was worth it. Bought myself some antique money to spend back here too.

So here I am.

And I'm on my way. It's been hard, it's been slow, but I've got only one chance at this so I've got to do it right. I picked the other band members carefully and trained them to play what I want. They need work so they go along with me, especially since they all think I'm a genius for writing such diverse songs as "Jumpin' Jack Flash," "Summer in the City," "Taxman," "Bad Moon Rising," "Rikki Don't Lose That Number," and so many others. People are starting to talk about me. And now Dylan has heard me. I'm hoping he'll bring John Hammond with him some time soon. That way I've got a shot at a Columbia contract. And then Dylan will send the demo of "Mr. Tambourine Man" to *me* instead of Jim McGuinn.

After that I won't need anyone. I'll be able to anticipate every trend in rock and I'll be at the forefront of all the ones that matter.

And so far, everything's going according to plan. I've even got a naked woman running around the apartment. I'm finally beginning to feel at home.

"Where'd you get these?"

It's Sally's voice. I open my eyes and see her standing over me. I smile, then freeze.

She's holding up copies of the first two Byrds albums.

"Give me those!"

"Hey, really. Where'd–?"

I leap out of bed. The expression on my face must be fierce because she jumps back. I snatch them from her.

"Don't ever touch my records!"

"Hey, sorreeeee! I just thought I'd spin something, okay? I wasn't going to steal your fucking records, man!"

I force myself to cool down. Quickly. It's my fault. I should have locked the music room. But I've been so wrapped up in getting the band going that I haven't had any company, so I've been careless about keeping my not-yet-recorded "antiques" locked away.

I laugh. "Sorry, Sally. It's just that these are rarities. I get touchy about them."

Holding the records behind me, I pull her close and give her a kiss. She kisses me back then pulls away and tries to get another look at the records.

"I'll say they are," she says. "I never heard of these Byrds. I mean like you'd think they were a jazz group, you know, like copping Charlie Parker or something, but the title on that blue album there is "Turn! Turn! Turn!" which I've like heard Pete Seeger sing. Are they new? I mean they've gotta be new but the album cover looks so old. And didn't I see 'Columbia' on the spine?"

"No," I say when I can finally get a word in. "They're imports."

"A new English group?"

"No. They're Swedish. And they're pretty bad."

"But that other album looked like it had a couple of Bobby's tunes on it."

"No chance," I say, feeling my gut coil inside me. "You need to come down."

I quickly put the albums back in the other room and locked the door.

"You're a real weird cat, Troy," she says to me.

"Why? Because I take care of my records?"

"They're only records. They're not gold." She laughs. "And besides that, you wear underwear. You must be the only guy in the Village who wears underwear."

I pull Sally back to the bed. We do it again and finally she falls asleep in my arms. But I can't sleep. I'm too shaken even to close my eyes.

I like her. I really like her. But that was too close. I've got to be real careful about who I bring back to the apartment. I can't let anything screw up the plan, especially my own carelessness. My life is at stake.

No ripples, that's the key. I've got to sink into the timeline without a ripple. Bob Dylan will go electric on his next album, just like he did before, but it will be *my* influence that nudged him to try it. "Mr. Tambourine Man" will be a big hit next summer, just as it's destined to be, but if things go according to plan, *my* band's name will be on the label instead of the Byrds. No ripples. Everything will remain much the same except that over the next few years Troy Jonson will insinuate himself into the music scene and become a major force there. He will make

millions, he will be considered a genius, the toast of both the public and his fellow artists.

Riding that thought I drift off to sleep.

Dylan shows up at the Eighth Wonder the very next night in the middle of my note-perfect imitation of Duane Allman on "Statesboro Blues," perfect even down to the Coricidin bottle on my slide finger. There's already a good crowd in, the biggest crowd since we started playing. Word must be getting around that we're something worth listening to. Dylan has about half a dozen scruffy types along with him. I recognize Allen Ginsberg and Gregory Corso in the entourage. Which gives me an idea.

"This one's for the poets in the audience," I say into the mike, then we jump into Paul Simon's "Richard Corey," only I use Van Morrison's phrasing, you know, with the snicker after the bullet-through-his-head line. After that I spend the rest of the set being political, interspersing Dylan numbers with "originals" such as "American Tune," "Won't Get Fooled Again," "Life During Wartime," and so on.

I can tell they're impressed. *More* than impressed. Their jaws are hanging open.

I figure now's the time to play cool. At the break, instead of heading for the bar, I slip backstage to a doorless cinderblock-walled cubicle euphemistically known as the dressing room.

Eventually someone knocks on the doorjamb. It's a bearded guy I recognize as one of Dylan's entourage tonight.

"Great set, man," he says. "Where'd you get some of those songs?"

"Stole them," I say, hardly glancing at him.

He laughs. "No, seriously, man. They were great. I really like that 'Southern Man' number. I mean like I've been makin' the marches and that says it all, man. You write them?"

I nod. "Most of them. Not the Dylan numbers."

He laughs again. From the glitter in his eyes and his extraordinarily receptive sense of humor, I gather that he's been smoking a little weed at that rear table.

"Right! And speaking of Dylan, Bobby wants to talk to you."

I decide to act a little paranoid.

"He's not pissed is he? I mean, I know they're his songs and all, but I thought I'd try to do them a little different, you know. I don't want him takin' me to court or–"

"Hey, it's cool," he says. "Bobby digs the way you're doing his stuff. He just wants to buy you a drink and talk to you about it, that's all."

I resist the urge to pump my fist in the air.

"Okay," I say. "I can handle that."

"Sure, man. And he wants to talk to you about some rare records he hears you've got."

Suddenly I'm ice cold.

"Records?"

"Yeah, says he heard about some foreign platters you've got with some of his songs on it."

I force a laugh and say, "Oh, he must've been talking to Sally! You know how Sally gets. The Speed Queen was really flying when she was going through my records. That wasn't music she saw, that was a record from Ireland of Dylan *Thomas* reading his stuff. I think ol' Sally's brains are getting scrambled."

He nods. "Yeah, it was Sally all right. She says you treat them things like gold, man. They must be some kinda valuable. But the thing that got to Dylan was she mentioned a song with 'tambourine' in the title, and he says he's been doodling with something like that."

"No kidding?" My voice sounds like a croak.

"Yeah. So he really wants to talk to you."

I'm sure he does. But what am I going to say?

And then I remember that I left Sally back at my apartment. She was going to hang out there for a while, then come over for the late sets.

I'm ready to panic. Even though I know I locked the music room before I left, I've got this urge to run back to my place.

"Hey, I really want to talk to him too. But I got some business to attend to here. My manager's stopping by in a minute and it's the only chance we'll have to talk before he heads for the West Coast, so tell Mr. Dylan I'll be over right after the next set. Tell him to make the next set – it'll be worth the wait."

The guy shrugs. "Okay. I'll tell him, but I don't know how happy he's gonna be."

"Sorry, man. I've got no choice."

As soon as he's gone, I dash out the back door and run for Perry Street. I've got to get Sally out of the apartment and never let her back in. Maybe I can even make it back to the Eighth Wonder in time to have that drink with Dylan. I can easily convince him that the so-called Dylan song on my foreign record is a product of amphetamine craziness – everybody in the Village knows how out of control Sally is with the stuff.

As I ram the key into my apartment door I hear something I don't want to hear, something I *can't* be hearing. But when I open up...

"Mr. Tambourine Man" is playing on the hi-fi.

I charge into the second bedroom, the music room. The door is open and Sally is dancing around the floor. She's startled to see me and goes into her little girl speedster act.

"Hiya, Troy, I found the key and I couldn't resist because I like really wanted to hear these weird records of yours and I love 'em I really do, but I've never heard of these Byrds cats although one of them's named Crosby and he looks kinda like a singer I caught at a club last year only his hair was shorter then, and I never heard this "Tambourine" song before but it's definitely Dylan although he's never sung it that I know of so I'll have to ask him about it and I noticed something even weirder, I mean *really* weird, because I spotted some of these copyright dates on the records – you know, that little circle with the littler letter C inside them? – and like man some of them are in the *future*, man, isn't that wild? I mean like

there's circle-C 1965 on this one and a circle-C 1970 on that one over there, and it's like someone had a time machine and went into the future and brought 'em back or something. I mean, is this wild or what?"

Fury like I've never known blasts through me. It steals my voice. I want to throttle her. If she were in reach I'd do it, but lucky for her she's bouncing around the room. I stay put. I clench my fists at my sides and let my mind race over my options.

How do I get out of this? Sally had one look at a couple of my albums last night and then spent all day blabbing to the whole goddam Village about them and how rare and unique they are. And after tonight I know exactly what she'll be talking about tomorrow: Dylan songs that haven't been written yet, groups that don't exist yet, and worst of all, albums with copyright dates in the future!

Ripples...I was worried about ripples in the time stream giving me away. Sally's mouth is going to cause *waves. Tsunamis!*

The whole scenario plays out inside my head: Talk spreads, Dylan gets more curious, Columbia Records gets worried about possible bootlegs, lawyers get involved, an article appears in the *Voice*, and then the inevitable – a reclamation squad knocks on my door in the middle of the night, I'm tranqued, brought back to my own time, and then it's bye-bye musical career. Bye-bye Troy Jonson.

Sally's got to go.

The coldbloodedness of the thought shocks me. But it's Sally or me. That's what it comes down to. Sally or me. What else can I do?

I choose me.

"Are you mad?" she says.

I shake my head. "A little annoyed, maybe, but I guess it's okay." I smile. "It's hard to say no to you."

She jumps into my arms and gives me a hug. My hands slide up to her throat, encircle it, then slip away. Can't do it.

"Hey, like what are you doing back, man? Aren't you playing?"

"I got...distracted."

"Well, Troy, honey, if you're flat, you've come to the right place. I know how to fix that."

In that instant I know how I'll do it. No blood, no pain, no mess.

"Maybe you're right. Maybe I could use a little boost."

Her eyes light. "Groovy! I've had my gear all set up in the bathroom but I couldn't find a vein. Let's go."

"But I want you to have some too," I say "No fun being up alone."

"Hey, I'm flyin' already. I popped a bunch of black beauties before you came."

"Yeah, but you're coming down. I can tell."

"You think so?" Her brow wrinkles with concern, then she smiles. "Okay. A little more'll be cool – especially if it's a direct hit."

"Never too much of a good thing, right?"

"Right! You'll shoot me up like last night?"

Just the words I want to hear.

"You bet."

While Sally's adjusting her tourniquet and humming along with "Mr. Tambourine Man," I take her biggest syringe and fill it all the way with the methedrine solution. I find the vein first try. She's too whacked out to notice the size of the syringe until I've got most of it into her.

She tries to pull her arm away. "Hey, that's ten fucking c-c's!"

I'm cool. I'm more than cool. I'm stone cold dead inside.

"Yeah, but it wasn't full. I only put one c-c in it." I pull her off the toilet seat. "Come on. Let's go."

"How about you, Troy? I thought you wanted–"

"Later. I'll do it at the club. I've got to get back."

As I pack up her paraphernalia, carefully wiping my prints off the syringe and bottles, she sags against the bathroom door.

"I don't feel so good, Troy. How much did you give me?"

"Not much. Come on, let's go."

Something's going to happen – 20,000 milligrams of methamphetamine in a single dose has to have a catastrophic effect – and whatever it is, I don't want it happening in my apartment.

I hurry her out to the street. I'm glad my place is on the first floor; I'd hate to see her try a few flights of steps right now. We go half a block and she clutches her chest.

"Shit, that hurts! Troy, I think I'm having a heart attack!"

As she starts retching and shuddering I pull her into an alley. A cat bolts from the shadows; the alley reeks of garbage. Sally shudders and sinks to her knees.

"Get me to a hospital, Troy," she says in a weak, raspy voice. "I think I overdid it this time."

I sink down beside her and fight the urge to carry her the few blocks to St. Vincent's emergency room. Instead I hold her in my arms. She's trembling.

"I can't breathe!"

The shudders become more violent. She convulses, almost throwing me off her, then she lies still, barely breathing. Another convulsion, more violent than the last, choking sounds tearing from her throat. She's still again, but this time she's not breathing. A final shudder and Sally the Speed Queen comes to a final, screeching halt.

As I crouch there beside her, still holding her, I begin to sob. This isn't the way I planned it, not at all the way it was supposed to be. It was all going to be peace and love and harmony, all Woodstock and no Altamont. Music, laughs, money. This isn't in the plan.

I lurch to my feet and vomit into the garbage can. I start walking. I don't look back at her. I can't. I stumble into the street and head for the Eighth Wonder, crying all the way.

❖❖❖

The owner, the guys in the band, they all hassle me for delaying the next set. I look out into the audience and see Dylan's gone but I don't care. Just as well. The next three sets are a mess, the worst of my life. The rest of the night is a blur. As soon as I'm done I'm out of there, running.

I find Perry Street full of cops and flashing red lights. I don't have to ask why. The self-loathing wells up in me until I want to be sick again. I promise to get those records into a safety deposit box first thing tomorrow so that something like this can never happen again.

I don't look at anybody as I pass the alley, afraid they'll see the guilt screaming in my eyes, but I'm surprised to find my landlord Charlie standing on the front steps to the apartment house.

"Hey, Jonson!" he says. "Where da hell ya been? Da cops is lookin' all ova for ya!"

I freeze on the bottom step.

"I've been working – all night."

"Sheesh, whatta night. First dat broad overdoses an' dies right downa street an' now dis! Anyway, da cops is in your place. Better go talk to 'em."

As much as I want to run, I don't. I can get out of this. Somebody probably saw us together, that's all. I can get out of this.

"I don't know anything about an overdose," I say. It's a form of practice. I figure I'm going to have to say it a lot of times before the cops leave.

"Not dat!" Charlie says. "About your apartment. You was broken into a few hours ago. I t'ought I heard glass break so's I come downstairs to check. Dey got in t'rough your back window, but I scared 'em off afore dey got much." He grins and slaps me on the shoulder. "You owe me one, kid. How many landlords is security guards too?"

I'm starting to relax. I force a smile as I walk up the steps past him.

"You're the best, Charlie."

"Don't I know it. Dey did manage to make off wit your hi-fi an' your records but, hey, you can replace dose witout too much trouble."

I turn toward Charlie. I feel the whole world, all the weight of time itself crashing down on me. I can't help it. It comes unbidden, without warning. Charlie's eyes nearly bulge out of his head as I scream a laugh in his face.

Edward Lee's The Bighead

Hits the Big Screen

by John Palisano

"What the hell's wrong with you?"

Someone asked Edward Lee at the first KillerCon convention in Las Vegas. The crowd laughed, because, well, if you've ever read one of Lee's books, you know he goes inside some very dark, depraved places. There's a little bit of hell on earth in most his works, and he doesn't stop there. This is the author who sculpted, over multiple books in the City Infernal series, what Hell would actually be like, should a person be able to visit and return.

Now Lee's first big hit, *The Bighead*, is making its way to the movies- by way of director Michael Ling and a talented crew of passionate filmmakers.

I asked Edward Lee how the film came to be. "It was just like my first movie, *Header*. A guy came out of the woodwork saying he wanted to option it (in this case the "guy" was Mike Ling) so I said 'Sure!' thinking that the guy was crazy, but I'd take his option money anyway. I never thought in a million years that a novel as hardcore as The Bighead could actually be made into a movie. A lot of reviewers called it 'the grossest novel every written.' How could someone in their right mind want to make a film adaptation of *this*? Mike Ling proved very quickly he was a really shit-together professional -and not crazy at all - and he kept renewing the option every year. Then one day not too long ago, he called me up, and I immediately thought he was finally giving up on the project and was going to tell me he wasn't gonna renew the option anymore. Instead, he told me, 'We're getting ready to shoot, and the preproduction is done!' If I had been sipping my diet Coke at that moment, I would've spat it all over the wall!"

✦✦✦

The sky was painted in pale pinks and blues as we arrived on the set of *The Bighead* nestled in the vast San Gabriel mountains. It was there I got to speak with director and writer Michael Ling, who turned out to be quite empathetic and warm. He told me how the movie came to be. "I read the book seven years ago. It was the most original, horrific, crazy, nutso thing I'd read. I'd never seen anything like it before. So I talked to the Overlook Connection about the rights. About a week later I got a call on the voicemail from Edward Lee. I'm like, 'Shit! The author called. This is great.' So I called him back and explained my vision. I wanted to keep the book intact. He was like, 'How are you going to shoot it?' I said it might not be rated 'R' and definitely not 'PG-13'. It's going to be like the book: extreme. I got an option for a year and a half and worked on the script. I sent the first draft to Ed the day before my wife and I got married. All through the honeymoon I was thinking, 'Did he write back?' And finally we were in Denmark and Lee liked the script and I thought, 'Thank God.'

Producer Jeff Skinner had a few people attached. We could find a director and no funding, or funding and no director. Never the right combination. For four years we kept doing that. In the meantime, we had our day jobs and such. With Kickstarter getting big, I said, 'How about we try and raise money through that and shoot this summer?'

We'd just shoot a short and use that to show people what we can do."

Producer Don Wygal added, "It was Mike Ling who brought this to life. I was a big horror fan when I was younger: Freddy Kruger, *Hellraiser*, *Friday The 13th*, the usual stuff. Mike Ling was into Ed Lee and Jack Ketchum and several other extreme writers. He said, 'Hey I've got this book and I really want to write a screenplay.' It was by far the grossest, most offensive book I'd ever read, but I knew no one was doing anything like that, and there have to be other people out there who were into horror so extreme it kind of becomes a Road Runner cartoon."

"Don called in favors from people on his day job," said Ling. "We got a fantastic crew for little to nothing. We got make-up for cheap. This show should cost us six figures. It's costing a quarter of that. It's going to look great: so professional and so well done. Hopefully people are going to like it.

The look we wanted was a Grindhouse look: 60s, 70s - without the scratches. With the cameras we had, we couldn't get that. The DP said, 'If we're going to do it, do it right.' So we used the RED camera, and so far? It looks amazing."

What drew the filmmakers to film an Edward Lee book?

"I think in a weird way, of the extreme ones, this is the most accessible one," Don Wygal said. "It's the gateway drug into the Edward Lee story. It says a lot about people that they don't even realize. Monsters aren't always monsters: sometimes they're redneck hillbillies. It spoke to me, and I think it will speak to people. Where else are you going to have nuns from hell and priests trying to reform a monster?"

"I was just looking for experience and I'd only done one other film," said Production Assistant Kimberly Conrad. "I love horror films. My favorite is the Friday the 13th series. On set, everyone is so nice and professional and they know what they want and how to get it." When asked if there were any memorable scenes, she said, "My favorite part is when the Bighead ate Wendy's brains. That was really awesome."

The first scene the crew shot during my set visit had a John, featuring Don Wygal in a clever cameo, patronizing prostitute Chrissy, played by petite blonde actress Ashley Totin. He said, "This is the first time you meet Dickie and Balls: the first time the audience sees what they're capable of. It sets the tone so the audience knows the Bighead isn't the only monster."

We got to hear from Orson Chaplan, who plays, "Balls."

"He's twisted," said Orson, who was warm and friendly off camera, but quickly turned psychotic in front on the lens. "He's the type of guy who enjoys fucking and he'll do it at any expense necessary, even with a colostomy bag. He seems to like to drag his buddy Dickie into everything. Dickie's scared they're going to get caught...that they're going to go to prison. I'm really looking forward to shooting today's scene with Rosie, the skinny string-bean prostitute

we're going to pick up in the clearing. I'm going to have fun with her."

Lance Trezona said, "Dickie's just an old redneck boy. Likes to go out with Balls, get into some mischief.

He's a crazy son

of a bitch. He'll do anything that comes to mind. Won't even hesitate. No filter. What you see is what you get. Him and Balls have been friends for a long time and he goes along with Balls' wacky ass plans. They like to go full force, pedal to the metal, balls to the wall."

How does one go about finding performers for such a brutal story? "We warned people it was extreme," Ling said. "Once they got the sides? Some of them would say, 'I can't do it.' One girl came in, Ashley, and was like, yeah, colostomy bag sex scene? Whatever."

"I found this great casting notice and met with Jeff and Michael," Ashley said, "In the audition I asked how far I could take it, and they said as far as you want. So I came in with my hair all ratty and oily and some scrubbed clothes and dark circles under my eyes. And here I am today."

"They had a description of the project and character. As soon as I read about Balls, that was me," Orson said. "That's what brought me to the audition and I guess they saw something they liked. I gather I gave it Balls out."

After Dickie and Balls pick up Chrissy, in the only way they know how (you'll have to see the movie. No spoilers here), the crew moved to a backwoods area. It was amazing seeing California transformed into the Deep South, complete with big Weeping Willows, ponds, and dirt roads. You could smell the dirt, the standing water, the mossy trees and the leaves. The occasional passing of a Union Pacific train only a few hundred feet away only added to the illusion. Unfortunately, the location also came with aggressive mosquitos even two coats of bug spray wouldn't deter.

Ashley gets raped and then has to eat poop and drink pee. "You'd think craft services would be a little more accommodating," Ashley joked.

Lance said: "This is the corn-holing scene. We're going to fuck the shit out of her and tie her to the trailer hitch and drag her around. I never played a part like this before in my life. You can live out some of your darkest fantasies. That's what brought me to this character and project. Where else can you do this shit? You can't. It's a once in a lifetime opportunity."

"This is my first horror project," Lance stated, "I'm jumping in with both feet. As far as the *Bighead*? It's just freakin' amazing, and the actor playing him is awesome. When you work in this industry, you work with a lot of different methods, and Michael's method is laid back. He has a tendency to put the actors at ease. It's nice to have someone just say 'have fun' when you're doing some of this crazy shit."

"Sometimes you work on projects that you know are going to touch millions of people," I overheard a crew member say during the rape scene. "Not sure if this is one of them." The scene was horrific. The actors brought

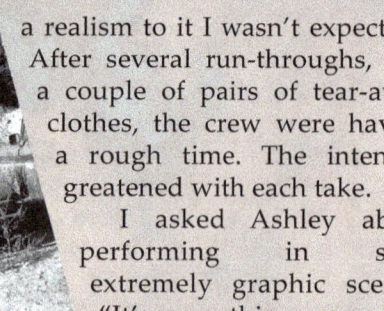

a realism to it I wasn't expecting. After several run-throughs, and a couple of pairs of tear-away clothes, the crew were having a rough time. The intensity greatened with each take.

I asked Ashley about performing in such extremely graphic scenes. "It's something you can't prepare for. You want that bone chill. As long as you're mentally there, your performance will shine through.

I can turn it on or turn it off. I don't think too much of it. It's harder for people watching it. You just 'get there.'

The crew is professional. After the first rape scene, everyone was so quiet. You're half-naked in front of people you don't know, and you're getting raped, so you never know."

I asked Michael Ling if there was an artistic reason to make such a violent film. "You have to do it the real way, close to the book. You can't do it half-assed. There's enough horror out there that doesn't cross the line.

Art is fearless. You can make horror movies at every level. You can make the great 'Z' with monsters. If you tell the story and it's done well, you can suck people in. Edward Lee knows how to tell good character stories. It's smart and well done."

I wanted to find out about the special effects, so I sat with the warm and funny Mark Villalobos of Monster FX. "They said they didn't have a huge budget and wanted minimal stuff. We weren't interested in that, so we said let's see what we could do. We enlarged his forehead and arms. An inflamed eye. Contacts. We amped up the gore. We did a fake head. We choreographed the effects so they had more impact and were scarier.

We did a fake head that cracks open and he eats her brains. We made extra stuff because we wanted it to look good and look cool, like the giant mutant.

I remember the book being super violent, and there's been a lack of that stuff lately. When we re-associated ourselves with those books, we wanted people to see and feel what was in the book."

As we wrapped for the day, I wondered what the long term goals of *The Bighead* were. Said producer Don Wygal, "Mike's got ideas about what he wants to do with the second one. We talked about one of the short stories. We're all into, 'The Pig' which would be interesting. Hopefully someone will see this and give us money for a feature."

I wrapped things up with director Ling as the sun set and the crew packed up. *The Bighead* is as cool as any other monster, but to see characters like Balls and Dickey in the flesh? They're so evil. They're almost likable because they're so over the top. The actors we had nailed it. We knew right away when we saw them.

As a duo, they work out perfectly.

I told Lee I just saw Balls and Dickey. Lee helped us with the Kickstarter campaign. Showed him a mold of the Bighead, and Lee was like, 'awesome.'

Hopefully it'll be a springboard to a feature, and the short will play a bunch of film festivals. We're doing a premiere in February, maybe tie it to one of Lee's new book releases."

I asked if there was anything he'd like to add. "This isn't just a guy in a suit. This is cross-the-line horror," he laughed as the sun set on the desert, casting a creepy purplish red glow.

"Getting to the set that first day and seeing sixty people, all insanely talented industry veterans, busting their butt for our 'little movie' was mind blowing. Seeing the Bighead in person was incredible. The work Monster FX did led to us showing more of the creature than we ever intended.

If I had to pick one bit of the shoot to single out, I'd go with the last day. We had seventy-five percent of our cast working, filming at the bar, we were well past the re-casting of Jerrica drama (and thanks one more time to the amazing Raquel Cantu for saving the movie), and by the end of the day, we had accomplished what we had set out to do: get *The Bighead* made. That feeling of excitement, relief, pride, and joy is one I will never forget."

I wondered what Edward Lee was most looking forward to in the finished movie. "Seeing my perverto, semen-slurping, innard-chomping, giant-phallused, super-fucked-up monster translated into a visual image, and that has now come to be. I've seen a few glimpses of Bighead and he looks AWESOME. Another awesome facet of all this is the photographic quality. I was expecting a mediocre production look like we see in a lot of independent movies (simply because the filmmakers can't afford expensive cameras and lenses) but what I got was production that looked so good I shrieked with glee when I saw the first clip. It looks like something a horror-fied Berman could've shot. You would think they used a 35mm Panaflex! And lastly, what I'm most looking forward to is seeing my version of the good old monster-in-the-woods theme done up in grand style the likes of which film audiences have yet to know. A horror movie that pulls no punches whatsoever, flinches not one iota, and delivers the goods in a big way!"

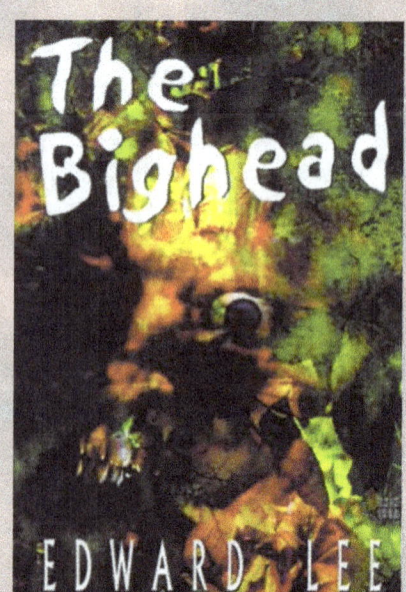

❦❦❦

JAMMING WITH JOHN SKIPP

John Skipp is one of the innovators of contemporary horror. In 1986, his punk vampire-in-the-subways novel The Light at the End (with Craig Spector) hit the New York Times bestseller list, helped launch the splatterpunk movement, and inspired the character of Spike in Buffy the Vampire Slayer. Their 1989 anthology Book of the Dead was the beginning of modern post-Romero zombie fiction. After their script for A Nightmare on Elm St. 5: The Dream Child was bastardized out of all recognition, the duo moved to Hollywood, wrote one more book (Animals), and promptly parted ways. Then Skipp disappeared from the scene.

Over a decade later, Skipp returned with a vengeance in 2002 with the solo collection Conscience, and has published 15 new titles since, including the coked-out zombie fungus epic Spore (with Cody Goodfellow), the Bizarro adventure favorite The Emerald Burrito of Oz (with Marc Levinthal), and most recently, the fem-o-centric horror triple-bill of solo screenplays, Sick Chick Flicks.

He also edited the massive landmark anthologies Zombies, Werewolves and Shapeshifters, Demons, and Psychos; launched his own Fungasm Press, devoted to wild fiction that defies all categories; edited five books for the Ravenous Shadows line of short, fierce genre work; and has embarked on a career as a film director with Rose: The Bizarro Zombie Musical and Stay At Home Dad, co-directing with Andrew Kasch (Thirsty, Never Sleep Again: The Elm St. Chronicles). But did you know he's also a musician? I chatted with John recently about his musical background for this Horror and Rock special of Dark Discoveries.

JRB: You were involved in music before writing books, right?

JS: Actually, I've been writing stories most of my life, and was the editor for the creative writing section of the school paper. And I helped write some of the music in a school play when I was 14 years old. So it was always there. But as a kid, I thought I was going to be a rock star. That's what I thought I was going to do.

It wasn't until eight insanely broken up bands later that I decided I would do something where I didn't have to worry about whether or not the bass player was puking in the parking lot. So I became a writer, and as such, self-sufficient. And almost immediately after becoming self-sufficient as a writer, I started collaborating. So much for *that* idea! (laughs)

JRB: Which is similar to music, right? Unless you're doing a solo thing, a band is usually a collaborative process to some extent.

JS: Totally. And what I like about collaboration as a writer is the jamming aspect of it. Bouncing ideas off people. Going in with a motif and finding out it's something cooler than you thought it was. So I've always enjoyed that process, which comes straight from the musical background. Working with a rhythm section, they would start to go into a groove and I would vamp over what they did. As opposed to just having to play rhythm, I could see the syncopation, let the wild notes flow, and the sparks would fly. That's always worked for me.

JRB: You had some stories published in the early 1980s in *Twilight Zone* magazine. And you were already collaborating with your first fiction partner, Craig, as far as the music side, right?

JS: We were in a band in high school. We were both dropouts and wound up in the same little private school for problem kids. And we started a band there.

JRB: That was the Philadelphia Children's Orchestra, right?

JS: Yeah. I actually taught Craig how to play guitar. He wanted to learn, and I knew how, so I showed him some shit. He picked it up real fast. He was a natural. So we started having fun and it spun out from there.

PCO was a freak show band. We came up with the name because you couldn't rent timpani and orchestra bells and so on if you were a rock band. Because we were the Philadelphia Children's Orchestra, we could theoretically get the weird instruments we couldn't normally get our hands on.

JRB: It sounds like you were definitely influenced by progressive rock then.

JS: Oh yeah. Frank Zappa, King Crimson, Todd Rundgren, Yes, Emerson Lake & Palmer… all the progressive rock guys, jazz fusion guys. Miles Davis. Mahavishnu Orchestra. Things kind of came together with all of the folkier elements, from Crosby, Stills, Nash, and Young to Jethro Tull and Gentle Giant.

You know I really am an old hippie, right? No matter how whatever-punk we were called… What was it John Waters said? For the early films, his audience was full of the hippies who hadn't figured out they were punks yet. So I was really like one of those types. A peace-and-love guy with a black sense of humor who wouldn't bust you in the teeth unless you really, really pushed me.

JRB: So you kept playing with Craig and some of the Children's Orchestra guys over the years. I read you also did a couple of records before starting to get your books published.

JS: That is true. I did a couple of independent records and projects that never got released. I was in a weird band in New York for a while. The singer put on a bald cap, pointed ears, and giant boobs, so he was this transsexual new wave demon, and he sang like Peter Gabriel. He was actually scary fucking talented. The guy could play all of the instruments. He would walk in with all of the parts and he would show the drummer what to play, the guitarist how to play it, the bass player, the keyboard player. And then we'd play what he said. I didn't last in it very long, but I learned a lot.

JRB: He sounds like a very knowledgeable guy - even if he was more into the performance aspect of it.

JS: Yeah, he was great. George Conrad, I think his name was. His band should have gone farther than it did, but it really helped me become a better groove player. I think I became a drummer after that. I could actually go over to the drum set and go wham-bam-de-boom, demonstrate where the accents were and shit.

JRB: That's interesting. I've known some drummers who knew everybody's parts (including their own) and have an incredible sense of what goes where, timing, etc. It sounds like it helped you develop that same instinct.

JS: As a writer, I think one of the biggest strengths I have is in pacing and laying down a beat. So yeah, it's all music-related.

JRB: William F. Nolan wrote a piece for me called "The Rhythm of Words" where he talks about just that. That there is a beat. There is a tempo. It's something that newer writers don't often have, and usually develop over time if they keep working at it. Or they don't in some cases. I've definitely noticed that in your work – a strong sense of pace and rhythm.

JS: Yeah. Not everybody is a good dancer. Not everybody has that sense of groove. They'll be running off a different set of metrics. Somebody who's visual and may not think in those terms of syncopation might float their images, whereas I tend to concuss them. (Laughs) Does that make sense?

JRB: Yeah, definitely. Now you did some music with Craig for your novel, *The Bridge*. I heard it was initially done for the remake of Night of the Living Dead that Tom Savini directed. Is that true?

JS: That's exactly right. We went to that set and were hanging out. I, in particular, heard some stoned music in my head while watching the zombies descend down the hill. I went back with Craig and we recorded some of this stuff, and then it just took off from there.

We were up for the soundtrack at the time with some really phenomenal people. None of the phenomenal people got the gig, a guy who was a friend of theirs did. I did not care much for that soundtrack. But we had this cool music sitting around that was very apocalyptic, and we were writing *The Bridge*. So we said "Oh, I guess this music will go here now." And that's how that happened.

JRB: It was an interesting soundtrack for sure. You worked with Brian Emrich on it –who's done remixing for various artists, for the record label TVT and so on.

JS: Yeah, he's Darren Aronofsky's sound designer, and the bass player for Foetus with J.G. Thirlwell. What happened with Brian was this: when I lived in New York I used to frequent Forbidden Planet, the great bookstore, and Brian worked there. He was a fan, and we would talk about music and say "Yeah we really need to do something someday." And he would show me all of his sampling and cool shit. One day we were talking and he's like "we're never going to do this, are we?" And I'm like, "Oh man, I'm a dick! I'm sorry. Let's go play!" And he was fantastic, and it was like, okay, I'm an idiot. So we ended up working together on some stuff.

JRB: You've also played with guitarist Chris Poland, right? Chris is most known for being on the first couple Megadeth albums and also does progressive hard rock /heavy metal. How did that project come about?

JS: And jazz. He was a jazz player who got strung out on heroin and helped invent speed metal. But originally, he was a jazz player, and this is where it wound up going for him. He brought that phenomenal jazz technique to metal, and really helped propel the virtuosity end of the genre, I think.

JRB: He's a phenomenal guitarist. Those first couple Megadeth albums were definitely ahead of their time. And quite a bit of it due to Poland's playing I would say.

JS: Yeah. You know those albums actually came out around the same time *Light at the End* and *The Cleanup* did?

JRB: So were you aware of what Chris was doing?

JS: I was *completely* unaware of what he was doing, and he was completely unaware of me. When we wound up playing together, it was a total discovery for both of us. Believe it or not, I'm not a huge metal freak. I love Led Zeppelin - and to me they kind of pioneered it – but what I loved about a band like Zeppelin was it was not all about how fast and mean they could play. There was also all of this beautiful nuance and so forth that was the other side of it. I mean I love aggressive metal power, but I don't like the angry teenage monocromaticism. I hope that doesn't make me sound like a dick. (laughs)

JRB: To me, Zeppelin was always a bit more of a progressive rock band – much like Queen – that had this huge mainstream following but with many different elements.

JS: Most definitely. And again, I also really like songs. I'm a song freak. So it isn't just the compositions, and it isn't just the virtuosity – although I greatly admire that – but I love all those things in the service of songs that communicate something to me - more than their velocity and their bad assitude. Sort of how rap and its constant fronting dilutes the massive power of the grooves for me.

JRB: So what happened with the Mumbo's Brain project with Chris Poland then? How come it didn't take off like it should have?

JS: Well, basically Chris and the guys wanted to leave metal and the progressive fusion place. Chris, in particular, wanted to work out some of his blues influences and things like that. It just so happened that I was perfectly positioned with the voice and the songwriting stuff to go there with him and push him into those directions. We had incredible songwriting chemistry. We wrote so many songs together. We wrote probably – in that two year period where we played together – 70 songs? Like an insane amount. The fucking day that I met him, we wrote three songs. He was providing the music primarily and I would go home, write lyrics and come in the next day. We rehearsed five hours a day, five days a week. We worked our asses off. We worked really, really hard.

One of the things I think was a problem was I'm not a metal singer, and my vocal stylings did not resonate well with a lot of his previous audience. The fact that I was a thirty-something-year-old guy with a beer gut who refused to keep his shirt on might have had something to do with it, too. (laughs) But for me, that band saved my life. I totally crashed and

burned in my writing, and my attempts at a film career, and I was about ready to die. I was about to explode and burst into flames. Mumbo gave me a chance to scream. To fly around the stage and scream. And much to the regret of those audiences, to tear my shirt off.

JRB: (Laughs)

JS: So it was the primal scream therapy I required. And we got a lot of great stuff out of it. I wish we recorded more than we did. We did record a lot more than has been released, but we were unable to get a deal.

One of the things is that I have the kind of voice that really benefits from a little bit of reverb on it. And we were in the Soundgarden/Pearl Jam/Nirvana era where all of that shit was stripped off. So when they took it off, it didn't sound the same. But with it on, they thought it was anachronistic. So here we were in a really great band, and everybody knew we were in a really great band, but we couldn't win. So it went where it did, down the tubes. But if it hadn't happened, I wouldn't be doing what I am doing now.

JRB: Well it sounds like regardless of what happened, it was what you needed at the time. And there is some of the music on the CD Chris Poland put out called *Rare Trax*. Hopefully more will surface in the future.

JS: Yeah Chris is monstrously talented. Talk about being devoted. He would show up and practice for three hours before we would. Then we would rehearse for five hours and then he would listen to the tapes. Then he would play some more. That's how you get that good. Talk about music saving somebody's life. It totally saved his.

JRB: In the spirit of collaboration, you've shifted back from the music and gotten back into writing again. You've had almost a second life in the last few years it seems. Both writing solo and collaborating with guys like Cody Goodfellow and Marc Levinthal. I know you've also worked on movies too – including doing a porno musical, *Misty Beethoven: The Musical*.

JS: I'm the only New York Times Bestselling author I know who has two Naked Oscars – AVN Awards.

JRB: I saw it! It was hilarious – especially the singing penis!

JS: Thank you. And I wrote those songs. It came out of loving crazy-ass songs. The chance to write a song about a singing penis that says it's the ruler of the world – which of course is revealed later on to *not be the truth* – that's the Frank Zappa in me coming out. The social commentary. The shameless crazy-assness.

Now there's *Rose,* the zombie musical. I wrote a lot of the music for that. *The Long Last Call,* our titty bar horror movie. I'll be doing some of the music there, too, and be deeply involved in the choices.

The great thing about film is that it combines everything that I dearly love. It combines stories, music, visuals, frenetic pace, and playing with creative other people. Collaboration on a grand scale. But I'm directing things on a larger scale. And I'm working with my co-director, Andrew Kasch, who's also an excellent film editor. He edits film like a great drummer. He's rhythmically precise. He totally knows how to work that stuff. So to me, film is like the place where all the things I love to do are synthesized into one.

JRB: I watched the trailer for *Rose,* which is pretty funny. I also read the scripts in your new book from Cemetery Dance, *Sick Chick Flicks,* which were all very good. All three in the book will lend themselves very well to the big screen, I think, and hopefully at least a couple of them will be made.

JS: Thank you. That's the idea.

JRB: That touched on pretty much what I wanted to talk to you about, John, except for one more thing. You've edited a number of anthologies over the years, right? The *Book of the Dead* series was a popular one, and now you've been doing a few new ones on werewolves, etc.

JS: The Black Dog set I've been putting together. *Zombies, Werewolves and Shape Shifters, Demons* and *Psychos.* Where this ties in musically is that as an editor, I basically approach it like I'm making a mix tape for someone I love. I'm taking the greatest stories -like I would take the greatest songs - and trying to arrange them in a way that they would love to hear, and would take them through the many moods, but still be continuous and make sense as a playlist, right?

JRB: I've seen that in the anthologies you've done – both recently and in the past. Things are chosen carefully and there's a certain rhythm to it. A certain reason that stories are in a certain place. I always wondered "Did he do that on purpose?"

JS: Always. Incredibly on purpose.

JRB: It sounds like you have a lot of fun with them for sure. Now you also have your own imprint now that you're in charge of editing for Eraserhead Press, right?

JS: I've got two. I've got Fungasm Press with the Bizarro guys (Eraserhead Press). I've also been doing a line over the last year called Ravenous Shadows where I've edited five books of horror, crime , mystery and suspense – all books that I totally love. *Tribesmen* by Adam Cesare is set during the Italian cannibal film era of the 80s. *House of Quiet Madness* by Mikita Brottman is like an Ira Levin novel, in his *Stepford Wives/Rosemary's Baby* period. Eric Shapiro's *The Devoted* is a tense thriller set inside a suicide cult, on the big day. *The Dark* by Scott Bradley and Peter Giglio, is a metaphysical Hollywood horror story about sentient darkness. And Jan Kozlowski's *Die, You Bastard! Die!*

is a psychotic crime story on the Jack Ketchum level of jaw-dropping hardcore-ness. They are all fantastic.

Fungasm is a line of books that are completely uncatagorizable, but completely knock me out. They straddle a weird line between mainstream fiction, genre fiction, and Bizarro. Sort of the literary equivalent of say, *Eternal Sunshine of the Spotless Mind.* What do you call that? Besides a really great fucking movie?

JRB: Yeah.

JS: Basically a woman named Laura Lee Bahr wrote a book called *Haunt.* She's one of my favorite people. We worked on some screen stuff together. She's a phenomenal actress, playwright, and screenwriter, and she spent seven years on this brain-melting Bizarro noir hall of mirrors. Then one day, she decided it was done, gave it to me, and said "Do you have any idea where I can sell this?" And I went "No, but I love this so much I'm going to form a publishing imprint to publish this motherfucker, and books like it." And that's what happened.

JRB: (Laughs) Yeah, that's how it happens sometimes.

JS: Yeah, "This is so good that I can't bear to see it rejected. So I'm going to put my ass on the line, and everybody needs to read this book!" And I'm looking for other books like it that follow in that crazed tradition. The only other one I've published so far is a short story collection by Violet LeVoit called *I Am Genghis Cum.* It has a picture of a warrior sperm riding a penis horse with a sword on the cover, while millions of dead sperm with X's for eyes are floating behind him. (laughs) The opening line is something like "There are 12 sperm banks in Southern California and by midnight I will have hit them all." Basically it's about a guy who wants to be like Genghis Kahn, repopulating the world with his own DNA, one cup of jizz at a time. Absolutely mindblowingly insane shit, written by this awesome woman. Violet LeVoit is sort of like the female Cody Goodfellow.

JRB: Okay, well that ought to do it! (Laughs)

JS: How the fuck are we going to top that? WOOOO!!!

THE LAST CHORD

By Douglas Wynne

I found the haunted guitar in a bus driver's garage. The bus driver was dead, had been for about a year, and his daughter Terry Sadowski was finally going through his stuff to clear it out and sell the house. She'd known he had a few guitars stashed away from the rock tours he drove in the seventies, had even heard the story of how he'd come by them, but it wasn't until she saw me on TV appraising some instruments for an episode of Rock n Roll Detectives that she realized the Stratocaster might be worth more than the house.

I didn't take her phone call myself, and I didn't have high hopes for authenticity—I spend most of my appraisal time looking at junk—but the house wasn't too far out on Long Island, only about a twenty minute drive from my shop in Greenwich Village, so I found time to head out on a Sunday afternoon and take a look.

Lo and behold, the first thing I saw when Terry led me into the living room was a black and white photo of her father with Cane Sinclair standing in front of what looked like a school bus finger painted by King Kong on acid. That was when my heart started picking up the tempo and I wished I had a better poker face. When it comes to Sinclair, I'm not just an appraiser. Hell, I'll admit it—the word fan isn't even strong enough. I'm a disciple.

It shouldn't have been me who found it. I'm sorry for that. If it had been someone less versed in the man's music, someone who couldn't play it, then that black Strat might have gone straight into a glass case and the world would never need to know how the song ends. But maybe I never had a choice and everything in my life, from the first time I heard him on the radio as a kid, has led me to this.

I had a briefcase full of photographs with me for comparing the wood grain and the paint scuffs, the hardware, and even that ghost of a bloodstain that had stubbornly refused to ever come out of the white pick guard. I flipped through the 8x10s mostly for Terry's benefit so she'd feel she was getting something for the fee, but I didn't need photos. I knew. As soon as I popped the latches and lifted the lid, I knew this was it: Cane Sinclair's 1966 black Stratocaster, the guitar he had called his *soul mate*.

"Tell me again how your father came by it." I was kneeling over the case, brushing my fingertips across the strings. I didn't dare pick it up, but I couldn't take my eyes off it. I sensed her shifting her weight from one foot to the other behind me, folding her arms, to recite the oft-told tale.

"He was driving Cane and the band on a little east coast promo tour. Just a few dates to promote a single. He had dropped Cane off at an airfield where a Cessna was supposed to hop him over the Long Island Sound to a radio gig in Connecticut. That was the plane that crashed and killed him. A few of the electric guitars were left behind on the bus."

"Because Sinclair only needed his acoustic for the radio show he never made it to."

"Uh-huh. My Dad was devastated like everyone— more so, because he thought of the band like family. People used to say the CIA made it happen, but Dad never believed that, even with all the near misses they had on that damned bus. Anyway, he didn't even check the cargo bay for a couple of months after Cane's death, and when he did, when he realized what he had, he called Mrs. Sinclair a couple of times, but she never took his calls. I'm sure it was a difficult time for her, what with the press, and the uh…"

"Time she spent in the clinic?"

"Yeah, that. It got harder to reach anyone at the compound after that, and the guitars just sat here. I'm not sure if the others belonged to Cane or his band, but everybody knows this one."

"So it never left this garage *in forty-two years?*"

"No sir."

"Okay. First thing you need to do is put it in a secure environment with temp and humidity control."

She put her hand over her mouth to stifle a squeak of giddy laughter, then got ahold of herself and said, "Mr. Brodie, are you saying you're gonna verify that this is…"

"Yeah. This is Dahlia. Congratulations."

If the guitar had gone to auction the Sadowskis might have made more money at the block, but they probably would have had to give a good chunk of it to Cane's widow anyway. And if it didn't even make it to auction, if Terry and her husband had to fight for it in court, they would have been seriously outgunned. I think Terry knew that, but I also think she cared about what her father would have wanted—for the guitar to finally find its way home after all those years. So when Myra Sinclair made a private offer within an hour of my public announcement, Terry and her husband accepted. I'd been storing the guitar in my vault for them, and when the deal was done, Myra Sinclair's people called and asked me to personally deliver it to the Sinclair ranch in California. I bought a seat for Dahlia on a 747, and flew out to L.A.

Most people think of the Appalachians when they think of Cane Sinclair because he grew up there and referenced the region so much in his music. But the fact is, he had left upstate New York for good by the summer of 1967, moved to California and bought the piece of land that he would dub *New Jerusalem*—a sprawling studio complex nestled in the Santa Monica hills. That's where he was working on a new album in fits and starts right up until he died, and it's where his wife Myra still lives today.

Conjure Man, Root Worker, Hoodoo Priest, Hex Doctor. All of those titles have been placed on Sinclair at one time or another. There are even college courses that seriously examine the question of whether or not the lyrics to "Deluge" prophesized assassinations of John and Bobby Kennedy and MLK. I'll admit that I've considered the notion myself. But nothing could have prepared me for what came into my life with that guitar.

I was expecting just a driver to pick me up at LAX, but when I found the placard in the crowd with my name on it, I noticed that Myra had also sent a security officer: a crew cut man in a navy blue blazer, wearing shades and probably a shoulder holster. Neither man offered to take the guitar case from me, but they fell in around me as I walked, and ushered me to a black town car. Now, I've handled some high profile items in my time, but this felt different. Riding through the hills I started feeling guilty and a little afraid. Not unlike a man carrying a suitcase full of money. A man who has skimmed some off the top.

I played it.

There you have it—a confession in writing. On the first night I had the guitar in my possession I played it. This was back at my shop on 8th Avenue after meeting with Terry, after photographing the instrument and logging it into my ledger.

I played one of Sinclair's songs on it. Don't think I did so lightly. Terry had told me that her father had no ability whatsoever on the guitar, so I knew the odds were good that the last man who had strummed a chord on the thing before me was Sinclair. I struggled with the temptation, and it felt a little like stepping into a dead man's shoes, or maybe more like bedding a dead man's wife, transgressing on the sanctity of something for the first time. It felt a little wrong because of how much reverence I had for him, and it was irresistible for the same reason.

Walking up to the studio door at New Jerusalem with the case in my hand, the conjoined scents of sweet lilac and bitter jimson weed wafting up around me every time the sea breeze shifted, I welled up with guilt. Sinclair told *Playboy* in 1970 that Dahlia was his soul mate. Watching my armed escort type a pass code into the box beside the door, I knew that when I met Myra Sinclair face to face, I would lie about what I'd done.

In the quiet and dark of my shop, the help gone for the day, the cream blue light of a neon sign smeared across the whitewashed brick wall like a divination of dawn, I had inserted a cable plug into Dahlia's jack, strapped her on, flicked the power switch on an old Fender tube amp, and strummed a chord. The sound was warm and deep. I dug my tender fingers into the strings knowing that the sweat of a legend had corroded all of the treble out of them over the decades.

I've never been a songwriter. I tried when I was younger, but figured out quick that I lack the knack. And yet, with Dahlia in my hands, I could hear something new emerging and diverging from my well-worn Sinclair riffs. It was something Sinclair had never written, but undeniably his. It was as if the guitar had taken hold of me and was showing me how to play it.

When the plate glass door of the studio swung open and my reflection slid sideways toward the dunes, I was relieved to find not Myra Sinclair but a member of the staff greeting my guilty face: a slender man about my age with short cropped graying hair and bright blue eyes framed by Buddy Holly glasses.

He shook my hand as I stepped over the threshold. "Hi Cal, I'm Jake Campbell, chief engineer."

My security escort had done an about face and was headed back to the car. Jake waved me in. "Don't worry, your bags will be delivered to your room." He pointed at a coffee bar in the foyer. "Can I get you anything before I show you to the studio? Coffee…tea… something cold? Myra will be joining us in the control room in a moment."

"No, thanks. *Jake Campbell*… why does your name sound so familiar?"

His poker face was better than mine, and he let me tick through it on my own. "Got it. You engineered that last Billy Moon album in the nineties, right? That one that uh…" He was nodding, but not smiling. "Well, excuse me for stating the obvious, but that was one helluva shit storm, huh?"

Now he smiled. "You could say that. Yeah."

"Shame what happened to him…" This was getting awkward. I'm usually better than this in professional situations, but my shame about the guitar, combined with my surprise at meeting the guy, had thrown me off. I flailed around for a conversational footing. "I can see why Mrs. Sinclair would have scooped you up—composure, discretion… Anyway…"

"Studio's this way." He led me down the hall to a control room that looked like it hadn't been touched since 1971. Guitars leaned against stuffed chairs and couches, legal pads with amp settings and lyrics scrawled over them in a familiar handwriting that raised the hair on the nape of my neck lay scattered atop effect processor racks. Even the cigarette butts heaped in glass ashtrays under lamps that looked old enough to belong at a yard sale but not quite old enough for an antique shop—and the way the

ashes had compressed—suggested a session in progress, but with a clock that had stopped ticking long ago. I had an idea, but it was crazy, so I decided to let Campbell walk me through it. "Is someone recording here?"

"No."

I waved my hand at the place, at the obvious evidence of work.

"The control room is just as Cane Sinclair left it."

My eyebrows told him to go on.

"My position here has more in common with a museum curator than a recording engineer. I keep the machines tuned up, and when Myra wants to hear some of Cane's unfinished music, I mix it for her. The console, that's my domain. I'm allowed to change settings as needed when we do the occasional vault release for a boxed set or something. But the guitars, the lyrics, and everything out there…" He gestured to the live room beyond the glass where a piano, a guitar amp, and some mics were waiting for overdubs that would never happen. "I don't touch it."

I pointed at an ashtray.

"Yeah, they're his."

"You're telling me those ashes have been here since 1970."

"Yeah."

"It's a *shrine*."

"Please don't touch anything, but have a seat." He rolled a chair over to me and spun it around. "Sorry for the inhospitable rules."

I sat down and laid the guitar case flat at my feet. We both stared at it in silence. Thankfully, it couldn't have been more than a minute before Myra Sinclair appeared at the glass door and entered to the sound of hissing hydraulic hinges.

It took me a moment to reconcile the woman in the room with the one I knew from photos and film. She had the same haircut—the same black bangs, no doubt dyed now—and her figure was as slender as ever, but I hadn't been expecting the deep lines etched into her face around hazel eyes that were a revelation because I had only ever seen her wearing her iconic sunglasses. She was dressed in blue jeans and a long black blouse that hugged her hips like a skirt with several layers of scarves blooming at the neckline. She squeezed my hand lightly, and settled into a black leather couch.

I noticed that her eyes never left mine, never once flitted to the guitar case at my feet. The expression on her face was neutral, could have passed for a smile in some noncommittal way. "Thank you for coming, Mr. Brodie."

"Cal, please."

"And call me Myra." She folded her fingers around her knee and said, "You're certain that this is Dahlia?"

My stomach dropped half a floor, like the elevator in the Brooklyn apartment I used to rent. "You must have read my report before you spent the money… I mean my reputation *is* at stake."

"Of course. But you know there have been some impressive replicas over the years. I'd just like to hear you say it."

"*Yes*," I almost whispered the word, then cleared my throat and opened the case. "The places where the black paint is worn through to reveal the factory sunburst finish all match up, the rosewood grain on the fret board is as telltale as a fingerprint, and the pick guard under UV light reveals— "

"You played it." Now she smiled. It brought no warmth.

"No Ma'am."

"You did, you played it." Her voice had a playful pitch to it, if a fishhook can be considered playful to a fish. "Don't lie."

I looked at the guitar.

"Did she give you a song?"

A chill passed through my shoulders, and I nodded.

"Cane used to say that old guitars sometimes have the ghosts of songs in them waiting for willing fingers to find them. What did it sound like?"

"Just a chord progression. It sounded like one of his. But I'm a fan, so…"

"Don't belittle it, Cal. I dreamed that you would come here and play it. I didn't know who you were, but I've dreamed of you for years."

I wasn't sure what to say to that. I looked at Campbell, but he was stoic and appeared to be waiting for some cue from his boss. Maybe he was used to this sort of talk.

"Aren't you going to play it for me?" Myra asked. Now she *was* looking at the guitar, and there was something new in her eyes, like the way you might look at an atomic bomb.

"I'm not much of a player," I said.

"How much do you suppose Cane was paid to play at the Royal Albert Hall?"

"A lot."

"I'll pay you the same amount to play me a few bars of Dahlia's song."

She didn't have to wait for a reply; she knew it was way more than I could turn down. She nodded at Jake, and he pulled his chair up to the console.

Dahlia's song. It was a crazy idea. And yet I knew I wasn't a songwriter, but here I was with a song. Or a fragment of one. "I'm afraid you'll be disappointed," I said.

"You said it sounds like Cane's music, so how could I be?"

"It's pretty dark. Minor."

"Do you know the meaning of the name *Dahlia*? It means 'dweller in the valley.' As in, *Yea, though I walk through the shadow of the valley of death.*"

Jake had threaded a master tape onto the machine and was rewinding it.

"What are you doing?" I asked him with an edge in my voice from the fear of little red RECORD lights.

"Nothing yet. Just being prepared. Relax." He tapped the STOP key, rose from his chair, and plugged a cable into the battered Stratocaster in my lap. He switched on an amp and handed me a pick—no doubt last handled by Sinclair.

I strummed an open chord to confirm that she was still in tune. Then I spun the volume knob up, took a deep breath, and played through the scrap of music that had come to me that night in the shop. I didn't know how to

finish it, so I just let the last chord hang in the air with all of its unresolved tension. It was an E flat diminished chord, and I only know that because I looked it up.

When the notes had faded into silence and the reverb springs in the amp ceased ringing, Jake pressed the PLAY button on the multitrack machine, and Cane Sinclair and his band spilled out of the monitor speakers, hot and wet like bourbon, playing the same song, but with words. The tune lurched along rough and ragged until the chorus climbed to an apocalyptic coda near the end.

Well I planted a seed
Now it's time for me to go
Them clouds are gonna bleed
But for now, they're movin' slow…

The vocal trailed off, the band unraveled, and I could hear Sinclair's husky speaking voice, off axis of the mic, saying, "S'all I got boys. Dunno how it ends."

Jake stopped the tape. The silence in the room was loud, but in my mind I could hear more: another line of lyric floating over the missing diminished chord Dahlia had given me, and then a final cadence. I felt like my anchor to reality had broken free of its chain.

I looked at Myra and she said what I couldn't. "It's the same song; the one Cain was writing when he died, and the one you're writing now. Do you know how it ends, Cal?"

I shook my head. "Not really, no. Probably a lot of chords could go there."

"What about the words?"

I laughed. "I'm a fan and all, and a bit of a guitar player, but a poet I am not."

"I didn't accuse you of being a poet. You know what I think you are? A conduit."

"For what?"

"Maybe Dahlia is the artist and *you're* the instrument."

"You think what? Cane's *spirit* is haunting the guitar, trying to finish his last song?"

"Don't you?"

I looked at Jake. He examined his fingernails. I noticed a long smooth scar running down his forearm.

Myra stood up and said, "Jake will show you to your room. Keep Dahlia with you. Change the strings, do a setup, get her ready for recording. And sleep on that song. In the morning Jake will record whatever you have." She held up a hand to stave off my protest. "Strictly for my edification, don't worry, we won't be releasing it. You'll still make your flight, and I'll send you home well fed and well paid. Do we have a deal?"

"I can't promise anything."

"I'm not asking you to. Just sleep on it."

My room was what a realtor might have described as "rustic luxury." There was a river rock fireplace and a lot of Mexican textiles, a large flat screen TV mounted like an onyx gem in the east facing cedar planked wall, and a larger picture window in the west. Rows of recessed shelves were well stocked with liquor and a comprehensive collection of Sinclair CDs, DVDs, and biographies.

I should have been tired, but I felt restless, nervous. I sat on the bed and gazed out the window. The Malibu sun was descending beyond the sage speckled hills toward the dark blue Pacific in the distance. My body was still on New York time, and I knew I'd need to sleep soon. I considered the guitar case and decided it would be best to do the maintenance now, before slipping under the sheets with a DVD on the screen and a scotch on the nightstand. With Dahlia in good shape, I could leave in the morning. No one could force me to write a song.

Jake had jotted a three-digit extension number on a pad beside the phone with instructions to call him at any hour if I had an idea for the song, so he could record it before it evaporated. Well, slim chance of that, it was already circling around in my head like a litany. I already knew how it ended. I had what Myra wanted, but I didn't know what it meant, or why it frightened me. I even had the last few lines of lyrics.

> Well I planted a seed
> Now it's time for me to go
> Them clouds are gonna bleed
> Gabriel's horn is gonna blow
> Where they gonna feed?
> Don't you know?
> Welcome to the show

I could hear the whole thing vividly, in Sinclair's familiar tones.

There was a desk in front the window, its surface bare except for a leather tool case and a fresh pack of strings. I draped a Mexican blanket over the desktop, laid the guitar down on it, and set to work: wiped it down, replaced the strings, adjusted the truss rod, and pricked my finger on the sharp steel point of the G string. A bead of dark blood welled up and dripped onto the fret board where the dry rosewood drank it right up. I put my finger in my mouth and heard a faint harmonic sigh ringing off of the strings, like a sigh of pleasure after a thirst has been quenched.

The pad of paper with Jake's number on it was paired with a pen on the bedside table. I knew I could write the lyrics and chords on it, but I didn't want to. I know how this sounds, and it wasn't the first time I've been pricked by a string, but I felt like Dahlia had *bit* me. I could sense her impatience, her anger that I wouldn't play her. How long had she waited in her little velvet lined coffin with the song?

I poured myself that scotch, and scanned the familiar spines on the media shelves. A memory teased the edges of my mind, like a shape under a sheet. My gaze was drawn back to the guitar, to the dim stain on the white celluloid pick guard where a fan's blood had splashed it at the Hanson's Field protest concert in 1968. Everyone over thirty knows the story—the clash between the protesters and the police in riot gear at the perimeter of the nuke plant. The newspaper photos of the massacre are flash burned into my generation's memory, and the official story, the story told by the police and the press with lock

step wording, about how the rolls of razor wire were picked up by the storm and raked across the crowd, has never been questioned.

There were other stories, though, nestled in the pages of some of those Sinclair biographies, and quoted in ones and zeroes on those DVDs. Heard in passing, they sound like evidence of the psychedelic delirium that defined the era, but taken together the eyewitness accounts paint a chilling picture. You'd have to believe in mass hallucination, *shared* hallucination, to discount them. Bassist Jerry Newcastle gives the most complete version, in the film *Mark of Cane*. He's still wearing a paisley shirt, but his hair is shorter these days. Looking beyond the camera, he says:

"Cane always talked about the spirit fish, called 'em the Qliphoth. Some of the hardcore fans used to send me mail about this stuff after he died, theories from Kabbalah and shit. Anyway, Cane, he said the fish were like hungry ghosts that fed on negative emotions. Like anger and fear and hate. Said it was part of the circle of life and we were helping people to purge those negative vibes. Cane used to put something in the fog juice for the light show, some kinda hoodoo powder so we could, you know, see them. Sounds crazy, right? I swear it looked like a shoal of silver piranhas feeding on the crowd. But they were just spirits, right? Most people didn't even know they were there. At Hanson's Field, though, they were real. They could cut you; they could *bite*. Flesh, not fantasy. They were getting stronger."

Newcastle rubs his arm and looks away.

It's the weirdest moment I've seen in a Sinclair documentary. The film goes on to talk about the drug culture. Sinclair's influence on it and vice versa.

The books hold other clues. Cane's music was always apocalyptic, but it got darker and more violent toward the end of his life. He's been called the godfather of heavy metal, and when his native scene in rural New York went all peace and love with Woodstock, some of his mystically minded peers hinted that they'd meant to use that festival to banish something dark unleashed by Sinclair on the left coast the previous year. In his published poetry, there's an oblique reference to "opening the door of judgment with the black axe". Is that Dahlia? The black Strat? I've often gotten the sense from his late-era lyrics that he thought the world was beyond redemption and in need of cleansing by a second flood. Tonight I wonder what might swim in that ethereal tide.

I think Myra wants me to end it. Not just the song, but maybe the world. Is that crazy? I wonder. I know how it goes. I can't get the tune out of my head. The black axe in the closet is calling me to take it up and play the tune… and God help me, *I want to.*

It's like an itch, like a sexual urge. Part of me needs to hear it, to channel it, to birth it into the world.

After the scotch I must have dozed off. The DVD was looping through the menu screen when I came to, and Dahlia was in the bed with me, tangled in the sheets, her curves looking more like a woman's than ever, but I don't remember taking her out of the case.

I swung my legs over the side of the bed, and picked the guitar up to put it away. But with the body in my lap and the neck in my left hand, my fingers just curled around in the shape of a chord. I tried to slide my hand off of the thing, but I could feel some kind of magnetic pull. I watched in horror as my fingertips were sliced open by strings turned to razor wire, my blood splashing out onto Dahlia, the sheets, the floor. I could hear my blood pattering on the polished wood, could smell the iron in the air. Then another sound: tapping on glass, like birds at the window, but when I turned my head to look at the window, it was like looking into an aquarium. Silver fish with needle teeth crowded the glass. A wave of cloud surged over them and the window shattered, raining glass on the bed. I curled my body inward and away from the tsunami, tucked my chin to my chest, and watched as the Qliphoth swarmed to the red ribbons of blood trailing from my fingers. That's when I woke up.

The DVD menu looped, reflected in the unbroken window. No blood on the sheets, just a lot of sweat.

❦❦❦

Dahlia is in her case in the closet, and I'm writing this account on my laptop at the desk. I called Jake Campbell. He must have been waiting up for the call because he answered on the first ring. It's three AM and the rest of the ranch must be sleeping, but I wonder about Myra. The moon hangs low, and I can see silver-washed thunderheads over the ocean, getting closer. Their shapes don't look quite right for clouds. More like dense flocks of starlings, or shoals of fish. They'll make landfall before dawn.

I told Jake that I might know how it ends, and he surprised me by saying, "Me too."

"The song?"

"No," he said, "The whole fucking mess."

"You mean the world?" I laughed. Nerves.

"Listen, Cal. It's a cold night for the valley. Bad weather's brewing. You might want to warm that room up. Do you need any wood for the fireplace?"

I looked at the closet. The song in my skull was so loud it almost drowned out what he was telling me.

"No. There's enough here."

"Good. Goodnight, Cal."

"I'll never work again, you know. If I do this."

"I understand. The price of action is high. The price of inaction may be higher."

"How did you get that scar on your arm, Jake… fishing?"

"No. Old war wound from the Billy Moon sessions."

"Well, if you're ever in New York again, look me up. We'll have a drink."

"Deal. Listen, Cal, you can dial nine for an outside line. You might want to have a cab meet you at the end of the lane before the ranch wakes up."

He hung up.

It's getting hard to write this with the music so loud it feels like the room should be shaking, that same coda going around and around like Hell's own calliope. I'm going to save this file to the cloud, shut the laptop down, and pack my things now. I might use some of the books on the shelf to get the fire going. Then I'll find out if I can take Dahlia out of her case and lay her down in a bed of flames without my fingers betraying me and reaching for that goddamned lost chord.

❦❦❦

THE NIGHTMARE RETURNS:

ALICE COOPER REVISITS A CLASSIC

By Trever Nordgren

A little over 35 years ago, the Godfather of Shock Rock, Alice Cooper, released his bonafide classic *Welcome to My Nightmare* and set the blueprint for every horror-influenced rock act since. Cooper had fully developed his grand guignol stage show and had also come up with an album that personified it. Now all these years later, Cooper is back with a sequel to WTMN called *Welcome 2 My Nightmare*.

Alice Cooper (whose real name is Vincent Furnier), is a Detroit native who dressed up in women's clothing and mostly offended audiences in the late 1960s. Backed by 4 able musicians who later became known as the Billion Dollar Babies band, they were discovered by Frank Zappa – who released their first two albums *Pretties for You* (1969) and *Easy Action* (1970) to little fanfare. Influenced by '50s Rock, West Side Story and horror films, Cooper and gang pushed the androgyny envelope and pre-dated glam rock by a couple of years. The music however, wasn't quite there yet. Unfocused lyrically and bouncing from one musical style to the next, producer Bob Ezrin (KISS, Pink Floyd) brought the much-needed focus to catapult the band to stardom and infamy with hits like: "I'm Eighteen", "Is It My Body", "Be My Lover" and "School's Out".

Barely touched upon with songs like "Return of the Spiders", "Refrigerator Heaven" and "Lay Down and Die, Goodbye", under Ezrin's tutelage Alice started to explore his darker side. With songs like "Black Juju", "The Ballad of Dwight Fry" (still part of his stage set to this day with Cooper being fitted for a straight-jacket), "Halo of Flies", "Dead Babies", "Killer", "Luney Tune", "Billion Dollar Babies", "Sick Things", "Mary-Ann" and "I Love the Dead" he started to write about the twisted themes he became known for. He also started developing the trademark makeup around his eyes (originally spider legs and eventually the harlequin/snake eyes he is now associated with) and some of the black leather and bondage look he still sports to this day (that was so influential on so many bands and artists down the road like KISS, King Diamond, etc.). By incorporating some of this horror imagery into his concerts, Cooper began to fully mine the Shock Rock persona he eventually became known for. Bands like Black Sabbath had previously touched on the Horror movie element with album imagery and songs, but Cooper went the distance. From getting the Electric

Chair, having his head cut off from a guillotine, getting shots from giant needles, being hung by the neck, brandishing boa constrictors, bloody baby dolls and more – Alice brought it to life on stage.

All of this fueled what became probably his crowning achievement in 1975 with *Welcome to My Nightmare*. Having just parted ways with his Billion Dollar Babies band, Cooper went in to the studio to record what became the first Hard Rock/Heavy Metal concept album (No doubtably influenced by The Who with their landmark album Tommy and Rock Operas like Jesus Christ Superstar). Bolstered by a solid band of studio musicians like Dick Wagner, Steve Hunter, Whitey Glan and Prakash (of Lou Reed's band) and even a guest spot by legendary horror film star Vincent Price (who does the fiendish intro to "The Black Widow" – and a number of years later would be tapped by Michael Jackson to narrarate "Thriller") – Cooper frames the songs around the premise of Alice inviting us to participate in his nightmare and to "feel at home".

Here we meet the aforementioned "Black Widow" who is "the unholiest of kings", Steven (a disturbed man-child), "Cold Ethyl" (a cold, dead object of Cooper's affections and a song he still does on stage parading around with a lifeless corpse (manikin), "Some Folks" (who "love to see red") and other twisted, disturbing characters and imagery. Cooper even cops a huge hit with his sensitive ballad, "Only Women Bleed", done only as Alice can.

The album went on to be a huge hit and has influenced countless performers like Rob Zombie, Marilyn Manson, Iron Maiden, King Diamond, Twisted Sister, GWAR, Slipknot and even Ozzy Osbourne himself (who employed a more visceral horror-influenced stage show after he left Black Sabbath). The TV special in April, 1975 did very well - as did a theatrical release of the tour (and later concert video) in 1976. Cooper became so well-known he even ended up doing the title track of WTMN on the Muppet Show, appeared on Hollywood Squares and eventually even humorously played himself in the movie Wayne's World. Alice Cooper was a born showman and his influences, ranging from Musicals to Horror had finally found a firm foundation. Rock Music would never be the same again…

So here we are all these years later and Ozzy is back with Black Sabbath, Twisted Sister is together again on stage and KISS has been in full makeup and costume making new albums and touring the world. Some acts like Queensryche and King Diamond are even revisiting their popular concept albums like Operation Mindcrime and Abigail respectively and now the master himself takes a trip back to Nightmare Land once again.

As they say, it's hard to capture lightning in a bottle twice - as most bands, directors, authors, etc. who do sequels or revisit classics have found. There are also varying factors to a successful album, film, book or creative endeavor. Timing is everything, they say. Nerves can be touched in the public consciousness and spark off in numerous directions. The original *Welcome to My Nightmare* came out in the mid-1970s as the first waves of glam rock and heavy metal/hard rock were dying out. The US wave of Hard Rock and Metal (the second wave of HM) led by KISS, Aerosmith, Ted Nugent, etc. had not yet hit and people were looking for something new. The successful UK and Broadway play of The Rocky Horror Picture Show (which very much fit along the lines of Cooper's twisted stage antics and the androgyny and 50's rock-inspired glam) was garnering more of a fan base and pushing the confines of sexual roles (and about to launch the film around the time of WTMN). The resurgence of Horror both in films (with the age of the drive-ins and cult favorites like Night of the Living Dead, Texas Chainsaw Massacre, The Last House on the Left and others) and fiction (the emergence of best-selling Horror novels from Stephen King, Ira Levin, Thomas Tryon and William Peter Blatty) after many years in the cellar also helped fuel the popularity of darker material in the public eye. Sex and violence were becoming more commonplace in the entertainment world and boundaries were continually being pushed. Then along comes Cooper on the music side to blow it out of the water.

So how about the new album, *Welcome 2 My Nightmare*? To start with, Alice smartly brings back producer Bob Ezrin to helm it. Ezrin was classically trained and uses the tried and true technique of incorporating a theme into a musical movement which helps tie it together. It's something he used to great effect in albums like Destroyer from KISS and The Wall from Pink Floyd – and especially in the original WTMN – with injecting orchestras (courtesy of the excellent Michael Kamen) as well. Cooper also invites back three members of his original Billion Dollar Babies band: Michael Bruce, Dennis Dunaway and Neal Smith (Glen Buxton passed away back in 1997). Also present are WTMN guitarist Dick Wagner, eighties-era band mate Kip Winger and longtime songwriting collaborator Desmond Child.

The album opens with "I Am Made of You" which incorporates a reworked theme from "Steven" from Welcome – as well as a guitar solo from WTMN alumni Steve Hunter. With the exception of a brief, goofy modulated voice it sets the tone right away. Next comes the up-tempo "Caffeine", which is what you would expect it to be about – an ode to something a majority of Americans are hooked on. "The Nightmare Returns" re-establishes the theme, followed by "A Runaway Train" (featuring a solo from Country star Vince Gill), "Last Man on Earth" (somewhat of a nod to "Some Folks" with its vaudevillian style) and "The Congregation" (a grooving rocker along the lines of "The Black Widow" and "School's Out" and features Rob Zombie as "The Guide").

Then comes the first single off the album, "I'll Bite Your Face Off", which is a bluesy hard rock song in the vein of "Be My Lover" or "No More Mr. Nice Guy". It's the sort of straightforward rock song that keeps Cooper from straying too far to the Heavy Metal side, but incorporates his typical black sense of humor. Next comes (in my opinion) the low point of the album, "Disco Bloodbath Boogie Fever", a silly song that harkens back to the likes of "I Gotta Dance" and "Guilty" when Alice discovered disco. Now he adds in some rap as well to it. Ugh. "Ghouls Gone Wild" is sort of a Beach-Party pop song that harkens back to some of Cooper's sixties influence and features Mark Volman (The Turtles, T. Rex and Frank Zappa's Mothers of Invention) on backing vocals. "Something to Remember Me By" is a ballad that is the "Only Women Bleed" of the bunch and nods towards "Cold Ethyl" as well. It was originally written by Cooper and Wagner back in the late 1970s but never used.

Moving back into harder rocking territory (and featuring the BDB band), "When Hell Comes Home", moves back into the psychological "Steven"/"The Awakening" territory, with a kid's memory of a dark upbringing. It also hints that Steven is the protagonist of this album-long Nightmare (much as WTMN did). "What Baby Wants" is a guitar peppered dance/pop song featuring Ke$ha (and has the feel of catchy Desmond Child co-penned hits of the late '80s like "Trash"), and "I Gotta Get out of Here" jangles with elements of Tom Petty and The Byrds country/rock. "The Underture" is a re-working of the theme of "Welcome to My Nightmare" from the original album (also incorporating elements of the other songs from WTMN and the new album like: "Devil's Food", "Steven", "Something to Remember Me By", "The Awakening", "Years Ago", "I Am Made of You" and others) and wraps things up neatly. (**Ed. Note:** *You can also hear strains of "The Black Widow" in the bonus track, "Under the Bed", a creepy ode to keeping our hands and feet away from those monsters' clutching claws*).

So it's certainly a mix of styles and a little disjointed at points, but then again Alice always has combined a lot of different types of music trends (Heavy Metal, Glam, New Wave, Art Rock, Broadway Musicals, '50s Rock, etc.). At times, it reminds me a bit more of *Alice Cooper Goes to Hell* (which was much more all over the place musically than *Welcome to My Nightmare*), but the re-occurring themes do help bring the focus back and the spirit of the original is present. And having a solid band and musicians from his formative years certainly helps. So probably not destined to be the classic that WTMN is, but definitely one of the better things Cooper has done in recent years. And peaking at number 22 on the Billboard 200, it's also the highest-charting album for Cooper since 1991's *Hey Stoopid*.

So can you go home again? Probably not, but it doesn't hurt to bring along some old friends for the ride.

TOP 10
ROCK & ROLL HORROR MOVIES

By R.B. James

Music has always had a place in horror movies, as well as in various films of other genres. Horror and Rock and Roll hold a special place as both have commonly been shunned by society (especially Heavy Metal and Punk Rock). There's always those people who think we're a bit bent for liking horror movies and loud music (and it's always been a tradition to piss off your asshole neighbors by cranking Motorhead or Slayer as loud as you can or offending that stuck-up cheerleader with a splatter film).

Some of the movies like *The Horror at Party Beach, Earth VS the Spider*, etc. are very dumb, but still have some silly charm and were the first to use Rock music in their films. Others like Stephen King's ill-fated directorial debut *Maximum Overdrive* had a great soundtrack but was a piece of turd. There are a few movies that stand out however. Some are influential films, some have music so ingrained in it that it's inseparable, and some are just plain cult classics. And since we're focusing on Rock and Horror in music and fiction, it seems a shame not to take a peek at music in the movies as well. So here's my list of favorites (in no particular order):

1   *Return of the Living Dead* (1985) – Alien screenwriter Dan O'Bannon's directorial debut and a wild, funny zombie romp with a great soundtrack and the lovely Linnea Quigley (naked quite often). What more needs to be said?

2   *The Rocky Horror Picture Show* (1975) – One of the biggest cult classics of all time. Translated from a successful run as a musical (in both the UK and on Broadway), Rocky Horror made its way to the big screen with a strong cast (Tim Curry, Susan Sarandon, Barry Bostwick, Meat Loaf, etc.). A take on Frankenstein, Rocky pushed the envelope with cross-dressing and bisexuality and put the perfect soundtrack along with it to become one of the first audience participation films. Let's do the Time Warp again!

3   *The Phantom of the Paradise* (1974) – Brian DePalma's musical riff on The Phantom of the Opera. Predating Rocky Horror by a year or so, De Palma diverted from his usual Hitchcockian efforts to do a rock opera. Not scary, but a fun, underrated film with Paul Williams as the villain and a good soundtrack.

4   *Repo Man* (1984) – Emilio Estevez stars as a Punk Rock car repossessor who runs across something out of the X-Files. Although sort of a science fiction film, it's dark enough to make my list and has a great Punk soundtrack to boot!

5 *The Crow* (1994) – Brandon Lee's moody last film based on James O'Barr's successful and equally moody comic series. A dark, atmospheric film along the lines of Blade Runner with an excellent soundtrack entwined in the film. Spawned two sequels and a short lived TV series, but the first is the best!

6 *Susperia* (1977) – Dario Argento's classic horror film set in a dance academy and haunted by one of the Three Mothers. A pounding, relentless soundtrack by Italian progressive hard rock band Goblin helps drive the movie. (Runner up award goes to Argento's previous effort Deep Red which features Goblin's screen & soundtrack debut)

7 *Spawn* (1997) – Bolstered by a soundtrack mixing Metal bands like Metallica, Slayer, Korn, etc. with DJ's and electronic music. The combination produced a solid soundtrack for Todd McFarlane's adaptation.

8 *The Devil's Rejects* (2005) – Rob Zombie's best film picks up where House of 1000 Corpses left off and features a great soundtrack that helps the film along.

9 *The Lost Boys* (1987) - The brat pack of the horror and fantasy scene with a solid music lineup. Kiefer Sutherland, Jason Patric, Bill and Ted's Alex Winter, the lovely Jami Gertz and the Coreys (Haim and Feldman). Nice town but too many damn vampires!

10 *Trick or Treat* (1986) – Okay, this one's kind of goofy, but I like it. Features Mark (Skippy from Family Ties) as a browbeaten Metalhead whose idol, Sammi Curr, dies in a fire. Gene Simmons plays a DJ who gives him Curr's last demo and when played backwards brings Curr back for mayhem. Features an excellent soundtrack by Motorhead guitarist Fast Eddie Clarke's band Fastway and a funny cameo from Ozzy Osbourne as a preacher.

AND

An honorable mention must go out to John Carpenter for his theme music in *Halloween, Escape From New York, The Fog*, etc. While not Rock & Roll music (with the exception of *Christine* which features classic '50s Rock & Roll mixed with John's instrumental score), Carpenter had a knack for making very memorable soundtrack music that set the tone for his films and is integral to them.

Books About Comics!

HOW **UNDERDOG** WAS BORN...

Buck Biggers & Chet Stover

IF YOU'RE **CRACKED** You're Happy!
A HISTORY of the WORLD'S 2nd GREATEST HUMOR MAGAZINE!
VOLUME 1: THE EARLY YEARS

DAMMIT! I Swallowed ANOTHER ONE!
"Kit's cartoons are sort of like *The Far Side*, but more offbeat and often much funnier."
Chip Rowe, Senior Editor, *Playboy*
CARTOONS BY **KIT LIVELY**
FOREWORD by New Yorker cartoonist **SHANNON WHEELER**
INTRODUCTION by **JAMES O'BARR** (creator, writer-artist of *The Crow*)

PRIVATE EYES in the **COMICS**
by John A. Dinan

FLIGHTS OF FANTASY
The Unauthorized but True Story of Radio & TV's **ADVENTURES OF SUPERMAN**
By Michael J. Hayde

STRONGER THAN SPINACH
THE Secret OF THE Appeal *Famous Studios* **POPEYE** Cartoons by Steve R. Bierly

YOU WOULDN'T LIKE ME WHEN I'M ANGRY!
A HULK COMPANION PATRICK A. JANKIEWICZ

Comic Strips & Comic Books of Radio's Golden Age
A Biography of All Radio Shows Based on Comics
by Ron Lackmann

THE SILVER AGE OF COMICS
Fantastic Four
WILLIAM SCHOELL

BLONDIE GOES TO HOLLYWOOD
THE BLONDIE COMIC STRIP IN FILMS, RADIO & TELEVISION
CAROL LYNN SCHERLING

GROWING UP WITH MONSTERS
My Time At Universal Studios in Rhymes!
by Carla Laemmle and Daniel Kinske

WHISTLING DOWN THE HALL
The Times and Cartoons of America's Original Pantomime Comic Strip Artist
From pre-Depression to mid-20th century; highlights from thirty years of those and other works of Francis X (Frank) Reardon, Virginia's premier cartoonist and one of America's greatest pen artists
By MICHAEL Y. KONNS

BearManorMedia.com

KING'S ROCK

By Michael R. Collings

Let me start by being honest: I don't care for Rock and Roll.

I don't dislike it particularly. It just never spoke to me.

Oh, I had a pre-teen flirtation with pop music—I still remember singing along with "One-eyed, One-horned, Flying Purple People-eater" and "Itsy-bitsy Teeny-weeny Yellow Polka-dot Bikini"—but by the time I was in my mid-teens and ripe for Rock, I was already enamored with classical music. Perhaps because by then I was playing the organ for my church, and most of the music I encountered was of the more staid and serious sort.

As a result, I've never quite understood the Rock-and-Roll phenomenon. In fact, for years, I rarely listened to *anything* composed after the death of Gustav Mahler in 1911. I've since upgraded my limitations to anything composed after the death of the great French organist Charles-Marie Widor in 1937—but it took me nearly two decades to make that concession.

What has this to do with the subject of this essay: Stephen King and Rock and Roll?

Well, it is kind of the basic point I want to make. If I—if even *I*—know that Rock is fundamental to King's life and to his writings, it must *really* be important…and obvious.

The briefest overview of King's life immediately suggests deep connections with Rock, both as a form of music and as a culture (or sub-culture). Perhaps the most conspicuous item, until recently at least, is his participation in a veritable Rock band—and lest anyone miss the correlation, the performers called themselves the "Rock-Bottom Remainders. Since its beginnings two decades agothe grouphas at times included such literary luminaries Mitch Albom, Dave Barry, Sam Barry, Tad Bartimus, Roy Blount Jr., Robert Fulghum, Matt Groening, Cynthia Heimel, Greg Iles, Barbara Kingsolver, James McBride,Ridley Pearson, Joel Selvin,Amy Tan, andScott Turow. They performed for a final time in August, 2012.

For the past decade or so King's name has also been associated with another unlikely endeavor—nothing less than a theatrical musical in collaboration with Rock-legend John Mellencamp. After innumerable revisions and adjustment among the two, *The Ghost Brothers of Darkland County* opened in April 2012. The play is described in one review as "Southern Gothic musical fraught with mystery, tragedy and ghosts of the past," highly appropriate for a performance with book by Stephen King. And, although the number of instruments is limited to half a dozen or so, the music partakes of the heartland rock that Mellencamp help to develop in the 1970s.

Even before these endeavors, however, King's participation in the media as a way of satisfying his love of Rock was nothing new. From 1983 to 1990, King was directly involved with Rock through the Bangor-based radio station, WZON. After he and his wife purchased it, the station initially showcased Rock; eventually, however, the station failed to earn a profit and was sold. In 1993, King received the station back and still operates it under a progressive-talk format. The Kings also own WZLO, a talk-based station; and, more to the point,another Bangor-based outlet, WKIT-FM, currently advertised as "Stephen King's Rock and Roll Station."

Even before King began pursuing outlets through radio, theater, and life Rock performances, King's love of Rock led to a different kind of decades-long engagement. Over three decades ago, as a young, relatively unknown writer, King found himself in a quandary. His publisher at the time felt (along with most major publishers) that more than one book per year would over-saturate the audience, reducing sales. Yet—as by now probably every horror reader knows—Stephen King is nothing if not prolific, with over 50 novels and 200 shorter fictions to his credit, along with countless reviews, articles, screenplays, and other bits of writing.

The solution to the problem was to publish additional books under a pseudonym. As a result, other than a single short story that appeared under the name 'John Swithen,' every pseudonymous work by King has highlighted the name 'Richard Bachman,' now almost as famous as King's own. Between 1977 and 2007, Bachman released *Rage* (1977), *The Long Walk* (1979), *Road Work* (1981), *The Running Man* (1982), *Thinner* (1984—the book that revealed King's use of a pen name), *The Regulators* (1996—sold as a set with *Desperation*, by Stephen King), and *Blaze* (2007—a re-working of an early attempt at a novel).

In 1985, the first four were published in an omnibus collection, *The Bachman Books*, which reached the bestsellers lists in October of that year. It was instrumental in definitively demonstrating that the publishers had been wrong about the danger of King over-saturating his market. In late November of 1985, King had no fewer than *five* titles on the lists: the hardcover editions of *Skeleton Crew* and *The Bachman Books*, and the mass-market and trade paperback editions of *The Talisman*, *Thinner*, and *The Bachman Books*. The achievement was repeated with the same titles in January 1986.

All right. That's interesting enough, I suppose, but what does it have to do with Rock? In a sense, every one of those novels was a tribute to Rock. The name 'Richard Bachman' came from two sources: Donald E. Westlake's 'Richard Stark' (King would pay homage to Westlake again by naming a character in the Bachman-dedicated *The Dark Half* 'George Stark'); and the Rock group King was listening to at the time he decided on the pseudonym, Bachman-Turner Overdrive.

Of course, there is more than just the appearance in a pseudonym to connect King with Rock. In book after book, novel after novel, on the reverse of the title page readers will find permissions to quote lyrics, more often than not Rock lyrics: Lennon, McCartney, Dylan, Springsteen, Joplin, Guthrie, and a host of others are includede, excerpts from their songs lending power, cadence, and rhythm to the stories King wishes to tell. In some cases, there may be only a handful of such permissions. In longer novels, such as *Christine* (1983) and *It* (1986)—not coincidentally written during the period when King was involved with the struggling WZON in its Rock format—the permissions extend over three pages, indicating King's massive indebtedness.

In addition, characters in his novels and stories associate themselves with Rock. Larry Underwood in *The Stand*, to name the most obvious, has just released his first single, a chart-breaking piece called "Baby, Can You Dig Your Man." The title, and the lasting effects of an almost stereotypic Rock-lifestyle on Underwood and his relationships with others, recur throughout the novel. Music becomes, in effect, a symbol for Captain Tripps and its influence on the readers' perceptions of life and death.

Perhaps the clearest—and simultaneously the most ambiguous—paean to Rock occurs in a short piece, first appearing in *Shock Rock* (1992) and reprinted in *Nightmares & Dreamscapes* (1993). In it, a young couple traveling the Oregon back country leaves the main highways and, largely due to the husband's stubbornness, gets hopelessly lost until they crest a final ridge and discover that they are in a small town—and almost perfect Norman Rockwell town—called Rock and Roll Heaven. As events unfold, however, Mary Willingham begins to suspect that the proper allusion would not be to Rockwell but to Ray Bradbury…specifically, to the story "Mars is Heaven," which appeared in *The Martian Chronicles* as "The Third Expedition."

In short, the idyllic town is a trap.

Gradually, the Willinghams discover that, except for a handful of people, Rock and Roll Heaven is populated by the ghosts of dead Rock stars: Janis Joplin, Rick Nelson, Buddy Holly, Elvis Presley, and a host of others. Initially, the couple is invited to stay for the evening's Rock Concert in the park, but before it even begins they intuit the worst. The Rock stars require audiences, living audiences, to give them the accolades they desperately need. And the Willinghams, the newest victims, are never leaving Rock and Roll Heaven. As Alan Freed screams in the penultimate paragraph, "Rock and Roll will never die." Neither do its prey.

The story is ambiguous because, in spite of King's affection for Rock, it is presented as in some senses life-threatening. Most of the revenant performers died young, some at their own hands, others as a direct result of the accompanying lifestyle. And even before the threat to the Willinghams becomes overt, there is something cloying, too-cute—but rapidly "not-cute"—about the names of businesses, including the Rock-a-Boogie Restaurant. Mary herself responds to Main Street with a *Twilight Zone* reference that, as the story progresses, becomes more and more appropriate.

Yet the couple remains, drawn into the illusion of a perfect town until, when they finally make a break for freedom and, ultimately, life, they are trapped. There is something about their surname—*Willingham*—that seems apt terribly. The meaning of the first part, *willing*, is obvious; the last part, still common in place names in Britain and the U.S., is the Anglo-Saxon word for 'home.' Rock and Roll Heaven is both seductive and destructive, like the music itself; but ultimately Clark and Mary are unwilling to leave the perfect *home*.

Every point made in this brief examination of King's connections to Rock could easily be expanded and explored to heighten readers' appreciation of how intertwined the man and the music are. But even in this cursory glimpse, it seems clear that the two are, on multiple levels, inseparable.

✹✹✹

ZOMBIE A GO-GO

From The Misadventures of Butch Quick

By Brian Knight

I've believed a lot of dumb shit in my life, but some shit is too dumb even for me to swallow. Vampires, werewolves, Santa Claus and honest politicians. Topping the list of things too outrageous for even me to buy—zombies.

I do not believe in zombies.

The western sky was red fading to black, the Paradise Valley light pollution just a distant lighter haze to the north. Below me, in The Pit, the party was still pretty much under control. As under control as X raves ever were anyway. There was a lot of heavy petting and ass-grabbing masquerading as dancing, but that's X for you. At least it doesn't make you psychotic like some of the new shit out there on the streets.

The Pit is one of those out of the way places that attracts partiers from time to time, an abandoned rock quarry in the hills south of the city. A stone dimple at the ass-crack end of a shit gravel road. The Pit was half a city block around and thirty feet deep, accessible by a single steep and rusting iron staircase. A few old sheds and ancient rock crushers loomed nearby to lend atmosphere, and did a nice job I thought. Part of an old conveyer gantry still jutted out over the edge of The Pit. The rest lay dismantled and scattered at the bottom.

It's not used as often these days. There's no cell reception at The Pit, and the current generation of creampuffs go to pieces without their cell phones.

I'd considered trying to keep a lookout from one of the old catwalks that seemed to hold the decaying mess together but decided against it. Just because everyone down there was stoned didn't make them blind. The guy standing at the top of the steps handing out goodie bags to the new arrivals would see me for sure, and I didn't want anyone to see me until I was ready to act. I didn't want *her* to spot me until it was too late to run away.

I'm Butch Quick, or as I'm somstimes known on the streets of Paradise Valley, that big, fuck-ugly, sasquatch-looking guy. It's an unfair comparison, since Native Americans don't have that much body hair. If you're looking for the missing link, there are plenty of rednecks in Eastern Washington who fit that bill better than I do.

I don't spend all of my time sneaking around abandoned quarries to spy on ravers. I don't think I could handle it, that techno crap they play makes me want to hurt people. Mostly I repo cars and collect bail jumpers for my Uncle Higheagle, owner of Higheagle Classic Cars and Eagle Eye Bailbonds. This wasn't a normal night though. It wasn't even a normal rave.

There were lights set up around the perimeter of The Pit, one pointing down from the catwalk above the rock crushers, another pointed down from a crumbling outcrop on the far side, probably a few more I couldn't see from where I sat with the binoculars. The lights were still dark, the only light came from a bonfire down in The Pit.

The partiers below me, the ones who hadn't already stripped naked – that 'X' just seems to bring out the nakedness in some people – were dressed up as zombies.

A zombie themed rave in an old-school horror movie setting.

I was in the right place, now it was just a matter of waiting for the right time and keeping my eyes peeled for The Director and his fresh young starlet.

Nikki Guerlain.

They arrived just when I was beginning to second-guess myself.

A small U-Haul rolled up and parked alongside the cluster-fuck of rust bucket vans, pickups and cars. The girl who hopped down from the passenger side was a slightly older and punkier version of the girl from my photo. She wore tight black pants and a muscle shirt. Bright red hair stuck up in sporty spikes around a pail, pixyish face. She was smiling, bouncing with each step. Excited.

The Director came around the other side and joined her a moment later.

He was an older guy, stalky, blocky, his gray hair buzz-cut and his face clean-shaven. Dressed in a crisp black suit. Not exactly what I'd expected, more than a bit out of place. He looked like a banker or lawyer, except for the cane he carried, black with a skull for a handle. It looked ornamental rather than functional. He rolled the U-Haul's back door up and motioned toward the leaning shacks at the pit's edge.

Three guys rushed from the darkness inside the nearest shack, the next to the edge of The Pit, and scrambled inside. They came out a minute later packing a camera, a big one on a tall tripod, and what looked like a lot of antique studio recording equipment.

They carried their load of shit back into the shed, and a few minutes later I heard the distant rumble of a generator. The spotlights joined the bonfire at the center of the pit, stuttering and flashing like strobes, and the ravers cheered when the lights fell on them. It gave the whole event the texture of an LSD nightmare, techno music and raving zombies in a Stone Age disco-tech.

The men collected short stacks of bills from The Director and bags of party supplies from Mr. Goodie Bags, high-fived each other and joined the fun below.

Nikki waited by the U-Haul, bouncing with anticipation. Ready to get the show started. The Director took her by the arm and she settled to listen to him. He pointed down into The Pit with the point of his cane and made lots of very directorly hand gestures.

Maybe they were discussing motivation and subtext.

She was on her way, Mr. Goodie Bags didn't offer her any of his chemical music enjoyment enhancers as she passed him by, and a minute later she was lost in the crowd.

The Director disappeared around the far side of the old shacks and appeared again a few seconds later climbing a dangerous looking spiral staircase that led up the catwalks.

There was no call of Action, but I thought the show had started. Maybe not a porn movie after all, which would be a relief to Nikki's old man. Still, she was sixteen, and The Director had encouraged her to run away from home to star in this cheap-ass movie of his.

He was damn lucky Nikki's old man hadn't wanted to get the law involved.

Which was why I was there.

I decided to sit back and wait it out, give The Director a chance to shoot his zombie flick, then follow them after the party broke up. Grab the girl when there weren't fifty or so ravers standing between us.

A few minutes later the screaming started down in The Pit, and my plan was shot to hell.

❦❦❦

Thad Guerlain was an old acquaintance, not quite a friend, whose company I was too often forced to endure out of obligation to my then girlfriend and future wife, Beth Trout. Thad's younger sister was one of Beth's best friends, and Thad was an unrepentant tagalong. I never cared for the guy much, but I don't care for most people.

Thad Guerlain was a pompous and upwardly mobile kiss-ass who majored in business management and had a five-year plan to marry rich so he'd never have to apply his education in the real world. Like him or not, you have to give him some credit. His five-year plan had worked, and he'd managed it in only three years. By graduation he was engaged to a cute little-miss-money-bags who smoked a lot of dope, dressed like a '60s hippy, and drove her daddy's hand-me-down Beamer. She was the youngest sister of Paradise Valley's currently reigning District Attorney, the spoiled baby-girl of the well monied Reynold's family.

I didn't see him much after college until Paradise Valley's very own serial killer, Redwolf, killed my wife. Thad's brother-in-law tried his hardest to hang the crime on me, and Thad got his own fifteen minutes of fame when he appeared on the news. He screamed for my blood and pumped out the tears in an Academy award-worthy performance that the local press ate up. They still play those clips from time to time, whenever Redwolf makes the news again.

So, when he called me at just after nine that Saturday morning quite naturally I suggested he fuck off and die. I may have even offered to help before I hung up. He called back, and I hung up again. On his third callback I realized it would be easier to just let him talk, and that was when he laid his sob story on me.

Sucker that I am, I swallowed it.

We met face to face for the first time in years an hour later, and you should be proud of me, I didn't even *try* to hit him.

❦❦❦

I was between cars at the time and using my Uncle Higheagle's favorite showroom eye candy, a restored 1927 Indian Ace, to get around. It was a beautiful machine, scarlet red with gold striping. A bit on the small side for a large guy like me, the poor machine seemed almost to cringe away every time I hoisted my seven feet, three hundred pounds onto it, but damn fun to drive.

Uncle Higheagle had reluctantly allowed me to borrow it, and his threat of a slow and painful death if I did anything bad to it sounded only half serious.

I had most of Main Street to myself, a slow Saturday morning downtown, and saw Thad before he saw me. I found a handy spot a few feet from where he sat and parked.

"Butch," he said. He put out his hand, then seemed to think better of it and dropped it to his side. "You're looking … uh, good."

He took in my face, the new scars and marks on it since the last time he'd seen it up close, and cringed back a step.

I indicated my disinterest in continued small talk.

"Cut the shit, Guerlain. What have you got for me?"

He blushed and took his seat.

We'd decided to meet on neutral ground. He suggested Starbucks. I vetoed it and told him to meet me at Greasy's Grill, a little place on Main Street in the east valley. Good food but a cramped dining room. I preferred to sit at the table outside on the sidewalk, which was where Thad was waiting.

It was a favorite of Beth's.

Not sure why I picked the place, I'm not normally given to nostalgia.

I took the seat across from him at the outside table and eyed his cup of coffee with a pang of jealousy.

He wasted no more time on small talk, slapped a sheath of folded pages down on the table between us.

"Butch, please help me. I know that I've …," and there he seemed to lose his guts again.

I decided to help out.

"You said I was a monster and called for my blood on national television," I said. "I remember. The clips are still on YouTube."

"Butch, please. It's my daughter."

I reached across the table and he flinched back again. I took his cup of coffee and finished it off in a gulp, then took the stack of printed pages and unfolded them. Figured if I was going to accept this ridiculous chore I might as well get started.

I ordered another coffee and read what he'd given me. Some social media chatter and private messages between Thad's daughter, sixteen-year-old wild child Nikki and a guy who called himself The Director. Then emails.

"Have you tried having his email address traced?" Simple stuff, and not one of my skills.

"Yes," he said. "The address is re-routed through random nodes, scrambled. Completely anonymous."

Whatever the hell that means, I thought.

I went back to the emails and spent the next several minutes being a semi-professional snoop.

In a nutshell: bored, over-privileged teenage girl meets creepy, and apparently anonymous independent film director online. Cue the slightly inappropriate relationship. Girl flirts a little and director compliments her on her obvious star quality. Things continue in that vein for a few months, then The Director tells her he's coming to Paradise Valley to shoot a new movie, a zombie flick he expects to be the next big breakaway.

Like The Blair Witch Project with raving zombies, he said, and *I'd like you to play the lead, if you're up to it.*

Her reply: *Fuck me 'till I cry … hell yeah!*

The last email from The Director the previous Wednesday: *On my way now. Will call you when I'm in town. Can't wait to meet you, Nikki. You're gonna be a star!*

I refolded the sheets and set them down.

Next he handed me a photograph, a year or so out of date, but unless she'd done something drastic to her colorful appearance it would be good enough. I'd have no trouble recognizing the real life Nikki if I spotted her.

"And what makes you think I can find her?" I already knew the answer but I wanted to hear him say it. I felt for him a little, I knew what it was like to lose a child. But he was a still an asshole.

He squirmed a little, blushed again.

"Because you know … people. You have connections." He was unexpectedly tactful. Then he said something that actually surprised me. "And you're smart about stuff like this. I've heard stories."

"From your good old brother-in-law?" The fact that DA Reynolds had once tried to have me locked up for life hadn't stopped him from getting mixed up in one of my more memorable misadventures.

Thad regarded his hands sitting on the table with apparent interest and nodded.

Having a reputation sucks. People always expect you to live up to it.

"Listen, Butch, she's only sixteen." His blush went a shade deeper, anger trumping embarrassment. "I don't know what this guy has in mind for her but it can't be good!"

I had a pretty good idea. I'm sure he did too. There may or may not be zombies involved, but creepy anonymous director plus rebellious sixteen-year-old girl says porn to me.

I pushed the folded sheets and photograph back to him.

"Call the cops. Sic your brother-in-law on them. This is their job, not mine."

"I can't." He spoke quietly and seemed to shrink a few inches on his seat. "She's been in too much trouble already, and …"

"*And what*?" My irritation was growing. My self-improving resolution not to hit the guy was getting harder to keep.

"If this gets out to the press … shit, I have to keep this quiet. We can't have another scandal in the family."

I took a few moments to absorb this, to try to rationalize around the obvious sub-text. I couldn't.

"You don't want to embarrass the rich relatives," I said. "You're afraid your little girl will then look bad and they'll punish you for it. Pull you off the cash-cow's tit?"

Thad said nothing.

"You're a real piece of work," I said.

"What do you want," Thad asked. "How much for you to find Nikki and bring her back?"

"I can't guarantee …," I started, and Thad cut me off.

"I know, goddamnit! I know!" Heads inside Greasy's turned toward us. A professorly looking fellow—lots of tweed and gray hair, a pipe dangling from the corner of his mouth and a pair spectacles perched on the end of his nose—gave us a very disapproving look as he passed. "Just do what you can!"

He didn't believe a word he was saying. In his mind it was a done deal. He cuts a check and I bring his girl back. A simple transaction that I was fucking up with semantics.

I named my price, a pretty outrageous one I thought.

He cut the check without a second's hesitation.

Well shit, now I was freelancing as a private investigator.

Thad Guerlain was right about one thing. I did know people.

I also knew a walking modern art exhibit called Boswell.

❧ ❧ ❧

"Quick! The fuck you doin' Chief!" Boswell seemed happy to hear from me, which is not always the case with people. Our last encounter brought a bit of extra excitement, not to mention a pack of armed lunatics, into one of his nightly raves, and apparently they had enjoyed it quite a bit.

Boswell was a local dealer and lunatic who hosted nightly raves in an unused warehouse basement. He favored chain mail and leather clothing. Every available inch of flesh was inked or pierced, and he wore his hair in foot-long spikes. Boswell sold a shitload of X to his ravers, but he kept them off the streets, and that was something.

"Still breathing." I caught myself smiling. Boswell was a scumbag dealer and a bit freaky for my taste, but he was a likable freaky scumbag dealer. "You still in business?"

"Hell yeah I'm still in business!" Talking to Boswell was an adventure. You had to brace yourself for every verbal repost. "You gonna grace us with your presence again? I didn't think that was your scene."

"You guys are too wild for me," I said. "But you keep your ear to the ground, right? You'd know if there's another party going on?"

"Abso-fucking-lutely, Chief! Whatchu lookin' for?"

"Zombies," I said, and managed not to laugh at myself.

Boswell did laugh. "That sounds wild! Maybe I'll do that for Halloween!"

"Nothing like that going down any time soon then?"

"News to me if there is," he said, settling back into normal conversation.

I was about to thank him and hang up when he said, "If you're not stuck on the whole zombie thing there is something big going down tonight at The Pit, and that place hasn't seen heavy action in years."

"There is?" It wasn't exactly gold, but maybe I'd struck something.

"Zero shit, my man. You know The Pit, right?"

I knew The Pit.

The screaming started, a single hysterical high-pitched voice ringing out impressively over the rotten tooth throb of bad techno music. I snapped out of the semi-doze I'd been drifting into and scanned the jumble of bouncing bodies, a few more naked now and more stripping down even as I watched. A second scream sounded and I found the screamer, a bald chick in black bra, panties, and combat boots was doing a really excellent job pretending to be bitten by a naked man in zombie makeup, splattered with fake blood.

I zoomed in on them and was impressed by the man's ferocity and the spray of fake arterial blood as he ripped a chunk of flesh free from her neck. The spray fanned out and drenched the ravers closest to them. More screams, as if that had been their mark.

I'm not a big fan of the zombie genre, but I could give credit where it was due. Even with a stoned all-amateur cast and the shoestring budget the setup suggested, The Director made it convincing.

Too convincing maybe, because the panic that spread out from the pair, zombie and victim in a blood-drenched death struggle, was real.

When the raver in the zombie makeup went for the bald girl again and tore most of her right cheek off with his teeth, I realized that was real too.

While I was trying to work out just what the fuck was happening below, more screams sounded around The Pit. More attacks, more blood, and now there were a half-dozen zombie ravers bearing down on a half-dozen victims.

Nikki stood in the middle of it all, Nikki stood, scared but keeping her cool. She then began forcing herself through any gap she could find, fighting her way slowly back to the steps.

I pointed my binoculars at the top of the steps, at the man with the goodie bags, saw him intercept the first panicky young man to reach the top. Mr. Goodie Bags pulled a small pistol from the waistband of his pants and popped the guy in the face.

The man flew off his feet and slammed into the people packed in behind him. The forward surge up the steps became a domino tumble back to the bottom. One of the tumbling bodies, a pretty Latino girl dressed in the height of zombie fashion, convulsed when she hit the bottom. When one of her friends tried to help her up she raked with her fingers and snapped at the helping hand with bared teeth.

More wildly dancing figures tumbled to the dirt. Eyes rolled, foam frothed from grinning lips.

Down in The Pit, shit was getting real.

More gunfire.

From high above on the old catwalks, The Director watched, hands on hips.

Behind me, hidden off-road, was the old Indian Ace and the glow of Paradise Valley. Ahead was The Pit, a whole lot of crazy, and one gullible sixteen-year-old girl I'd agreed to return to her family.

I had to pick a direction, and damn quick.

I do not believe in zombies.

What I did believe in was good old-fashioned human fuckery. *That* I'd seen proven time and again.

I picked a direction and ran.

Guess which direction I picked.

As I've said, the old Indian was a favorite of my uncle's, another old Indian, and the young Indian riding it was going to get his ass kicked if he cracked it up. I tried to put that out of my mind as I rode full throttle toward the sound of techno and screaming.

This is usually the point at which I'll cobble together some god-awful Rube Goldberg style exit strategy. This time I gave it a pass and decided to play it by ear.

I do not believe in zombies.

Mr. Goodie Bags was my immediate problem. He was the one with the gun.

The old rock crushers loomed into view, backlit by the glow of the flashing lights and the bonfire blazing in The Pit. I could see a speck up in the catwalks, The Director overseeing his current masterpiece no doubt, and then I was weaving through the jumble of cars and trucks. A second later Mr. Goodie Bags was turning my way, the grin on his face withering when he registered the giant Indian zooming toward him.

He raised his gun and fired. The wind from his first slug tugged at my shirtsleeve, the second sprung off the front wheel well. My uncle was going to skin me for that. The third didn't even come close.

He screamed as I plowed into him and sent him flying up and over the jumble of bodies on the steps. He hit the chaos below and disappeared in a mass of bodies, some still dancing, oblivious to the deadly dance going on around them, some attempting to climb over the bodies piled in front of them.

The flashing lights and screaming made the scene feel even more like a bad acid trip, unreal but still dangerous.

Was I really about to throw myself down into that mess?

I spotted Nikki again, near the center and working

her way toward the steps.

A few more zombies, or whatever the hell they were, pounced and tore at wide-eyed, Xed-out ravers. More bodies hit the ground convulsing, either from the strobe lights or the shit Mr. Goodie Bags handed out.

One of the chompers, a big gruesome fucker in threadbare cutoffs and metal mixing bowl helmet was bearing down on Nikki. He looked like an undead Viking, a lot of long, dirty blonde hair, a long, braided beard that wagged energetically with each stride he took, thick mustache and face dripping with blood.

A red-faced fat guy dripped with sweat and tore at his T-shirt. His scream was silent in the overall racket. When the shirt was gone he tore at the skin of his bulging belly.

Young people these days, with their raves and techno music and drug-induced zombie rampages ... they make my generation look almost sane and respectable.

I twisted the old Indian's throttle and went over the edge with a slight whimper of anticipation. The ride down those rusted metal steps was quick and bumpy, like a jackhammer to the nuts. I consoled myself by causing even more havoc as I rode down toward the bottleneck at the bottom.

Most scattered. A few who'd made it through the bottleneck bailed over the handrails. The ones still in my path were either bleeding out or foaming. One ran up to meet me with a gurgle of rage, and I amused myself further by running him down. There was a moment when I thought I was going to end up on my head, this was not an off-road bike and I was about as off-road as I could get, but I kept it upright and hit the bottom of The Pit with great relief and a burst of speed.

So far so good, and no one else was trying to shoot me yet.

The way ahead of me emptied rapidly, those still mostly in their right minds giving me plenty of room. Those who didn't ... well, I was here to rescue one girl, not save every brain-blasted fucktard who'd turned up as an extra in The Director's movie.

Most were getting away now, leaving the foamers and chompers behind to focus their attention on the biggest and noisiest distraction in The Pit.

Me.

I spotted Nikki in the thinning crowd. She was on the ground, pushing herself away from the Viking.

He loomed over her, shaking and shambling, his face splitting in a bloody grin.

I do not believe in zombies.

And to prove it to myself, I aimed the Indian at him and twisted the throttle.

We hit with a crunch and he flew backward and landed in a sprawl.

The Indian reared up and threw me in a sprawl next to him.

Before I could shake off the tumble and rise the chompers were surrounding me.

I do not believe in zombies, but these guys were going to have a try at changing my mind. The first one

bent, lunged, and I kicked his feet out from under him. The second and third went for me, a stubby little guy in skid-marked briefs and a pretty little thing with a blue mohawk and a nose ring the size of a door knocker. I kicked most of the guy's teeth out, but hesitated when the girl came at me. My uncle had raised me not to hit girls. No exceptions.

This one bit though, and really fucking hard.

I shook her off as the next one went for me, a scrawny guy in baggy black pants, a torn net shirt, and a lot of bad jailhouse ink.

He grinned and leaned down toward me as two others grabbed hold of my arms and bit. I brought their heads together with a satisfying smack and they hit the dirt twitching.

Almost on my feet, The Pit nearly empty now, the ravers split and the chompers scattering in search of easier pickings, when the dickweed in the net shirt grabbed me by the throat and went for my face with his broken and bloodied teeth.

There was a clang, blood trickled from his greasy mop of hair, and he tipped over sideways.

Nikki stood there, holding the long handle of a flat edged shovel in her hands like a baseball bat. She looked pleased with herself.

"An Indian riding an Indian," she said. "Gotta love the irony."

I did a quick dust off while she crouched in a menacing manner with her shovel. Another chomper charged us and she whacked him in the face with the flat of the shovel's head.

A moment later I mounted Uncle Higheagle's old Indian, and Nikki jumped into the seat behind me. I spun a quick circle, almost mandatory when making a desperate escape on a cool motorbike, and threw a rooster tail of gravel at a fat, lurching chomper. He cried out, threw his hands over his face, stumbled off in another direction.

Nikki whooped, clearly enjoying herself.

I found the steep steps to the slightly saner world outside The Pit and went for it.

Nikki shouted something unintelligible at me, between the echoing roar of the Indian and the warbling syntho-screeching of the music, normal communication was out, but when I turned my head to her I found a finger pointing at two o'clock near The Pit's far wall. Two lady chompers advanced on a skinny little guy who looked like Justin Beiber in cargo pants, suspenders, and not much else. His back was to the granite and he raised his arms over his face to block the approaching menace.

I got the idea and turned toward them. It was against my deeply ingrained personal code to hit women, even the ones who bit from time to time, but Nikki was free to wallop whoever the hell she wanted. She did so with obvious relish, hanging onto the back of my shirt with one hand, gripping the shovel's handle high up with the other.

Her swing was short, but momentum was on her side. She knocked the closest lady chomper off her feet, and when the other turned our way with a snarl, the Justin Beiber look-alike made a run for it.

"More!" Nikki screamed, and I obliged. I drove twice around The Pit, veering close enough to the menacing chompers to give Nikki a swing, and she swatted them like flies. One fell backward against a rusted oil drum where a battery powered boom-box blasted that shitty techno. It fell to the dirt, ejected the CD and switched to a local FM station. The Ramones belted out Committed and improved my mood considerably. She knocked another into the bonfire, where he flailed and screamed and sent sparks up in a cyclone.

I decided to get the fuck out while we were still capable and turned the Indian back toward the steps.

I wasn't exactly happy with the night's work, there were too many bodies in the dirt to call my intervention a success, too many crazed chompers still nibbling on them, but I'd earned my paycheck. Nikki was safe and apparently enjoying herself, and most of the hapless fuck-nuts who'd shown up for this fun little get-together were running or driving away.

I saw Goodie Bags crouched under the steps.

Goodie Bags saw us coming, and stepped out to greet us. He'd found his gun and pointed it at us.

I jigged left and avoided his first shot, right and avoided the second. I was close enough when he aimed again that he couldn't have missed, but he'd fired his big revolver dry. I buzzed by close on his left and Nikki swung her shovel like a pro.

He went down flat on his back and a few lonely chompers jumped on the chance to get some face time with him.

"More!" Nikki screamed. "This is fucking fun!"

I'd had enough fun for one night though, and gunned it up the steps.

This second helping of the jackhammer to the nuts experience was muted slightly by the collection of bites and bruises I'd picked up, and Nikki had to drop her chomper club to hold on with both hands.

A wild half-minute later we were on flat ground again, and I was about to let myself experience a bit of relief when The Ramones ended and The Director shouted down at me from his high place in the catwalk above the old rock crushers. I wanted to get down the road, back to town and relieve myself of my teenage passenger, but I was curious to hear what he had to say. I stopped and searched the catwalks above until I found him.

He stood behind one of the flashing lights. He was too far away for me to see the smile on his face, but I could hear it in his voice.

"Holy shit! What a show!" The Director seemed ecstatic, overjoyed at the unexpected turn of events. "Excellent improvising ... and what a face! You were made to be in horror movies!"

"You're a fucking asshole!" Nikki jumped off the back of the bike and started toward the crusher. "You tried to kill me!"

"Yes," The Director said. "And I'm going to be a rich asshole! This is going to sell a million copies!"

He laughed and danced in place.

"Nikki, get back here."

She ignored me and I reluctantly dismounted to follow her.

"I'm going to call it ...," The Director spread his arms wide and stared up into the night sky. "Zombie A-Go-Go: Dancing With The Dead!"

"Fuck your movie," Nikki shouted back up at him, and ran toward the nearest shack. The makeshift studio.

"No!" The Director screamed. "Don't go in there!"

She ignored him and sprinted toward the gaping hole in the side of the shack that used to be a door.

The Director screamed and jumped up and down like a toddler having a tantrum, then ran down the catwalk, toward the spiraling steps that led back to the ground, waving his prop cane over his head.

A quick check around showed a mostly deserted parking lot: a half-dozen rust buckets of varying make and model, The Director's U-Haul, and my Indian. The groans and screams from inside The Pit were tapering off. The Director's chompers seemed to have run out of juice. Now there was only The Director, Nikki, and me.

And whatever new surprises The Director might have up his sleeves.

I decided not to give him the chance to surprise us again.

I ran past the shack, where Nikki was energetically smashing equipment, and found the dizzying twist of steps.

I got a good look down into The Pit as I climbed, saw the dead and injured, the wound-down chompers looking almost as pathetic as their victims. A familiar slow burn started in my guts, a mostly unwelcome sensation that meant I was about to loose my temper and do something very anti-social. I usually try to squash the rage before it blooms, but this time I let it come. I welcomed it back like the old troublesome friend it was. I decided to close down The Director's little operation for good.

I heard a final smash below followed by Nikki's laughter, The Director's hurried footfalls from above, my own heavy breathing as I stomped up the stairs. I reached the top and found The Director waiting for me in the stuttering disco-tech lights.

He lurched forward, his cane raised over his head, and I dodged his first swing, almost falling over the rickety railing. He hit the handrail instead of my noggin, and I looked up in time to see him raise the cane again. The strobing lights made him look like a figure from an old film, a gaudy black and white silent movie psycho.

He scowled, screamed, swung the skull-topped cane down at me. I caught it on the downswing with one hand. It hurt, but not as much as what I did to him next.

"You big dumb oaf!" he shrieked at me. "I have to stop her! She's ruining my movie!"

I considered informing him that I didn't *have* to do shit, and decided to let my actions speak for me. Still holding onto his cane with my left hand, I stepped forward, reached down, grabbed a handful of his crotch with my right. He squealed in pain and I gently heaved him up and over the catwalk's old rusty railing.

The Director's descent into The Pit was mostly silent. There was a lot of useless arm flapping and kicking, quite comical, but only a brief squawk just before he hit, as if he had only just realized it wasn't a part of his script, that it was for real. There would be no second takes.

A few of the livelier chompers scuttled over to him and began to do what they did best.

The flush of anger began to drain from my face, and I started to feel ashamed of myself. I always went too far when I lost my temper. Shit like this was the reason I had my unwanted reputation.

Screw 'im, I thought. *He had that coming.*

I took the downward steps slowly, and by the time I'd reached dirt I mostly felt okay about it. He wouldn't be making more of his shitty movies now.

I found Nikki standing beside the Indian Ace, The Director's laptop closed under one arm, a satisfied grin on her face.

"That was fucking awesome," she said. "You should have told me you were doing that! I could have filmed it!"

"I can drag him back up and throw him over again," I said.

Nikki, clearly immune to my sarcasm, almost bobbed with excitement. "Would you?"

A scream broke the tense silence and Nikki spun at the sound. I turned in time to see the Viking coming at me but not quickly enough to do anything about it. He hit me like a sweaty side of beef, still screaming, and drove me into the ground. I had an easy fifty pounds on the guy, but he was insane with whatever crazy shit Goodie Bags had set them up with for the party. Sure as shit not X.

He pressed his face up against mine and for a crazy moment I thought he was trying to kiss me. That might have been preferable. He snapped at my nose and I jerked my head to the side in time to avoid loosing it. We grappled for a moment. I smashed his nose and he bit my hand. I head-butted him and got another bite on the brow. He forced his face down toward my neck, teeth snapping, and I kneed him in the crotch.

A handy FYI for everyone reading this, a zombie-viking's nuts are just as vulnerable and sensitive as the next guy's. Remember that. Might come in handy some day.

The Viking groaned and seemed to loose interest in the fight, so I took the opportunity to put a few feet between us. Nikki finished it for me with a nicely placed crack to the cranium that would have caved his skull in if not for his mixing bowl helmet. He hit the ground and began to snore.

Nikki stood, regarding him with the discarded shovel back in her hands. "You know, I'm kind of bored with this shit. I don't even like zombies."

It was as good a time as any to scram, so we did.

I drove the old Indian Ace back toward town with Nikki seated behind, The Director's laptop pressed between us.

"*Who are you anyway?*" she yelled in my ear.

"*Your father sent me looking for you.*" I wasn't sure how she'd greet that bit of info, but I was reasonably confident that she wasn't going to bail at 45 miles per hour however much she hated him.

There was a long moment of silence, then, "*So you're a friend of the old dickhead?*"

"*I wouldn't call the old dickhead a friend,*" I shouted back.

"*Then why did you come for me?*"

Because I'm an idiot, while factual, was too hard to admit aloud, so I lied.

"*Because I'm nice!*"

The Paradise Valley PD, with a few exceptions, would have been happy to toss me back into The Pit with the remaining chompers, or a cozy holding cell at the very least. It's not an attitude I like, but I'm used to it by now. They'd seen too much of me over the years, and you know what they say about familiarity. But after interviewing Nikki and reviewing the evidence on The Director's laptop they had to let me go.

Of course a nice cozy holding cell might have been my best short term option considering the state I'd brought Uncle Higheagle's bike back in. It was still running, but I'd knocked most of the pretty off of it.

"I think it looks more … rugged this way," I offered as my uncle stood next to me in the Higheagle Classic Cars lot.

He didn't say anything for a long time.

I was about to start backing slowly away when he grabbed hold of my arm and examined one of the freshly bandaged bite marks. "Are you sure those weren't real zombies?"

"Uncle, there's no such thing as zombies."

The zombie outbreak had been limited to a few dozen who The Director and Goodie Bags had dosed with a new street drug they called Rave. The initial effects were indistinguishablefrom X: the euphoria, the urge to get naked and rub up against anyone who strayed too close; then nausea, confusion, a rapid rise in body temperature, and severe paranoia. The bloodlust that followed was a purely chemical reaction, a kind of misfiring of synapses in the prefrontal cortex. Nothing supernatural or biological, just a bunch of drugged up degenerates dancing to bad music. A Typical Saturday night in Paradise Valley in other words.

"Too bad," Uncle Higheagle said, and dropped my arm. "It would have been an excellent excuse to shoot you."

  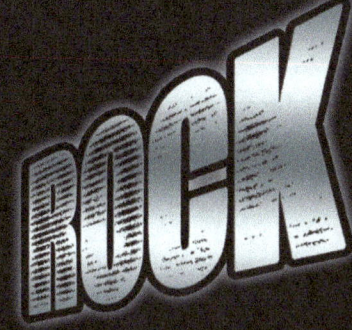

HORROR and ROCK

By James R. Beach

In the Beginning…

There was Rock & Roll itself. Shocking and controversial in its own right, it spawned a new phenomenon. Black Rhythym and Blues music melding with white Country & Western to form a new hybrid. Elvis Presley causing girls to faint with his gyrating pelvis and his cruel good looks. Wild men Little Richard and Jerry Lee Lewis pounding on the piano keys (and also shocking for open homosexuality and underage marriage). Crazy-haired and wild-eyed Chuck Berry strutting his Duck-Walk on stage. These were horrific images to many a parent and preacher in the mid-1950s.

As far back as the Dark Ages, Classical composers often employed certain motifs in their pieces with dissonant chords, minor keys and overall themes. Elements of what we identify as horrific and creepy sounds have long been incorporated into popular music and many of these were later adopted by Rock & Roll bands – most notably in Heavy Metal and Hard Rock acts – but also in Progressive Rock, Punk Rock and early Goth and Electronic Music.

The horror and mock-violence on the stage dates back to the Grand Guignol theater in France of the 1800s. (Although a case can certainly be made for the crowd's thirst for violence as a spectacle in the Roman Coloseums – that wasn't fake though). With the continued popularity of Horror in the cinema during the 1900s, the stage was set (so to speak) for the Shock Rockers to come. By combining the darker elements of the music world with the darker elements of stage and screen, a new genre was born.

The first Rock and Roller to incorporate Horror elements into his act was Screaming Jay Hawkins. Way back in 1957, Hawkins emerged on stage from a coffin, wore leopard skin costumes and sang songs like "I Put A Spell on You" (his biggest hit). He also set off smoke bombs on stage (shades of KISS many years later) brandished rubber snakes (Alice Cooper) and waved a stick with a skull mounted on it named "Henry" (King Diamond). The Voodoo trappings were a tad comic, but his onstage antics were very shocking in the day and he continued to record and tour for many years afterwards. Some of the early Rock and Rollers were scary because of greasy long hair, hoodlum-like leather jackets and boots, and wild libidos, but Hawkins was something out of a horror movie itself. And Hawkins also went on the influence many bands and artists in the sixties and seventies with what later became known as "Shock Rock".Many rockers have covered "I Put A Spell On You" such as: Creedence Clearwater Revival, Bette Midler, Nina Simone and even current Shock Rocker Marilyn Manson.

In the early sixties, English royalty and sometime rocker Screaming Lord Sutch (real name David Edward Sutch) emerged from his manor to emulate some of Hawkins' stage act while singing about Jack The Ripper (often dressing as Saucy Jack) and coming out of a coffin. He also brandished knives and skulls and lugged around "bodies"(manikins). (**Ed. Note:** *Sutch also had a habit of hiring session musicians such as Jimmy Page and John Bonham (Led Zeppelin), Ritchie Blackmore (Deep Purple, Rainbow), Keith Moon (The Who) and Noel Redding (Jimi Hendrix Experience) to help him in the studio. He released two studio albums,* Lord Sutch and Heavy Friends *and* The Hands of Jack the Ripper, *followed by a handful of live and compilation albums*).

Arthur Brown (*The Crazy World of*), emerged shortly after Sutch in the late sixties wearing extreme makeup and a flaming helmet on stage. Brown had a big hit with "Fire" and also covered Hawkins' "I Put A Spell on You". A big influence on Alice Cooper and Kiss (whose "God of Thunder" is a nod to the "I Am the God of Hellfire"- the opening line of Brown's "Fire"). Other bands and musicians also started doing more visual displays on stage throughout the 1960s, with The Who and The Move smashing their instruments and television sets respectively and later Jimi Hendrix lighting his guitar on fire. Roy Wood of The Move (later to morph into Electric Light Orchestra) was also an early pioneer of bizarre stage makeup in the late 1960s and early 1970s.

In the late 1960s the godfather of Punk, Iggy Pop (real name James Osterberg) emerged from the streets of Detroit, Michigan. Inspired by the on-stage disrobing and dark side of The Doors' Jim Morrison , as well as performance artists, Pop was ably backed by the Stooges (often called the "dirtiest band"). The shirtless (and sometimes – a la Morrison - completely naked) singer careened around on stage (often bumping into his bandmates), vomited, covered himself in peanut butter, rolled around on broken glass and launched himself into the crowd (he was the first person to introduce the "stage dive"). Iggy also sang about drugs, sex, death and boredom with songs like "Death Trip", "Your Pretty Face Is Going to Hell", "1969", "Open Up and Bleed", "I Wanna Be Your Dog", "No Fun", "Gimme Danger", "Penetration" and the often covered "Search and Destroy". The Stooges broke up first in 1971,reformed in 1973 and then broke up again in 1974 - with Iggy heading over to work with David Bowie and become a bit more polished (later acting in movies and on TV and still making records and touring – and much later reuniting with two of the Stooges). But the foundation was set. Later Punk bands emulated not only the Stooges rough Stones/Sonics influenced riff-rock (like The New York Dolls, who followed Pop a couple of years later with much of the same style, wearing women's clothing and makeup and singing about drugs, sex, death and nothing to do. And subsequently self-destructed after two albums), but also elements of his onstage act as well. Some notorious performers like G.G. Allin (known for defecating, coprophagia, self-mutilation and attacking audience members) even threatened he would commit suicide during a concert. He ended up overdosing on heroin instead.

Alice Cooper, whose real name is Vincent Furnier, started riling up audiences in the late 1960s by wearing women's clothing and makeup and was soon discovered by Frank Zappa (who signed the band to a three album deal on his own label). Early pioneers (and often uncredited) in the Glam Rock movement, Cooper and his band (later to be known as the Billion Dollar Babies) soon evolved into a much darker theatrical stage group with elements of horror fiction and movies. By 1971 Cooper was already starting to refine his concert routine by adding live Boa constrictors, electric chairs, guillotines, bloody baby dolls, straight-jackets and gallows. Cooper set

the blueprint for the modern Shock Rock practitioners with his live set and also twisted, disturbing lyrics about insanity, death, necrophilia, voodoo and other horror tropes. With the help of producer Bob Ezrin (KISS, Pink Floyd), Alice Cooper also had a string of popular hit songs like "I'm Eighteen", "Be My Lover", "School's Out", "Billion Dollar Babies" and "Go To Hell". With his classic 1975 solo LP, *Welcome To My Nightmare* (featuring a creepy introduction to "The Black Widow" by Horror movie icon Vincent Price – later to be used by pop star Michael Jackson for an intro tohis song "Thriller"), he forever cemented his reputation as the king of "Shock Rock". Cooper continued to develop his stage show and repertoire over the years and at age 64 is still touring and making albums in the same vein.

Not long after Alice Cooper came on the scene, a band out of Birmingham, England by the name of Earth adopted a new moniker (from a classic Italian Horror film by Mario Bava), Black Sabbath and launched their debut album in 1970. Guitarist Tony Iommi had to adapt his playing style due to an injury to his fret hand. He developed a method of tuning down and playing thick bar cords to make up for having to use prosthetic fingertips to play. That coupled with bass player Geezer Butler's love of Horror movies, his dark lyrics and imagery about death, the devil, magic, paranoia, war and drugs, set the basic foundation for Heavy Metal. Employing some of the minor chords and keys from Classical music, along with non-typical jazz-influenced heavy drumming by Bill Ward and braying vocals by John (Ozzy) Osbourne – it would influence countless bands over the years. After a number of successful albums (all without much radio play and critical support) Ozzy was gone by the late 1970s and went on to emulate some of Alice Cooper's horror show elements with his shows in the eighties. With his various antics of biting the head off a live dove and gothic stage sets and imagery, Ozzy became synonymous with "Shock Rock" during that decade and those to come (even when he toned things down in following decades and became a reality show star). Black Sabbath rebounded in 1980 with Rainbow and Elf singer Ronnie James Dio, and continued to record albums with him and others until finally reuniting with Ozzy in the 2000s. Bands like Coven and Black Mass also mined horror and black magic elements in the late 1960s and early 1970s, but without the heavier direction and volume of Black Sabbath (which made it much more sinister) nor the impact.

A couple of years after Black Sabbath came out, two struggling New York musicians named Gene Simmons and Paul Stanley (real names Eugene Klein and Stanley Eisen respectively) formed a new band called KISS out of the ashes of their band Wicked Lester. Adding guitarist Paul (Ace) Frehley and Peter Criss(coula) to the mix, the four started wearing thick kubuki-style makeup and developed distinctive stage personas. Paul was the Starchild, Ace the Spaceman, Peter the Cat and Gene the Demon. From the start, KISS came up with a big stage show to accompany their larger-than-life image with a distinctive logo, a lot of lights, flash bombs and fireworks, and flashy costumes. Gene was able to breathe/blow fire like circus performers and spit blood from his mouth, Paul directed the crowd with Pete-Townsend style windmills and audience banter, Ace shot fireworks out of his guitar and inserted smoke bombs into the frets and Peter played extended drum solos and got the crowd riled up. KISS was shocking to many parents and were controversial at the time (some religious groups speculated that their name even meant Knights In Satan's Service), but most of their songs were fairly tame. KISS played simple, catchy, anthemic hard rock/heavy metal and, much as Alice Cooper did, ruled the radio waves in the 1970s. KISS continued on after Frehley and Criss left in the early 1980s and eventually reformed around the millennium to huge success. Gene and Paul continue to make music and tour the world with their current lineup (featuring longtime off and on drummer Eric Singer and Black N' Blue guitarist Tommy Thayer).

While most of the shots fired in the Shock Rock direction were from the Heavy Metal/Hard Rock acts, there were also some rumblings in other areas of music. Progressive Art Rock band Genesis, led by Peter Gabriel, was one. Starting

out as sort of an arty pop rock band, they added jazz-influenced drummer Phil Collins and Classically trained guitarist Steve Hackett in 1971 and started moving in a darker direction.

Hackett's choice of odd time signatures and darker scales enhanced the ever-increasingly strange lyrics of singer Gabriel. By the time they were into their landmark double LP, *The Lamb Lies Down on Broadway* there was almost a Lovecraftian/Cthulhu vibe to the songs. Peter also enhanced the stage shows by dressing up in strange costumes and makeup as various characters from his songs (he also sported the first "reverse" Mohawk as well) with dark lighting and imagery. Bands like King Crimson, Van der Graaf Generator also incorporated darker themes and elements into their music.

An early pioneer in the Goth and Industrial music was the band Chrome. Formed in 1975 by singer/drummer/keyboardist Damon Edge and Bassist/Violinist Gary Spain they released their first record in 1976 with guitarists John Lambdin and Mike Low. Guitarist Hellios Creed replaced Low after the first album was recorded and remained in the lineup thereafter. The band fused punk rock with experimental synthesizer music and feedback and predated the later Goth and pre-Industrial bands like Killing Joke, Joy Division, Gary Numan, etc. Their music very much incorporated horror and other dark elements into their sound. They continued on with various solo projects and talk still swirls of reunions even though Edge passed away in 1996.

Formed in London in 1976, The Damned was led by singer Dave Vanian –a former gravedigger who dressed up like a vampire with slicked back dark hair, white face makeup and black formalwear (pre-dating the Goth movement by a few years). Backed by bass player (and later guitarist and keyboardist) Captain Sensible, guitar player Brian James and drummer Rat Scabies, they released the first British Punk Rock LP the same year. As the band progressed and changed members, Vanian's crooning started morphing with the band's sound and started moving even more towards a darker, gloomier pre-Goth sound.

Not long after The Damned surfaced in the UK, another horror-influenced band emerged from New Jersey. Formed in 1977 by singer Glenn Danzig and Jerry Only (Ciafia) on bass guitar (with a revolving lineup up guitarists and drummers over the years). Influenced by Horror and 'B' movies and Punk Rock, the band adopted a look they would come to call "horror punk" with dark makeup, the traditional long "devilock" widow's peak hairstyles, black clothing and horror imagery (including forming an independent label called Plan 9 records after Ed Wood's classic bad movie). Danzig also crooned along to songs like "Last Caress" (later covered by Metallica and featuring the infamous line "I just came to say I killed your baby today"), "Night of the Living Dead", "Vampira", ""London Dungeon", "Who Killed Marilyn", "Halloween", "Death Comes Ripping", "Green Hell", "Die, Die My Darling", "Horror Business", "Skulls", "Mommy Can I Go Out and Kill Tonight?", "Devil's Whorehouse", "Astro Zombies" and "Bloodfeast". The titles alone were straight out of horror film history. Danzig eventually left the band in the early 1980s and formed Samhain and later his own band Danzig (which he is still performing with). Only and brother Doyle eventually got the rights to the name and reformed the Misfits and are still making albums and touring now.

While The Misfits were hammering out their following in New Jersey, across the river a band was forming with the spirit of KISS fully in mind. Twisted Sister was formed out of the ashes of a band called Silver Star by Jay Jay French in the early 1970s–and was a glam rock band in the vein of David Bowie, Slade and T. Rex. Singer Danny (Dee) Snider joined in 1976 and the band moved in a heavier direction influenced by Led Zeppelin, Alice Cooper and Kiss. The band became more and more popular on the club circuit, eventually selling out clubs repeatedly without a record deal. Finally after self-financing and pressing a couple independent singles, they got the attention of a small UK label called Secret Records and they released a 12″ EP and their first album in 1982. By then the band lineup was solidified and their glam image and feminine look had evolved into a darker, almost horror-clown type makeup and leatherwear look more along the lines of Heavy Metal acts like KISS and Alice Cooper. With dark lyrics and imagery making its way into their songs like "Burn In Hell", "Shoot 'Em Down", "Under the Blade", "Horror-Teria" (The Beginning: featuring "Captain Howdy" and "Street Justice" - which would later become the basis of Snider's 1999 horror film Strangeland), "Death Run", "Come Out and Play" (a nod to the 1979 movie The Warriors) and "Kill or Be Killed", the band mined some of the typical HM trappings, but injected a sense of humor (most notably in their popular videos with actor from the movie Animal House) and catchy pop-metal anthems like "We're Not Gonna Take It" and "I Wanna Rock". The band broke up in the late 1980s after a couple unsuccessful albums and tours but Snider went on to not only helm his solo band Widowmaker, but also write and direct a popular horror movie called *Strangeland* and recently reformed with their original lineup performing small tours in full-makeup.

Also formed in New York in 1976, was the band The Cramps. Fronted by singer Lux Interior (who looked a bit like Boris Karloff in high heels) and guitarist Poison Ivy Rorschach, the band used a unique 2 guitar,drums and no bass lineup, and were influenced by Screaming Jay Hawkins as much as The Ramones. They fused rockabilly with punk and what

became known as Goth later on and coined the new term for their brand of music ("Psychobilly"). Along with androgyny, they also incorporated elements of horror in their look and image and songs like "I Was A Teenage Werewolf", "Sunglasses After Dark", "Zombie Dance", "Voodoo Idol", etc. and also the humor of songs like the classic "Can Your Pussy Do the Dog?".

Fronted by Lead Singer/Porn Star/Weight Lifter and performance artist Wendy O. Williams, The Plasmatics were formed in New York in 1978 and quickly became popular at clubs like CBGB's. Known for smashing up the amplifiers and sets and chainsawing guitars, Williams often sported a large Mohawk, electrical tape over her nipples and fondled herself on stage and even simulated masturbation with a sledgehammer (which got her busted for indecency charged a couple of times). Bolstered by songs like "Corruption", "Butcher Baby", "Living Dead", "Sex Junkie", "Test-Tube Babies", "The Damned", "Put Your Love in Me" and even a duet with Motorhead's Lemmy on a cover of Tammy Wynette's "Stand By Your Man", Wendy went on to be called the first female Shock Rocker and also went on to successful solo albums (the first produced by Gene Simmons), and even a Grammy nomination, but later took her own life in 1998 after a couple unsuccessful suicide attempts.

After numerous incarnations of his band Iron Maiden, Bassist Steve Harris finally had a solid lineup and recorded and released a demo EP in 1979–spearheading what became known as The New Wave of British Heavy Metal. Followed by an LP on EMI records in 1980, the band eventually went on to be one of the most popular Heavy Metal bands in the world. They developed a mascot named "Eddie" (a zombie-like corpse) who adorned their covers and prowled their stages. They also incorporated a huge amount of influence from horror/dark fantasy movies and fiction (and even the bible) into their lyrics with songs like: "Phantom of the Opera", "Prowler", "Transylvania", , "Murders in the Rue Morgue", "Killers', "Purgatory", "Twilight Zone", "The Number of the Beast", "The Prisoner", "Rime of the Ancient Mariner" and "Hallowed Be Thy Name". The album *The Number of the Beast* was huge and also started the controversy that they were Satanists and worshiped the Devil and so on due to the title track and cover artwork. The band is still selling out arenas worldwide and Eddie still adorns the covers and prowls the stage sets.

In the midst of the New Wave of British Heavy Metal movement in the late 1970s and early 1980s, a band named Venom emerged in 1981 with what became the blueprint for

"Black Metal" (a term they coined by way of their second album title). Venom took the hints of Satanism and black magic from Black Sabbath and went full-on into it. Critics hated the band and criticized their somewhat sloppy playing and shoddy sounding records, but the band was hugely influential in later metal acts in Thrash, Black and Speed Metal. A three-piece in the model of Motorhead (a big influence on them), they played louder and faster than other bands of the time and mined much darker material. Songs like "Welcome to Hell", "In League With Satan", "Witching Hour", "At War With Satan", "To Hell and Back" and "Raise the Dead" confirmed a more serious embracing of the dark side, but the band always had a bit of the tongue in cheek regardless.

While the NWOBHM was taking over the UK, Los Angeles band Motley Crue was taking over the club scene very rapidly. Bassist Nikki Sixx had formed London with guitarist Lizzie Grey in 1978 (a pioneering Glam Metal band that wasn't to see an album release until much later). Sixx left the band in 1981 to start Crue with drummer Tommy Lee, vocalist/guitarist Greg Leon – who left the band soon after. They soon met guitarist Mick Mars (Bob Deal) who replaced Leon and suggested singer Vince Neil. The lineup was cemented and remained the same (with Neil leaving for a solo career in 1990, but coming back a couple of years later to remain in the band since). The band quickly started developing their sound (a continuation of the London Glam Metal – New York Dolls, Sweet, Slade, Mott The Hoople, etc. sound) and stage show (in the vein of KISS). They went for more of the KISS and Alice Cooper gothic horror and bondage look initially (lighting themselves on fire and lighting off flash pots, etc.) and a much heavier metal sound, but after a couple of albums drifted more towards the glam rock look and sound and hits like a cover of "Smokin' in the Boys Room". Their "hedonistic" antics off the stage with booze, drugs, women, etc. definitely continued the "Shock" element though over the continuing years (and inspired many other acts in years to come).

King Diamond (real name Kim Bendix Petersen) was the next to take up the mantle directly from Alice Cooper in the early 1980s. Starting out in the late 1970s, Diamond started developing his makeup and stage act with his band Black Rose. After morphing into the band Mercyful Fate, Diamond and the band released an EP in 1982 followed by 2 albums (in 1983 and 1984 respectively) to much controversy for his

outspoken Satanism and shocking stage show and presence. What Cooper and Black Sabbath hinted at, and Venom had recently embraced more fully, Diamond took to a new level. Wearing heavy black and white face makeup in the KISS mode (often adorned with upside down crosses) and brandishing a microphone made out human bones and a real human skull (named "Melissa"), Diamond sang about "Black Masses", "A Corpse Without A Soul", "Evil", "Come To The Sabbath", "Into the Coven", "Satan's Fall" and "Desecration of Souls". Unlike Venom, Diamond was backed by a strong band with a duel lead guitar attack in the vein of Judas Priest and Iron Maiden and their music was very influential as well in the Black Metal movement. King left in 1985 to head up his solo bands, but eventually did double duty as Mercyful Fate reformed in the early 1990s. After successful bypass surgery in 2010, he's back to performing shows around the world.

Slayer formed in Los Angeles in 1981 and was influenced by Motorhead, the Sex Pistols, etc. Taking up the Satanism mantle from Venom, singer Tom Araya, guitarists Jeff Hanneman and Kerry King and drummer Dave Lombardo played fast, technical metal as part of the first wave of what became known as "Thrash Metal" in 1983 – along with Metallica, Anthrax and Exciter. They incorporated much horror imagery in their stage show and lyrics and were continually one of the fastest and loudest bands in the movement and stuck pretty much to their sound and formula over the years. They are still making records and touring the world to this day.

W.A.S.P. formed in 1982 amidst the Glam Rock inspired Hard Rock/Heavy Metal acts like Motley Crue, Ratt, etc. in the Los Angeles area. Circus Circus, Singer and Bass player Blackie Lawless (originally on rhythm guitar) and lead guitarist Randy Piper joined forces with bass player Rik Fox and drummer Tony Richards. Their stage shows were very much Alice Cooper and Kiss and horror movies and were often shocking and controversial. Lawless would often tie half naked women to torture racks and toss raw meat into the audience. They also dressed in leather, studs and spikes and pushed the bondage quotient in their songs as well (with titles like "The Torture Never Stops", "On Your Knees", "Savage" and others). Their first single "Animal (Fuck Like a Beast)", was pulled from their debut LP (as a number of record stores wouldn't carry it for fear of offending people). That didn't stop them from three consecutive Gold albums. Lawless continued on with the band through various lineup changes over the years.

GWAR is a tongue in cheek band that formed in Virginia in 1984. Vocalist and Bassist Dave Brockie (Oderus Ungerus) developed the over-the-top grand gignol horror/sci-fi stage show with his Punk band Death Piggy and realized it completely with GWAR. After a couple short-lived vocalists, Brockie assumed the vocal duties and has handled them since. Truly a stage spectacle, the band dresses up in elaborate costumes and acts out gross and offensive songs that developed out of "The Slave Pit" – originally intended for a movie that Brockie's bandmates Hunter Jackson (Techno Destructo) and Chuck Varga (Sexecutioner) were developing back in college (called Scumgdogs of the Universe). Brockie had the idea to take the costumes from the set and turn it into a stage show for the band. GWAR released their first album, *Hell-O* in 1988 and were signed to Metal Blade records in 1990. The band continues to tour and make records and their shows have to be seen to be believed (don't sit in the front rows unless you bring a raincoat). Combining elements of Horror and Science Fiction movies, H.P. Lovecraft's Cthulhu Mythos, Splatterpunk, etc. they are the epitome of a "Shock Rock" band. Dave Brockie also recently saw the release of a novel with "Bizarro" book publisher Eraserhead Press offshoot Deadite Press in 2010.

The Mentors stand pretty much in a (low) class by themselves. Formed in Seattle in 1977 by drummer and singer Eldon Hoke (El Duce), guitarist Eric Carlson (Sickie Wifebeater) and bassist Steve Broy (Dr. Heathen Scum). They were three overweight guys who wore black executioner hoods and sang about pornographic sex and depravity. Starting with their first EP in 1981, the music itself was pretty standard Heavy Metal and Punk riffing, but the offensive lyrics and imagery degrading women (often times featuring scantily clad stripper-looking women being led around on dog leashes or on their knees) led to much controversy and separated them from the pack. After fighting with GWAR on the Jerry Springer show and claiming Courtney Love paid him to kill Nirvana singer Kurt Cobain, Hoke died after being hit by a freight train while intoxicated.

Rob Zombie was born Robert Cummings and met soon-to-be girlfriend Sean Ysuelt in 1983. They formed White Zombie a short while later and their first EP came out in 1985. A tribute to the Bela Lugosi horror film of the 1930s, the band used much of the horror imagery and trappings and it was obvious from the start that they worshipped KISS and Alice Cooper. Cummings initially went by "Rob Straker" but by the time the band was signed to Geffen Records in the early 1990s he had adopted "Zombie" as his stage surname. After three very successful albums (boosted by popular MTV videos in a Russ Meyer/Ultravixens style homage), Zombie launched a solo career and also wrote and directed four popular horror films, *House of 1000 Corpses, Devil's Rejects* and remakes of *Halloween* and *Halloween 2* (as well as producing the animated film *The Haunted World of El Superbeasto*). Zombie continues to tour (including a successful joint package with Alice Cooper not long ago and currently one with Marilyn Manson) and is also working on a new album and movie called The Lords of Salem. Gene Simmons and Alice Cooper both dabbled with movie acting from time to time, but Zombie moves successfully from directing the horror on stage to directing the horror on screen.

Marilyn Manson(Brian Warner), started out as a writer doing music articles and horror stories and poetry for small press publications in both fields. He formed Marilyn Manson & The Spooky Kids in 1989 with

guitarist Scott Putesky (Daisy Berkowitz). Out of a couple side projects, Jeordie White (Twiggy Ramirez) and Stephen Gregory Bier Jr. (Madonna Wayne Gacy) joined Manson and the basic lineup was cemented. They released their debut album in 1994 which was produced by Nine Inch Nails frontman Trent Reznor and by 1995 had begun to build their cult following. With the serial killer based names, bizarre makeup and costumes, Cooper and KISS-inspired stage show and controversy following him around, Manson became the next big cog in the Shock Rock wheel. Manson has also dabbled in acting (David Lynch's Lost Highway, Party Monster and then-girlfriend Rose McGowan's Jawbreaker) and now has turned his attentions to directing as well (with a proposed bio pic on Lewis Carroll which he would also star in as Carroll).

Deathklok is a band formed out of a death metal band cartoon show parody (sort of Spinal Tap in the future if the Taps ended up becoming the biggest corporation ruling the world's economy) created by Brendan Small. Small not only writes and voices most of the characters on the show, but also plays most of the instruments (besides the drums played by Gene Hoglan) and tours with a full-on band expanded out of that. The show pushes the boundaries of sex and violence on Cartoon Network and continues to amass fans all over the world. "Celebrity" voices (Mark Hammil, King Diamond, Kirk Hammett and James Hetfield, etc.) pepper the show as well.

There are many other bands that incorporated horror elements into their music or stage show over the years. Lucifer's Friend, AC/DC, Judas Priest, Accept, Holocaust, Blitzkrieg, Witchfinder General, Satan, Ratt, Exodus, Anthrax, Celtic Frost, Bathory, Dark Angel, Death Angel, Death, Sodom, Destruction, Forbidden, Testament, Morbid Angel, Iced Earth, Alice In Chains, The Toadies, The Dwarves, Mudvayne, Slipknot, Korn, Tool – and the list goes on and on. Most Heavy Metal and Hard Rock bands have incorporated at least some of the recognized Shock Rock tropes at one point or another.

So like horror movies and fiction that continue to disturb, thrill and scare people over the years, "Shock Rock" does much of the same. People continue to try and find ways to push the boundaries but it's tougher and tougher to do in this age of "We've seen and heard everything". So who will be next? And what will be considered shocking? One can only guess, but my prediction is it won't be "pretty".

༄ ༄ ༄

by David Agranoff

Jeff clicked his drumsticks together to signal the rest of the band. Brian strummed an open E-chord and let it hang while Gregg started picking the bass line. As soon as Brian hit that chord the entire audience knew Reaction was opening their set with their most intense song 'Filled with Anger.' The slam pit swirled like a gathering tornado. Ron walked on to the stage and wrapped the microphone cord around his wrist. Flash bulbs ignited as Ron dipped forward into the crowd. The band launched into the song and Ron held the mic out toward the audience. They sang for him almost drowning out the band.

"Filled with Anger!"

It was the first big show of the summer of '84. There were rumors of a Minor Threat show or the much talked about Rock Against Regan tour, but this was the first must see in D.C. for months. Reaction were not the headlining band at the 9:30 club; that honor was bestowed to the touring TSOL. Most of the D.C. hardcore scene had come to see Reaction play the show that was the warm-up for their first North American tour.

The crowd came alive like an angry mob. The tough, angry punk singer motif was a challenge for Ron: he couldn't hide how happy playing shows made him. He just had to smile, no matter how angry he had been when he penned most of the band's lyrics. He had known that the record was popular. He had hand stuffed the inserts in all 2,000 of both vinyl presses, and all 1,000 of the tapes. The tapes had been a pain in the ass, but they sold out quickly. No matter how many they sold, he was still surprised when the song ended to thunderous applause.

Ron tried to catch his breath; with his hands on his knees, he spit on the stage. Brian tuned his fender behind him. Desandra Copeland, the other love of his life was at her normal spot, stage left with her camera freeze-framing the history of the D.C. hardcore scene. Ron winked from his catcher's stance. She ignored it for a moment before laughing. Her smile was what he needed to summon the strength to fight the exhaustion and stand. He was ready for the next song.

Brian stepped on his distortion pedal and his guitar crunched. They were ready, hard fucking core.

❋❋❋

After the show ended it took Ron five minutes to find Dee. It should have been easier. Considering how white the D.C. hardcore scene was. Dee was the oldest child of Liberian diplomats, which had lived in Silver Springs Maryland since she was seven years old. Outside of the guys in Bad Brains Dee was one of the few blacks at most of the shows. She was a stunning dark African woman with Red and Green stripes weaved into her shoulder-length braided hair.

Dee found him first by hugging him from behind. "Your best show yet."

Ron kissed her before leading them to the back of parking lot where Jeff was putting the last of the equipment away in a van paid for by the hard working taxpayers of the state of Maine. Reaction's drummer was son of Maine's four-term republican congressmen after all. Ron sat on the bumper while Dee exchanged high fives with the rest of the band.

The only member that seemed unhappy was Jeff who struggled to pack the last of the gear as Ron moved out of the way. Jeff slammed the door hard. Brian and Ron shared a knowing look. Ron knew they were destined to have this argument; half way through the show, he knew it. His biggest problem was that Brian was starting to listen to him.

"We need a second guitar player," said Jeff.

Ron looked at Dee; she shrugged. It wasn't the argument he had expected. Just the same he decided to play stupid.

"I thought we sounded great tonight," Ron said and smiled. Gregg nodded in agreement.

"Not the point," Jeff said.

"We're not a metal band," sighed Ron.

Jeff rolled his eyes. "Crossover man, the metal labels pay for everything. Agnostic Front and DRI are both talking about it. What is so evil about making a few extra dollars?"

"I don't want to sing about Hobbits or air battles dude," said Ron.

"War songs are pretty cool," Brian added.

"Says the guy who still has Iron Maiden posters." Dee laughed.

"Nothing wrong with Maiden," said Brian.

"I'm serious," Jeff said. "We work our asses off. Our music is good, kids like it. We should make a living."

"Money?" Ron shook his head. "Is that what punk rock is about?"

With Jeff's dad in congress, his sister at Harvard and older brother heading into his father's political circle it was clear what was happening. The family black sheep felt the need to make something of the life he had chosen. Brian and Jeff shared a look. That told Ron everything he needed to know about where this talk was heading.

"Money helps Ron, why not make a little. That means more records, more shows."

Ron had started this band. His powerful screams were unique like a fingerprint. A one-in-a-million voice that made their sound pop, but his stubborn drive and independence also held them back. At least it did in Jeff's eyes. They did this head-butting with each milestone the band achieved. Ron knew if they kept playing shows like tonight, the tour would be like this every night.

"Fuck it." Ron took a step back. "I won't get in your way."

He turned and walked away. Dee grimaced, and Jeff looked shocked.

"What are you doing?" Brian asked.

"I quit!" Ron yelled back.

Dee put her hand up. "I'll talk to him; we'll see you at the house."

Ron went straight to his room and slammed the door. The house was known as the 'The React House,' since the entire band lived and practiced there. The basement was tiny, but it had been big enough to stuff some friends in for their first "show." It wasn't official, but It also became Dee's de facto house since it was two blocks from the edge of the American University campus where she and Ron were starting their sophomore years.

The living room was a mess where they were assembling T-shirts and records for the tour. It reminded Ron of how angry he had been this morning that Jeff had not helped. Jeff viewed that kind of task as something they should have a record label to do for them.

Dee opened the door to their bedroom, which was basically a closet with a window that opened up on a brick wall inches away. She waited for Ron in the doorway. He knocked his boots off and stumbled into the room, which was barely big enough for his record player, their 7-inch record collection and the bed they raided from Ron's childhood bedroom.

She shut the door and sat on his bed, but she wasn't smiling at him.

"You want to express yourself, they do too. It's not horrible that they want to make a career out of Ronny."

"They wanted a career, they should have started a new wave band."

Ron felt hurt and deep frustration. He hated that they did this so soon after they played such a great show and to make matters worse Dee was defending them. She moved closer, rubbing the stress knot that was forming on his neck. She knew how to disarm him.

"Go on the tour," Dee said softly into his ear.

Ron laughed. "Trying to get rid of me?"

"Oh no, I would love for you not to go away for two months. Just sleep on it. I think you'll regret not doing this."

He was sure she was wrong. He didn't like what they wanted to turn the band into.

"Sleep now?"

"Well." She kissed him. "Maybe not right away."

Ron woke suddenly; he was pressed up against Dee, his hand on the curve of her hip. It was dark, but he had a strange feeling the room was larger than normal. In his hazy half sleep he looked around the window and the brick wall beyond. It wasn't there.

"You awake?" Dee asked as she sat up. Ron watched her shape in the dull light as she pulled on her pants. Ron sat up and his head felt heavy. He leaned forward resting his forehead against the smooth skin on the small of her back.

"My head," Ron groaned.

It felt like he slept hard, but he didn't remember dreaming. The last thing he remembered was falling asleep in Dee's arms. Exhausted from playing the show of his life he barely had the energy to kiss Dee. They made love gently before falling asleep in a tight embrace.

Ron reached out expecting his hand to hit his tape and record player. His hand hung in the empty air. That was weird. He reached further and the wall wasn't where it was supposed to be. Dee shook him off and dropped a T-shirt on. Ron lifted the shirt slightly and kissed her back softly. The curving valley on her back was his favorite spot.

He didn't want to think about last night, or even the show because that meant thinking about the band. He knew he would have to walk out there soon and finish the fight with the band. They would tour or they wouldn't but they would have to figure it out soon.

"We have to talk," Dee said softly.

Ron's lips froze on her back. He didn't need those guys. He didn't want to deal with them. He was almost as good of a guitar player as Brian. Dee could sing and they could start a band together. He had already started to teach her to play.

Ron pulled her down so she was sitting on his lap.

"Before you say it I have an idea."

Dee smiled. "I don't want to start a band, not now."

Ron was surprised. Had she read his mind? Was he that predictable, or did she just know him that well?

"We need to talk about the show."

Ron sighed. "I know you think I shouldn't quit, I don't want to betray my ethics. There is no point in doing this band if it betrays my beliefs."

Dee smiled and listened. She waited until he was done. "That was a legendary show."

Ron laughed.

"No listen to me," Dee said. "That was the last Reaction show. Senator Eheim's daughter borrowed the family's camcorder. It was 1984, but it was the best technology available at the time. She filmed the whole thing standing on a chair. Do you know that video has been bootlegged and sold over 10,000 DVDs in Europe alone before it was uploaded to You Tube."

"Dee what are you saying?"

She smiled. "Lights."

The lights came on in the room. Ron looked around suddenly feeling dizzy. His bedroom was gone; this looked like a fancy hotel room. Ron slid back onto his bed, almost dropping Dee. The only thing that looked right was Dee standing there in her sleeve-less government-issued 'Boycott Stabb' shirt she had worn to bed.

She put up her hands to signal calm. "This is going sound unbelievable, but you have to trust me. Believe me." She paused. "It's not 1984."

Ron squinted. Dee could be a practical joker, but she was not this good at it. He had known her for four years, two before they dated when he had a serious crush on her. She looked serious enough.

"Did I sleep for six months or have an accident?" Ron asked and wondered if he was in some kind of hospital.

"It's not 1985 either," said Dee.

Ron looked at his handmade Rites of Spring T-shirt. It was the one he put on after he took off his sweat-soaked show shirt. Ron felt a sudden wave of pain in his head. Dee reached up and held his arm. It's May 25th, 1984 he thought, first day of tour.

Dee hugged him. He looked over his shoulder. The phone looked weird, there was no TV just a flat plastic square stuck to the wall. The small kitchen was filled with all kinds of equipment he didn't recognize.

"If it's not 1984…"

"It's 2041."

Ron laughed. "Sixty years?" He shook his head in disbelief. Dee looked the same. She was wearing the same shirt. His jeans that he took off last night were bunched at the side of this strange bed. Dee took his hand and pulled him up. They walked toward the window.

"I think you need to see this."

Dee pushed the curtains aside. The space needle broke through the gray skies in the distance; beside it traffic continued in each direction, some on the ground, some in the levels through the air. The window registered their presence and suddenly traffic and weather information appeared in the glass like a computer screen. Ron felt woozy as a high speed commuter train rolled by on the street to stop a block away. A few dozen people exited and a few boarded the train. A voice spoke from a speaker at the window base.

"Welcome, guest. The next downtown train is in five minutes."

Dee kissed his cheek.

"Welcome to Seattle of the twenty-first century."

"Come with me and I'll explain." Dee opened a drawer and pulled out Ron's denim jacket. It was his all right. 7 Seconds back patch he made out of a worn out T-shirt, SSD, DYS, and Bad Brains patches. They were in the right spots sewn into the jacket he wore in the picture on back cover of their first 7-inch record. The only patch missing was Minor Threat. The patches looked too clean.

"I know it's summer, but it's a little chilly out there. Put it on and we'll go get answers, I promise."

Ron put on the coat and followed Dee out the door and down a set of stairs. They were staying at a hotel. The staff addressed her as Miss Copeland before they walked outside.

Dee waited silently; Ron looked around at the strange style of clothes and dress around him. Several people were focused on small pieces of plastic in their hands. Others stood in place looking catatonic.

"*Your train will arrive in forty-five seconds,*" a voice spoke from the small plastic rectangular object in Dee's hand. It looked like a tiny television in her hand.

"In this time, there is a second virtual world called 'The Verse.' It's entirely digital, it's like the internet, but of course you haven't heard of that either. It's based on information, like this world is based on water and air."

Ron didn't know what to say. The white commuter train pulled up to the station. When the doors opened Dee pushed him in the train. She continued.

"I know it sounds strange but this 'Verse world is as real to these people as *this* world. You enter or interact with this 'Verse-world through this." She held up the tiny TV in her hand. "It's called a H-Phone. Most people these days don't even use these; they have the interface implanted and they interact inside of their minds."

"It's a phone? That tiny thing," Ron said as Dee set it in his hand.

"It can be, but it's a 'Verse controller too, just speak to it and it can provide any information you want or interface you with any portal inside the 'Verse."

Ron shook his head; it didn't make sense to him. Dee smiled and spoke into the phone. "Search Reaction – D.C. hardcore 1980 photos."

Ron couldn't believe it as Dee scrolled through photos of his band on the tiny screen. She touched one and expanded it to a full screen. There in black and white was a photo of Ron singing *'Filled with Anger.'* He knew the exact moment because to him it was just a day in the past. He remembered being blinded by Dee's flash at that moment.

"You took that photo."

Dee nodded. "From this interface I can listen to Reaction, watch videos of shows, or look at every photo taken of the band. You can do this with almost any band you can think of. Same with movies, books – there is a whole web of information for a small interface fee."

"That's totally crazy."

"These days most people have implants and they are interfaced every waking moment." Dee pointed at two zoned-out people sitting near them on the train. "They could be playing video games, scanning the news, watching a movie."

"In their minds? That's horrible."

"You *always* say that." Dee bit her bottom lip slightly, enough that Ron saw it. "I mean I knew you'd feel that way. It's normal now."

The train stopped. The H-phone told them it was their stop. Dee took his hand and lead them out of the train.

"The 'Verse has affected the music industry in lots of ways, but one thing the it can't provide is the energy of live music."

Ron listened to her, but wondered how Dee had become an expert on the year 2041 while they slept. They walked the block, passing two stores that looked like record stores, and a few restaurants. A few people turned and looked at them. One couple even stopped and pointed at them.

Dee stopped at the edge of an alley, pointing to a doorway. Ron looked around the corner before following her. The sign on the building which stretched the next entire block said – *'Hall of Fame.'*

After walking in a back door and up a long staircase they stopped at a door that had another sign on it. *Post Anger Records.* Dee paused with her hand on the door.

"Jimmy is a bit of a dork and a poser. Don't tell him I told you. Just listen, he'll explain."

The door opened on a room that looked like a history of 80's punk as told by show flyers. Ron stared in awe at flyers that were dated in '86 or '88, beyond his time. Dee pointed at a flyer for a band called Gorilla Biscuits.

"They will become your favorite band, trust me."

"Stupid name," Ron said, staring in amazement. There were flyers for shows all over the U.S., Europe and Japan. Dee sat on a couch and pointed to the cushion next to her. Ron was too busy looking at the flyers.

"Ron React."

Ron turned around to see a gray-haired man who had a mohawk pulled back into a ponytail. He was wearing a brand new looking Black Flag shirt. They shook hands.

"You have no idea what it took to get you in here."

Ron nodded. "Your're right about that. Dee promised you'd tell me."

"The how is not important," Jimmy said.

"I think that is important. I can't believe I'm saying this, but considering all of the things I have seen… Do you have some kind of time machine?"

"I suppose you could put it that way," Jimmy said as a screen came to life behind him. "There are lots of ways to time travel - pictures, old vinyl records can help your mind travel back to the good old days am I right?" Jimmy pointed at the video screen hanging like a painting on the wall. "Videos are time capsules."

The video came to life. Ron watched stunned as the show he just remembered performing a day ago appeared on the screen. The sound wasn't great, but he couldn't believe he was watching his own band perform.

"I've watched it a thousand times," Jimmy said. "One of the most intense and raw hardcore shows ever."

"Legendary," Dee said with a smile.

"You should have lived it," said Ron.

"Fuckin' A right, Ronny. I should have been there." Jimmy patted Ron on the back. "I've watched it many times but I can't ever live it, not like those lucky assholes in the pit. Most of them had no idea they were witness to history."

Ron was still in shock. He had a hard time accepting that sixty years had passed, but the idea that people still listened to his band blew his mind.

"By the way my name is Ron; only Dee gets to call me Ronny."

Jimmy put his hands up in a silent apology.

"If you won't tell me how, then at least tell me why?" Ron asked.

"Right." Jimmy shook his finger. "Ever since Slayer and Metallica covered Reaction songs the attention your band got just grew and grew. That last Reaction show is considered to be one of the best of the 20th century. The video is one thing most people have seen many times, but as you said to live it, well that is what the fans crave."

"The band broke up, huh?" Ron looked at Dee.

"That was your choice."

Ron watched the video unfolding. The band had been great, he loved the music, but the feeling didn't matter to him if the band was functioning like a bank teller handing out money. It wasn't about money to Ron. He always wanted to express himself, and if it was about money the other guys should have tried to be Van Halen.

Dee reached up and pulled him down on the couch next to her. She looked excited.

"They have Brian, Gregg and Jeff ready to play. A week of shows here at the Hall of Fame in Seattle. It's for history and most of the money goes to charity."

"Most?" Ron looked at Jimmy.

"You can't imagine the resources it took to make this show happen. We need to make up a good deal of our expenses. Think about it, Ron. Pick a charity in this century or back where you came from. Hell, both if you like."

Dee rubbed his legs and looked at him with passionate eyes. That wasn't like her. She disagreed with him at times, but she wasn't normally this eager to change his mind. Something was off.

"I need to sleep on it."

Dee and Jimmy shared a look. Ron didn't like the silent communication that passed between them. They were both clearly bothered by his answer. Jimmy's face contorted into a big fat smile that dripped bullshit.

"Of course, sleep on it."

Dee wanted to make him dinner. She seemed entirely focused on Ron's wants and needs all night. Ron smiled through all of it, the whole time thinking that it wasn't right. She sounded like Dee, felt like Dee, kissed like Dee. She just didn't behave like Dee. She was too eager to please.

Ron waited until she fell asleep. He slipped out of bed and pulled the H-phone off the charger. He shut the bathroom door and hoped he had watched her enough to know how to use it.

"'Verse Interface," the device told him. He was sure he just asked it what he wanted to see. Jimmy had told him he was better off not knowing his future past 1984, but the less they told him, the more he felt he had to know.

"Search Reaction – D.C. hardcore band."

The screen lit up. He knew he could either touch or ask for options.

"Select band members Ron React, display biography."

"Ron Bennett," the device said. "Also known as Ron React, he was born in Bethesda, Maryland October 29th 1964. He is most commonly known as the lead vocalist for the classic early 1980's Washington D.C. based hardcore band Reaction. The band released one 7-inch single and a full length LP just before it broke up on the eve of its first North American tour. The vocalist was known for his powerful and unique screams, but also his stubborn insistence that the band remain true to its do-it-yourself ethics, causing the band's break-up. The band went on to play a few shows and even recorded a demo with a different vocalist, but all attempts to continue the band were considered failures."

The device stopped. Ron told it to continue.

"Ron React went on to play guitar in Artic Flowers, one of D.C.'s early post-hardcore emo bands fronted by photographer and his longtime girlfriend Desandra Copeland. The couple broke-up after Bennett refused to sign the band to a three record deal with an imprint of Atlantic Records in 1989."

Ron looked at the door, knowing that Dee was on the other side. Well, a Dee who looked the same as she had in 1984.

According to the history they had broken up. The device continued.

"Bennett still believed in punk ethics even though the musical sound and fan base for his new band had evolved beyond a punk rock sound. The couple ended up in a long court battle as Copeland and the record label attempted to win back rights to re-press the Artic Flowers back catalog. Bennett next made headlines when he refused big contracts to do Reaction reunion shows before his death in…"

"Stop!" Ron took a deep breath, this was too much information. He had refused reunion shows before. He knew they must have been offering him huge sums of money, but he also knew he didn't want the band to become a circus.

"Search Desandra Copeland. Display in text."

Ron looked over the information; he didn't know who that woman lying in the hotel bed, but he knew it wasn't Dee. He opened the bathroom door slowly. The woman was out, breathing deeply. Ron grabbed his jacket and slipped the H-phone in his pocket. He carefully opened the door and slipped out.

If the real Desandra Copeland was alive, he would find her.

Dee was alive. Eighty-one years of age, but she was alive. She lived the last forty-three years of her life in Portland, Oregon. She played acoustic Artic Flowers songs at rock festivals into her sixties and played bass in a locally popular band called *Beta-test*, who the H-phone said sounded like a sub-pop version of The Pixies. Ron had no idea what that meant.

He used the H-phone to talk him through getting to Downtown Seattle and a ticket on a southbound Bullet train to Portland. Forty-five minutes later he almost slept through his destination. In another two hours he would have been in the Bay Area.

The H-phone had not found a listing for Desandra Copeland, so on a whim he searched for Desandra A'Razi, the name her parents had in the old country. Within seconds he had an address and a public bus route that would take a short walk from her front door.

All the funds were coming through the phone from the fake Dee's account. He knew that as soon as she woke up, they would be able to trace him by that phone. He only hoped he could talk to the real Dee first.

The sun poked up over a snow-capped mountain as the city bus crossed a large bridge. Bikes by the thousands passed beside the bus, with more lanes devoted to them than cars. Ron smiled. He'd never seen anything like it. He looked at the H-phone as they passed off the bridge; they were a mile from Dee's home.

The phone suddenly buzzed to life. A picture came up on the screen and it said *'Jimmy calling.'* He didn't answer, he didn't even know how to do that, but he assumed that fake Dee was awake and had found their hotel room empty of him.

The phone dinged and said. 'This is your stop.'

Ron got off the bus and walked the block before he arrived at the address. It was a small house. An old black woman with a puffy gray natural sat on the porch in a rocking chair. The woman had her eyes closed as she rocked with a slow rhythmic creak.

Ron walked up the steps and smiled when he saw steam rising from a hot drink in the handmade cup with a faded Discord records logo painted on its side. He made the cup in a freshman pottery class at AU.

"Dee?"

She didn't respond.

"Dee?"

She opened her eyes and almost jumped out of her chair. She pulled two headphone cords away that had twisted up under her hair. For a moment Ron heard Bad Brains blasting from the tiny earpieces, but it stopped when she pushed a button on the H-phone sitting in her lap.

"Ronny? Again?"

Ron looked at her. The older Dee laughed.

"What a stubborn persistent fucker you are. It's gotta be in your DNA."

Ron sat on the stone ledge of her porch feeling a little dizzy. Dee smiled, it was a beautiful smile accented by lines on her face that came with age and experience, but it was really her. She rubbed his cheek with her worn wrinkled hands. He looked into her eyes and saw amazing wisdom and humanity that could not be faked.

The H-phone beeped in Ron's hand. Dee grabbed it from him. She didn't even look at it.

"It's hers, isn't it?"

Dee pulled out the battery not even waiting for an answer. Ron reached out to stop her. Dee grabbed his hand.

"Trust me," Dee sighed. "So what did they tell you this time?"

Ron told her the story in detail. Dee listened, never stopping him. As he spoke he could tell she was getting angrier with each minute.

"They won't ever let you go free, and if you don't return soon and agree to the show they are going to kill you."

"That's crazy."

"This is big business, your favorite," Dee grinned.

"But I have to get back to 1984."

Dee shook her head. "You need to go back to Seattle, go straight to the club. I could explain, but it is so hard to believe. See the truth for yourself and you'll have to make an informed decision."

Dee leaned forward and gave Ron a kiss. He hesitated briefly, but relaxed as her lips met his. Her hand reached up to the back of his neck. They remained locked in the kiss for a long moment. After they parted she rested her head on his forehead and stared into his eyes. She couldn't pull away from him.

"I never loved or hated anyone as much as you," Dee whispered and kissed his lips again gently. They both cried, and Ron couldn't believe he had ever lost this woman in his life. How could he have been so stubborn?

"Play the show, you pain in the ass," she said before kissing him for the last time.

Ron waited for three hours in the line, and wouldn't have gotten in at all had the real Dee not given him a ticket. She offered to join him, but Ron didn't want to disrupt her life any more than he already had. The show was in full swing when he walked in the door. He made his way through the crowd toward the bar.

The band played a note for note version of the Doors classic 'Riders on the Storm.' The eerie piano played as he made his way through the crowd. A few were dressed in 60's style, while others still dressed in modern clothes. Ron double taked when he saw a woman holding her phone up to take a picture with a dead ringer for Jimi Hendrix.

The vocalist sung, from behind Ron heard a pitch perfect Morrison. Ron turned toward the stage and saw a band that looked identical down to each member. They were the Doors. The singer didn't just sound like Morrison, he acted like him on stage. Ron spun and looked around the club. The crowd danced and drank, but sprinkled throughout the room were familiar faces. Faces he knew from album covers. Phil Ochs and Dylan were drinking together at a booth; Joplin and Lennon were laughing together and bobbing their heads to the beat.

Ron looked up at Morrison and back at his own hand.

"What the fuck am I?" he whispered. He looked up as the song ended. Through the applause he searched. The Doors launched into 'Break On Through.' The crowd swelled and danced. Ron reached the bar and found the man he was looking for. He'd dropped the punk look, but Jimmy sat at the bar with two young women who looked dressed for Woodstock.

Jimmy turned and looked shocked as he saw Ron walking up to him.

"Ronny? Where have you been man? We've been worried sick."

"We need to talk."

"Fuckin' A right we do."

Jimmy opened his office door. The fake Dee had been waiting; she ran at Ron and hugged him.

"Oh, baby, I was so worried."

Ron pushed her away. "Dee would never call anyone baby."

Jimmy waved her off. She suddenly went cold and sat down with an angry face. "Oh, great, here we go again Jimmy."

Ron didn't sit, he just stared at them. Jimmy took a big swig of his drink before Ron finally spoke first.

"So what is it? You bring all these musicians through time?"

Fake Dee and Jimmy both laughed.

"Well sweetheart, we had to try something different," Jimmy said addressing fake Dee.

"Four times now." Fake Dee shook her head. "No matter how we do it, this asshole always says no."

Ron paced. Jimmy took another drink.

"Relax Ron. Time travel is impossible. The real natural born Ron Bennett lived and died over forty two years ago."

"Natural born?"

"Is it that hard to believe?" Jimmy pointed at the fake Dee, then he pointed out a window overlooking the club. The Doors were just starting to play "LA Woman." After a few moments Jimmy closed the window. "I'm a genetic engineer by training, but twentieth century Rock and Roll is my passion. The problem is I was born in 1991 and missed several important musical experiences. That's OK, because collectors save amazing things. DNA, my man! Sweat-soaked T-shirts, towels, hairbrushes... and best of all, used condoms. You'd be amazed."

Ron put his hand on his chest. Jimmy nodded.

"You were the tricky one to track down, but then someone gave us an envelope you hand addressed and licked to send out a demo tape. I know that you, and certainly the first four clones of you we did, don't have the first clue how bad your fans want this. Most bands did reunion shows, but not Reaction."

"It's not about money," said Ron.

Jimmy opened and shut his hand. "I agree man, I want to see this show as bad as anyone, but clones cost money. A this point you owe me five times over, dickhead."

Ron looked at the fake Dee for empathy, but she had none for him. Why would she? She was a clone and knew it.

"It's wrong to clone artists against their will."

Jimmy shook his head. "I have only four fucking clones that ever pissed and moaned about being a legend, and they all had your fucking DNA."

"Make that five then."

Ron turned to walk out the door but when he opened it, he saw a wall of huge humans standing in his way. He remembered the real Dee's warning: If you don't play the show, they will kill you. Ron turned back but there was nowhere to escape.

"Let me go."

"I have invested far too much money for that," Jimmy said. "Besides you need to get over that idea that you're a real person. I made you, I can destroy you and it's legal."

Ron tried to push past the body guard who held him in place.

"I think, Ronny, the only way we'll convince you next time is if we take your young lady's advice."

Ron looked over at fake Dee.

"I've said all along we have to fool you into thinking it's 1984."

"Wait," Ron begged.

"Let's hope the sixth time is the charm Ronny," Jimmy said as Ron felt something smash into the back of his head. He thought about the real Dee; even she thought he should just play the show. He wanted to live, to see her again. He fought to keep his eyes open as his body fell to the floor.

Desandra knew that as an eighty-one year old, she'd look out of place at this 1984-styled punk show.

Fuck that, and fuck all these twenty-first-century-born posers, I was there for me, she thought to herself as she walked in.

She got there early so she could find a prime spot at the front of the balcony. The Hall of Fame was three times the size of the 9:30 club in D.C., and she wasn't used to be being so far from the stage. She had a hard time believing a Reaction show was actually going to happen after sixty years, and this was the first time she wouldn't be on stage with her camera.

Dee got a kick out of seeing the 80's style punk fashion even if several of the modern kids looked goofy in similar, but not quite right clothes. She assumed they had simply cloned Ron again; this time the strict period clothes policy told her they were trying to fool him into accepting that it was still 1984.

Her first real moment of pure joy came when a perfect clone of Brian walked on to the stage to tune his Fender. Jeff looked nervous behind his drums. Gregg who was always calm signaled that his bass levels were set. Dee scanned the stage and saw the young version of herself on the left behind the bass cabinet holding a camera that was almost a century old.

She supposed she'd always been a part of D.C. hardcore, standing behind all the great bands holding that camera. Always a part of history.

Jeff clicked his sticks, Brian hit the crunching E-chord, and Gregg started picking the bass intro. Ron ran out on to the stage and dived into the crowd as the music swelled behind him. He screamed with the audience, more than a thousand voices raised together.

"Filled with Anger!"

Through the cyclone of bodies, Ron screamed the vocals as he crawled across a forest of heads toward the stage. Unlike the `84 show the massive crowd sang each and every word. It was so loud that when Ron finally rolled back on to the stage he simply held the microphone out and let the crowd finish the song.

Dee banged her fist on the balcony banister and sung along. The band played with a power she hadn't heard in decades. Her hips ached, and her feet were sore, but she felt drawn to jump in the pit.

When the song ended, she cheered with the crowd, watching Ron put his hands on his knees as he always used to do after a song wore him out. Dee smiled, remembering with fondness how he winked at her during the last show.

Ron stood up straight. Brian was ready to play the next song, but Ron put up his finger to ask him to wait. Ron put one foot on the front stage monitor and looked out into the audience. Dee's heart almost stopped when his eyes landed on her. Ron winked, then lifted the mic.

"This next song goes out to the real deal." He smiled one last time before launching into an hour of angry hardcore.

✼✼✼

DARKREGIONS PRESS AND CHRIS MOREY: JOINED AT THE HIP

By Joel B. Kirkpatrick

Who can read and not be inspired to write? Who can work in publishing, immersed in creative stories, poetry and art, and not be bitten by the desire to have a title on a bookstore shelf? Can anyone, by all appearances, be born to publishing and avoid getting their own fingers bloody?

No one can avoid it. Certainly not anyone named Mr. Morey.

There are two at the helm of Dark Regions Press, one of the largest specialty presses in the United States. One, Joe Morey, who founded the company and the second, his son Chris, who is the young wizard-behind-the-curtain at Dark Regions. He handles all matters web-related, and also manages the online marketing and customer relations. His work to print and promote hundreds of other authors has certainly put some colorful, creative fire into his own fingertips.

JBK: Chris, you and Dark Regions Press came into existence in the same year—1985. You were already connected to D.R. at birth it seems. Has it ever felt like a sibling to you?

CM: I've only been truly involved the past six years or so. My old man is the one who actually pulled me into it. It started with working on a new version of the DarkRegions.com website then evolved into me becoming the anything-to-do-with-the-internet guy. Now I own the whole damn thing. Just when I thought I was out….
If Dark Regions Press is a sibling then he's a big brother who kicks my ass on a regular basis, but damn he shows me some cool new things on a regular basis too.

JBK: Do you challenge one another creatively, or complement one another? Are you fans of the same themes in books? Do you share the same favorite authors?

CM: Both, I'd say. My dad is creatively brilliant. He has an endless well of ideas, and it's great for brainstorming new projects. We don't agree on everything, of course, but we can often take a good idea and make it great by working together. I can't count how many times he's helped me with my own writing, telling me "say, what if this character wasn't such a jackass?" Then I will consider it and say "you're right, I'll make him a complete asshole!" Not really, but you catch my drift.

JBK: How much design input does an author have when their book is accepted for production by Dark Regions? How many authors can you get to meet face-to-face?

CM: Well, it depends on the author. Some say "Hey, here's my book, do what you will," while others might say "Hey, here's my book, do what I want." I understand both perspectives (and there's obviously plenty of middle-ground, too) and we work with the author as best we can. It's most fun when it's a collaborative creative effort, in my opinion. That's what Dark Regions Press is, after all; a creative collaboration.

I've had the privilege of meeting quite a few of our authors face-to-face, thanks to the fine folks in the HWA who hold the fantastic World Horror Convention every year. I've met Bruce Boston, Mort Castle, Weston Ochse, G.O. Clark, Marge Simon, James Chambers, Gene O'Neill, Gord Rollo and even the cigar-smoking Jim Gavin. So far I've been amazingly impressed with each and every one of our authors. Fine people capable of real conversation. Something you don't get enough of these days. They have inspired me through their words—written and spoken—more times than I can count.

JBK: You recently launched your first imprint; Black Labyrinth, a line of original psychological horror/thriller novels and novellas. What pushed you to launch this line?

CM: I love me some ghoulies and ghosties, don't get me wrong, but I was seeing some pretty common trends in horror fiction for the past ten years: monsters (vampires, zombies, werewolves) and apocalyptic/post-apocalyptic fiction. I'm a sucker for both, but I wanted to see something more.

I've always been fascinated by the psychological aspects of horror, the mind's reactions and defense mechanisms. After all, human plight is our deepest, most instinctual source of excitement in dark fiction. What greater test than of the strength of your mind? What greater despair than experiencing or witnessing a descent into madness?

My dream is for the Black Labyrinth imprint to be the definitive line of psychological horror, so that when someone says "I've read all the zombie stuff, but what about the stories that show us who we really are? The stories that reveal the darkest parts of what terrifies us most: our own minds?" They are directed to the Black Labyrinth imprint. For this imprint will consist of ten books written by the masters of psychological horror and thrillers. All ten books will be novels and novellas, because I want the reader to join each protagonist on their journeys through the depths of their minds and all that affects them.

Fair warning, dear readers: these are going to be some intense psychological tales. Enter Black Labyrinth with caution, and readiness for masterful storytelling.

JBK: Black Labyrinth begins with the new novella *The Walls of the Castle* by Tom Piccirilli, who was diagnosed with brain cancer recently. Did you find out before or after the book was published?

CM: It was after we just about finalized the manuscript with Tom that he found out about the tumor. Shortly thereafter he underwent surgery and a fund was started to support him. Thanks to helpful friends like Brian Keene and many others who helped spread the word the fundraiser was a success, but brain cancer is an ongoing struggle. We decided to give 20% of hardcover proceeds and 100% of ebook proceeds from the book directly to Tom to try to give him some more help. By the time this interview is published, I'm afraid all hardcover editions will be sold out, but the trade paperback and ebook editions will be available.

The Walls of the Castle is currently on track to becoming the best-selling Dark Regions Press title of all time, giving the Black Labyrinth imprint an amazing kick-start.

Oh, and by the time this is in print, our customers should have the hardcover editions in their hands—and man oh man are they going to be happy campers.

JBK: The imprint is going to last until 2015, is that right? There will be ten books in the line?

CM: That's correct. I wanted readers and collectors to know that this is a finite imprint with a fairly small amount of books. I think that makes it more of an exciting product, and prevents it from being overextended and exhausted. For Black Labyrinth I'm trying to assemble the masters of psychological horror and thrillers. Your

readers will discover one of the next authors in the imprint on the page after this interview, and we are elated to have him as part of the line.

One of my goals? Well, you might think I'm nuts, but I want the master, the King of kings, to finish out the Black Labyrinth imprint with Book X. If the imprint is successful enough we can make it happen. Keep your fingers and toes crossed.

JBK: Argentinian artist Santiago Caruso is illustrating all ten books. The cover artwork and what interior illustrations we have seen that he did for The Walls of the Castle by Tom Piccirilli have been spectacular! What is it about his style that made you choose him for Black Labyrinth?

CM: First, his style is very Gothic and heavy with blacks and darker colors, so I was naturally attracted to this style. But Santiago also has a graceful, poetic nature to his illustrations. He takes a concept and recreates it with artistic metaphor, and this challenges the viewer to analyze it rather than simply digest it. I've always appreciated a story that made me consider it; that didn't spoon-feed me the answers. I found these stories in Santiago's artwork.

Santiago will illustrate all ten covers and we plan on having him do interior illustrations for every book as well. It will be a glorious day when all ten Black Labyrinth books can be sitting on our shelves with Santiago's artwork gracing all of the covers!

JBK: Can you tell us any of the other names in the Black Labyrinth line yet?

CM: No, besides the one we're announcing (or may have already announced by the time this reaches print). But rest assured: when I say the masters of horror and dark fiction, I mean it.

JBK: Playfully, you invite readers to connect with you on the web, assuring them you are not as creepy as you look. Ironically, it is nigh impossible to find a photo of you anywhere. That quirky fact illustrates that there is so much on the internet…nothing is visible. How does that complicate your work as a marketer for Dark Regions?

CM: As much as I appreciate what the internet has done, I would like to retain an anonymous identity to a certain extent. Just preference I suppose. It hasn't really affected my marketing work. People just see me for the creative weirdo that I am. However, it does seem to intrigue people, and that's just fine.

JBK: Do any of the Dark Regions releases have your illustrations on the cover? Have you designed any book covers which you would like to mention?

CM: Nope. This sort of falls back to the no self-publishing thing. I'd feel sort of like a cocky prick publishing a book with my artwork splashed all over the front cover. I did, however, design *Lullaby for the Rain Girl* by Christopher Conlon and *Crooked House* by Joe McKinney. There might be another one, but those are the two that jump to mind.

JBK: It takes more than a fishing pole to be a fisherman. It takes much, much more than a printing press to be a publisher. Please explain what makes Dark Regions a specialty press.

CM: We offer premium, signed hardcover editions of both original fiction and reprinted fiction. These hardcover editions have limited print runs, ranging from thirteen worldwide copies to three hundred or more. The books are bound in premium materials like leather and are often signed by many of the contributors, including the author, artist and sometimes the editor, introduction writer, etc. The prices for these editions range from $35 to $300. Working in the business has made me a bit of a collector myself. It also helped me realize what collectors are looking for. That's why in the Black Labyrinth imprint we're offering our highest-end specialty edition yet.

All ten books in the Black Labyrinth imprint will be offered in an oversized 8.5"x11" tome bound in black cowhide and printed with oil-based ink on premium 70lb Classic Crest paper and Smyth sewn. These oversized tomes will all feature exclusive essays written by each Black Labyrinth author regarding their writing process and other topics. These editions will also feature special edition traycases with the BL logo stamped atop the covering. We plan on limiting each oversized tome edition to thirteen copies, but may need to increase the runs as the imprint gains popularity and we release titles from bigger authors. I'm getting excited just describing it!

JBK: 1985 preceded the computer revolution by several years. Some small press publishers are entirely computerized. What elements of DR have never been computerized, throughout its busy twenty-eight year history?

CM: You know, since we moved the business to Ashland, Oregon we're going through the tedious, meticulous and sometimes painful process of digitizing many aspects of the business. The bookkeeping, of course, takes priority. Keeping track of the numbers is crucial to any business, and we're in the process of getting all of the numbers in the computer (as much as we love having papers scattered all over the office).

We're getting there, though, and looking forward to having everything set up in an easily accessible and fluid digital format soon.

JBK: Publishing has been described as corrupt as politics, and as dogmatic as religion. The reading public is witnessing a massive change in the industry but still mostly believes that anything outside traditional publishing—is vanity publishing. Explain what vanity publishing really is, and why it cannot do what Dark Regions does for authors.

CM: Vanity publishing is the act of publishing your own work through the means of LuLu, CreateSpace and other self-publishing services. Sometimes these self-published titles can be good, but often the reason they had to self-publish the book is because no legitimate publisher would take it.

What self-publishing can't do for authors is have a book that is professionally edited, proofread and vetted to be presented to the reading public. Self-publishing doesn't provide you with a professional marketing campaign. It also makes readers more skeptical about the title, and in my opinion it can damage your reputation as an author.

We also provide renowned artists to do cover artwork for the authors' books and experienced designers to give the books a professional external appearance. Finally, since we are a specialty press, we offer most authors' books in signed limited edition hardcovers. As far as I know there aren't any self-publishing services that offer this.

JBK: Your submission portal is currently only open by invitation. Is Dark Regions a viable printing option for the first-time, unpublished writer?

CM: As much as we've grown, Dark Regions Press is still a small company. When we open up submissions we get thousands—and I do not exaggerate when I say thousands—of submissions. This forces our already small staff to focus much of their efforts on wading through growing slush piles, which hurts productivity in other areas.

We all watch the industry closely, and can identify rising stars in the genres pretty easily. Our editors are also very involved with the writing community. That's how we get the debut novels and books from authors like *Hard Boiled Vampire Killers* by Jim Gavin.

As a young writer myself, I understand the desire to have open submissions, but sometimes it's important to think about it from the other side. We always work to make each of our books a success, but that becomes difficult when we have hundreds or thousands of manuscripts to wade through. But perhaps one day….

JBK: How many projects can DR juggle within the same year?

CM: Well, that's what got us into a bit of trouble the past couple of years. We started juggling too many projects and it got us behind in our production schedule. Now we're playing catch-up. I'm not very fond of preorders, and understand as a customer and a publisher the desire to get your product as soon as possible after you order it. I'd say realistically we can juggle about twenty-four books a year before we really start going nuts. Personally, I like having a full month to dedicate to each book to really make it a success, but these days we're doing around two a month.

JBK: Dark Regions was presented with the 2010 HWA Specialty Press Award. How did that honor come about? Was that a nomination by your peers, or authors in the industry?

CM: It was a nomination from the HWA trustees. They decided that we deserved it for the year of 2010, and it was humbling and an honor to receive it. Both DRP and myself are members of the HWA, and I'm always looking for volunteer work. I really appreciate what the HWA has done for the genre, and it keeps our little community of authors, artists, publishers, editors and more grouped together and organized. We've gone the past two years and will be going to New Orleans in 2013.

JBK: The foremost truth about traditional publishing is that change is coming, and cannot be avoided. Readers are finally leading the industry in new directions. Are there any serious changes coming to Dark Regions, and if there are, will they only make a difference behind the scenes?

CM: One of the biggest changes is the launch of Dark Regions Digital. We understand the shifting market, but feel quite comfortable in the sector of the industry that we're in. Actually, I feel pretty bad for the mass paperback guys. Heck, I own a Kindle Fire HD, and the sheer convenience immediately made me realize the eventual demise of the paperback. But guess what digital books can't replace? Signed, collectible hardcovers.

Indeed, in the future it's likely that physical books will be considered specialty items. Dark Regions Press is a specialty publishing company. I feel like we're in the right place when it comes to the future of literature. For my generation, at least.

JBK: Which of your own short stories have been published? Were they printed in magazines, anthologies or collections?

CM: I've had some stories and poems published in *Ghostlight* Magazine, *Aoife's Kiss*, *Demon Minds* (Halloween 2010) and so on. Personally, I only want to be published with folks that will pay me, and preferably in print.

If I can manage—while running the press—I'm planning on releasing a new short story/other pieces of fiction every month leading up to my first book release. Let's hope I can follow-through while maintaining my sanity.

JBK: Are you on track to complete your own first novel in 2013? What can you tell us about that project?

CM: I'm afraid my own writing has taken a halt since I've been given the task of running the company. I have a short story that I will be launching for free, titled "The Boy and the Abyss," hopefully a month or more before this reaches print on all ebook platforms. I'm hoping to release a new story for free each month leading up to my first book launch. Just. Need. More. Coffee.

JBK: Will Dark Regions help you publish your first full novel, or will you be going gonzo with it?

CM: No. I refuse to have anything published (that wasn't intended to be a freebie) where I am not paid, and refuse to have DRP in anyway be involved with the publishing of my first book. Makes me a lot less lazy and makes for sharper writing. I'll publish my first book when I feel like I've written something important, something that could affect people. I care more about that than pumping out 99 cent ebooks. As Ray Bradbury so perfectly stated: "If you don't write for one day, you'll notice. If you don't write for two days, your critics will notice. If you don't write for three days, your audience will notice." Well, that makes me pretty damn rusty these days.

JBK: You're as young as the latest explosion in new, creative Horror fiction. Historically there were no images, beyond canvas and paint, to give color to the authors' macabre creations. Today, anything that can be written can be photographed, filmed, illustrated or computerized. Are modern writers being influenced by images they have already seen? Are you still discovering writers with new visions?

CM: It really is exciting to see the expansion of the creative spectrum. People are doing amazing things now and really expanding the reaches of art. The delivery methods of writing have fundamentally changed (and are changing) the way we access fiction. The barrier is so low that people from all over the world are submitting their writings (for better or worse) for others to analyze. It makes you wonder about the future of art culture, and how the depleting well of original ideas is beginning to shine the spotlight through Hollywood's bullshit. I can see sub genres like Bizarro and surrealistic horror becoming more popular, once people realize how interesting and different they often are (even from one another). Maybe I'm just being a narcissistic downer, but I feel like there's a lot of the same, or twists of the same. Give me something new! Using a different instrument or hitting a different body part doesn't change the act of beating a dead horse, for crying out loud!

JBK: Can we expect more editing work from you in the future?

CM: My primary editing work will be for the Black Labyrinth imprint, but I will be doing other work as well. I recently edited Jeff Strand's *Dead Clown Barbecue*, which was a thrill because I've been a Strand fan for years. It's been an honor to edit the work of Tom Piccirilli and Jeff Strand, and I can't wait to work alongside more of my literary inspirations in the future. Keep your eyes peeled on the Black Labyrinth page at DarkRegions. com/BlackLabyrinth as there are many exciting things to come.

Thunder Perfect Minds:
Thomas Ligotti and Current 93

By Aaron J. French

In the late 1990s, one of the most unusual collaborations took place between weird fiction author Thomas Ligotti and British poet, singer, and artist David Tibet of the music group Current 93. Their first project, *In A Foreign Town, In A Foreign Land* (1997, reissued 2002), was followed by *I Have A Special Plan For This World* (2000), *This Degenerate Little Town* (2001), and *The Unholy City* (2003). All were released in limited quantity on Tibet's Durtro label and feature original artwork and sometimes a hardcover edition of Ligotti's stories. They are highly prized among collectors; rare, too. *This Degenerate Little Town* currently goes for $490 on Amazon.

While Thomas Ligotti needs no introduction for readers of Dark Discoveries, I would like to take a moment to introduce David Tibet. Current 93 formed in the early 1980s out of another experimental British punk band Psychic TV, and Tibet has been the only full-time member of the group since their first release, *Nature Unveiled*, in 1984.

Most of Current 93's earlier music could serve as the soundtrack for a haunted house or a ritualistic murder scene, utilizing abrasive tape loops and droning synthesizer noises over Tibet's distorted, grating vocals. Later the group would develop into what is called Apocalyptic Folk, a combination of acoustic instruments and ambient sounds, with Tibet's mystical poetry spoken over it.

I remember seeing a 1988 interview with Current 93 in which a young Tibet stood before a ruinous collection of rubble buildings somewhere in the UK, speaking vehemently into the camera about the spiritual emptiness and rampant materialism afflicting the West, and how he could no longer stand it and would be leaving Europe for India. This kind of intense spirituality is a hallmark of Current 93's music, and what makes it such a profound listening experience.

Tibet's religious beliefs are difficult to pinpoint. They begin with Aleister Crowley and his quasi-Masonic magical orders, the Ordo Templi Orientis (Order of Oriental Templars) and the A∴A∴ (*Argentium Astrum*). These groups practice a form of ceremonial magic promulgated by Crowley known as Thelema. Tibet most likely joined one, if not several, of these groups, and the philosophy behind Thelema is strongly represented in his poetry and music. The name Current 93 is taken from Crowley, 93 being the most important numerological value running through Thelemite magical practice. These days, however, Tibet claims to be simply a Christian, his focus tending toward Christian mysticism and esoteric Christianity.

So of all the people Tibet could be hooking up with, American-born writer Thomas Ligotti seems the most unlikely—owing to the fact that Ligotti's worlds appear, at a glance, fully devoid of spirituality. Yet if you look closer you find something spiritual at work, something that aligns with the "abyss" ideas of Thelemic practice, a kind of inner netherworld which one must traverse in order to reap the "spiritual fruits" growing on the opposite side.

David Tibet proclaimed in 1996 that "for anyone who has an interest in the work I have created with Current 93 over the last thirteen years, I *must* say: Read Ligotti." He then instigated their first collaboration by sending Ligotti a package containing all Current 93's recordings and a letter.

Despite the mistaken conception, the two have never actually worked together in person. Ligotti wrote and recorded his stuff without much input from David at his home, using inferior equipment and without much knowledge of home recording. Tibet then did his thing over and around what Ligotti had sent him.

In A Foreign Town, In A Foreign Land comes with a CD and a small hardcover featuring IV interconnected Ligotti stories and artwork by David Tibet and Steven Stapleton. Instructions suggest one to "listen ... at a low volume, at dusk," then to read each Ligotti story over the corresponding track. These tracks consist of bells, ringing chimes, soundscapes, ghostly wails, and Tibet's eerie voice uttering short passages from the text.

My favorite track is III, "A Soft Voice Whispers Nothing," because the Ligotti passages uttered by Tibet here are so striking and disturbing that, if listened to correctly, they can produce a very strange feeling. "A Soft Voice Whispers Nothing" was reprinted in 2008 in Jeff and Ann VanderMeer's *The New Weird*.

I Have A Special Plan For This World was released as a twenty-two minute long single on both CD and limited edition vinyl. For this one, Tibet narrates the entire story and does an excellent job, cutting in and out like an old cassette, interspersing passages with tape noises, samples, and an extremely unsettling circuit-bent Speak & Spell gibbering.

Their final releases, *This Degenerate Little Town* and *The Unholy City*, I don't actually own since they are seemingly harder to come by and more expensive. But both can be listened to on YouTube and suchlike. *This Degenerate Little Town* comes with a beautifully-printed book containing lyrics and a Tibet color illustration. The music is sparse, but the story is narrated by Ligotti himself. *The Unholy City* receives a similar treatment, however this time with lush and melodic musical accompaniment. Again, Ligotti's voice shines through.

I don't know if there has ever been an artistic collaboration quite like the one between Thomas Ligotti and David Tibet. And I don't know if these two will ever collaborate again. But we have their previous efforts to enjoy and to remind us what unique strangeness can be dreamed up and breathed to life. It also seems to have formed a bond of mutual respect among the two artists. In a recent email to me, Ligotti had this to say about David: "I haven't communicated with David for years now ... [but] he's easily the most complex person I've ever known, and at the same time I've always sensed a solid core of decency, generosity, and genuine goodness in the man."

✹✹✹

HELLNOTES REVIEWS

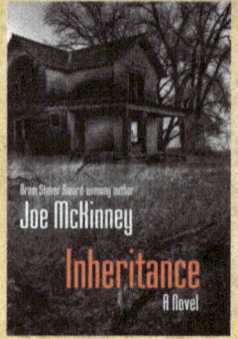

Inheritance
by Joe McKinney
Evil Jester Press
ISBN-13: 978-0615690896
2012; (US) $16.43
Paperback

Thinking back over the horror novels that I have particularly enjoyed, I've decided that they divide relatively neatly into two large categories. For lack of better terminology I've chosen Narrow and Broad. These are not necessarily qualitative terms; a Narrow novel may be powerful, evocative, even great. A Broad novel may be thin, superficial, formulaic. But in some senses the two words suggest my responses to the storytelling each attempts.

Narrow horror novels concentrate on the horror, the monster. They are about a creature, in some cases more than they are about the humans that interact with it. For readers intrigued by the darkness, the monstrous, these may be ideal. The story begins with intimations of evil; expands through revelations of the extent, focus, and purposes of the evil; and concludes with the destruction (permanently or temporarily) of the evil. To a degree, perhaps the most famous monster book of all, Bram Stoker's brilliant *Dracula*, is a Narrow novel. Even though he does not feature in the book for some time, Dracula overshadows everything else, and when he is gone, there is nothing more to say.

Broad horror novels work in the opposite way. Their concern is primarily for the people, the individuals involved, and the ways in which they must deal with the intrusion of darkness and evil into their lives. The monster is every bit as vital, every bit as threatening, every bit as repellent (or, conversely, as seductive) as in a Narrow horror novel. But in a Broad novel, humans count for a bit more. Even without the evil, there is a story to be told, often multiple stories; and the evil may in fact link otherwise unrelated tales into a complex of narration and revelation.

To achieve this, Broad novels tend to be long, or at least longer than most Narrow novels. No one would argue that *Dracula* or King's *Salem's Lot* or McCammon's *Usher's Passing* are 'short' novels, but for me they are better considered Narrow than Broad. King's *It*, *The Shining*, and *The Stand*; McCammon's *Swan Song*, *Stinger*, and *The Wolf's Hour*; Simmons' *Carrion Comfort* — these and many others are Broad, in no small part because they are provided with a broad canvas upon which to trace the movements of evil through human lives.

Joe McKinney's latest novel, *Inheritance*, is Broad horror. It extends beyond the limits of a monster or a creature to explore the world in which horror can find its place. It is a ghost story, with ghosts evil and ghosts benign ultimately contesting against each other for a human soul.

It is a story of black magic and witchcraft, in which the forces of darkness and destruction manipulate the heart of a scapegoat (literally!) to bring about a final dissolution.

It is a story of the walking dead … although not the zombies of traditional fiction but something crueler, something closer to the original conception in which the dead are controlled by the living and forced to perform acts that would have been anathema to their living selves.

It is a story of cults that reach out and, almost invisibly, trap an unknowing city, drawing it piece by piece into a whirlwind of evil.

It is a police procedural. In it readers see the inner workings of a large city police force — in this case San Antonio — as it systematically follows clues that lead to … the impossible.

It is a story of brotherhood among officers, of pranks and games that only thinly disguise the fact that any of them would sacrifice anything, up to and including their lives, for the welfare of their colleagues.

It is a story of domestic violence, in which small matters only hint at the horrendous truth behind abuse, exploitation, and perversion. It demonstrates how easily violence perpetrates itself across generations and what is required to stop its progress. And it is ultimately a story of an Apocalypse waiting, drawing nearer, its threat gaining strength with every passing page…and a final moment of redemptive sacrifice.

In all, it is a thoroughly imagined, thoroughly developed, masterfully written novel of broad horror.

And one final thought. All of these points developed gradually but inexorably through the course of the story. They were, of course, not the first thing I noticed about the book. The first thing — and the worst thing — struck my eyes when I first opened the book. The typeface is ridiculously small. Especially when set next to unusually wide margins (the better to take notes in, my dear!).

Then I started reading, and I noticed the second thing — and the best thing — about *Inheritance*. The size of the type made no difference. Once I began reading, I was caught. *Inheritance* tells its story of ghosts and possession inordinately well, engaging readers through 350 pages (which would be perhaps double that with a larger type), never flagging, never introducing any irrelevancies or digressions.

Highly recommended.

-Reviewed by Michael R. Collings

The Last Final Girl
by Stephen Graham Jones,
Lazy Fascist Press
ISBN: 978-1621050513
2012; (US) $11.95 Paperback;
$6.95 Kindle Edition

A novel written both as a slasher flick and a love letter to slasher films? Yes please! See, I grew up during the golden age of slasher movies. I devoured them all, like a zombie does brains, and I know my favorite masked maniac movies line by line; every scene—and more importantly—every kill. I do deeply love them, from the acknowledged greats like *Halloween*, to the cheesy and forgotten gems like the slasher in a supermarket flick, *Intruder*. Furthermore, I'm a fan of the author of this new book, Stephen Grahm Jones, and his off kilter sense of humor. In fact, the novel I read before picking up this book was Jones' wonderfully weird *Zombie Bake-Off*. So I love the genre to pieces and I dig the author…then why am I not completely in love with this book?

Maybe because it is too much like *Scream* and not enough like *Halloween, Black Christmas, Friday the 13th, My Bloody Valentine*, and other earlier classics that put slashers on the map. By that I mean the characters are far too glib, snarky, and hip—that they just don't read as believable. If this was just a single character, that would be one thing, but it is most of them here. Now I can't totally begrudge a novel about slasher films for having not entirely realistic characters in it. After all, every slasher film ever made had people in them that strained the suspension of disbelief to the breaking point. But, that has always been part of their charm. However, the real reason for my earlier *Scream* reference is because of all the self-aware, wink-wink, meta name-dropping of horror movies that happens on almost every other page of this book. Again, if it were a single character in this novel that was a walking, talking slasher movie encyclopedia, that would be one thing. But it's not, and all this nudge-nudging gets old remarkably fast.

Another gripe is this: if this was actually a slasher flick like it wants to be, it would be known for being one of the slowest moving stalk and slash movies ever made. More than half the novel goes by without any of the "good stuff" happening, and by that I mean any sort of action other than lots of pseudo-hipster horror dialog. To drop some of my own meta slasher knowledge that only the tried and true horrorheads will get, remember the 1984 slasher, *The Prey*? Well that flick moves along at a quicker pace than this book. See, I can do it too.

Now all is not dire here. The book can be quite funny and on more than one occasion I literally laughed out loud while reading it. Also the idea of a killer in a Michael Jackson mask was suitably silly, if a little bit out of place for a modern novel, and the high school setting seemed more than appropriate. Overall I did enjoy my time with this *Last Final Girl*, and most of the characters were fun,

if not at all believable. But if you're a fan of the slasher movies that inspired this novel then you're likely to be left wanting something more than what this novel has to offer. So consider this one recommended, but sadly not highly. Three bloody butcher knives out of five sounds about right.

-Reviewed by Brian M. Sammons

Cannibal Corpse
by Tim Curran
Permuted Press
ISBN: 978-1618680587
2012; (US) $14.95 Paperback;
$7.99 Kindle Edition

John Slaughter is an outlaw biker, one of The Devil's Disciples. He is traveling to the Deadlands, the area West of the Mississippi River. The country is in a shambles, and the dead walk among its citizens. Bioengineered "corpse worms" have been unleashed on the world through "worm rains," and they turn the living into the walking dead. But these zombies aren't "normal" zombies–they're area cognizant and can brandish weapons. They can carry out revenge.

Slaughter is captured by the Army and blackmailed into traveling to an old NORAD base to rescue a bioengineer who can help get rid of the virus. He must return her safely to her destination if he wants his brother released from prison instead of given the death penalty. They reunite him with his incarcerated fellow bikers and equip him with weapons and an outfitted school bus. They head West, running into "worm boys," militia group Red Hand and other evil beings. Slaughter also runs into a mystical being who brings more death and destruction to the country and is interested in Slaughter's talent for murder and mayhem. They finally make it to the NORAD base, only to be confronted by the Cannibal Corpses–an undead biker gang and bitter enemies of The Devil's Disciples.

Cannibal Corpse is different from the usual zombie stories that are overrunning the genre lately. Not only are they aware of what they are, they are able to talk and some are pissed about their situations. Some of them know things. And they can fight back with weapons as well as their teeth. I enjoyed that aspect; it was interesting having the zombies actually interact with the humans.

There were many horrific scenes throughout the story, and Curran describes them in loving, disgusting detail. Worm people, mutants, and other monstrosities have taken over the Deadlands, and nobody living is safe.

I wasn't as interested in the mythical aspect of the story, though. I thought it took away from the human aspect of the zombie genre that I like. I did enjoy the camaraderie among Slaughter and his fellow bikers; although Slaughter is a cold-blooded killer, he does have redeeming qualities that make him a great character. However, even though I didn't care for the mystical sections of the story, the book was overall a great read. I don't know if this is intended to be a series, but it could be a great series if continued. Curran's post-apocalyptic world would be interesting to explore further.

If you're looking forward to the zombie apocalypse, this is the book for you.

-Review by Sheri White

Fresh Blood & Old Bones
Edited by Kasey Lansdale,
Biting Dog Publications
2012; (US) $6.99 e-book

There are monsters ... and then there are monsters.

The truly fun thing about *Fresh Blood & Old Bones* is the sheer number of monsters captured in the eighteen tales collected by Kasey Lansdale in this offering of short fiction by established and neophyte horror writers. At one extreme, one finds multiple award-winner Joe R. Lansdale's riff on traditional "Black Car" lore, complete with murderous nuns (or anti-nuns) and an unstoppable monster that slaughters its way through a Halloween landscape. At another (and there are more than two extremes in this book), the totally unexpected and wonderfully comic appearance of Wanda and Earl in Rhonda Eudaly's initially unassuming "Crocodile Rock," a title that must be taken in at least two ways to do justice to the outré assumptions and rough-and-tumble actions that develop.

Some of the best reading doesn't seem to entail actual 'monsters'—that is, until the stories begin to unfold, until characters reveal themselves more and more fully, and yet another definition of monster emerges. Perhaps the best example of this occurs in John Paul Allen's "Little Miss." At every key point in the story, readers must abruptly alter perceptions and understanding as what seems at first a censorious account of a metaphorical 'monster' mother and her long-suffering child pageant-contestant becomes increasingly pointed. Cast as an interview with the imprisoned mother (for what crime and for how long is only gradually explained), intercut with dialogues between parent and child just before various pageants, the story twists into increasingly disturbing byways as the true relationship between mother and daughter inexorably emerges.

Or, to take another example by a relative newcomer, Monica J. O'Rourke, "Celler" (an unfortunate typo there) seems in the beginning to be a straightforward tale about another kind of human 'monster,' an unnamed man who has abducted a child and kept her in the cellar, in a state of numbed fear and terror blended with something like perverted love. The child has no name but "Girl"; the man is simply "Him." Nothing is said explicitly about what he has done to her, but the suggestions are manifold. Now she finds herself alone, starving, thirsting, and terrified to climb the steps to freedom. Somehow, she finds the courage to do so, and when she does…well, suffice it to say that child-abductors are not the only monsters little girls should fear.

And again, Stephen Mertz's "The Lizard Men of Blood River" is an almost perfect pastiche of an Indiana Jones-style action-adventure romp, complete with—as the title tells us—Lizard Men…and a Lost City; a millennia-old evil magician; a swooning, scantily clad damsel in distress; and a doughty hero named, appropriately enough, Speed McCoy. He works fast at resolving problems, such as a sudden attack by Amazonian headhunters, and at getting the girl. And all encapsulated into the space of a novelette.

I'm tempted to continue with an assessment of each story in *Fresh Blood & Old Bones*, since there is something interesting, intriguing, or just plain fascinating about each, but to do so would take too long and possibly deflate the power of the individual tales. Certainly, a piece titled "Jimmy and Me and the Nigger Man," by Scott Cupp, or the errily haunting "Seven Devils," by Nancy A. Collins, or the sheer insanity-in-the-making of "If Mama Ain't Happy," by Sam W. Anderson richly deserve additional discussion.

Instead, however, let me simply note that one of the most conspicuous strengths of *Fresh Blood & Old Bones* is that in spite of the title, which indicates that the stories were written by new as well as established writers, unless one is familiar with the authors' names, it is almost impossible to tell which is a first appearance and which comes from the imagination of someone with decades of writing experience. All of the stories are strong, all invite readers into dark worlds—literally and metaphorically—in which monsters dwell, and all are a credit to their authors and to the genre.

Highly recommended.

-Reviewed by Michael R. Collings

Nightwhere
by John Everson,
Samhain Publishing,
ISBN-13: 978-1609289225
2012; $10.20 Trade
Paperback,
$4.24 Kindle Edition

I'm going to start off by saying *Nightwhere* by John Everson isn't for everybody. This book is extremely intense, violent, sexual, and horrifying. In fact, the squeamish are not allowed into the Red Room. This is only for the readers who can handle this particular type of in-your-face terror. Think *Hellraiser* meets *Basic Instinct*, and you have some idea about the dark contents of this novel. That being said, I loved *Nightwhere*.

I knew in the first couple of pages that I was going to be hooked, and I mean that in a painless way. This novel grabbed me by the throat, shook the loose coins from my pockets, and threw me against the wall like I was a ragdoll. I was so worn out by the time I finished reading it that I had to check my body for marks to make sure I hadn't secretly paid a visit to the Red Room.

The macabre story focuses on a young married couple, Mark and Rae, who need a variety of sexual stimuli to feel satiated and content. They experience this stimulus through swinger's clubs and sessions filled with light bondage and S&M. It's really Rae who's in desperate need for more lovers and in search for a place where anything goes, and I mean anything. She wants to be taken to different realms of unbelievable pain and intense psychological humiliation. But, she needs to find that place first. Mark constantly follows after her in order to keep her happy and pretty much does whatever she wants. He doesn't need the types of experiences she craves to remain in love or to feel complete with his spouse. Mark does, however, derive some sexual pleasure from watching his wife seduce other men and then experience the sexual pleasures that the strangers have to offer her.

Everything is revved up several notches when they receive an invitation to attend the premier club for S&M—Nightwhere. The club is a legend; yet, nobody knows how to find it. The dark things that go on there are only whispered about. It's said that not only are patrons whipped to within an inch of their lives, but that many disappear, never to be seen again.

Rae is eager to attend this legendary club of darkness and pain. Mark agrees to their visitation only because he wants to keep an eye out for his wife to make sure nothing terrible happens to her. What he fails to understand is that the floodgates have now been opened. And, once the door opens, there's no turning back.

While Mark sits at the bar in the Blue Room of Nighwhere, nursing drinks and talking to other people in the same boat as he, Rae begins to get a delicious taste of the many different and unusual things that the club has to offer her. But, a taste is just what it is. She instinctively knows that more goes on behind closed doors, and she wants to experience that depravity to the utmost.

It's the second invitation that does the trick for her. Rae gets a brutal whipping from another woman that causes her eyes to light up in excitement and to finally realize this is exactly what she's been looking for all of her life.

On the third invitation (I should point out that Nightwhere is in a new location each month, making it impossible to find without a personal invitation), Rae is invited to experience the Red Room. Not Mark, just her. He has to stay in the Blue Room and settle for some dancing and drinking, while Rae gets a shocking taste of pain and blood that simply causes her to yearn for more. She literally doesn't care what's done to her as long as that insatiable itch is scratched.

Once they get home and her husband sees the whip marks and scars on her body, he forbids her to attend Nightwhere again. But there's no stopping Rae. She's not about to give up what she has longed for over the years and that now fills the emptiness inside of her.

The next invitation is for Rae only. Mark isn't even invited to Nightwhere. The Watchers who run Nightwhere (think of the pale creatures in *Hellraiser* with the pins sticking in their faces) know of his resistance to what they have to offer and decide to leave him out of the equation. Rae doesn't care as long as her dark cravings are met, and they are in every way imaginable. Mark soon begins to understand that his wife no longer needs him and is ready to give up their life together just to stay at Nightwhere on a more permanent basis. Mark, however, isn't ready to give up on his marriage, no matter what Rae wants. He becomes determined to save her at all costs. What he doesn't realize yet is that the only true thing he has to offer is his own life because Rae has now been invited into the Black Room. He will have to be prepared to suffer in the most hideous and painful manner in order to see Rae and to try and win her back from the utter depths of depravity. Good luck, buddy, is all I had to say.

John Everson has written what I already consider to be a true classic in every sense of the word. The author has invited the reader on a journey into the depths of Hell, knowing that once the last page is turned, the individual (man or woman) will never be the same again. I kid you not. This is a journey where the ugliness of humanity is revealed in all of its glorious, retched detail, and most won't have the stomach to deal with it. I know about these things and was once involved with a woman much like Rae, who was more than willing to sacrifice me in order to achieve the ultimate orgasm. What Mr. Everson writes about does exist (this doesn't include the *Watchers* and the creation of *Nightwhere*), and if a person is willing to give up everything, a club tailored to one's desires can be found quite easily in Los Angeles, San Francisco, New York City, London, Paris, Berlin, and who knows where else. For every top, there's a bottom. For every sadist, there's a masochist who wants to feel the touch of pain. These places do exist and in greater numbers than ever before.

This is an addiction that's ten times stronger than alcoholism, drugs, gambling, eating, starving, and whatever else you can think of. The author has captured it perfectly in its total essence of blackness and in some cases, true evil. I should also point out that John Everson is definitely a master of words and character development and plot. He weaves a story here that is like stepping into a bear trap. Once the trap snaps shut on your leg, the only way out is to either cut your leg off or die in a most horrible manner.

Read *Nightwhere* at your own risk, and don't say you haven't been warned. What's inside this novel may just change the world as you know it, and not necessarily for the better.

-Reviewed by Wayne C. Rogers

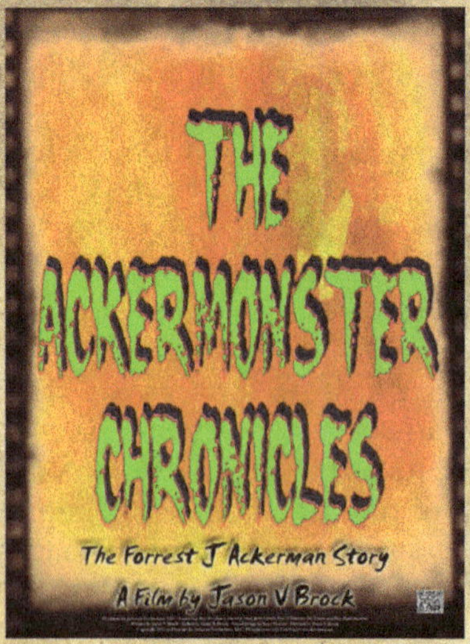

The Ackermonster Chronicles
Directed by Jason V Brock
Jasunni Productions
2012; DVD Format;
$19.95

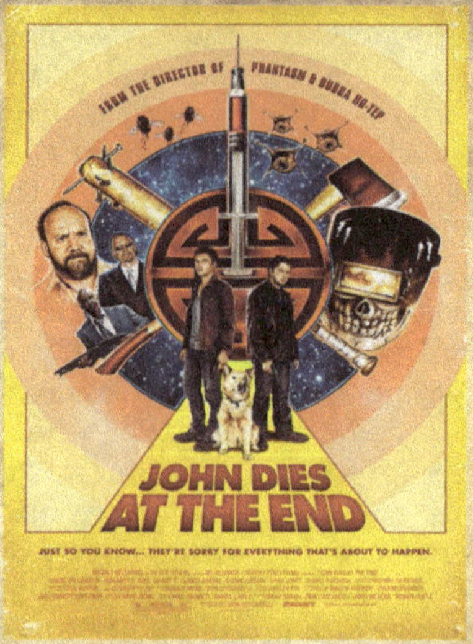

JOHN DIES AT THE END
Directed by Don Coscarelli
Magnet Releasing
2012

Most of you probably know Jason from his tenure as Managing Editor and Designer/Art Director for Dark Discoveries up until earlier this year. Jason's gone and started his own magazine, Nameless, and already kicked it off with a strong debut issue. He's also a filmmaker and helmed an excellent documentary on Charles Beaumont (Twilight Zone, Roger Corman's films, etc.) with his wife Sunni Brock handling the editing chores. It's called *The Short Life of Twilight Zone's Magic Man* and it came out a while back. It received a number of excellent reviews and hit the film festival circuit to great success (and I'd recommend checking it out as well).

Now the Brocks are back with a new documentary. This time it's on Fandom's longtime ambassador, Forest J Ackerman (Uncle Forry to many of us Monster kids). Most people know Ackerman from Famous Monsters magazine or his extensive museum of a house for many years (home to many monster collectibles), but did you know he was also an early agent to many writers such as Ray Bradbury, A.E. Van Vogt, Charles Beaumont and others. He also created Vampirella, wrote articles for nudist publications and was an honorary Lesbian (I'm not kidding!). So there's things even the die-hard fans might not know about Forry.

The tone of the movie is lighthearted and fun – much like Forry's life overall. There are the sad situations with publisher Ray Ferry and the lawsuits and Forry having to sell off a lot of his vast collection, but overall it's pretty upbeat and quite funny. Pretty much everybody who knew Ackerman is in the film like John Landis, Joe Dante, Ray Bradbury, Dan O'Bannon, Ray Harryhausen, William F. Nolan, John Tomerlin, and the list goes on.

I liked it a lot myself. There's definitely a need for this movie to celebrate Forry's life and it succeeds in that I think. It's probably not for the kids or easily offended as there is a good bit of nudity, but it's all pretty tame overall (and probably nothing your kids haven't seen already). I liked it a lot better than the couple previous documentaries on Ackerman that skimmed over a lot of things in his life that happened (especially the nudist stuff, etc.).

Highly recommended!

- Reviewed by Trever Nordgren

John Dies at the End is the new film from Don Coscarelli (*Phantasm, Bubba Ho Tep, Beastmaster*) making the film festival and theater rounds. I wouldn't call it a horror movie outright, but put it more in the vein of *Bubba Ho Tep*. There are horrific elements, but it's more of a dark comedy and reminded me of movies like *The Frighteners* and *Ghostbusters*. It's really all over the map though as far as genre with elements of Science Fiction, Psychedelia, Horror and teen buddy comedy. Even so, I would say it's one of his more mainstream films.

Based on a book by David Wong (a pseudonym for Jason Pargin), it tells the story of two friends, Dave (Chase Williamson) and John (Rob Mayes), who try and stop the spread of a drug called Soy Sauce and the creatures its use results in. Paul Giametti (*Sideways, American Splendor*) plays a reporter who Dave tells their story to. Angus Scrimm (the Tall Man from the *Phantasm* movies) is present as well as Father Shellnut and Clancy Brown (*Highlander, Buckaroo Banzai*) and Doug Jones (*Hellboy, Pan's Labyrinth*) are also featured.

The movie itself is kind of indescribable in some ways. It will definitely keep you guessing from one minute to the next. I liken it to a drug trip in high school and it felt a bit like I was having a flashback myself while watching it. Hallucinogenic is a perfect word for it. It's on par with *Naked Lunch* in that Coscarelli, much like David Cronenberg, has taken a book that was pretty much unfilmable and pulled it off. He took some liberties with the original novel, necessary I'm sure to adapting it. I think it's a much more successful end product than Cronenberg's Burroughs film, though, and would definitely recommend it. My favorite movie of 2012 actually!

-Reviewed by Justin Giallo

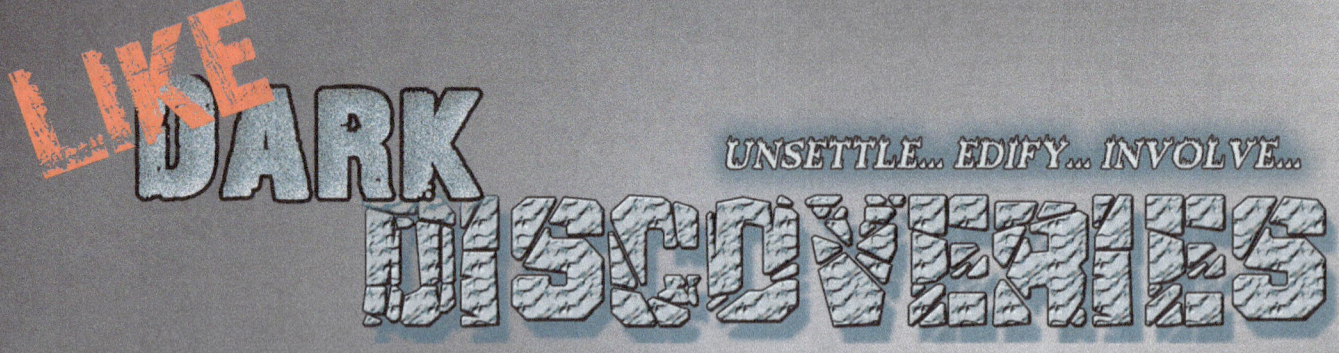

LIKE DARK DISCOVERIES?

UNSETTLE... EDIFY... INVOLVE...

Then **SUBSCRIBE** and never miss another issue of...

FEATURES:

Weird Fiction & Film, Extreme Horror, Comics & Pulps, New Blood, Dark SciFi,

Twilight Zone, H.P. Lovecraft, Horror in Rock, Forgotten Horror & SF TV...

INTERVIEWS:

Ray Bradbury, Bruce Campbell, Christopher Lee, Joe R. Lansdale, William F. Nolan,

EC Comics Al Feldstein, Brian Keene, Jack Ketchum, David Cronenberg...

FICTION:

Richard Matheson, Ray Bradbury, Thomas Ligotti, Richard Laymon, John Shirley, William F. Nolan, Ramsey Campbell, Joe R. Lansdale, Lisa Morton, Edward Lee...

"Dark Discoveries is a very handsome publication..."

--Dean Koontz

"A bright new force in Dark Fantasy."

--William F. Nolan

"Dark Discoveries is a high quality mag... and it keeps getting better..."

--Horror Fiction Review

PRINT SUBSCRIPTIONS

4 issues (1 year): US ($37.95) Canada ($46.95) Overseas ($69.95)

8 issues (2 years): US ($74.95) Canada ($92.95) Overseas ($139.95)

(*Shipping is included on print subs)

DIGITAL SUBSCRIPTIONS

4 issues (1 year): $19.95

8 issues (2 years): $39.95

Payment accepted via PayPal:

christophercpayne@journalstone.com

Also by Check/M.O. (Payable to) JournalStone

199 State Street, San Mateo, CA. 94401, USA

ON THE WEB:

www.darkdiscoveries.com

ADVERTISERS!

Inquire via E-mail for rates!

Please Note: Future content subject to change without notice. All rights reserved.

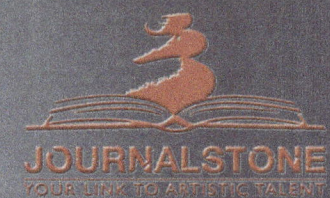

JOURNALSTONE
YOUR LINK TO ARTISTIC TALENT

www.ingramcontent.com/pod-product-compliance
Lightning Source LLC
Chambersburg PA
CBHW081214170626
46811CB00010B/3290